TIMEWEB

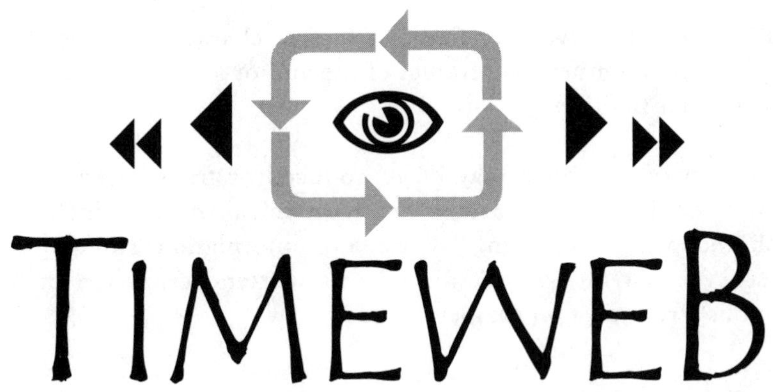

TIMEWEB

Book 1 of the Timeweb Chronicles

BRIAN HERBERT

Five Star • Waterville, Maine

This novel is a work of fiction. Names, characters, places and incidents are either the product of the author's imagination, or, if real, used fictitiously.

First Edition
First Printing: May 2006

Published in 2006 in conjunction with
Tekno Books and Ed Gorman.

Set in 11 pt. Plantin.

Printed in the United States on permanent paper.

Library of Congress Cataloging-in-Publication Data

Herbert, Brian.
Timeweb / by Brian Herbert.—1st ed.
p. cm.—(Timeweb chronicles ; bk. 1)
ISBN 1-59414-216-5 (hc : alk. paper)
I. Title.
PS3558.E617T56 2006
813′.54—dc22 2005036144

TimeweB

Chapter One

We are but one of many galaxies,
wheels moving the cart of the universe.
—Ancient Tulyan Legend

He stood profiled against the blood-red sunset as bulbous ships took off, a swarm of mechanical insects transporting contaminated materials to dump zones. It had been another long day. Normally the muscular, freckled man liked the buzz of activity in the air, the sense that he was restoring a planet that had been severely damaged by the industrial operations of the merchant princes. At the moment, however, he had something else on his mind, a surprising turn of events.

Noah Watanabe glanced again at a brief telebeam message, a black-on-white holo letter that floated in the air beside him. He had been estranged from his father, Prince Saito Watanabe, for so long that he had never expected to hear from the old tycoon again. Touching a signet ring on his right hand, Noah closed the message. In a wisp of smoke, it disappeared into the ring.

Brushing a hand through his reddish, curly hair, Noah considered the unexpected offer of a meeting between them. His initial thought had been to send a scathing response, or to simply ignore his father altogether. But other possibilities occurred to him.

In the din of aircraft, soil-processing machines, and the

shouts of workers, he became aware of an oval-shaped hoverjet landing nearby, raising a cloud of dust. Moments later, the craft settled to the ground, and an underbelly hatch swung open, followed by a ramp that slid to the ground. Men wearing the green-and-brown uniforms of the Guardians—his ecological recovery force—hurried down the ramp, dragging with them a disheveled young woman, a prisoner. A trickle of blood ran down the side of her face. Her eyes were feral, and she kicked at her captors, without much success.

"Caught her trying to rig explosives to our biggest skyminer," one of the Guardians said, a rotund man with a purple birthmark on his chin and chestnut hair combed straight back. In his early forties, Subi Danvar was Noah's trusted but sometimes outspoken adjutant. "She and two men—we killed both of them—stole one of our fast recon ships and locked onto the miner. They were about to set the whole rig off when we caught them and defused the charges."

"Who sent you?" Noah demanded, stepping close and looking down at her.

Sneering, the woman said, "I don't do anything for free. What will you give me if I answer your questions?"

"You're a mercenary, aren't you?"

"You haven't paid for my answer yet."

"Talk and we'll let you live," Subi snarled. "That's our offer." With a round belly and a puffy face he looked soft, but in reality he had the strength of three men.

Having never mistreated prisoners, Noah scowled at his adjutant, who should know better. The man was bluffing, but was doing so without Noah's authorization.

"Maybe the princes sent her," another Guardian suggested, a large man who held the woman's arms and danced away whenever she tried to kick him.

"Do you think it was your own father, Master Noah?" Danvar asked.

"I'm not sure," Noah said, recalling the telebeam message. Remarkably, old Prince Saito had offered an apology for their failed relationship, and had expressed the hope that they might be close again. But warning signals went off in Noah's mind; this could be a trick, even from his own father.

Noah and his Guardians had to be on constant alert against sabotage. In the past year, attacks had come from his business competitors and from enemies of the powerful Watanabe family, people who didn't believe the stories about the estrangement between the business mogul and his son, and thought they must be working together in some clandestine way.

"Take her away for interrogation," Noah said, with a dismissive gesture toward the young woman. "And treat her well, with respect."

The woman looked at him in astonishment. "No torture?"

"Of course not. We don't do things that way."

"I am very pleased to hear that." With a sudden movement, the woman writhed free of her captors and lunged toward Noah, brandishing a long dagger that she seemed to have produced from thin air. She moved with surprising speed.

Displaying athletic grace, Noah sidestepped the thrust and grabbed her weapon hand. But in his grip, her hand seemed to melt away, and the dagger, too.

"Mutati!" Danvar shouted.

It was a shapeshifter. For centuries Mutatis like this one had warred against the Merchant Prince Alliance. In a matter of seconds, her entire body metamorphosed into a long, serpentine form. She coiled, and struck out at Noah with deadly fangs.

But he whirled to one side and rolled away. His men fired a volley of ion-pistol shots at the creature, bursts of energy that flashed and sparkled in the air. Purple blood oozed from the Mutati, and the wounded creature began to change form again, this time to a startlingly large and ferocious beast with sharp barbs all over its body and face. But it only half metamorphosed, with its rear—more injured than the rest of the body—still a writhing snake. Using its front legs to propel itself forward, the monstrosity lunged at the Guardians, but they kept firing, and the Mutati finally fell, spurting gouts of blood.

On his feet, Noah drew his own sidearm and pointed it. Holding his fire, he took a step backward, watching the Mutati in fascination. His men stopped shooting.

Once more, the creature shapeshifted on its front, and the barbs on the face dissolved into torn and jagged flesh. A tiger-like beast began to take form, with desperate, wild eyes. But when it was only half formed, it abruptly shuddered and twitched, and then stopped moving entirely.

"Are you all right?" Subi Danvar asked, running to Noah's side.

"I'm not hurt. Doesn't look like any of you are, either."

"My fault, sir. I thought for sure our prisoner was Human, but the red blood on the side of her face was obviously faked, something she wiped on her skin."

"They used a new trick on us," Noah said, "but that's no excuse. From now on, stick all the prisoners in the finger to see if they bleed purple. It's the one thing about their bodies they can't change."

"I'll check them myself," Danvar said, referring to half a dozen men and women saboteurs that they had captured here on the planet Jaggem in recent weeks.

"Guess this lets my father off the hook," Noah said, staring at the motionless blotch of purple flesh on the ground.

One of the men used a knife to dig a small white object out of the body. "Implanted allergy protector," he said, holding it up. Mutatis were strongly allergic to Humans, so the shapeshifters often wore medical devices that encased the cells of their bodies in a prophylactic film.

After a worried, guilt-ridden nod toward his superior, Danvar departed with his men.

Shaking his head as he watched them go, Noah realized that he should have taken precautions earlier to prevent Mutati incursions. Especially here, on a planet that could have future significance to the Merchant Prince Alliance as a military outpost, by virtue of its strategic location. With all the planets that he had restored so far, Noah had never experienced even a hint of trouble from the shapeshifters, and for years he had relied on local police security operations to detect them if they ever tried to get through. The possibility of Mutati incursions had been in the back of his mind all that time, but from now on he needed to move such concerns to the forefront. He would have Subi Danvar work up new security measures in coordination with the MPA.

Noah's thoughts returned to the communication he had just received from his crusty, septuagenarian father. How odd to hear from him after all this time, after all the bad feelings and bitterness between the two of them. Their last encounter—more than fifteen years ago—had been a shouting match that had become physical when the prince struck his son in the face with a closed fist. The blow from the big man had been considerable, and Noah had reeled backward in surprise and shock. Out of a sense of honor, the younger man had not even considered striking back, not even for a moment. As a result of the altercation, he had not expected to ever see his father again, except on newsreels that documented the businessman's comings and goings.

Now he watched Danvar's hoverjet take off and thread its way through the crowded airspace, flying toward the Guardians' base of operations on a nearby plateau. The sky was deep purple, almost a foreboding Mutati shade, and Jaggem's small, silvery moon was just rising above a distant escarpment. He wished his father was here to see how successful he had become in his own right.

Noah had not needed any inheritance from Prince Saito. The younger Watanabe had become wealthy beyond anything he could ever hope to spend, from the ecological recovery operations he conducted on numerous planets around the Merchant Prince Alliance. Before embarking on that career, Noah had considered becoming the industrialist that his father wanted him to be.

But, after long consideration, Noah had come up with a better line of work, one that did not conflict with his own strongly held environmental beliefs. His ambitious, conniving sister Francella was more suited to following in their father's footsteps anyway, so by default Noah had given her what she wanted, his own spot as the heir apparent of the family's huge commercial operations, spanning countless star systems.

After making his momentous, life-changing decision, Noah had proceeded to carve out a business niche of his own, bringing efficiency to what had previously been a fledgling, loosely run industry. His timing had been exquisite, and now he ran the largest ecological recovery operation in the galaxy, with skilled teams working on blighted worlds, restoring them to habitability after their resources had been stripped by merchant prince industrialists.

It was a career path in which Noah restored many of the planets that his own father's operations had nearly destroyed. But he had not selected this particular business just to irritate the old man—at least not consciously. Noah had only done what he thought was right, and as a Watanabe he felt he had an obligation to make up for the environmental wrongs committed by his family.

In memory, he reread his father's short telebeam message. Then he activated his ring and transmitted a polite but reserved response, agreeing to the meeting.

Chapter Two

Lorenzo the Magnificent . . . Should he be described as Machiavellian, or as a Renaissance man? Perhaps he is both: a leader who will do *anything* necessary to advance the business and scientific ideas that he holds dear.

—*Succession: a Concise History of the Doges*, one of the underground press books

Of all the worlds in the Merchant Prince Alliance, none came close to rivaling the elegant capital world of Timian One, a domain of fabulous palazzos, villas, and country estates, with ambassadors and nobles coming and going on important business. The planet was guarded from space attack by orbital military platforms and by extensive installations on the surface.

And yet, in all of this opulence and grandeur, there existed on the homeworld of humankind a high and sprawling prison known as the Gaol of Brimrock, filled with blood-stained walls and floors, musty rooms, and filthy corridors . . . a structure that reeked of bodily decay and the most excruciating, horrendous deaths. At any hour of the day and night, victims could be heard screaming as they were tortured and killed.

In the largest chamber of the gaol, a vaulted room with barbed straps hanging from the ceiling and hideous machines arrayed along the walls, the aged but still-spry Doge Lorenzo del Velli sat at the Judgment Table between a pair of princes. At one time the Doge had been a classically handsome man with a prominent chin, strong nose, and dark, penetrating eyes, but now the skin sagged on his cheeks and under his chin, and his gaze had lost its luster. The leathery face was etched with the concerns of high command and the depravities of endless nocturnal liaisons. He rarely ever smiled, and when he did, it had a steely edge to it. Lorenzo and his companions wore cloaks, brocaded surcoats, silkine shirts with dagged collars, and golden medallions. Their liripipe hats, in the varying colors of their noble houses, rested on the table in front of them.

The trio of noblemen watched dispassionately as their top military officer used a nerve induction rack to torture a flesh-fat Mutati. The air around the rack sparked and flashed with green light, from the strong threads of a jade laser held by the inflictor, a delicate little man in a baggy red uniform with gold braids and an oversized officer's cap. Supreme General Mah Sajak, despite his high rank, enjoyed coming here on occasion to perform tasks that were normally reserved for men in black hoods.

The high-intensity device, a golden staff that shot threads of green fire from the tip, had been manufactured by the Hibbil race, specialists in computers and high-performance machines. The electronic wand inhibited the movements of the Mutati, and was used in lieu of physical cords or other restraints.

An expert in the application of the laser, Sajak intentionally left small segments of the victim's flesh only lightly secured, thus providing apparent escape opportunities. Every few seconds, the Mutati would shapeshift and try to squirm through one of the "openings," but each time the General would quickly close it up, while leaving another space free.

It was all a game, and the Doge noted a cruel smile

twitching at the edges of Sajak's scarred mouth. After each escape attempt, the officer adjusted controls on the nerve induction rack as punishment, to intensify the pain.

Looking puffy and red-faced, the victim coughed and sneezed, and emitted the foul odor of Mutati fear. In order to intensify the suffering, General Sajak had removed the creature's implanted allergy protector.

The agonized, high-pitched shrieks of the Mutati gave the Doge a warm, toasty feeling because he hated the shapeshifters so much and always had. From a young age he, like billions of people, had learned to loathe the arch enemies of humanity. He looked forward to these sessions as much as Sajak did, the way children looked forward to sugary treats.

On the wall behind Lorenzo hung a stylized painting of the Madonna holding technological devices. A composite artwork, it depicted a synthesis of the leading religious and scientific disciplines of humankind . . . tenets that dated back to the origins of Human life on Earth eons ago, and to the subsequent migrations to Timian One, Siriki, Canopa, and other planets.

The ruler of all Humans, the stocky, wrinkled Doge Lorenzo was the ninety-fourth person to occupy the Palazzo Magnifico and sit upon the legendary Aquastar Throne. He held strong theoscientific beliefs himself, and employed them to keep his citizens in line. The officially sanctioned text of the Merchant Prince Alliance was the *Scienscroll*, whose origins lay in the murky, legendary past. An electronic copy lay open in front of the Doge, and he read a passage from it aloud while the Mutati screamed in agony. A wager box also sat on the table, a black mechanism that the three noblemen used to keep track of their bets concerning how long the victim would survive. Lorenzo loved games of chance.

This notorious prison was linked to the Palazzo Magnifico by a covered walking bridge over a narrow waterway, a man-made tributary of the Royal Canal that ran through the heart of Elysoo, the capital city. Named after a mythical economist of millennia past who led the first corporate migrations from Earth, Elysoo became the most beautiful of all cities created by the affluent princes, one of the Wonders of the Galaxy. Even Mutatis (those foolish but brave ones who ventured here in disguise) said so; everyone admired the magnificent municipal designs, and especially the intricate dancing lights on the canals and the illuminated, lambent waterfalls that made the metropolis such a magical wonderland at night.

To prevent the features of his beloved city from being duplicated elsewhere, the doges always blinded the architects and engineers after they had completed their work. But the biggest threat to the Merchant Prince Alliance was not the theft of urban designs, or even of industrial secrets. It came from the Mutati Kingdom. Lorenzo wanted to annihilate the entire race of shapeshifters and make them suffer as much physical pain and humiliation as possible in the process. In his view they were the lowest form of life imaginable, the biological dregs of creation. He could not understand why the Supreme Being had contrived such organisms, unless it was to test Humans, to see how they would respond to such a dreadful enemy. The Mutatis were not just a military threat; they were a supreme challenge to all that any decent person held sacred. . . .

This hapless torture victim (captured in a space skirmish between Humans and Mutatis) was still trying to metamorphose his flesh in order to escape, but Sajak handled him deftly with the strong green threads of his high-intensity light. As the Mutati assumed different physiques, the laser threads still held onto him, tightening their grip on his cellular structure and causing him to howl in agony and frustration. Exhausted, he reverted to his original fat, fleshy form.

With a sardonic laugh, the General turned up the pain amplification mechanism to its maximum setting, causing the Mutati to squirm even more frantically. The creature reached the highest note of a blood-curdling scream, and then babbled everything he knew about the military operations of his people. In a cracking voice, he said he was a mid-level officer, a sevencap who had been the adjutant for one of their top admirals.

"He has told all he knows," General Sajak announced triumphantly, as the victim slumped on the rack, bleeding purple fluid from his ears and giving off fitful gasps. The small officer stood over him, smiling. . . .

One of the noblemen sitting in judgment with Lorenzo was the gray-haired Jacopo Nehr, inventor of the "nehrcom," the instantaneous, cross-galactic communication system. Fabulously wealthy, he also manufactured efficient, low-cost robots in leased facilities on the Hibbil Cluster Worlds, and engaged in precious gem mining and distribution.

The other noble at the Judgment Table was Saito Watanabe of CorpOne, a tall, obese man with jowls that hung loosely on each side of his face. He and Nehr, both born commoners, had been promoted by the Doge to "Princes of the Realm," in honor of their business successes. Now their companies were affiliated with the all-pervasive Doge Corporation, which received a share of all merchant prince profits.

Prince Saito did not like these sessions, but attended them out of necessity, in order to maintain the favorable economic position of his own business empire. When the interrogation of a prisoner became most intense, he tried to tune it out discreetly and think of other matters. At the moment, he was remembering back a decade, to a time when his estranged son Noah had been in his late twenties and had worked for him. Once they had been close, though it had developed into a strained relationship, filled with disagreements over environmental issues.

Thinking back, he wondered if the young man had been right after all.

Sadness filled the Prince as he recalled their emotion-charged final argument. As the details came back, he felt tears forming in his eyes. With sudden resolve, he fought the emotion and pushed it deep inside, where it would not be noticed by his companions.

Only hours ago, Prince Saito had sent his son a letter suggesting a meeting. A telebeam response had arrived moments before this interrogation session, as indicated by a change in the color of Saito's signet ring, from ruby to emerald. He had not been able to look at it yet.

At long last the victim issued a horrendous, shuddering scream and died. As he did so, the wager box metamorphosed from black to gold, and cast a bright beam of light on the face of the victorious contestant. It was Lorenzo the Magnificent, as usual. He loved to win, and set the machines to make certain that he always did.

Presently, the Doge and Nehr went out the door, bantering back and forth over the results of the bet, while Saito remained at the table. Men in black hoods swung a hoist mechanism over the corpse of the prisoner. They grunted with exertion as they moved the heavy body onto a sling.

Prince Watanabe took a deep breath, anticipating a negative response from his proud, willful son. To activate the telebeam projector, he touched the stone of the signet ring. The mechanism identified him from DNA in the oil of his skin and flashed a black-on-white message in front of his eyes, floating in the air.

He read it, and allowed a tear of joy to fall down his cheek. Given a fresh opportunity, he would listen to his son this time, would do everything humanly possible to bring them back together again.

Chapter Three

There is a legend that the Creator of the Galaxy can alter his appearance, like a Mutati.

—From a Mutati children's story

Paradij, the fabled Mutati homeworld. . . .

High atop his glittering Citadel overlooking the capital city, the Zultan Abal Meshdi stood on a clearglax floor inside a slowly spinning gyrodome. An immense terramutati who could take on many appearances, he now looked like a golden-maned lionoid in flowing robes and jewels, clinging with the suction of his bare feet to the moist, revolving surface.

Around the majestic leader spun two other compartments, visible to him through thick, clear plates. One contained waterborne Mutati variations that swam gracefully . . . while the other enclosure was filled with genetic variations that flew about at hummingbird speed.

These were the three types of Mutatis—terramutatis, hydromutatis, and aeromutatis—functioning on the ground, in the water, and in the air. Within their own environments, the variations could shapeshift, becoming a panoply of exotic creatures.

From the gyrodome, Meshdi saw Royal Chancellor Aton Turba in the room outside, pacing back and forth as he awaited the instructions of his superior. A mass of flesh with a small head and centipede legs, Turba had been in this shape for less than a day.

If a Mutati remained in one form too long, his sensitive

cellular structure locked into place, so that he could no longer metamorphose. Normally it was safe to maintain one appearance for weeks, but Turba changed himself on a much more frequent basis, fearful that if he didn't he might slip into cellular rigidity. And, despite the chancellor's fluid appearance he remained instantly recognizable to the Zultan, who possessed a rare gift. Meshdi was one of the few Mutatis who could look at another, no matter his appearance, and see beyond the surface to an intricate combination of aural hues and electrical charges that were unique to the individual.

The Zultan's gyrodome made a faint squealing noise specially tuned to give pleasure to him, and he smelled the sweetness of santhems, tiny airflowers that glowed faintly mauve in the moist, humid air . . . a barely visible field of color.

Abal Meshdi inhaled deeply, absorbing millions of the scented flowerets. A sensation of deep relaxation permeated his entire body, and he sighed with pleasure.

A wonderful gift from his Adurian allies far across the galaxy, the gyrodome spun faster and faster, raising the pitch of its whine, heightening his pleasure to one of the highest levels he had ever experienced. Everything became a blur around him. The mechanism sent the Zultan into a trance in which all of the problems, decisions, and challenges of his position were aligned, and he could consider them in detail.

Foremost in his mind: the continued Human threat. Each day he considered what to do with the ones that were captured, assigning the trickle that came in from various sectors of the galaxy to hard labor or execution through horrific, screaming deaths. He enjoyed watching them die, since they suffered so much. Like his counterparts on

Timian One, he knew how to heighten the pain of his enemies.

He also worried what to do with his own son, Hari'Adab, who seemed overly independent, almost rebellious at times. It especially troubled him that Hari had expressed opposition to him privately about the "Demolio" program, a top secret, highly ambitious military weapon that the Mutatis had under development. The Zultan, with no patience for naysayers, had thus far been unable to change the young Mutati's mind, but had obtained his sacred promise to keep his feelings to himself. And, in an effort to provide Hari with administrative experience for the maturation of his thinking processes, he had assigned him as Emir of another planet, Dij. For some time, however, Hari had not been submitting the required reports to his father. As a result, the Zultan would need to apply stern discipline.

Gradually the dome slowed, and Abal Meshdi stood upright. The water and air creatures around him had grown quiet, and the Zultan's head was clear and calm. By the time he emerged from the dome, he had made a decision about his arch enemies. The matter of his errant son would have to wait.

Aton Turba bowed, then stood submissively with his three hands clasped in front of his round belly.

Above all, the Zultan hated Humans. It was an enmity that went back for millennia, to disputes among the distant ancestors of both races. He didn't remember what started it all, but had an exacting memory of the events that had occurred during his own lifetime. There had been a number of military skirmishes, and in most of them Humans had prevailed. Because of limitations on space travel, however—with faster-than-light speed only achieved by mysterious, sentient podships that operated on their own schedules—

neither side had been able to mount a large-scale attack on the other.

According to Mutati mythology, the galaxy was once pristine, before Humans defiled it tens of thousands of years ago. The Mutatis knew this from an oral tradition that went back to a time before Humans existed, when there were only a handful of galactic races.

The Zultan scowled at his chancellor and announced, "The gyrodome has just shown me exactly how to use the new weapon my researchers are developing."

Turba looked perplexed, for he had not been told anything about this. But he knew better than to ask questions of his superior. As always, the information would flow in due course, and the chancellor would be required to remember every detail.

"When the device is perfected I will institute a new policy," the Zultan announced in a pompous voice, "and trillions of Humans will be exterminated, like hordes of insects."

Abal Meshdi went on to explain the terrible new doomsday weapon to Turba, and told the astounded chancellor that he would need to tend more carefully to the affairs of the Citadel in the future, since the Zultan would be occupied with other, more far-reaching, matters. . . .

Within days, an elite corps of "outriders" was selected and trained . . . Mutatis who were looking for opportunities to attack their enemies with the most frightful weapon of annihilation in the history of galactic warfare.

Overseeing the operation from his busy War Room in the capital city of Jadeen, the Zultan gazed out on banks of data processors that projected space-simulation images of the merchant prince worlds . . . and of planets farther out, at the fringe of the enemy realm. A tiny spaceship, represented by a larger-than-scale point of orange light, flew toward one of the outer worlds.

Abal Meshdi chuckled, and thought, *The Humans believe they are such masters of technology, but we have a surprise for them.*

Chapter Four

> Timeweb ensnares the past, the present, and the future. As each moment becomes the past, it folds into the web and seems to disappear without actually doing so. Simultaneously, in a great cosmic balance, the future opens up for us . . . little by little.
>
> —Tulyan Imprint

Seated in the back of a maglev limousine, the man gazed out a tinted window as the car hummed along a mountain track, snaking downhill. Through morning vistas that opened between sun-dappled trees, Noah Watanabe saw immense factories and office complexes below in the Valley of the Princes, facilities that were operated by the titans of industry who controlled the multi-planet Human Empire. For a few seconds, he barely made out the high-walled perimeter of his father's CorpOne compound, with its radically-shaped structures, an imaginative variety of geometric and artistic combinations.

On the opposite side of the valley, Rainbow City—the largest industrial metropolis on Canopa—clung to a shimmering, iridescent cliff. Workers occupied homes on the lower levels of the community, while the villas of wealthy noblemen studded the top like a crown of jewels. For decades Prince Saito had owned one of those palatial residences, and Noah recalled some happy times growing up there . . . but only a few. There had been too many family problems.

It was early summer now, with the canopa pines and exotic grasses of the valley still bright green, having gorged themselves with moisture in anticipation of the coming dry months. Noah viewed it as a survival mechanism, and thought that plants were just as intelligent as other life forms, but in different ways. This and other controversial beliefs frequently put him at odds with the wealthy industrialists of the Merchant Prince Alliance, including his own father.

Noah wore a velvis surcoat and a high-collar shirt with a gold chain around the neck. His muscles bulged under the fabric. He was accompanied by six men dressed in the green-and-brown uniforms of the Guardians, his force of environmental activists who were known as "eco-warriors." The men were armed with high-caliber puissant rifles, as well as sidearms and an arsenal of stun-weapons, poisons, and plax-explosives. They sat silently, staring outside in all directions, ever on the alert for danger. Ahead of the black car and behind it on the maglev track—as arranged by Prince Saito—were nine other identical vehicles, thus preventing potential aggressors from targeting Noah too easily. An air escort of CorpOne attack hellees flew overhead, and the entire area around him had been scanned by infrared and other devices.

Enemies could still defeat any of these systems. Technology was that way; you could never be certain what your adversary knew, or what he had developed to use against you in the eternal dance of offensive and defensive advancements. People wishing to do Noah harm might still be lurking in the woods or in the air, but he believed in fate; if something was meant to get him, it would.

This was how he felt about the upcoming meeting with his father, which he had not expected to occur. Upon receiving the message from the old man, Noah had experienced a visceral sensation that a greater power was at work, drawing them together. Perhaps the two of them, who had disagreed so vehemently about industrial and environmental issues in the past, might find some common ground after all. Noah had always held onto a thread of hope that this might happen, but had taken no steps in that direction, until he replied to his father's recent message.

Noah's strong belief in fate did not mean that he just sat around and waited for things to occur. Far from it. The penultimate activist among activists, he was an assertive leader who constantly pushed events, implementing large-scale transformations on the worlds of the Human-controlled Merchant Prince Alliance.

In the process, Noah had become fabulously wealthy in his own right, so he cared nothing of rumors reaching him that he had been disowned by his father; he really only cared about the loss of a relationship with Prince Saito . . . the riches of emotion, knowledge, and experience that they were not sharing with each other. Maybe that was about to change.

The procession of maglev vehicles reached the valley floor, where the single track widened into ten, with a variety of conveyances whirring along on them . . . luxury cars, truck-trailer rigs, and buses filled with workers. Presently Noah and his entourage passed through a security beam at an ornate gate, and entered the CorpOne compound. A pair of diamonix elephants with red-jeweled eyes stood on either side of a grassy planting area just inside the entry. Ahead, Noah could see the main building. He knew it well, from having worked there with his father at one time, before their blowup.

A marvel of engineering and aesthetic design, Prince Saito

Watanabe's office headquarters was an inverted pyramid, with the point down. As if by magic, the large structure balanced perfectly in that precarious position, while the foundation—a broad platform that included gardens, flagstones, and ornamental fountains—spun slowly beneath it. But Noah Watanabe (with his scientific knowledge and curiosity) knew how it worked; the structure was held in place by a slender core-pillar of pharium, the strongest metal in the galaxy. Elaborate geomagnetics were involved as well, and as a last recourse, a backup system would shoot stabilizing outriggers into receptacles if the tilt meters indicated trouble.

Noah's car hummed up to the edge of the slowly revolving platform and locked into position at the edge of an exotic rose garden. He gazed up at the improbable building above him as it rotated with the platform, and considered the practical benefits of such a design. As the headquarters spun, it gave off electronic pulses that absorbed and processed important data. The system could identify known agitators from all galactic races, profile criminal types, and make highly sophisticated statistical predictions.

Noah wondered what his father wanted; their emotion-charged enmity had lasted for a decade and a half. In memory, he went over the conciliatory message he had received from the old patriarch, reviewing every detail that had been in the telebeam. His father was a precise man, who said exactly what he intended every time he communicated in any form, but Noah suspected hidden meanings:

In the past we have not understood one another as a father and son should. I blame myself almost entirely, and you not at all. It is my duty to bridge our differences.

The electronic transmittal had gone on to suggest a time

and a place for a meeting. Now, as Noah watched a white-uniformed escort secretary march primly toward the hover-limousine, he recollected his own written response:

Father: I appreciate your sentiments, and look forward to meeting with you as you have specified.

From her office inside the inverted pyramid, Francella Watanabe stared in rage and disbelief at a closed-circuit screen that showed the escort secretary leading Noah and his entourage through a wide corridor. At various points along the route, Francella—as Corporate Security Chief—could activate detonations by remote control and kill the entire party. The thought was tempting, but she had something even more devastating in mind.

With a heavy sigh, she activated a copy of the telebeam messages her father and Noah had exchanged, and continued to seethe over them, as she had done since seeing them for the first time three days before. To the very depths of her soul she loathed her twin brother, resenting the preferential treatment he had always received at her expense. Before the big disagreement between Noah and his father over environmental issues, the young man had been the heir apparent, the favored one. In those days Noah had even dressed like his father, in a cloak, brocaded surcoat and liripipe hat, while she was expected to remain in the shadows and say very little. She was, after all, only a female in an interplanetary society run by men, for the benefit of men.

Now her bête noire had entered the building only a few floors down. She wished their father had consulted her about such an important matter, for she might have used her considerable wiles to steer him away from making the invitation. Recently, though, the old man had seemed distant and had been making excuses to avoid or delay the appointments she had requested with him.

He would regret that soon, because Francella had set in motion a new and climactic plan . . . one that would take both her father and brother out of the picture, while allowing her to obtain everything she so richly deserved.

A two-pronged attack.

She wished it didn't have to be this way, and her conscience had been giving her some trouble over it. But she had been driven to do this, with no other choice. Events . . . and people . . . were conspiring against her, and she needed to strike fast, in order to protect her position.

Hearing familiar noises behind her, she felt her pulse quicken. Francella flipped off the telebeam and turned to see her aged father opening the door and lurching into the room in his stiff-jointed way, tapping the hardwood floor with one of his ornate walking sticks. He had arrived only the day before from Timian One, where he had been attending to his duties on the Council of Forty, a powerful clique of noblemen who ruled with the Doge.

Prince Saito Watanabe had a large collection of fancy canes, many of them carved in the images of animals. This one, of canopa white teak, had a bull elephant head carved on top of the handle and the end of an elephant snout at the bottom.

All around the CorpOne complex, as well as in his lavish homes and vehicles, the obese old man had representations of the grand, extinct beasts. Images of the pachyderms were on wall hangings, pillow cases, and statuary; even articles of furniture were carved in their likeness. In addition, Prince Watanabe had commissioned paleontology expeditions to Earth and other far planets where the creatures used to roam . . . scientific ventures that brought back remains of elephants for genetic testing.

"You requested an urgent conference with me," the industrialist said to her, in a coarse tone. "I grant you five minutes, before my appointment with Noah."

"Five minutes?" She felt her face flush, and noticed her father looking at her closely with his intense, dark eyes.

"My schedule is very tight," he said.

"Too tight for your own daughter?"

"I'm sorry if it appears that way, but I have been planning for this important rendezvous with Noah, going over what I will say to him."

"Are you certain it is wise to do this now?" she asked, already knowing his answer.

Saito Watanabe studied his statuesque, redheaded daughter, who wore a white lace dress with gold brocade, and a high, star-shaped headdress. For an additional fashion statement, she had shaved off her eyebrows and hair at the front of her head, creating a high forehead.

He heard the displeasure in her voice, saw it etched on her face . . . and wondered what had gone wrong with the relationship between her and Noah. For years Saito had not failed to notice the raw hatred between them, the destructive sparks and flames that flared whenever they were together.

"I will see your brother alone," he said to her. "It is best for the two of you to remain apart."

"Daddy, Noah hates us. Don't you realize that?"

With deep sadness, the heavyset man looked away. He felt his eyes misting over, and didn't say what had been in his heart for a long time, a primogenitary hope that Noah would take over for him.

A son should follow in his father's footsteps, the Prince

thought. *It is the natural order of things.*

But Noah had been defiant and headstrong. So much so that the Prince had not expected him to accept the invitation. But he had.

What is Noah thinking? What are his wishes, his dreams?

"It is time," the Prince announced to his daughter. And he ordered her out of his office, hardly noticing the fiery glare she shot back at him.

The reception room where Noah had been told to wait was on the fourth level of the upside-down pyramid, with a wide picture window that looked out on the gardens and fountains below. Since each floor was larger than the one beneath it, he saw an overhang outside the window, and knew that each floor all the way to the top was like this as well, in a dizzying arrangement of inverted tiers.

He was pondering the upcoming session with his enigmatic father, and only half noticed a number of CorpOne security police in silver uniforms gathering on a flagstone area outside. Over their heads, blue-and-silver CorpOne banners fluttered, each bearing the stylized designs of elephants.

Suddenly he heard the violent pop-pop of gunfire. The private police took cover behind plants, benches, and fountains, and drew their weapons. But many of them were not quick enough, and they fell under the onslaught.

Stunned, Noah saw a squadron of green-and-brown uniformed soldiers running onto the flagstones, all carrying shiny blue puissant rifles, setting up a ferocious volley of high-intensity fire that drove the defenders for cover. Many died in the onslaught.

The uniforms looked like those of Noah's own Guardians! But they couldn't possibly be his people. He had not ordered this! Oblivious to any danger, he pressed his face against the window glax. He didn't recognize any of the individuals. Who were they and why were they doing this?

Noah's thoughts went wild. He couldn't imagine what was occurring. Now the attackers were hurling explosives that detonated and shook the building.

Furious and confused, Noah hurried into the corridor, where he met his entourage of six Guardians, all with their weapons drawn. "Follow me!" he shouted. And he led them back the way they had come in.

Only moments before, Saito Watanabe had been standing at a window of his large office, considering what he would say to his son. It had been a long time since the two of them had spoken at all, so it would be an extremely awkward situation. Lifting a tall glass to his lips the old man took a long drink of sakeli, a syrupy liqueur, and admitted to himself that he was afraid the meeting would not go well. A tiny remark could set off yet another argument, so he would be careful about what he said . . . and try not to take offense too easily.

We need to get to know one another again.

His dark gaze flickered around the room and settled on a scroll attached to the wall. It was his Document of Patronage from Doge Lorenzo, the legal instrument attesting to the fact that Saito had been elevated to the status of a nobleman, even though he had not been born to such a station. Saito's entire corporate empire rested upon that piece of inscribed tigerhorse skin, and upon the ancient political system that supported it.

My son should receive this some day.

Like other merchant princes, Saito believed that a strong son could carry on the family traditions in ways that a daughter could never do. Francella had been trying to fill that role, but something had been missing. The Prince knew it, and she must as well.

Canopa, one of the wealthiest Human-ruled worlds, was dominated by CorpOne, the mega-company owned by Prince Saito Watanabe. Under grant from Doge del Velli, the Prince owned industrial facilities on more than a hundred moons and planets, including distant Polée, a mineral-rich but sparsely populated world that generated immense profits. With a wide range of operations, Watanabe was especially proud of his medical laboratories, which had developed remarkable products to extend and improve the quality of life through "cellteck"—advanced cellular technology.

In recent years, Noah had become wealthy in his own right as Master of the Guardians, demonstrating considerable business acumen. The young man's operations were on nowhere near the scale of the Prince's, but nonetheless they showed great ability. In sharp contrast, Francella had never accomplished anything on her own. She just whiled away her time as an officer of the firm, without showing any creative spark of her own.

An eruption of gunfire brought the old man out of his thoughts. As if in a bad dream, he stared in shock at the outbreak of violence and pandemonium outside. Guardian forces were attacking CorpOne! He could not believe that his own son would commit such an atrocity against him, no matter the differences they'd had in the past. They were the same blood, the same heredity, and the Prince had sought a reconciliation with him. Was there no honor in Noah, no familial loyalty?

Dark fury infused Saito Watanabe, the raw, unforgiving rage brought on by deception and betrayal. Somehow his son's Guardians had disabled the building's electronic-pulse security system to gain entry!

Why would Noah do this?

All hope for rapprochement between the two of them exploded. A gloomy darkness settled around the Prince. Prior to this, he had been reconsidering his entire business philosophy, wondering if his son's environmental activistism might have some merit after all. Saito had wanted to suggest to Noah that perhaps CorpOne's polluting factories might be dismantled or redesigned after all, no matter the cost.

Now they would never have that conversation.

The door of Watanabe's office burst open, and his silver-uniformed security police rushed in. Their faces were red, their eyes wild. "This way, My Prince!" one of them shouted, a corporal.

The police formed a protective cocoon around the big man, and rushed him out into the corridor.

Chapter Five

The noble-born princes have too much time on their hands.

—Doge Lorenzo del Velli

General Mah Sajak stood impatiently while an Adurian slave put a clean red-and-gold uniform on him, replacing one that was covered with fresh purple blood stains. The General had been torturing a Mutati with an evisceration machine, and the prisoner of war had not died well.

The next time, Sajak would stand in a different position while supervising the interrogation and punishment process, to avoid being splattered with the filthy alien fluid. Sometimes when he got excited and stepped too close to a captive this sort of thing happened. It was all part of the job, he supposed, but he didn't like it. A stickler for decorum, he wanted everything clean and tidy, in both his profession and his personal life.

"Hurry up, hurry up," Sajak admonished the slave, for the General was anxious to get back to Regimental HQ and take care of other business.

The captive Adurian was a male hairless homopod, a mixture of mammalian and insectoid features with a small head, bulbous eyes, and no bodily hair. His skin, a blotchy patchwork of faded colors, poked out around the wrinkled but clean rags he wore. He perspired profusely as he worked, and made the mistake of leaving spots of moisture on the General's new uniform. Because of this, Sajak marked him for death, but would keep it a secret until a suitable replacement had been trained, and administered the necessary psychological testing.

This one should have received a perspiration test.

"Sorry, sir," the Adurian said, as he noticed the sweat dripping from his own wide forehead onto the clothing. "Shall I get another jacket?"

"No time for that now," Mah Sajak growled. "Do you really think I have time to wait for such things?"

"No, sir. It's just that . . ." The slave's oversized eyes became even larger from fear, and he perspired even more, a torrent that ran from his brow down his face.

Grumbling to himself, Sajak left the nervous alien and stepped into the hot, silvery light of a security scanner that identified him and allowed him to pass through to a corridor. His body and uniform glowed faintly silver, and would until he reached the next security checkpoint.

A slideway transported him through a long series of corridors in the Gaol of Brimrock, past dismal cells, torture chambers, and body-handling rooms. Unpleasant odors seeped into the hallways, mixed with sweet disinfectant sprays that never quite masked them. Other officers, guards, and civilians passed by, all glowing with metallic illumination that indicated which checkpoints they had been through. Here and there, through tiny windows, he caught glimpses of another world outside, the blue waters of the Grand Canal and the glittering buildings of the opulent city.

The officer barely noticed any of it, however, so engrossed was he in his own concerns, which were extremely important. Mah Sajak—in his oversized uniform and cap—took seriously his duties as Supreme General of the Merchant Prince Armed Forces. Eleven and a half years ago, he had dispatched a military fleet to attack the Mutati homeworld of Paradij, where the Zultan lived in his ostentatious citadel. That fleet should be arriving soon.

I'd like to hoist Meshdi's fat carcass onto one of my interrogation machines, the General thought, and he considered the wide array of torture devices at his disposal—automatic, semi-mechanized, and manual. Each had a specific, deadly purpose, and worked to great effect on the Mutati race.

Beneath the small, bony-featured officer, the slideway squeaked as it flowed forward jerkily. He gripped a shimmering electronic handrail that moved alongside.

So much responsibility on his shoulders, and sometimes it weighed heavily on him. Especially now, with the climactic moment approaching. The "Grand Fleet" of MPA fighter-bombers was aboard a bundle of vacuum rockets that had been traveling through space at sub-light speed for all those years, moving inexorably toward the Mutati homeworld of Paradij. He expected complete military success, but there were always little nagging worries that kept him awake at night.

The General had assured the Doge that all would go well. The renowned Mutati-killer, Admiral Nils Obidos, headed the task force, a man who had won two important military victories against the shapeshifters. He had selected more than twenty-four thousand of the finest men and women in the armed forces, including the top fighter-bomber pilots in the Merchant Prince Alliance. In addition, all ships had redundant mechanical systems and even a backup crew of the finest sentient robots from the Hibbil Cluster Worlds . . . intelligent machines that could operate the whole fleet without Human involvement, if necessary. In some respects the General considered them better than Humans; if he told them what to do they did it, without delays, complaints, or questions.

Doge Lorenzo del Velli was so convinced of a huge victory that he had begun preparations for a gala celebration on Timian One, with the exact date to be announced. It was widely known that there would be a festival, but the Doge had not told anyone what the occasion was. Rumors spread like fire on oil. The best entertainers—Human and alien—would be brought in from all over the galaxy. Even Mutati captives would participate. Under the high security of a huge containment field, terramutatis, hydromutatis, and aeromutatis would perform shapeshifting acts in a golden amphitheater.

At Sajak's thought command, he felt the tiny computer strapped to his wrist imprint his skin with a nubraille pattern, telling him what time it was at that moment. The device, containing a vast encyclopedia of information that he could access, required only that he think what he wanted to know, and the message would be received almost immediately. Now it was early evening, and in the zealousness of his interrogation he had neglected dinner.

During the first six years in which merchant prince fleet had been advancing toward the enemy, General Sajak had received coded nehrcom transmissions from the task force admiral informing him that the operation was progressing well. Nehrcoms (invented by Prince Jacopo Nehr) were audio-video signals transmitted across the galaxy at many times the speed of light . . . an instantaneous communication system in which messages were fired from solar system to solar system at precise angles of deflection, using amplified solar energy. Nehrcom Industries, with a monopoly on the system, had installed transceivers in key sectors of the galaxy—sealed units that would detonate if anyone tried to scan or open them, thus protecting the priceless technological secrets. But the inventor still worried about military and industrial espionage by military enemies and business competitors, and refused to install transceivers in locations he did not consider secure.

And, although the remarkable transceivers could transmit instantaneously across space, they only operated to and from land-based facilities . . . for reasons known only to the secretive Nehr. The General and his staff had discussed sending status reports via messengers on board podships . . . but it had been known from the beginning that this would be an unreliable, dangerous method. Podships operated on their own schedules, often following circuitous routes with numerous pod station stops—thus risking detection by Mutati operatives. The mission planners agreed that it would be better to transmit no messages at all than to take such chances.

So, during the more than five years that the fleet had been beyond nehrcom range, the General had heard nothing at all. His huge task force was taking the long way to the Mutati homeworld, approaching it from an unexpected, poorly patrolled direction. If the Grand Fleet encountered Mutati forces, they would only be small ones, easily crushed.

The arrogant Jacopo Nehr irritated Sajak, for more reasons than one. The self-serving inventor should be forced to share his technology with the Merchant Prince Armed Forces, so that military strategists could employ it more effectively. It might even be possible to improve the system, so that it was no longer dependent upon land-based installations.

The Supreme General sucked in a deep breath. That would be a tremendous advance. But Nehr would not give up the information easily. Attempts had been made—through friendly persuasion and otherwise—and all had failed.

Jacopo Nehr and Prince Saito Watanabe were often seated beside the Doge during torture sessions that the General conducted. For Sajak, this created an awkward situation. Born to a noble station, he secretly resented princely appointments such as the ones received by the two business tycoons, and would prefer a return to the old ways. While Sajak had done well personally through his own efforts, many of his relatives and noble friends had suffered setbacks—having been supplanted by the new breed of entrepreneurs and inventors that the Doge favored. Even worse than his father, Doge Paolantonio IV, who started all of this foolishness, the merchant prince sovereign was surrounding himself with scientists and industrialists, upsetting the old, proven ways of doing things.

Someday the General would do something about that. It was one of his vows, and he always did what he set out to do. From an early age he had been that way. The trick was to conceal his desires from persons more powerful than he, so that they could not prevent him from achieving his goals. Fortunately for him, that list was quite small now, and one day it might not exist at all. He didn't mind taking orders from a commander in chief; but he had to respect the commands, and their source.

General Sajak stepped off the slideway and strolled through a short corridor, then paused at another security checkpoint. This one scanned him with golden light and left him glowing that color when he left. He made his way down a short set of steps through a hallway where the lights were not functioning, and his own glow cast an eerie illumination on the walls. He took another slideway in a different direction.

At a casual wave of his hand, a red-cushioned seat popped up beside him on the conveyor, and he sat upon it. The transporter went through a long tunnel that sloped gently downward toward the Military HQ complex, a heavily fortified bunker deep underground.

In a few moments, he saw a cavern of bright white light ahead, and presently he was immersed in a scanner, this one with a rainbow of metallic colors that left him without a glow. Despite the security checkpoints, one could never be too careful when your mortal enemy was a race of expert shapeshifters.

Robotic guards greeted the General with stiff salutes as he stepped off the slideway and strode through a wide entrance into the War Chamber. Each of the mechanical sentinels was a weapon in itself, featuring a destructive array of guns and explosives that the General could set off at a thought command.

The machinery and personnel of tactics and strategy filled the immense War Chamber. Officers in red-and-gold uniforms rose stiffly and saluted as he entered. Those in his way stepped aside, enabling him to reach the red velvis command chair on a dais at the center.

"Give me a full report," General Sajak said, as he sat down and gazed about impatiently.

His adjutant, Major Edingow, was an angular, square-jawed man who favored single malt whiskey and the camaraderie of officers' clubs. He had halitosis, and to counteract it often chewed mints. This time he seemed to have forgotten his manners.

Irritated, Sajak stepped back to escape the stale odor.

Oblivious to the offense he was committing against his fastidious superior, the Major activated a telebeam bubble—a bright light that floated in the air—and moved it to a comfortable distance in front of the General. In a wordless broadcast, data flowed from the bubble into a receiver implanted in Sajak's brain, and from there traversed the circuitous neural pathways of his mind. He felt a soft hum inside his skull. The facts unfolded in an orderly fashion, and he considered them.

Concerned about the obsolescence of military technology in the eleven-year-old attack force that he had dispatched, General Sajak had sent advance men to the Mutati homeworld, covert agents who were assigned to sneak in and commit acts of sabotage against Mutati infrastructures and military installations, softening them up for the bigger attack. Now he learned the results of the most recent forays, that many agents never got through, and that some were missing and possibly apprehended.

At the edge of the glistening data bubble, Sajak saw his staff officers watching him alertly, ready to comply with his commands the moment he issued them. At a snap of his fingers, the bubble popped and faded away.

Ignoring the faces that were turned toward him expectantly, General Mah Sajak considered the new information. For a century and a half—since galaxy-spanning podships first appeared mysteriously and began to increase contact between the races—Humans and Mutatis had been in an arms race, with huge research teams on both sides striving to make quantum leaps in military technology. He did not know what the Mutatis were working on now, but hoped it was not significant.

A career soldier, it had been frustrating for him to deal with the limited cargo capacities of podships, which had prevented him—and the enemy—from mounting large-scale offensives. He needed the element of surprise to work in favor of his forces . . . but gnats of worry reminded him that the Mutatis might have their own surprise in store for him.

Chapter Six

These machines are designed to mimic only the best aspects of their creators. To permit the opposite, either through something intrinsic or of their own volition, would be to invite disaster.

—Hibbil product statement,
sent out with each AI robot

The jewel-like volcanic planet of Ignem was a favorite for those who liked to travel the back ways of space. Shaped by a series of volcanic cataclysms that belched up rainbows of porous silica, the glittering world looked like an exotic treat for giant gods, one they could just scoop up and swallow as they flew past it on one of their journeys across the cosmos.

Each day Ignem looked a little different, depending upon solar conditions and the amount of glassy dust that was kicked up by powerful winds blowing across the surface. No known life forms existed on the planet, since conditions were too severe for carbon-based, chemical, electrical, or other living creatures. Humans, Hibbils, Mutatis, Adurians, and other galactic races could only go on the surface in expensive, specially-crafted spacesuits that contained layered filter systems. Deep-space adventure companies took wealthy tourists to Ignem several times a year, and the visitors always returned home in amazement, gushing about the natural beauty they had seen.

All expeditions stopped first at the Inn of the White Sun, a comfortable machine-operated way station that had been constructed in a dense orbital ring more than eighty kilometers above the surface of the planet. At the inn, bubble-windowed rental spaces had been fitted with an atmosphere that was breathable to most of the galactic races. Adventurers checked their equipment and purchased anything they needed from a wide array of vending machines. At premium prices, of course.

Sales conventions were also held at the inn, usually for members of the Human-run Merchant Prince Alliance. At the moment, however, many of the rooms were filled with Heccians and Diffros, races of artisans and craftsmen from the far-off Golden Nebula of the Seventieth Sector. They were making quite a commotion as they drank foul-tasting venom extracted from snakes . . . a traditional kickoff ceremony for their conventions.

Now it was the month of Dultaz in the White Sun solar system. A flat-bodied, gray robot named Thinker paced back and forth on the main observation deck of the Inn. The deck ran along the top of the thickest ring section, and was not atmospherically-controlled. Beneath him and stretching along the rings were the beehive-like rooms of the Inn, positioned so that they offered spectacular views of the shimmering jewel-like world below. For travelers on a budget, less expensive rooms were available without views, or with vistas of the twinkling darkness of deep space.

Far below the robot, Ignem glowed with a million colors as the last rays of the setting sun pierced the faceted, layered surfaces of the planet, lighting up the globe and the thin atmosphere surrounding it. He watched the hypnotically subtle chromatic changes, and the translucent effects on Ignem's surface, as the planet held onto the last rays of light before they were sucked away into the stygian night of space.

Thinker often came to this spot late in the day and stood by himself. These were reflective times for him, when he could consider significant issues, utilizing the immense amount of information in his data banks. As the leader of the sentient machines in this galactic subsector he had many responsibilities, and took them all seriously.

In a continual quest to improve himself, Thinker periodically went around the galaxy to collect material for his data banks, which he then brought back to the Inn of the White Sun to catalog. Whenever he traveled, he sought out other sentient machines, conversing with them and making interface connections, to download whatever data they had. Sometimes their security programs would not permit them to interface with him, and if that happened he had the ability to force a connection and override their internal firewalls. But he only rarely did that, not wishing to create controversy or call unnecessary attention to himself. Usually it was easier to just move on. There were always machines that would help him.

The sentient machines under his command had done quite well for themselves, rebuilding mechanical life forms that had been discarded by Humans and putting them back into operation. They even manufactured popular computer chips and sold them around the galaxy. Sometimes, though, they seemed overly dependent upon Thinker. At the moment, two of his assistants, Ipsy and Hakko, were standing at a thick glax door staring out at him, as if they could not do anything further without his advice. He waved them off dismissively, and they stepped back, out of his view. He knew, however, that they were still close by, waiting to talk with him the moment he went back inside.

I should reprogram them, he reminded himself. But this had occurred to him before, and he had never done anything about it. He knew why. Despite the minor irritations he actually enjoyed the relationships, because his subordinates made him feel needed.

Far off, in the perpetual night of the galaxy, he saw something flash and disappear. He would never know for certain what it was, and could only speculate. Perhaps it was a shooting star, a small sun going nova, or the glinting face of a comet before it turned and veered away from the reflective rays of sunlight that seemed to give it life.

It is so beautiful out there.

Since Thinker was a mechanical creature with few internal moving parts, he did not breathe, and was able to function outside the boundaries imposed upon biological life forms. The machines that operated this facility were the sentient remnants of merchant prince industrial efforts. Thrown away and left to rust and decay all over the galaxy, the intelligent robots had sought each other out and formed their own embryonic civilization.

Among Humans and other biological life forms that visited the inn, these mechanical men were something of a joke, and non-threatening. After all, the machines had an affection for Humans, referring to them in almost godlike terms as their "creators." The metal people were an eclectic assortment as well, and amusing in appearance to many people. Some of the robots were Rube Goldberg devices that performed tasks in laughable, inefficient ways, taking pratfalls and accomplishing very little. This explained why many of them were abandoned. Others had been cobbled together with spare parts. In all they looked quite different from the standardized robots manufactured by the Hibbils on their Cluster Worlds, under contract to the Doge and to the leaders of various galactic races.

Thinker didn't really care how he and his loyal compatriots were viewed. His emotional programs were limited in scope, and while he became mildly irritated at times he did not take offense easily. His thoughts tended toward the intellectual, toward questions of deep purpose and matters involving the origins of the universe. Most of all he found it exhilarating to stand out here in the vacuum of space, gazing into eternity . . . into all that was, and all that ever would be. Some marvelous power had created this galaxy, and in his most private thoughts he liked to imagine the Supreme Being as a machine, and not some cellular entity. It seemed plausible . . . perhaps even likely. The galaxy was a machine after all, one that operated on a vast scale, ticking along moment by moment in its journey through time.

Lights blinked on inside the rooms and public chambers of the Inn of the White Sun. Far below, Ignem gave up its ephemeral translucence and faded to darkness, casting an ebony shadow against the cloth of stars beyond.

The cerebral robot was about to go back inside when he felt a rumbling in the metal plates of his body, and his metal-lidded eyes detected a distortion in the fabric of the cosmos, with star systems twisted slightly out of their normal alignment. A section of space in front of him became opaque and amorphous, with a wobbly effect around the edges. He noted a slight change of pressure around him, too, as if a door into another dimension had opened for an instant, and something altogether different was entering.

Podship.

The opacity glowed bright green for a moment, then flickered. A blimp-shaped object took form and made its way toward a faint, barely visible pod station, floating nearby in the airless vacuum of space. The mottled, gray-and-black podship had a row of portholes on the side facing Thinker, with pale green light visible inside the passenger compartment. From his data banks the robot drew a comparison. The sentient creature was reminiscent of a whale of Earth, but without a tail or facial features, and cast off into space.

The pod station, after fading from view during the entry of the podship, solidified its appearance. A globular, roughhewn docking facility, it was nearly as mysterious as the podships themselves. For tens of thousands of years the sentient podships—hunks of living cosmic material—had been traveling at faster-than-light speeds through the galaxy, on regular routes. The ships were of unknown origin, and so too were the orbiting pod stations at which they docked—utilitarian facilities positioned all over the galaxy, usually orbiting the major planets. Some of the galactic races said that the podships and their infrastructure were linked with the creation of the galaxy, and there were numerous legends concerning this. One, attributed to the Humans of ancient Earth, held that the podships would come one day and transport religious and political leaders to the Supreme Being, where all of the great secrets would be revealed.

Thinker signaled for a sliding door to open, and then strode into the lobby of the inn on his stiff metal legs. There he encountered Ipsy and Hakko, who had been waiting for him, as he'd suspected. "Later," he told them. "For once, handle something on your own."

"We need to plan next month's sales convention," Hakko said, "so that the necessities can be ordered."

"Yes," Ipsy agreed. "There is a great deal of printing to be done—announcement cards, menus. You know the trouble we had at the last convention when we tried to serve Blippiq food to Adurians."

"Well, take care of it then," Thinker said, with mock impatience, since it was like playing a game with them.

He continued on his way, and entered a lift that took him down to the lowest level of the inn. There, through a thick glax floor, he could see the dark gray pod station floating perhaps a thousand meters away, and the sentient ship that had just entered one of its docking bays.

Presently he saw a shuttle emerge from the pod station, burning a blue exhaust flame as it closed the gap between the station and the orbital ring. The little craft locked onto a berthing slot, and Thinker saw men step out. He counted twenty-two.

His first impression was that they were Humans, a group of tourists. Unlike other galactic races, Humans did that sort of thing. They just went places to be there, to experience them. Most galactic races considered this sort of thing a waste of time, but Thinker understood. Like the Human technicians who created him, he had a sense of curiosity and wonder about the cosmos.

But the new arrivals were *not* Human. As they walked across a deck toward the main entrance to the Inn of the White Sun, he noted subtle differences that only a highly trained observer such as himself could detect. The bodily motions were slightly different. Oh, they were very close to authentic, but not quite right. They moved like what they really were.

What are Mutatis doing here?

In order to contemplate without distraction, Thinker folded his dull-gray body closed in a clatter of metal, tucking his head neatly inside. To an observer he might look like a metal box now, just sitting silently on the deck. Inside, though, he was deep in concentration, organizing the vast amount of information in his data banks, trying to solve the conundrum that had presented itself to him suddenly.

Unlike Humans, Mutatis never traveled for leisure. They always had some important purpose in mind . . . usually military, political, or economic. In memory, Thinker recalled the bodily movements of the Human impostors. Remnants of their true identities could be seen in every step they took.

They were Mutati soldiers, led by an officer.

This worried Thinker, and he wondered if word had gotten out about the machine operations here. Down on the surface of the volcanic planet, in a region not visible from the orbital ring, the machines were secretly building a military force of their own, a collection of patched-together fighting robots. One day he would use them to prove that his sentient machines had value, that they should not have been discarded.

Were the Mutatis here to spy on that operation? Or had they come for another reason?

Chapter Seven

Our entire galaxy is in motion.
The *Scienscroll* tells us this.
But where is it going?
—Master Noah of the Guardians

At CorpOne headquarters on Canopa, Noah Watanabe had been shocked to see soldiers in green-and-brown Guardian uniforms, firing puissant rifles and setting off booming explosions. He came to realize that they were impersonating his own environmental activists, but there was no time to determine the reason. Instead, he'd led his small entourage to the rooftop of the main building, where they ran toward a dark blue, box-shaped aircraft.

From the days when he had worked there, Noah knew the layout of the complex, and the main building had not changed much in fifteen years. Here and there, doorways were marked differently, but the corridors and lifts remained the same, and it was unchanged on the roof. The aircraft, one of the grid-planes kept on the premises for Prince Watanabe and his top officers, was familiar to Noah, for this was a technology so successful that it had not been significantly altered in nearly a century. The onboard semiautomatic systems were relatively simple to operate, and many people knew how to handle them from an early age.

Noah and his men leaped aboard, and his adjutant Subi Danvar squeezed into the cockpit. Using voice commands and pressure pads, the rotund Danvar activated the takeoff sequence. Red and blue lights flashed across the instrument panel.

The vessel extended four short wings and lifted off. Within moments it engaged the multi-altitude electronic grid system that was part of a planet-wide transportation network. Through the open doorway of the cockpit just forward of Noah's seat, he saw automatic systems begin to kick in, as parallel yellow and blue lines on an instrument panel screen merged into each other, and became green.

Danvar activated touch pads beneath the screen, then reached down for something in the flight bag beside his chair. A scar on the back of his right hand marked where doctors had attached cloned knuckles and fingers, after he lost them in a grid plane crash. Noah had his own moral objections to cloned Human body parts, but he'd never tried to force his views on other people.

He felt a characteristic gentle bump as they locked into the grid, but this was followed moments later by a disturbingly sharp jolt. The screen flashed angry orange letters: TAIL SECTION DAMAGED BY PROJECTILE.

Before Noah could react, the screen flashed again, this time in yellow: BACKUP SYSTEMS ENGAGED.

The craft kept going with hardly a variation in its flight characteristics, and presently Noah felt a reassuring smooth sensation as the grid-plane accelerated to the standard speed of three hundred kilometers per hour.

"Permission to seal the cockpit," Danvar said. "I need to concentrate on the instruments."

"Do it," Noah responded. Almost before permission was granted, the pilot slid the cockpit door shut, placing a white alloy barrier between them.

Through a porthole Noah could see that they were leaving the Valley of the Princes behind, a landscape of trees and fields, spotted with industrial complexes. Had his father betrayed him, faking a Guardian attack to bring him and his organization into disfavor?

Unable to suppress his anger, Noah slammed his fist on the armrest of the chair, so hard that pain shot through the hand. He scanned the sky and the land below, looking for threats.

Obviously, Subi was concerned about this himself. He was Noah's most trusted Guardian, but somewhat eccentric at times, and very outspoken. Noah had learned to give him free rein, but new thoughts began to occur to him now.

Could this man betray me?

After all that he and Subi had been through together, it seemed a preposterous, paranoid thought, and Noah discarded it out of hand. While the two of them were careful to maintain their distance, keeping their relationship professional, Noah had always felt an affinity for the adjutant, a strong bond of friendship. The feeling seemed mutual.

Master Noah heaved a deep sigh. He sat back in his bucket seat and listened to the smooth purr of the gridplane.

If I am meant to die today, so be it. If I am meant to live, that will happen instead. He flicked a speck of black off the long sleeve of his ruffled shirt, where the garment poked out from his surcoat.

Ever since boyhood, Noah Watanabe had sensed a presence guiding him, a force that was always there, constantly directing his actions. He often felt it viscerally, and was convinced that it told him whether or not he was doing the right thing. His stomach was calm now, but the sensation didn't always provide him with consistent indicators. It seemed to have lapses . . . unpredictable and disconcerting gaps.

The grid-plane left the valley far behind and flew over a rugged mountain range, irregular peaks that looked like the heads of demons. On the far side of the mountains the aircraft streaked over an industrial city perched on the edge of a high cliff whose stony facets glittered and flashed in midmorning sunlight.

Known as the "canyon planet," Canopa was unlike any other world in the charted galaxy, with deep rainbow-crystal gorges, powerful whitewater rivers and spectacular scenery. Cities such as the one they were flying over now were engineering marvels, clinging to cliff-faces of iridescent rock. Long ago, superstitious aborigines had lived in these areas, but had been driven out by Human traders who were the economic precursors of the modern-day merchant princes. Primitive people still lived on Canopa, but kept themselves out of view, with the exception of a few men and women who were captured on occasion and brought in for observation. Curiously, aboriginal children were never seen by outsiders, not even in pre-merchant times.

Canopa was steeped in mystery and legend, and was said to have been the domain in ancient times of a race of alien creatures . . . people who had gone extinct, with their bodies now on display in museums. At a number of archaeological sites around the planet, their eerie exoskeletons and personal effects had been dug up. After studying the bodies, galactic anthropologists determined that they were a race of arthropods of high intelligence. Through rune stones that had been recovered, their language had been only partially deciphered. It was known that they had referred to themselves as Nops and that they had engaged in off-world trading, but very little else had been discovered about their activities.

Following an hour's flight, Noah's compound came into

view atop a verdant plateau, bounded by river gorges on two sides. Restoring land that had once been the site of industrial operations, he had converted it to an impressive wildlife preserve and farm that he called his Ecological Demonstration Project, or "EDP." The facility was far more than just structures and compounds and set-aside areas. It was a high-concept dream shaped into reality, one that included projects designed to show how man could live in harmony with the environment.

One of Master Noah's oft-repeated admonitions to his loyal followers was, *Excess is waste.* This was linked to his concept of balance, which he saw as a necessary force in the cosmos, as true for microorganisms as it was for higher life forms.

This way of thinking had been a source of friction between Noah and his father, building up to their terrible argument. On that day, only moments after Prince Saito struck him, Noah had quit his job at CorpOne and stormed out, never expecting to return or even to speak with his father again. Noah's environmental militancy had proven too much for the Prince, who had refused to accept any of the concepts. Like Earthian bulls the two men had butted heads, with each of them holding fast to their political and economic beliefs.

After Noah's resignation, his father had publicly and vehemently disowned him. Noah wondered how much of a part his twin sister Francella had played in encouraging the old man's willful behavior. She had always hated Noah. Certainly there had been jealousy on her part; he had seen too many examples of it. But her feelings of enmity seemed to run even deeper, perhaps to her own biological need to survive and her feeling that Noah was a threat to the niche she wanted to occupy.

At the troubling thought, Noah cautioned himself. One of his father's criticisms of him might have been valid, the way Noah constantly saw situations in environmental terms. Sometimes when Noah caught himself doing this, he tried to pull back and look at things in a different way. But that did not always work. He was most comfortable thinking within a framework that he knew well, which he considered a blueprint for all life forms, from the simplest to the most complex.

The grid-plane locked onto a landing beam. Subi Danvar opened the cockpit door, and Noah saw the parallel green lines on the instrument panel diverge, forming flashing yellow and blue lines.

"All systems automatic," Subi reported. He swung out of the pilot's chair and made his way aft, turning his husky body sideways to get past banks of instruments on each side.

Noah felt the grid-plane descend, going straight down like an elevator, protected by the electronic net over his EDP compound.

With a scowl on his birthmark-scarred face, Subi plopped his body into a chair beside Noah and announced, "I'm not getting any sleep until I get to the bottom of this. Somebody copied our uniforms exactly . . . or stole them from us."

"I didn't see any of our people out there," Noah said.

"That doesn't mean they weren't involved, Master. I'll start with the most recent volunteers and work back from there. Maybe one of them is disgruntled."

"Could be."

In an organization as large as Noah's, with thousands of uniformed Guardians, it was impossible to keep every one of them happy all the time. It was company policy to recruit people with high ideals, capable of thinking in terms of large-scale issues . . . rather than petty private matters. Still, there were always personality conflicts among workers, and unfulfilled ambitions.

The aircraft settled onto a paved landing circle and taxied toward a large structure that had gray shingle walls and elegant Corinthian columns, shining bright white in the midday sunlight. This was Noah's galactic base of operations, the main building in a complex of offices and scientific laboratories.

In his primary business, he performed ecological recovery operations around the galaxy, under contract to various governmental agencies, corporations, and individuals wanting to repopulate areas devastated by industrial operations. On some of the smaller worlds he also operated electric power companies, having patented his own environmentally-friendly energy chambers. The merchant princes, and not just his father, had shown absolutely no concern for ecology; they routinely raped each planet's resources and then moved on to other worlds. Canopa, despite the wild areas that still existed along the route Noah was flying now, was nowhere near what it used to be. Huge areas of the planet had been stripped of their resources and denuded of beauty, leaving deep geological scars that might never heal.

As far as Noah Watanabe was concerned, the galactic races tended to be interlopers in the natural order of things, and Humans were the worst of all. His ideas were much wider than humanity, though, or any of the races. While performing his business operations on a variety of worlds, he had begun to see relationships within relationships, and the vast, galaxy-wide systems in which they operated.

The grid-plane came to a stop and a double door

whooshed open. As he stepped down onto a flagstone entry plaza, Noah inhaled a deep breath of warm, humid air, and watched aides as they hurried to greet him. This moment was a gift. For a while, he had not been certain if he would ever make it back here.

Chapter Eight

The art of business is not a pretty one; it requires blood-red pigment.

—Francella Watanabe, private reflections

In her white-and-gold dress and star-shaped headdress, Noah's sister gave the appearance of a lady of leisure. It was just one of the subterfuges the tall, redheaded woman employed to conceal the fact that she was responsible for the assault on CorpOne headquarters, and that she herself had received training in the most advanced styles of combat and tactical warfare.

"Faster!" Francella shouted to four company policemen who carried her injured, comatose father on a hover-bier. With her leading the way, they ran through a dimly-illuminated corridor, just one of the tunnels that formed a maze beneath the office-industrial complex of more than twenty buildings. Originally these subterranean passageways had been the streets of an ancient Nopan city, but the community had been abandoned long ago when the inhabitants fell victim to a mysterious malady.

Old Prince Saito, with his head bandaged, came to life suddenly on the bier. His eyes opened wide and he groaned loudly, then flopped one of his beefy arms over the side. "Noah?" he said, while lifting his head and looking toward Francella.

She wanted to scream her rage and pound on him, but instead pressed a small skin-colored pad against her own neck, right over a throbbing vein. Almost immediately she felt a custom drug take effect, deadening her emotions and dampening twinges of personal guilt she had been feeling, concerning the things she had to do.

Abruptly the nobleman's eyes closed again, but he kept murmuring Noah's abominable name. Finally he fell silent and his face went slack, though his chest heaved up and down as he clung stubbornly to life. She stared at a sapphire signet ring on his right hand and vowed that Noah would never possess it. She considered slipping it off the old man's finger at the first opportunity, but hesitated. Soon she would have everything she wanted anyway.

In order to maintain appearances, Francella fell back beside her father and re-secured his arm inside the electronic strap that had been holding it. His eyelids fluttered, but didn't open.

She spoke his name, but he did not respond. His breathing remained steady.

Prince Saito had been injured by a hail of alloy-jacketed projectiles fired into his office building by the phony Guardians, who were *conducci,* mercenaries she had hired secretly. Murdering her father had been the primary objective of the professional fighters, but they may not have succeeded. She hated sloppy workmanship.

"You'll be fine," she assured Prince Saito, though he seemed unable to hear her. "We're taking care of you."

"Noah?" he murmured, with his eyelids still closed.

"I'm *Francella,*" she said, arching her hairless brows in displeasure. "Noah tried to kill you."

"He wouldn't do that . . . wouldn't do that . . ." Prince Saito's face became a twisted mask as he struggled to think, struggled for consciousness, and finally gave up the effort . . . but kept breathing.

She studied the heaving of his chest, and thought, *Die, damn you!*

They ascended a corrugated alloy ramp to a platform and ran across to the opposite side, where they boarded a small maglev rail car. Francella took a seat at the rear of the vehicle, while the others placed the bier on the floor in the center of the aisle, and then took seats themselves. Armored doors closed and the car accelerated quickly, throwing Francella against her seat back.

Only half an hour earlier, fifty-eight heavily armed *conducci* had attacked the CorpOne complex. She had hired them through a series of middlemen in such a circuitous chain that no one knew who had originally paid for their services. As the Security Chief for the company, Francella Watanabe had ways of getting things done discreetly. She had, however, put out the word that any mistakes would be handled brutally . . . and the killers had not done their job cleanly, as she had demanded.

The CorpOne policemen in the rail car with her had known nothing of the plot and had interfered, going to the aid of the Prince and whisking him off to safety, with Francella in tow . . . trying to figure out what to do.

Her thoughts racing, she touched an electronic transmitter at her waist, setting off explosives in the tunnel behind them. The company security men chattered excitedly and stared out the rear window of the railway car at the flaming tunnel.

But Francella had other matters on her mind. Privately, she was considering how best to finish the job on her father, but she needed to do it carefully, so that no one suspected a thing. For years she had been monitoring the old man's declining health, and had hastened it along by seeing to it that the "cellteck" life extension drugs and other medicines he took were of less effect than they should have been. With those products at full strength—many manufactured in CorpOne laboratories—he might have lived to a hundred and ten, another twenty-seven years.

Too long for her to wait. She wanted control of all family corporate operations as soon as possible, before anything could erode her position.

The alterations in her father's pharmacopoeia had been slight but cumulative, so that over a period of years they undoubtedly subtracted time from his life. An actuary secretly in her employ (his services obtained through another circuitous series of middlemen) had prepared projections showing how much she had probably shortened the unnamed subject's life. Based upon raw medical data that she had provided for the actuary, he had originally estimated a reduced life span of seventeen months, twenty-four days, and a few hours.

Unfortunately that had been modified by the interference of the Prince himself, who had unwittingly compensated for her tricks by improving his diet and instituting a moderate exercise program. In the process, the big man, unaware of her actions, had been bragging that he'd lost two kilos over the past few weeks. Undoubtedly the net effect on his health had been minimal, since he had always been sedentary and had such an enormous girth. She had been waiting for him to slip back into his old ways, but the crisis had interfered . . . the meeting between Noah and her father that she could not allow.

At Francella's instigation another explosion sounded behind the maglev car in which she rode. The vehicle shuddered, but kept going. It entered a brightly-illuminated tunnel, and moments later a heavy alloy door slammed shut behind them, keeping them safe from pursuers or the fire and detonations that she had set off.

A rapprochement between Francella's brother and father

would have unraveled much of her carefully-crafted efforts over the past decade, allowing her hated brother to gain a toe-hold on CorpOne operations.

She and Noah, her fraternal twin, had never gotten along very well, and the problems started early. After the babies were born, they thrashed around on a table and gave each other bloody lips. Over the years there had been respites between them, cease-fires, but they were few and far between . . . and tense. The siblings had always loathed one another, and had exchanged few words in the last fifteen years.

Their mother Eunicia, the only woman Prince Saito ever married, had almost died in childbirth. She had lived for years afterward, but never fully recovered, and was always a frail woman, finally dying in a grid-plane crash at the age of fifty-one. Prince Saito had never been the same afterward.

In recent weeks the old man had been wavering about Noah, and had mentioned the possibility of revamping his business operations in order to satisfy his son. This could involve bringing her hated twin back into the corporation, with all of his costly, meddlesome ideas about environmental issues. Francella could not tolerate that.

Upon learning of the scheduled meeting between the men, she had gone into a crisis mode. Setting aside her attempts to erode the Prince's health, she had moved forward quickly. Her military-style attack with phony Guardians was a risky course of action, but offered the potential of distinct benefits. It could eliminate the Prince much more quickly, while placing the blame for his "tragic death" on Noah.

It might still work, if the old man died of his head injury.

On the bier beside her, Prince Saito groaned again. Francella felt like stuffing something in his mouth to shut him up, but resisted the temptation. She would take the rational course, not letting her emotions get the better of her.

Chapter Nine

We Parviis are the most powerful of all galactic races.
And, with good reason, the most secretive.
—Woldn, the Eye of the Swarm

A towering black cloud hung over Canopa's central plain like an anvil, threatening to strike the land with a hammer-blow of rain. Summer was late getting underway this year, as the weather had been unseasonably stormy and cold, almost a month into the season. There had been some warm days, but not many.

As Tesh Kori stood on cobblestones near the center of a large courtyard, she wished her boyfriend did not have such a quick temper. Dr. Hurk Bichette stood with his hands on his hips, shouting at the maintenance man for his country estate. The prominent physician had a strong jaw and closely-set green eyes. A vein bulged and throbbed at his temple, a sign that he was losing control.

"You're not paying enough attention to your duties," Bichette thundered in his basso voice. "It seems that other things interest you more." He shot a glance in Tesh's direction and glared at her for an instant before looking away. This courtyard was between the doctor's palatial home and the stables for his expensive tigerhorses. The buildings were constructed in the classical Canopan style, of smoky-white marble with inlaid ruby and emerald gemstones. A colorful kaleidoscope of imported tulips bloomed in flower beds around the perimeter of the courtyard, and in planter boxes on the balconies of the three-story main house.

The target of Dr. Bichette's rage, Anton Glavine, wore a short blue-and-white tunic buttoned down the front, with high, tight leggings and black boots. Remaining calm all through the verbal onslaught, the blond, mustachioed maintenance man stood taller than the doctor, and stared down at him dispassionately, saying nothing in response.

Tesh tried to be understanding, but in recent weeks she had been growing increasingly irritated with her boyfriend's possessive, even paranoid, attitude. Bichette seemed to fear that he might be losing her affections to this rough-and-tumble young upstart, who enjoyed tramping around in the woods and living off the land. Glavine—only twenty years old—had been working on the opulent estate, performing handyman tasks and yard work.

Concerned that the situation would escalate, Tesh stepped forward and said, "Hurk, he's hardly spoken to me at all. I assure you, there's nothing for you to worry . . ."

"You stay out of this," he snapped. With one arm, he shoved her away, and she stumbled backward before regaining her footing.

The muscles in Glavine's face tightened. He studied Tesh, as if to make certain she was all right.

Standing off to one side with her arms folded across her chest, Tesh had to admit to herself that she was physically attracted to Glavine. With a tan, ruddy complexion and hazel eyes, he carried himself with an air of maturity. Despite his youth, he was well-spoken and knowledgeable on a wide range of subjects. He had a tendency to exude an air of arrogance, though, and this seemed to grate on Dr. Bichette at times.

Human males have interesting means of combat, Tesh thought.

She hoped this pair didn't come to blows, but she had seen other Human men fight for her attentions, and even an unfortunate instance where one man had killed another. Among her own Parvii race this sort of verbal . . . and potentially physical . . . battling never occurred. But her true identity remained a complete secret here on the merchant prince planet of Canopa. With long black hair, emerald green eyes, and a full figure, Tesh looked like an attractive Human woman of around twenty-seven years.

But all of her people *looked* Human, with one significant exception. Parviis were exceedingly tiny, no taller than the little finger of a typical *humanus ordinaire*. In order to conceal their true identities when traveling to foreign planets such as this one, the diminutive humanoids used a personal magnification system that made each one of them look as large as the Humans of the merchant prince worlds. The ingenious apparatus, undetectable to scanners or the most sophisticated scientific instruments, even caused anyone touching Tesh's "skin" to think it was real, and permitted her to experience sensory feelings. Her projected skin and hair, and the atomic structure of the clothing she wore, were in reality crackling molecular energy fields, technologically-created illusions that involved no magic whatsoever.

Emerging from her thoughts, she noticed that the doctor was taking a deep breath and gazing off into the distance. After several moments he resumed talking, in a lower, more controlled tone. He seemed to be holding back a little, perhaps because he knew that he could not easily find another person who would maintain the structures on the large estate as well as Glavine. In the few months that the young man had worked on the property, he had already completed important repairs to the larger of two stable buildings.

Among other operations here, Dr. Bichette provided a tigerhorse stud service for nobles on the merchant prince planets. This had been his family business for centuries, begun by a great-great grandfather and continued to the present day as a highly successful enterprise. Bichette himself had extensive veterinary knowledge, in addition to the medical services he offered to important noblemen and their ladies. A renowned medical expert with a handful of powerful clients, he was Saito Watanabe's personal physician. He also directed CorpOne's Medical Research Division.

Presuming that the dispute between the men would dissipate, Tesh went inward again. She did this sometimes in order to revisit the fondest places of her memory and heart, and for deeper ruminations, to better understand her position in a cosmos of staggering dimensions. The voices of the men droned on, a fuzzy background noise in her mind.

Linked inextricably to the fate of her own people, Tesh could extricate herself somewhat from them during occasional inward journeys in search of her own personal identity, but these were no more than ephemeral trips of the mind, vagrant sparks of thought that were soon washed away in the streams of time. She was linked to every other Parvii, part of a collective organism that stretched into the most distant sectors of the galaxy, into light and into darkness.

The personal magnification system of each Parvii provided only superficial benefits, a defense mechanism for each segment of the much larger organism that allowed it to avoid detection in certain situations . . . and thus to survive.

The Parviis were a powerful race. Secretly, they held dominion over another galactic race, the Aopoddae, that fleet of podship spacecraft that carried travelers and goods across the entire galaxy. One tiny Parvii could, in fact, pilot a much larger sentient pod through deep space. It had been this way for countless millennia, since the early moments following the Moment of Creation. And Tesh was herself a pilot. She had learned her skill from an early age, in the time-honored method by which all children of her race were trained.

However, since there were many more Parviis than podships, she had a great deal of time off-duty . . . as much as a decade without interruption. During the current interlude she had been getting to know Human men better, while on previous breaks she had dated the men of other star systems. By galactic standards she was quite old, much more than she appeared to be. It was like this with all of her kinsmen, but each Parvii was not eternal. On average they lived for twenty or twenty-five standard centuries, and sometimes for as long as thirty.

Parviis were a traveling breed, galactic gypsies without a homeworld. They lived all over the cosmos, and communicated with one another across vast distances through a mysterious, arcane medium that was known by many appellations, the most common of which was Timeweb.

Timeweb!

Even after the seven-plus centuries of her life, the thought of the gossamer connective tissue between star systems never failed to amaze and confound her. The web meant so many things beyond its physical reality.

A shout startled Tesh to awareness. It was the deep voice of Dr. Bichette, and she saw him shove Glavine in the chest. The younger man, much stronger than his feisty, smaller aggressor, hardly moved backward at all. Enraged, Bichette took a wild punch, which Glavine eluded with athletic ease, and then grabbed both arms of his boss to restrain him.

"Let go of me!" Bichette demanded, as he struggled unsuccessfully against the stronger man. "If you value your job, take your filthy hands off me!"

Instead, Glavine spun him around and forced him toward a wrought-alloy bench on one side of the patio. "Our relationship is no longer employer and employee," Glavine said in a flat tone. He glanced at Tesh, and then looked away as he shoved the doctor onto the bench. "Sit there until you're ready to talk reasonably."

"Nothing happened between you two?" Bichette looked first at her, then back at him.

In response, both of them shook their heads. But Tesh knew it was a lie; there *had* been sparks between her and the young maintenance man, a mutual attraction that they had not acted upon. Not yet. Parvii women, like their Human counterparts, knew such things intuitively.

With a sudden, startling clang, a heavy metal door slammed open on the perimeter of the courtyard, and a heavyset man in a purple uniform burst through. Wearing a frilly white shirt with lace at the collar and sleeves, he was a *messagèro,* one of the bonded couriers who worked for the Merchant Prince Alliance. Breathing heavily and perspiring, although his run had not been far from the circular parking area outside, he bowed as he reached Bichette.

"Doctor Sir," he gasped, "most urgent news. A car awaits you."

Narrowing his eyes, Bichette accepted a pyruz from him, a rolled sheet of white ishay bark on which matters of life and death were written. The doctor touched an identity plate on the seal, causing the pyruz to unfurl and become rigid. He read it, then rose to his feet.

"We must continue this later," Bichette said to Glavine. "I am certain we can resolve it." Without another word, he handed the pyruz to Tesh and strode out of the courtyard, behind the sweating *messagèro*.

Tesh read the communication.

"Prince Saito has been gravely injured," she said to Anton Glavine. But as their gazes met, she knew they were thinking of something else, with each of them wondering where their relationship would go from there.

They stood near each other, and drew closer, with almost imperceptible movements. Out at the front entrance, the maglev car hummed. Then, with a high-pitched whine, the vehicle left.

Anton took Tesh in his arms and drew her to him. She had been waiting for this moment, expecting it. However, she had learned that one of the interesting things about physical relationships was that neither the timing nor the exact circumstances were ever known in advance. Of course, Tesh reminded herself, it was that way with the rest of life as well. But she had never anticipated anything quite as much as this particular first kiss, had never wondered about anything so much.

As Anton held her tightly, the Parvii woman had the pleasurable sensation of floating away, on a journey to a far-off place.

Chapter Ten

It is said of merchant prince schooners that they are as numerous as raindrops from a cloudburst. The small red-and-gold vessels, filled with the most wondrous products imaginable, are transported by podship to all sectors of the galaxy.

—*Jannero's Starships*, tenth edition

On Timian One, the stocky, gray-haired Doge Lorenzo del Velli sat upon his great throne, perusing a folio that his Cipher Secretary had just delivered to him, the translation of an intercepted Mutati communiqué. The gangly secretary, Triphon Soro, stood at the foot of the dais, awaiting instructions.

Such messages (which the Mutati Kingdom sent by courier since they did not have nehrcom transceivers) were of interest to Lorenzo, but he always eyed them suspiciously. The shapeshifters were tricky, and had been known to plant false information.

The missive was brief, and he reread it several times, then spoke it aloud with a query in his voice, " '*Demolio is almost ready.*' " Leaning forward a little, he handed it back to Soro. "What in the inferno does this mean?"

Shrugging, the lanky man responded, "No one knows. It is the first time I have ever heard the word, but it might be a code name for something. Perhaps the letters *d-e-m-o-l-i-o* represent a deeper cipher, or an acronym. We are working on it."

"Well get on with it," the Doge snapped. He waved a

hand dismissively, causing the royal functionary to scurry away.

With a sigh, the aged leader retrieved a rolled parchment from a golden receiving tray at his elbow. He opened the document and let it roll out so that it stretched all the way to the plush crimson carpet at his feet.

The immense chair on which he sat, the legendary Aquastar Throne, had been cut in the shape of a merchant schooner. Presented to Lorenzo the Magnificent by a wealthy nobleman in exchange for the granting of a lucrative trade route, it was the largest piece of blue aquastar ever found, and one of the Wonders of the Galaxy.

At the side of the royal dais and only peripherally noticed by the Doge, his Royal Attaché fidgeted, having signaled that he needed to speak with his superior . . . an entreaty that had been ignored. Dressed in an oversized gold and platinum robe, Pimyt was a Hibbil, a soft-fleshed creature with black-and-white fur that made him look somewhat like an Earthian panda bear. Despite the cuddly appearance of his galactic race, they were vicious fighters, and extremely fast; no one could outrun them. Over the course of centuries, they had formed political and business alliances with Humans, and were most renowned for their innovative machines, which they manufactured on their Cluster Worlds and provided to Human allies at reasonable costs.

Pimyt was an extraordinary individual. Even though he was not Human, he was so trusted that he had been made the Regent of the Merchant Prince Alliance decades ago, when the princes on the Council of Forty could not agree on the election of a new leader. The aging Hibbil had flecks of gray fur and a thick, salt-and-pepper beard. His red eyes still remained bright and youthful, and at the moment they flashed impatiently as he moved around restlessly. He did not like to be kept waiting, but Doge Lorenzo sometimes made him do so anyway, just to remind him who was in charge.

"Your Magnificence," Pimyt said, "if you could just . . ." He paused, as Lorenzo raised a hand to quiet him, and read the long parchment.

The document was a long list of "requests" from the Princess Meghina of Siriki, whom he had married after divorcing three of his previous five wives and executing two others. He had married all of them for political reasons, to cement alliances between the noble houses and to gain assets. Everything was a business proposition for him, and the current spouse was the most expensive of all. Still, Meghina had undeniable physical talents to go with her excellent pedigree, and he intended to keep her around. This did not mean that he was faithful to her, or that he expected her to be, either. She was, after all, a celebrated courtesan . . . and they had reached an understanding in the beginning of their relationship that neither of them would ever be tethered. For his own part, Lorenzo had always liked to "dabble" with the females of the various galactic races.

In her mid-thirties, the Royal Consort was much younger than her husband, and he had given her virtually everything. On their wedding day Meghina had asked for her own golden palace, and he had commissioned one for her on the Human-ruled planet of Siriki, complete with two hundred servants and a private zoo of exotic, laboratory-bred animals.

Now she was pressing him for a larger ballroom and a royal hall to entertain important guests. The new construction would require adding another wing onto her palace. She also wanted a more modern stable for her thoroughbred tigerhorses, and sculpted carriages to be pulled by those powerful animals. This would require new access gates for the coaches to enter and leave the grounds, and a spiral ramp to traverse a steep incline down to the cobblestone streets of the village below.

Lorenzo fiddled with the gold medallion that hung from his neck. He was not feeling well this morning, from an attack of the gout. Within the hour his physician had administered a kaser injection, which had dulled, but not eliminated, the pain and swelling in his feet. He took a deep, exasperated breath and continued reading.

Meghina's document included a construction cost estimate, which he presumed she had inflated grossly—one of her many tricks to extract extra money from him. Adding to the expense, she wanted a fast-paced construction schedule, requiring some of the highest paid artisans in the galaxy. Fortunately, Doge Lorenzo had no shortage of funds. In his position at the top of the merchant prince food chain, he had an efficient tax collection network that brought in a massive flow of money. All of it was managed by his Finance Minister, but the Doge—ever cautious and suspicious—had an elaborate system of checks and balances to prevent embezzlement.

In her transmittal, the Princess explained why it all had to be done quickly. She had given birth to the first of seven daughters for the Doge when she was only fifteen, and now Annyette—the eldest—was making her society debut. The party for her would be a grand affair, with guests invited from most of the galactic races . . . with the exception of the Mutatis and their allies, of course.

With a sigh of acceptance, Lorenzo signed the parchment and instructed Pimyt to attend to the necessary details. As the Doge gave his orders, it amused him slightly to see the Hibbil twitching and clearing his throat, wishing to say whatever was on his mind but having to wait.

"Yes, yes," Pimyt said when he had heard the commands. "I will attend to all of them."

"Immediately."

Confusion reigned in his expression. "Yes, of course, but don't you wish to hear . . ."

"One matter at a time. I don't want anything to be forgotten. You would not wish to displease me or the Princess Meghina, would you?"

Stammering, he replied in a voice that squeaked with agitation: "N-no."

"Go then, and come back."

The furry man bowed and scurried away.

When he finally returned, it was nearly lunch time and the Doge could have put him off again. But he did not, and instructed him to speak.

"My Lord, I am sorry to report that Prince Saito Watanabe has been seriously injured and clings to life. He is the victim of an attack on CorpOne by a force of Guardians."

"Guardians?"

"They call themselves environmental warriors, Sire. They also use the term eco-warriors."

"Oh yes, now I remember. We only permit them to operate because they are led by Prince Saito's son. But why would they attack him?"

"No one knows. They have never done anything this rash before. Most of their efforts have been confined to political maneuvering and to ecological restoration projects on distant worlds. On a couple of occasions they have attempted to block certain industrial efforts, demanding changes in corporate practices . . . but it was our understanding that the Prince was keeping them under rein."

"Obviously that understanding is wrong." Lorenzo scowled, and listened as Pimyt provided details on Prince Saito's medical condition. The corpulent industrialist was an important business and political associate of the Doge, one of the most trusted men in the Merchant Prince Alliance. This was a crisis situation that would require action at the highest level. He knew only too well how fragile allegiances could be.

Shifting on his throne, Lorenzo gazed out a stained glass window high on one wall, through which he could see dark gray clouds hovering. "I need accurate intelligence reports," he said in a sharp, urgent tone. "Important decisions must be made."

Chapter Eleven

In the final days of the galaxy, there will be many clever schemes and designs for power.

—Tulyan Prophecy

The Citadel of Paradij was not one of the Wonders of the Galaxy, but only for political reasons that the Zultan resented deeply. The quintessential example of neoclassical Mutati workmanship, the breathtaking structure seemed to float above the rugged surrounding plateau, with slender, glittering spires rising to impossible heights . . . more ornamentation, it seemed, than practicality. Ordinary Mutati citizens never knew what really went on inside the palatial fortress, where Abal Meshdi kept some of the most remarkable technological devices ever developed. The people could only whisper among themselves, and imagine.

He stood inside a spire on one of the highest levels of the Citadel now, and peered through a window slit at the distant horizon. Silvery gray clouds and the pastel oranges of sunset were darkening, becoming the homogeneous indigo of night. Abal Meshdi liked to watch this transitional process of light into darkness, and the reverse as well, at dawn. It was a cosmic, eternal march of illumination and color. Sometimes he equated his interest with the fact that he was a changeling himself, a Mutati who could metamorphose into a panoply of shapes and functions.

He held the fleshy palm of his third hand against the window, and for several moments felt subtle temperature variations in the clearglax as it grew cooler, despite the warmth of his touch. Intrigued by change in its variety of forms, he had included this as a design feature of the fortress, with tiny sensors in the glax that transmitted data to him.

It was rumored among the common citizens that the spires of the Citadel contained electronic signaling or receiving units, for communicating across the entire galaxy. After all, Humans had the nehrcom instantaneous communication system . . . and weren't Mutatis every bit as good as Humans when it came to the latest technological advancements? Hadn't the Mutati High Command halted the earlier flow of Human military victories, leading to the present stalemate?

He sighed at the questions, knowing there were still doubters among his people, despite his impassioned speeches. At least he had a refuge here from the problems of leadership.

The totality of secrets within the Citadel were known only to the Zultan himself. His closest advisers, as well as the scientists, architects, and builders they employed, knew some of the mysteries, but nowhere near all of them. Ever-wary, the Zultan liked to compartmentalize important information, letting it out piecemeal to those few aides that he trusted the most. In addition, his special police, the Dubak, had surveillance methods that provided him with reports on even the tiniest nooks and crannies of his empire.

Reports, reports, and more reports.

They arrived in a variety of forms, and for decades he had been thriving on the details contained within them. His grandfather once told him, "A ruler is only as good as the information he receives, and only as strong as the organization that supports his power." It had been excellent advice, and Abal Meshdi had never forgotten it.

This morning, however, he didn't feel like reading innocuous reports, or even receiving holosummaries of them. Normally he studied information from all over his realm during breakfast, and by midday he decided what to do about most of the matters. He was a leader who made many decisions, but at the moment he didn't feel like dealing with ordinary activities of state. He almost felt like canceling all of his appointments for the entire day with the exception of the Adurian ambassador who was calling on him . . . hopefully with progress information on the new doomsday weapon, their joint project.

With a little time available before the arrival of the foreign dignitary, Meshdi strolled around the Citadel and rode the lifts inside the spires to high vantage points, each of which provided him with a slightly different view of the fortress and the surrounding ornamental gardens. Sometimes he needed a break from the flow of information, curtailing its steady inward current. Especially now, after all the time he had spent in coordinating development of the ferocious weapon that would destroy humankind. He did not consider such breaks wasted time; far from it. They restored his mental capacities.

Dressed in a white-and-purple royal cloak, tunic, and matching beret, the Zultan had eight chins of fat beneath a puckish little mouth, a snout, and two oval, bright black eyes. His body, among the largest in the realm, was a lumpy mass of salmon-colored flesh with a broad hump across the shoulders. It had the traditional complement of three slender Mutati arms, along with six stout legs.

Often when he scuttled around the Citadel, he liked to make subtle alterations in his appearance, since it was so pleasurable for a Mutati to shapeshift. Large changes were extremely gratifying while small ones were lesser, but still sensual, joys. A complete transformation in the way he looked, however, could send a Mutati into waves of hedonistic ecstasy, from which he might not emerge for hours or even days on end. The Zultan, ever conscious of this and of the priorities required of his position, could not afford such a diversion now, not with the important visitor about to arrive.

As Meshdi exited the lift at the base of a spire, he scurried through a wide corridor. Set up on a grand scale, the main passageways of the Citadel of Paradij were as wide as boulevards. Commensurately, the ceilings in the great rooms were as high as government buildings, and were adorned with frescoes, lacy platinum filigrees, and even necropaintings, a macabre Mutati art form in which the artists prepared their pigments from the bone powders of Human corpses.

As the royal personage rounded a corner, he used his Mutati mental powers to shift his facial appearance slightly, adding one more fatty chin . . . so that he now had nine of them instead of eight. Just ahead, a black-uniformed guard noticed the alteration, and stared more closely than usual when the immense leader passed by, so that the guard saw beyond the outer shell of the Mutati leader and analyzed the spectral aura beneath.

Satisfied at the identity of his superior, the guard nodded stiffly and looked away.

On a whim, Abal Meshdi whirled and returned. He stood in front of the guard and studied him closely, peering all the way to the glowing yellow aura beyond the skin. "Is that really you in there, Beaustan?"

"I am here, Sire," the guard said, with the faintest hint of a smile. He tapped the butt of his jolong rifle once on the floor, a gesture of respect. For a Mutati, Beaustan was small, weighing only around one hundred and fifty kilograms. He had obtained his position by family connections, and was descended from a long line of loyal guards.

"I have a better idea," the Zultan said. "I don't feel much like attending to my duties today, so let's trade places." As he said this, he began unsnapping the golden clasps of his royal cloak.

"You want me to meet with the ambassador, too, Sire?" The guard looked shocked and frightened.

"Yes, he's scheduled to arrive at any moment. I think you'll do a fine job."

"But Sire, I am a much smaller terramutati than you are. Even if I shapeshifted to look like you to an outsider, I would not have the requisite mass."

"You aren't proficient at puffing up, expanding your cells? No? Well then, just tell him you've been on a diet. He can't see your aura, won't know the difference. It will be a good test to determine how smart he is, to see if he really believes it."

"Sire, I am not trained in diplomatic matters. I do not have your consummate interpersonal skills, and I do not wish to cause a galactic incident by making a major faux pas."

"You are much too intelligent to be a guard," Abal Meshdi said, nodding. "I have known that for some time. Perhaps I can find some more suitable job for you in my administration."

"I am happy wherever you assign me, Sire." He smiled nervously. "With certain exceptions, of course."

At that moment a white-uniformed aide ran through the corridor. Stopping in front of the Zultan he saluted and said, "The Adurian ambassador has arrived, Sire."

"Tell him I'll be right there," Meshdi said.

When the aide was out of earshot, the Zultan re-secured his tunic and said, "Perhaps you are right, Beaustan. We wouldn't want to create an embarrassing incident."

With a noticeable sigh of relief, the guard nodded, and stood even more rigidly at attention than before.

Actually, the Zultan had not intended to trade places with an underling. He had simply made the ludicrous suggestion on impulse, using absurdity to relieve (albeit only slightly) the matters that weighed so heavily on his mind. The Mutati leader was not known to have a sense of humor, which undoubtedly contributed to the confusion of the guard.

Meshdi shrugged his entire body in the way he had been trained to do by his dancée master, a spiritual counselor who taught him time-honored ways of controlling the mind and body. But even the most skilled dancée instructor could only do so much.

In his position, the Zultan needed more, and his magnificent gyrodome usually provided what he needed. He would reenter it later this evening.

In Abal Meshdi's opulent Salutation Chamber he greeted Ambassador VV Uncel of the Adurian Nebula, a region of spiral arm star systems. This large room in the west wing of the Citadel featured a mosaic dome, with rabesk designs on eight interior columns that supported the dome's weight. Statues of great Mutati statesmen filled alcoves around the perimeter of the room, next to high-backed merchant prince chairs that had been taken from the Humans in one of the Mutati military victories. Even the most petite Mutatis were too big to sit on these exquisitely-carved articles of furniture, but Meshdi liked to keep them around for display anyway, as reminders of past successes.

Larger, more practical chairs stood on an orange-carpeted section at the center of the chamber, furniture that had deep cushions bearing the likenesses of legendary Mutati rulers. The Zultan pointed in that direction, and led the way.

The Adurian diplomat had arrived with two attendants, who waited off to one side with a heavy gold and crystal chest, which they held by the handles with considerable difficulty. Like his assistants, Uncel was a hairless homopod, a mixture of mammalian and insectoid features with a small head, bulbous eyes, and no bodily hair. Dressed in a tight black suit and long white cape, the Ambassador's skin was, in contrast, a bright patchwork of pink, blue, green and red caste markings. The intense colors and arrangements symbolized his high social status, but the large chair made him look very small.

VV Uncel waited while a servant brought two trays filled with tiny ceramic cups of irdol, an imported wine that was reputed to enhance virility. One tray was placed in front of each of the dignitaries. Quickly, the Zultan quaffed a cup of the bright orange liquid, then hurled it to the floor with a small crash, grabbed another and drank it too, before his visitor had even reached for one.

The Adurian dignitary rubbed his wiry fingers together, making a grating sound, as if a microphone had been placed next to an insect. "I shall partake of your fine wine," he said in his whiny alien accent, "but first allow me to present you with a gift." He nodded toward his two attendants.

At his signal the homopods stepped forward, carrying the heavy chest. They set it down on the thick carpeting in front of Abal Meshdi and swung open the lid.

After discarding his irdol cup, the Zultan leaned forward expectantly and looked inside. Seeing a pale blue polyplax bubble sitting on black velvmink, he wondered if this was a prototype of the terrible weapon. He had been told that the device was easily transportable, but had no idea what it actually looked like. The Adurians, with their inventive and manufacturing skills, were building it on one of their industrial planets, using funds provided by the Mutatis.

"Is this a Demolio?" Abal Meshdi whispered. His ring-bedecked fingers danced over the top of the box. He wanted to touch the object, but was not entirely certain if it was a prototype.

Uncel laughed with an abruptness that startled the Zultan, causing him to recoil, and then to scowl.

"Certainly not," the diplomat said, in a squeaky voice. "This is a portable version of the full-size gyrodome that we gave you earlier. We call it a minigyro, and soon it will be the most prized thought-enhancement device in the entire galaxy. Everyone will want one, but few will be able to afford them. The gold and crystal chest is yours as well, with my personal compliments."

"But I thought you were bringing me news of my Demolio program."

"My apologies, Zultan. Did someone say I was?"

"No, but I assumed . . . the last reports I received said that it was very close to completion, requiring only a few more tests and some fine tuning. I thought you were bringing me the good news that it is ready."

"I am not a scientist, but I can report that I too have heard the same thing. I would be happy to check immediately upon my return and get right back to you. Will that be satisfactory?"

"Yes, yes, of course." Meshdi felt flush in the face, from embarrassment. He reached into the box and brought forth the polyplax bubble, which was lightweight.

"Here, permit me to show you how it works," Uncel said. "It is a minigyro, a small version of the gyro we gave you earlier."

"I can do it myself," the Zultan responded, for he was quite proud of his ability to figure things out. Soon, however, he gave up the effort. With an awkward grin, he shrugged and waved all three of his arms.

The Adurians were always creating new, wondrous objects from their marvelous collective imagination, often involving biological and biotech products. Like a small child, Meshdi was intrigued by the polyplax bubble. He felt a rush of excitement, and his pulse quickened.

"You wear it like this," the Adurian explained, as he placed the minigyro high on the Zultan's forehead, where it stuck to the skin with suction. When the device made contact it flashed on, bathing the Zultan's flesh-fat face in spinning circles of multicolored light.

"Intriguing," Abal Meshdi exclaimed, as images floated and gyrated in the air before his eyes like organisms under a scientist's high-powered magnifying glax.

The Adurian looked on, and finally said, "You are seeing Mutati cells. A precise mixture of them, including all three variations of your people—those that walk upon the ground, fly, and swim."

"Cells?" The pitch of the Zultan's voice rose in alarm. "But how did you acquire them? I thought they were too complex to extract."

"One of your own companies has developed a method." He smiled. "Quite expensive, I must say. It's one of the matters I would like to discuss with you. Perhaps you can help us obtain better prices."

The Zultan nodded as he continued to watch the dance of the organisms before his eyes, projections that came from inside the housing of the minigyro. He felt his thoughts merging with the mechanism, sorting themselves into categories that he could analyze in the same manner as the much larger gyrodome.

It was quite ingenious, really, which he came to realize when he used the thought-enhancement quality of the minigyro to determine some features of its design. As the Zultan removed the mechanism from his forehead and felt the effects diminish, he asked how many units had been manufactured.

With an enigmatic wink, the Adurian said, "The production lines will start soon, but I wanted to meet with you first to go over . . . details."

"Yes, that is wise." After a moment, Meshdi added, "I wish to be your only customer for the product." He turned the unit over in his hands, studying it from every angle. Through a clear plate on the underside he saw multicolored swirls, which Uncel explained were the Mutati cells, going about their tasks without complaint.

"You want our entire production?" Uncel said, after a moment of silence. "But we had hoped to export them all over the galaxy. The demand for something like this could be enormous."

"But you need my cooperation in order to obtain the most essential ingredients. At a word from me, I could put you out of business."

"That may or may not be true. We are talking about cells, after all, and the ones we have could be divided."

"Without a loss of quality? Remember, Mutati cells are unique in the galaxy, and very sensitive."

"Perhaps you are right. To be honest, I am not certain. In any event, I wish to be cooperative." The Ambassador narrowed his eyes. "But must you have *all* of our production?"

With a firm nod, the Zultan said, "I can arrange for excellent wholesale prices and I will pay you fairly. You deserve to be rewarded, but all minigyro manufacturing must be performed on Paradij, or on another planet in the Mutati Kingdom."

The Adurian's insectoid eyebrows arched. "Why, if I might ask?"

"We are concerned about security."

"With all appropriate respect, sir, I do not understand. You permit us to develop and manufacture Demolios on one of our own planets, but not minigyros?"

Meshdi nodded energetically, causing his many chins to quiver like the layers of a trifle. "The idea of extracted Mutati cells troubles me a great deal. It is no reflection upon your people, for I trust them completely. It is just that our cells are . . . sacred . . . and I do not wish to have them or your interesting product fall into the wrong hands." He spoke with all the solemnity of his high position. "There is tremendous potential for harm here as well as for benefit."

Abal Meshdi did not really trust the Adurians that much. With their permission he had stationed his own military forces on the industrial world where Demolios were being developed. Since it was well-known that Mutati forces were far superior to those of the Adurians, the conspirators agreed that it would be best to have the Mutatis provide security for this highly important, ultra-secret project. Still, the Adurian military had made significant advances recently and would need to be monitored, even if they were an ally. . . .

VV Uncel hesitated, and considered the situation. He thought it would be better to do the work on Adurian property, but didn't envision problems doing it the Zultan's way. The Adurians were so adept at their biomanufacturing processes that they could keep certain information secret from the Mutatis, even if the shapeshifters were watching them all the time.

With authority from the Adurian Council to make his own decisions in this matter, the Ambassador proceeded to reach an agreement with the Mutati Zultan. The diplomat-salesman accepted a large order for the new minigyros, which he knew Meshdi would distribute to his own people, despite his professed security concerns. The gyrodome and minigyros would suggest this course of action to him subconsciously, and he would not be able to resist.

This Adurian was much more than a diplomat, or a salesman. As VV Uncel departed, he was exceedingly pleased. Soon a large segment of the Mutati population would be influenced in their decision-making processes by the minigyros.

The Zultan was not going to get what he expected.

Chapter Twelve

The love between father and son should be simple, but the reality is far different.

—Prince Saito Watanabe

On the grounds of his Ecological Demonstration Project, Master Noah Watanabe knelt in a meadow and dug his hands into soft, loamy soil around the roots of plants. The sun-warmed Canopan dirt had a calming effect on him, especially now, shortly after a warm summer rain. The muscular man wore a khaki, sleeveless tunic and short, matching breeches. His knees were damp, but he hardly noticed.

This planet is alive, he thought. *Just like the back country people say.*

He was thinking of a superstitious legend, one found all over the galaxy, among various sentient races. On Canopa the primitive people called their planet "Zehbu," while on other planets the living entity was referred to as "Gaea" or other names, but always in conjunction with a similar story. So-called intellectuals dismissed it as a commonly held myth, but Noah believed it was much more than that. Millennia ago there had also been a legend of a great flood that swept across the planet Earth, and another story about a race of sentient spaceships that traveled the galaxy at tremendous speeds. Both "myths" proved to be accurate, so he was confident that one day everyone would also come to accept the fact of living planetary organisms. He could only hope this would be the case. His entire environmental movement was closely allied with the concept.

Zehbu. The people living on your surface are only as healthy as you are.

A tiny yellow field sparrow swooped low, and landed on the grass a couple of meters away. As Noah watched from his kneeling position, the bird looked up at him, tilting its head comically.

Noah smiled softly, then gazed at the distant blue-green hills. Philosophically, he believed that all galactic races, as well as every genus of flora and species of fauna, functioned best if they worked in harmony, filling ecological niches. He loathed the rapacious industries of his father and the other merchant princes, valuing profits above all else. They were ruining every planet where they were involved, stripping minerals and polluting the air, water and ground, caring nothing of the future generations who might live in those places. Most Human businessmen took the short view of events, doing whatever it took to fill their purses with money. Noah, also an entrepreneur but with environmentally friendly operations, took what he considered to be a much longer view.

He had attempted to contact a number of third world alien races to enlist them into his activist organization, but the vast majority of them were suspicious of him, and preferred to keep to themselves. With the exception of the Tulyans, they scoffed openly or paid no heed when his representatives told them that his beliefs were similar to theirs, that all planets needed to be treated with respect and preserved for future generations. As far as most of them were concerned, no matter the promises or assurances of Noah Watanabe, he was not worthy of trust.

He was, after all, the son of a greedy merchant prince.

Something touched the back of Noah's shoulder, and he

straightened. The little yellow bird came into view again, perched close to his face. After a few seconds, it chirped and flew away.

Noah heaved a sigh, and prepared to catch a shuttle. In less than an hour he would be inside EcoStation, his laboratory complex in geostationary orbit over Canopa, always directly above his unique wildlife preserve and farm. Up there he conducted genetic studies on exotic plants and animals under strict, uncontaminated conditions. . . .

Just before boarding the shuttle, he received word about his father's grave injuries, and that he had fallen into a coma. Hearing the news, Noah went cold inside. Prince Saito Watanabe had betrayed his own son, and had somehow been caught in his own trap. It seemed fitting.

Nonetheless, a small part of Noah grieved.

Tesh no longer had feelings for him.

For almost a week, her former boyfriend had not returned to the country estate that was his principal residence. Instead, Dr. Bichette stayed in a CorpOne apartment near the Prince's cliffside villa, where his important patient lay, gravely wounded. According to a telebeam message that the doctor sent to Tesh at the estate, he wanted her to join him at the apartment.

But she wasn't interested.

His first message had arrived three days ago, and she had not responded to it yet. Additional demands arrived each day, and this morning he had sent her two more . . . each more importunate than the one before.

Since Bichette's departure, Tesh Kori and Anton Glavine had spent a lot of time together, but had remained in separate quarters. There had been no sexual intercourse, but not due to any reticence on her part. She had tempted the young man in every way she knew (short of disrobing), and he *had* shown considerable interest. He did not appear to be a homosexual in any sense, either, but for some reason he was resisting his own natural urges, holding back and not saying why. Perhaps he wanted to get to know her better before committing himself; he certainly asked her a lot of questions about her background.

But Tesh felt she was making progress anyway. They had taken walks together through the forests on Dr. Bichette's property, and Anton had kissed her once on the mouth for a few seconds before pulling away, revealing in his demeanor that he was struggling with his own willpower. Soon he would come to her; she sensed it.

In response to Anton's queries, Tesh had provided him with creative answers, fragments of truth painted on wide canvases of lies. She couldn't possibly reveal her real identity to him, for that was beyond the comprehension of a *humanus ordinaire*.

The Parvii race, like its distant Human cousins, required regenerative sleep, but not nearly as much. That night as Tesh slept alone, she remembered . . . and remembered. Her unconscious thoughts seemed to drift off into deep space, to a far-away galactic fold where her people swarmed by the millions whenever there was trouble. . . .

She awoke with a start and opened her eyes. The images had seemed so real, as if she were again with all of her companions in their hidden sanctuary, responding to the commands of Woldn, their revered leader.

From her bed she heard a noise, and saw a crack of light at the doorway that soon widened, as illumination streamed in like yellow sunlight. A shape filled the doorway, profiled against the brightness.

Anton Glavine.

He closed the door, and she heard him moving around inside the room, without seeing him. Moments later he crawled into bed with her, and she felt the warmth of his body against hers. She had been hoping for this, and had kept her physical magnification system in operation, making her appear to be a normal-sized woman. Otherwise, she thought with a smile, he might not have been able to find her tiny body under the bed coverings.

Soon Tesh forgot about her dream, and about everything else. Except for her mounting passion.

Chapter Thirteen

> Tulyans and Parviis pilot podships in different ways. In both methods, it involves telepathic control over the Aopoddae, but Tulyans—unlike Parviis—actually merge into the flesh of the pods, changing the appearance of the spacefaring vessels so that they develop scaly skin, protruding snouts and a pair of narrowly slitted eyes. Why, in view of that remarkable symbiosis, are we Parviis more dominant over podships than Tulyans? This is a great enigma, and a blessing from the Universal Creator.
>
> —The Parvii View of Divinity

A creature with bronze, reptilian skin piloted a grid-plane low over the surface of Canopa, a small aircraft that bore the green-and-brown markings of the Guardians. From the air Eshaz surveyed conditions below, blinking his pale gray eyes as he searched for subtle signs on the ground, for even the smallest indications of trouble. Like all of the people in his race he was extremely old, dating back to a time when Tulyans were stewards of the entire galaxy.

Those times were long gone. Now the Tulyans filled in where they could, performing their specialized, unselfish tasks . . . even if they had to work for others. Eshaz's Guardian superior, Noah Watanabe, had complete faith in him and in scores of other Tulyans in his employ, permitting them to operate unsupervised on a number of planets, monitoring ecological conditions. In the process, the reptilian men and women submitted regular reports to Noah . . . but they also performed other tasks on their own that they could never reveal to any Human.

Wherever possible, Tulyans tried to meld into society, be it Human or otherwise. In the process, they visited planets, asteroids, moons, and mass clusters, and in some of those places they found environmental protection measures already in place. None, however, were as extensive or as well thought out as those instituted by Noah Watanabe and his Guardians. That one man had, to his credit, found a way to enhance and restore natural systems while making a great deal of money.

How odd Humans are, Eshaz thought. *The worst polluters imaginable, and the most careless, but they are the most creative, too.*

For a moment the Tulyan had an unexpected thought, that Humans, despite their glaring flaws, could possibly be the greatest hope for the salvation of the cosmos, for the restoration of Timeweb. How ironic that would be, if it proved to be true. But every Tulyan knew differently. Only Eshaz's own people could save the web, through the caretakers they sent out on clandestine missions.

As Eshaz flew over a dry river bed at the base of a cliff, a cloud of glassy dust rose from below and blocked the large front porthole of the grid-plane. The normally quiet engines whined and sputtered, and the craft spiraled toward the ground. He fought desperately for control, jabbing his fingers against the touch pads on the instrument panel.

Tulyans could live for hundreds of thousands, even millions of years, but were subject to accidental death. Eshaz bore the scars of countless injuries, yet he had been fortunate, exceedingly fortunate. He and his kinsmen were immune to disease or any form of bodily degeneration, and had remarkable powers of recovery from injury. But they were not immortal.

At the last possible moment, just before it touched the ground, the grid-plane pulled up and then swooped back into the sky, rising above a looming, rainbow-crystal cliff face. Eshaz went higher this time, to avoid whatever was occurring down there. Moments later he brought the plane around, circled the glittering cliff, and descended toward the riverbed. He saw the swirling dust again, but this time he remained at a safer altitude.

A small golden circle adorned the lapel of his Guardian uniform, which had been custom-fitted by a Human tailor to conform with the unusual contours of his alien body. The golden circle was the sigil of the Tulyan race, representing eternity. It was a design found everywhere in their arcane society: on their clothing, on the hulls of their ships, and on the sides of their buildings.

Today the mission of this highly intelligent race was much more limited than it had been in ancient times. Now a comparatively few Tulyans traveled the galactic sectors, performing fine ecological adjustments wherever necessary, trying to restore delicate environmental balances that had been disturbed by the careless practices of the galactic races. Humans were not alone in the damage they caused.

He brought the grid-plane as low as he could over the trouble spot, for a better look. Below him was a wide, dry riverbed with a rough, disturbed surface of crystalline soil and black volcanic rock. The disturbed area was pulsing, surging with ground and air action and then diminishing . . . as if breathing. He had seen this before, and needed to wait for just the right moment.

Most of Eshaz's people remained back at the Tulyan Starcloud, their home at the edge of the galaxy. In that sacred place they thought of the old days . . . or tried to forget them. His brethren harbored secrets that could never be discussed with any other race, things known only to the Tulyans since time immemorial, and perhaps even before that. Much of the highly restricted information had to do with Timeweb, the way everything in the galaxy was connected by gossamer threads that were only visible to certain sentients, and then only during heightened states of consciousness.

There had been signs of increasing problems on Canopa and in other sectors of the galaxy, causing the Tulyans great concern. Handling the touch-pad controls of the grid-plane expertly, Eshaz watched the swirls of glassy dust diminish. He would have to move quickly.

Without hesitation he set the aircraft down, off to one side of the broad riverbed, a couple of hundred meters from the debris. He didn't like to think about what would happen if Timeweb continued to decay.

It would mean the end of everything.

He stepped from the craft and made his way across the rough, rocky terrain. Every few steps Eshaz knelt to examine the ground, touching its disturbed surface, studying stones, small broken plants, and dirt. He moved closer, and confirmed his suspicions. This was no ordinary debris field, nothing that had been caused by the natural geological or weather forces of Canopa itself. He studied a blast-pattern of dirt and fragments that had been broken away from the planetary crust, and shook his head sadly. It was exactly as he had feared, a very serious situation indeed.

He watched as a patch of crystalline soil and debris began to swirl only a few meters from him, then faded from view. Unmistakably, he was looking at the early stage of a timehole, a defect in the cosmos through which matter could slip between the layers of the web and, for all practical purposes, disappear from the space-time continuum.

Bringing forth a sorcerer's bag that he always carried in a body pouch, Eshaz stepped forward carefully, until he reached the edge of the flickering area. He sprinkled a handful of green dust on it, raised his hands high and uttered the ancient incantation that had always been used to ward off Galara, the evil spirit of the undergalaxy.

"Galara, ibillunor et typliv unat Ubuqqo!"

Now the Tulyan bowed his scaly bronze head in reverence to Ubuqqo, the Sublime Creator of all that was known and all that was good, and uttered a private prayer for the salvation of the galaxy.

"Ubuqqo, anret pir huyyil."

This was the strongest form of invocation that he knew, for it did not request anything for himself, and not merely for this small section of Canopan crust, either, only a pinprick in the cosmos. Rather, Eshaz's prayer stretched and stretched along the cosmic web . . . the miraculous filament that connected everyone, ultimately, to the Sublime Creator.

But agitated by the Tulyan's magic, the timehole grew larger, and Eshaz felt the ground crumbling beneath him. Bravely, he held steady and refused to retreat. Each timehole was a little different, and all shared something in common: unpredictability. But this one seemed to be in its beginning stages.

Debris swirled all around him, and he felt a powerful force tugging at him, drawing him toward a realm of existence where he would no longer have thoughts and would no longer experience independent movements. It was not entropy, for that natural force of cosmic decay and disorder did not discard matter into another realm. Entropy did not waste energy in that manner.

No, this was something else . . . the eternal, unyielding and opportunistic force of the undergalaxy, working on every weakness, trying to exploit it for its own voracious purposes. He had no doubt that the undergalaxy—like the galaxy that he wanted so desperately to save—was a living entity, with a powerful force that drove it. And this timehole, like so many others, threatened to cast the galaxy into oblivion.

The ground cracked and shook, and the heavy Tulyan fell to one knee. He felt aches and pains in his joints and muscles, something he had never experienced before in his long life.

Timeweb's pain is my pain, he thought, since his own condition seemed to run parallel with the recent precipitous decline of the web.

He repeated the invocation.

"Galara, ibillunor et typliv unat Ubuqqo! . . . Ubuqqo, anret pir huyyil!"

A rift opened beneath him, as deep as a grave, and he tumbled into it. As he struggled to climb out, the ground rolled and knocked him back in. Swirling dirt piled on top of him, and though Tulyans did not breathe, he knew what might happen next. The hole could open up completely, and send him hurtling through into the stygian oblivion of the undergalaxy. Still, like a bird struggling to fly against the wind, he fought to stand up and free himself.

Fumbling in his pocket, he located the sorcerer's pouch, and scattered its entire contents around him. A thunderous noise sounded, followed by a cacophonous grating sound, like huge continents rubbing together. He felt warm air.

Suddenly, with a flash of green light, he was tossed out of the hole and onto the rocky ground. The air was still, and there were no sounds. The rift had disappeared and the land looked almost normal, with hardly any sign of disturbance. Even his grid-plane, which he had parked away from the center of the disruption, appeared unharmed.

Eshaz rubbed a sore shoulder, and felt the pain diminishing already. With his recuperative powers it would not last long. He tested the surface of the ground carefully by putting a scaly foot on it, and then taking a step. It felt solid. Presently he walked on it, toward the waiting aircraft.

As he entered his plane to leave, worries assailed him like a swarm of insects. There had been too many timeholes appearing . . . and too many missing Tulyans, who presumably were being sucked into the openings. Symptomatic of the heightening crisis, fifteen of his people had disappeared in the past year . . . and hardly any before that.

The grid-plane lifted off, and he looked out through the window. Amazingly, the ground hardly looked disturbed at all, and even had wildflowers and small succulent plants growing on it. He clutched the empty sorcerer's pouch in one hand, and wondered if he had actually repaired that timehole, or if it had just shifted position in relation to the strands of Timeweb. He had ways of finding out, and would do so.

Eshaz tapped the touch pads of the instrument panel, causing the aircraft to accelerate along the planetary flight control system. With a little stretch of his imagination he could see similarities between this airgrid, with its unseen web of interlocked electronics, and Timeweb, which encompassed so much more. In each case, ships traveled along strands that guided them safely. Where Timeweb was the work of the Sublime Creator, however, the airgrid networks on various Human planets had been invented and installed by much lesser beings . . . and the equipment operated on infinitely smaller scales. It could not be overlooked, either, that Timeweb was a *natural* system, while airgrids were not; they were intrusions. Airgrids were, however, ecologically benign, and not known to cause damage to plants, animals, or other aspects of nature.

The Tulyan wished he could do more for the empyrean web, that his people were again in control of podships as they had been in the long-ago days when he had been a pilot himself—before Parvii swarms came and took the pods away. At one time, Tulyans could travel freely around the galaxy, performing their essential work on a much larger scale.

An entire sorcerer's bag expended for one timehole. It would take him nearly a day to restore the ingredients in the repair kit. For a moment he despaired, as the efforts of the Tulyans seemed so inefficient. But in a few moments the feeling passed, and he vowed to continue his work for as long as possible.

He was fighting more than timeholes, or the inefficiencies of dealing with them. On top of everything else, Eshaz and other Tulyans had been experiencing bodily aches and pains . . . for the first time in the history of their race. This suggested to them that their bodies might be undergoing a process of disintegration into homogeneous chemical soups and dust piles . . . along with every other organism in the dying galaxy.

Chapter Fourteen

> The Theoscientific Doctrine tells us that our religious and scientific principles are indistinguishable from one another.
>
> —*Scienscroll*, 1 Neb 14-15

After gambling all night in the palazzo casino with members of the royal court, Doge Lorenzo took a ground-jet to the dagg races on the other side of the broad river that bisected the capital city of Elysoo. This was one of his favorite haunts for placing bets.

It was Monday morning, and he should be attending theoscientific services at the Cathedral of the Stars. Right about now, the Moral Instructors—elderly women in silver robes—would be reading passages from the *Scienscroll*, perhaps even admonishing the parishioners about the sins of gambling. He didn't care. The meddlesome old maids of the Cathedral would not dare to speak directly against him, the powerful leader of the Merchant Prince Alliance. Still, he would not want a confrontation with them; he was a devout believer in the holiest of all writings, the *Scienscroll*. He even knew the most famous verses by heart, such as the one from the Book of Visions:

> *Know ye the Way of the Princes,*
> *for it is the path to gold and glory.*

He liked another passage even more, and frequently quoted it:

May mine enemies tumble into space,
and crumble to dust!

There! he thought, after murmuring the verses to himself. *I've fulfilled my theoscientific obligations for the day.*

As usual, he went to the dagg track with no fanfare whatsoever, accompanied by only a handful of plainclothed security guards. His Hibbil attaché, Pimyt, went along as well. Dressed in red-and-brown capes and matching fez hats, the two of them entered the Doge's private box, which was decorated in wallpaper that featured sports calligraphy and holos of race champions in action.

Lorenzo stood at one of the windows of the enclosure and watched spectators stream into the stands. Out on the track—over slopes and around hairpin turns—daggs made practice runs, dusty brown-and-tan animals that resembled the canines of Earth but with tiny heads . . . proportionately less than half as large as those of greyhounds. Each dagg had a large, bulbous eye in the center of its face—dominating the front like a headlight—and a snout-mouth beneath the boxlike jaw.

"While we await the first race, I thought you might like to use the time productively," Pimyt suggested. After removing his cap the furry Hibbil knelt and tried to open the clasps on a shiny black valise that he had brought with him. He pressed on the release buttons, but only two of the four fasteners popped open.

"Must we discuss business here?" Lorenzo protested, watching him with irritation. He heard the crowd roar and looked to see the daggs and their trainers—many of them alien—parade in front of the main viewing stands and private boxes.

"You've said yourself that every bit of time is useful,

Sire, and you are extremely busy . . . so there is hardly a moment available to show you the latest in Hibbil technology." He waved casually at the valise. "Of course, if you would prefer not to see this. . . ."

The Doge sighed. "You know me too well, my friend. Aside from my weakness for betting, I do have a fondness for gadgets . . . and for women, lest I forget, and not necessarily in that order."

With a curt smile, Pimyt struggled to open the lid of his valise. "I think you will like this, Sire." He slammed a furry fist on the bag, but the last clasp resisted him.

As Doge Lorenzo gazed dispassionately at his attaché, he had a hard time believing that Pimyt had once been the Regent of the Merchant Prince Alliance. A *Hibbil.* Though he hadn't realized it at the time (and still didn't), Pimyt had not been given any real power or responsibility during his term in office. It had only been ceremonial, and something of a well-concealed joke, a way of treading water between doge regimes while seeming to show respect for the Hibbil Republic, an important economic ally who provided the best machines available, at reasonable prices. His tenure in office had only lasted for a few months, until the Council of Forty elected a new leader, but it had helped cement relations between the Human and Hibbil societies.

Finally, Pimyt won his argument with the stubborn clasp and swung the lid of the valise open.

Intrigued, Lorenzo leaned closer to look.

"We call this a 'hibbamatic,' " Pimyt announced proudly, as he brought out several flat, geometric pieces and snapped them together on the floor, forming a box with octagonal sides. He slid open a little door on the structure, permitting Lorenzo to see that it glowed pale orange inside, as if from an internal fire.

"Strange device." The Doge reached out and placed a finger against one side of the box, which was around a meter in height. It felt cool to the touch.

"This is one of our smaller models, a machine that can be programmed to build a variety of small consumer and military devices out of programmable raw materials." Pimyt had noticeable pride in his voice. "Here, let me show you."

The Doge squinted as he watched the Hibbil remove a hand-sized cartridge from inside the lid of the valise. The selected cartridge had a keypad on one side, and Pimyt tapped a code into it. He then tossed the cartridge into the geometric structure and slid the door shut. Moments later, a tray opened on the opposite side and a small, red-handled weapon slid out and clattered onto the tray.

"An ion gun," Pimyt said. "Fully loaded. The hibbamatic can create anything except a copy of itself." He grinned. "Or so our promotional literature says. Assuming we provide enough raw materials."

"How about a beamvideo of *Capponi's Revenge*?" Lorenzo asked.

"Ah yes, that patriotic war story."

Seconds later, like a wish fulfilled by a genie, a silver-colored video cylinder clattered into the tray. After examining it, Lorenzo smiled craftily and said, "Now make me a nehrcom transceiver."

Since this was one of the most secret devices in the galaxy, with its workings known only to Prince Jacopo Nehr, the Hibbil responded, "Don't believe everything in our promotional literature, Sire."

With a guffaw, the merchant prince leader said, "Nonetheless, I rather like your hibbamatic, as a novelty item for the amusement of my court."

"Shall I transmit your order to my homeworld?"

"Later." Lorenzo glanced out the window. "The race is about to begin."

Twenty daggs in racing colors took off and dashed around the track, going up and down the slopes and around the sharp turns. But the top daggs were not as fast as usual. Doge Lorenzo smiled, for he had taken steps to influence the result, having arranged for the sedation of the favorites . . . just enough to slow them down slightly.

As expected, Abeeya's Dowry, the underdagg he had bet on, won easily.

"Now I have enough to buy your products," Doge Lorenzo said. "Big payday . . . minus operating expenses, of course."

Beside him, Pimyt smiled, but a bit too broadly for the occasion, as he envisioned the Hibbil-Adurian master plan unfurling, moment by moment. Timing was everything. . . .

Chapter Fifteen

Life is about changes, and adapting to them.
—Tulyan Wisdom

Only moments before the arrival of the *conducci,* Tesh Kori and Anton Glavine ran through the front gate of the estate and hid in the thick woods outside. Flushed with anger and outrage, Tesh parted the leaves of an aixberry bush and peered through the red-leafed foliage. A groundjet stopped at the gate and waited for it to slide open slowly. These mercenaries had their own transmitter key.

It was a warm afternoon, with hardly any clouds in the azure blue sky. Beside her, Anton breathed hard from the exertion of running across the large compound. His brow glistened with perspiration. In contrast, Tesh showed no signs of physical effort. Parviis, who could survive in outer space without the necessity of any breathing apparatus, did not have cardiovascular systems. Rather, they were complex electrochemical creatures, with tiny, highly sophisticated neurological systems.

Six large men wearing black coats and tinted eyeglasses sat inside the oval-shaped vehicle, which discharged orange flames from the rear as it idled. To Tesh they looked like barroom brawlers, or street thugs. The tip telebeamed to her by a girlfriend had been correct. Dr. Bichette had hired muscle to bring her back to him . . . and had sent enough men to handle not only her, but Anton as well. Judging by the puissant rifles that Tesh saw in the rear of the passenger compartment, she judged that the men had been given strict orders to do whatever it took to accomplish the task.

She had long suspected that Bichette had a mean streak, and this confirmed it. Despite his attempts to show her a gentle, compassionate side she had seen behavioral lapses in him, moments when a darker aspect showed through and then scurried for cover, like a creature not wishing to be discovered. It had taken months for this nature to reveal itself, but it had not escaped her attention, as she noticed the way he treated servants and even his valuable tigerhorses when he didn't know anyone was watching. Two of the animals in his stable had died of poisoning, and while he had insisted that it must have been committed by an intruder, he had also collected large insurance payments. Humans could be so unethical.

"I have a bad feeling about this," Anton said. He held a four-barrel handgun that he had grabbed on the way out of the palatial home.

"So do I," she said. "Let's go deeper into the woods. Maybe there's a way out on the other side."

Not a person to run from a fight, no matter the odds, Anton hesitated.

She tugged at his arm. "Come on!"

The groundjet roared fire and entered the compound. The gate closed behind it with a hard click of metal. Tesh and Anton scrambled deeper into the woods, tromping their way over thorny underbrush and through stands of gray and yellow-barked trees.

Ten minutes later they heard a commotion behind them, barking daggs and shouting men. A second vehicle must have arrived, carrying the animals. To Tesh they sounded like keanu tuskies, known to be fast and deadly. A hundred years ago she had seen one run down a fugitive and chew off his legs before handlers arrived to collect what was left. Ever since, the memory had been etched indelibly in her mind.

"Faster!" she said, without explaining what she knew.

Anton didn't need any encouragement, but he had trouble keeping up with her. His hands were bloody from thorn bushes, but hers were not, since Parviis did not bleed.

Abruptly, Anton stopped and turned the other way. Kneeling, he flipped a toggle and pressed a button on the handgun. Flames belched out of all four barrels and ignited the tinder-dry underbrush. He scurried to one side and the other, setting up a wall of fire to block the pursuers.

Then he turned and rejoined her, where she awaited him. "That'll slow 'em down," he said. "My dad and uncle were hunters and had a lot of guns, including a couple like this one . . . handy for flushing wild treegeese out in the open."

"That doesn't sound very sporting," Tesh observed.

"Maybe not, but it works."

The pair sprinted ahead, while fire raged behind them, turning the brush and trees into a popping, exploding conflagration. Birds screeched and flew off.

"We have a favorable wind direction," Anton said. "It could switch on us, though. We need to hurry."

She glanced longingly at her companion as he ran alongside her. He seemed to be in complete control and unafraid . . . capable of handling virtually any situation.

In the seven centuries of her life, Tesh had enjoyed countless sexual experiences with the males of almost every galactic race. Two of the most memorable had been a tryst with a Vakeen swordsman in the Dardar Sector and months of lovemaking with a handsome Ilakai merchant, who entertained her at his various chateaux around the galaxy.

She sighed, remembering her first physical relationship, with a powerful Adurian lord who looked like a humanoid ant, with bulbous eyes and puffy black cheeks. She had been little more than a child at the time, and he had been so ruggedly handsome, enhanced by the keloid scars on his face and arms. The touch of his antennae had been almost electric on her skin, so stimulating that she had been hard-pressed to find anyone afterward who was anywhere near his sexual equal.

Her current love interest, Anton Glavine, was perhaps the most perplexing of all. In her many relationships, she had learned a great deal about the various races and cultures, including Humans. But this was an entirely new experience for her. She found him intelligent, sensitive, and extremely irritating. With males, she was used to getting her own way.

Their first night of lovemaking had been passionate, but nowhere near the most stimulating of her life. Still, the sexual experience had been adequate, and she'd wanted to continue the episodes, hoping they would improve with time. After that, though, Anton had refused to make love to her again, saying he'd made a regrettable mistake with her. He said he wanted to get to know her better before repeating what they had done.

"But it was so wonderful," she'd told him in exaggeration, blinking her emerald green eyes. She and Anton had been in the living room of the main house, sitting in front of a warm, cheery fireplace. Tesh had set it all up, even providing wine to lower his resistance.

With surprising determination, Anton had said, "I like to be in control of myself, and with you around that presents a challenge."

Then he put down his wineglass and gave her a hard

stare, as if he could see through her superficiality. He seemed to look deep into her soul with his penetrating hazel eyes . . . all the way through her personal magnification system to the tiny Parvii inside. Of course that was impossible, but she had been unnerved, and bewildered. He was not like any Human male she had ever encountered; instead he behaved more in the manner of a Human *female,* who typically wanted to develop an emotional relationship before becoming intimate.

Things were topsy-turvy. Tesh was even playing more the part of a Human male, as she pursued him aggressively. But she was not a *humanus ordinaire,* and could not be judged in the terms of that race. As a Parvii, she had her own ways, her own traditions and genetic makeup that drove her actions. She was not sure how to control this man; the more time she spent with him the more she wanted him, and the more he befuddled her.

Privately, she had to admit that she rather liked his gallantry, the way he treated her with courtesy and respect. He showed great bravery in the face of danger as well, and a strong desire to protect her from harm. She could outrun him, but usually held herself back and checked to see how he was doing.

Behind them, the keanu tuskies yelped in confusion. "The smoke of the fire is interfering with their ability to smell," he explained. "My uncle used them for hunting daggs, and said that was their weakness."

Tesh smelled the acrid odor of the fire.

"The wind is changing!" Anton shouted. He pointed down a steep, brushy hill, toward a small lake. "I think we've lost the daggs, but we need to get into the water."

Suddenly Tesh heard a loud noise overhead, and peered up through an opening in the trees. A green-and-brown grid-plane hovered above them for several moments, profiled against the sky, and then flew back toward the fire. She heard the popping of the flames, and loud hissing noises.

"That's a Guardian aircraft," he said. "They're a bunch of radical environmentalists, and wouldn't be happy if they found out I started the fire. They're always patrolling Canopa, like self-proclaimed eco-police."

"You make them sound kooky."

"Actually, I admire them. I wouldn't have set fire to the woods if we weren't in a life or death situation. For days I've seen their spotter craft operating in the area, and hoped they would show up here . . . but not too soon. I just wanted to use the fire as a temporary shield, without causing too much damage. They'll put it out now."

"I see."

He helped her down a steep embankment, over granite boulders and through thorny bushes. The lake was only a short distance away, deep blue in a rock bowl.

The aircraft noise returned, and Tesh saw the same Guardian grid-plane fly low over the lake. Pontoons emerged from the undercarriage, and the aircraft set down on the water with a splash, near the closest shore. A hatch opened in the fuselage, and a reptilian creature stepped out onto the short wing. Larger than a Human, he had bronze, scaly skin and a protruding snout. He wore a green-and-brown uniform.

"One of the Tulyans who work for Noah Watanabe," Tesh said, identifying a race that was at least as ancient as, and perhaps even older, than her own . . . going all the way back to the earliest known days of galactic habitation.

"I'm familiar with them," Anton said in a low tone, "but I've never seen one this close. I hear they are non-violent?"

"That is correct."

"Hurry," the Tulyan said in a throaty voice. He motioned with one arm, which seemed too small for his substantial body.

Anton and Tesh looked at each other for a moment, then waded through cold water to the grid-plane and boarded it.

"What a coincidence," Anton said to the Tulyan as the two passengers found seats in the rear of the craft. "We were just on our way to see Noah Watanabe and volunteer as Guardians."

"We were?" Tesh said, surprised.

"I wanted to surprise you," Anton said. "Noah and I go way back."

The Tulyan looked at him skeptically through slitted, pale gray eyes, and said, "Your friends were asphyxiated by the fire. One of our crews picked up their bodies."

Tesh wanted to say they weren't friends, but caught Anton's hard stare and read the message there. It was best not to say anything about being chased, or about starting the fire.

The reptilian man identified himself as Ifnattil, and said he was a caretaker, responsible for protecting the natural resources in this region. With no further comment, he plopped his large body into a specially-designed pilot's seat and began tapping the instrument panel with stubby fingers. The grid-plane lifted off with a smooth whir into the smoky sky.

"Noah was a friend of my parents," Anton told Tesh. "Just working-class people, but he always took a special interest in me when I was growing up. Noah is seventeen years older than I am, like a big brother to me. I told him I wanted to join the Guardians someday, and engage in his style of environmental warfare."

Tesh grinned, and curled an arm around Anton's waist. "It looks like that someday is now," she said.

Chapter Sixteen

The path of honor is a narrow ridge,
with deep crevasses on either side.
—Princess Meghina of Siriki

Dr. Hurk Bichette wanted his patient to get better. Certainly he was administering every technique known to medical science, some of them the result of advice he had received from experts he'd brought in for consultation. Money was no object; Prince Saito Watanabe had unlimited funds.

But in Bichette's thoughts, grating on his conscience like sand between his skull and brain, he wished the Prince would just die, if that was going to occur anyway. It was irritating the way the old man kept straddling the fence between life and death, not heading in either direction.

From the foot of the bed, Bichette watched the regular breathing of the comatose man. Following brain surgery, the rotund patient had been fitted with a mediwrap around his head to enhance the healing of damaged functions, along with a clearplax life-support dome. The injury was severe, but with modern technology this patient could live indefinitely, well beyond his normal life span.

But this is not living, the doctor thought.

Two women stood on one side of the bed. . . . the Prince's redheaded daughter Francella and the blonde Princess Meghina, who had a distinctive heart-shaped face. Occasionally they glared at one another, without saying anything.

Located within the Prince's cliffside villa, this had been an elegant reception chamber, until its conversion to a high-tech hospital facility. The large room had gold Romanesque filigree on the walls, a vaulted ceiling with dark wood beams, and brightly-colored simoil murals. The paintings, by the renowned artist Tintovinci, depicted the life of Prince Saito Watanabe, from the time when he had been an itinerant street vendor to his years as a factory worker and his rise to the very highest echelons of merchant prince society.

Life-support equipment hummed and clicked softly as it kept the body's vital functions going. The big man's chest heaved up and down within the clearplax dome, and occasionally he coughed, but did not awaken.

Meghina wiped tears from her eyes, and appeared about to say something. Her generous lips parted, then clamped shut as she seemed to change her mind. Though married to the Doge, she was also a well-known courtesan, and had relationships with a number of noblemen. She and her powerful husband lived separately—she in her Golden Palace on Siriki and he in his Palazzo Magnifico on Timian One. Though Bichette did not approve of such relationships himself, they were commonplace among MPA noblemen, and the source of much braggadocio.

Beside her, Francella Watanabe shifted uneasily on her feet. She had a reddish makeup splotch on her high forehead, but neither Meghina nor the doctor were about to tell her.

Dr. Bichette looked away from them, back at this great Prince who seemed so helpless now and so peaceful, with his eyes closed and a calm, almost pleased expression on his round face. Even if the doctor wanted to disconnect him for humanitarian reasons—or for other reasons—he could not do so. Watanabe had left specific, signed instructions that he was not to be taken off life support, not even if he became brain dead. He had not reached that stage yet, but his mental functions had been damaged by oxygen deprivation, and he seemed unlikely to recover. Since his injury he had lapsed in and out of consciousness several times, and had spoken a few garbled, unintelligible words.

Frustrated by the amount of time he had been required to spend here, Bichette would rather deal with Tesh instead, to see if they could resurrect their relationship . . . a relationship that might be in worse shape than this patient. Bichette didn't like Anton Glavine, and didn't trust him around his attractive girlfriend.

A method of tipping the medical balance occurred to him. *If I make just a slight adjustment in the nutrient lines, or administer a quick injection of protofyt enzyme, Saito will slip away, with no evidence remaining of what I did.*

Anxiously, the doctor weighed the possibilities. Certainly this client paid him high fees, but there were other nobles who wanted his medical services, and if he lost this one he would have more time for the others. Prince Saito was something of a hypochondriac anyway, constantly summoning him for perceived, but not real, ailments. If he died, Dr. Bichette could take on three or four additional important clients who would pay him more in total, and cause less trouble.

Of course, there must be no suspicions cast upon me . . . and no suggestions of incompetence, either.

He would decide what to do after speaking with Tesh. The *conducci* he had sent to retrieve her should be bringing her back at any moment, with or without Anton. If the maintenance man happened to get in the way and sustained an injury, so be it. Bichette would not even provide him with a healing pad.

* * * * *

Princess Meghina did not like the hard expressions on the faces of Francella and the doctor, the way they stared coldly at the man she loved, as if impatient for him to slip away. A highly sensitive woman, Meghina prided herself on her ability to detect the hidden emotions of others, picking up on little mannerisms, tones of voice, and ephemeral expressions that suggested hidden thoughts and motivations. It did not seem to her that either of these people were overly concerned about Saito's welfare. Rather, they appeared to be thinking of other matters, of other priorities. Meghina didn't see how that could be possible. Still, she was detecting this.

To protect Prince Saito, Meghina would spend more time at his side, to monitor what was being done for him. If he died, it would be a terrible tragedy, not only for him but for Meghina. Even though they were not married, they were deeply in love and by all rights should have at least another twenty-five years together. Yet, if this wonderful man was going to pass away, it seemed fitting for him to do it here, surrounded by murals depicting the stellar accomplishments of his life.

Fighting back tears, she envisioned one last painting of Saito Watanabe lying on his death bed, and her administering to him.

Hold on, my darling, she thought.

Princess Meghina loved the fine things that were provided for her by the Doge and other noblemen—fancy clothing and jewels, the best food and wine, luxurious living and travel arrangements. But above all, she had a special fondness for Saito, and had provided him with honest business and financial advice for CorpOne operations, in addition to her physical and mental comforts.

Meghina shot a sidelong glance at Francella, who gazed dispassionately at her father, a man she should care about. On a number of occasions, Saito had confided to Meghina that he suspected his daughter only wanted money and power from him, and nothing else. The woman seemed to bear no love for anyone but herself, but her father kept hoping he was wrong.

Princess Meghina shook her head sadly. Francella was probably everything he feared she was, and maybe even worse. It seemed obvious that she thought Meghina was interfering, preventing the old man from lavishing money on her. Francella treated the courtesan like an enemy, a competitor for her father's affections and wealth.

We live in a universe of secrets, Meghina thought. *Everyone has them.*

She considered her own secrets, especially one that would send shock waves across the entire Merchant Prince Alliance if it was ever revealed. Only two people knew it, herself and Prince Saito.

In reality, Princess Meghina was a Mutati who could not change back because she had remained in one shape—Human—for too long, allowing her cells to form irreversible patterns. This did not make her internal chemistry, or the arrangement of her organs, Human at all. Her DNA was radically different, and her blood was of a purplish hue. Thus it was quite easy for her to be revealed through a medical examination or a security scan—none of which had ever been required of her, because of her purported noble status and lofty connections. Even a pin prick could reveal her true identity, so she had to take extra care to avoid injury.

Meghina had in her possession falsified documents attesting that she was of noble merchant prince blood, the last surviving member of the House of Nochi. In fact she was a princess, but a *Mutati* one . . . a distant cousin of Zultan Abal Meshdi. Ever since her childhood on Paradij she had wanted to be Human, and now she was living her dream under an elaborate subterfuge. And, making her task somewhat easier, she was one of the few people of her race who did not display any of the typical allergies that Mutatis felt toward Humans. She had discovered that benefit inadvertently, after her implanted allergy protector stopped functioning.

The Princess had spent a great deal of time and money setting up her clandestine life, and each day she paid close attention to how well the artifice was going, and what she might do to strengthen it. For her own sake, and for that of Prince Saito, it was necessary to remain on constant guard. If anyone ever discovered her, it would ruin her and the Prince, since he knew her true identity and sheltered her. Without any doubt, it would rock the foundations of the Merchant Prince Alliance if the dirty little secret ever got out—despite the fact that she was, at heart, more Human than Mutati.

Her husband Lorenzo was at risk as well, though she did not love him. He was a cruel, selfish man who cared nothing for anyone but himself. Still, he was enamored of her, and provided her with the luxuries of a queen. She used her feminine wiles to manipulate him, like a flesh-and-bones puppet.

Purportedly, Meghina had given birth to seven daughters for the Doge. But each of her pregnancies had been false, since Humans and Mutatis could not interbreed. The "births" were among the most elaborate of her subterfuges, since she paid for children that had been carried in the wombs of other women, and she always went away to a remote planet, without her husband or any of his cronies, to "give birth."

Without realizing it, Princess Meghina had been holding one of the large, limp hands of Prince Saito, and had been massaging it. Suddenly he jerked free of her. His eyes opened wide, and his gaze darted around in all directions. Finally he looked in Meghina's direction, but not directly at her. Instead, he fixed his attention on a point somewhere beyond.

"Noah?" he murmured in a ghostly voice. "Is that you, Noah?"

Without waiting for an answer, he closed his eyes suddenly and slumped back on the bed.

Watching this, Francella grimaced. Nothing, it seemed, could dissuade the foolish old man from loving Noah. She had not planned on her father surviving the attack, so now she had to work on a contingency plan. As in a game of nebula chess, she needed to visualize several moves ahead.

Moments passed while she let the game play out in her mind. When a particularly delicious possibility occurred to her she smiled, just a little. Then, remembering suddenly where she was, she stiffened and looked directly into Meghina's penetrating sea-green eyes.

Chapter Seventeen

> The technology of war is a perilous, but fascinating game. As each side makes an advance, the other attempts to learn its secrets and counter it. Thus, the information provided by spies becomes the most precious commodity in the galaxy.
>
> —Defense Commander Jopa Ilhamad
> of the Mutati Kingdom

The Citadel of Paradij glittered in morning sunlight like a huge, multifaceted bauble, casting emerald, ruby, and sapphire hues across the rooftops of the capital city. Despite the early hour, the air was already warm and the air conditioning system had broken down, causing the Zultan to perspire heavily and exude foul smells. Someone would die for this incompetence.

In Abal Meshdi's satin-gold dressing chamber, a small Vikkuyo slave stood on a step stool and placed a cone-shaped wax hat on the head of the Mutati leader. In the warmth, the hat would melt a little at a time, releasing perfumes that would mask his body odors. He would be calling upon his concubines today, and did not wish to offend them.

Eight hundred star systems away, General Mah Sajak paced the outdoor patio of his penthouse, fretting and muttering to himself. Around him towered the geometric buildings of Elysoo, the capital of Timian One. Between the structures he saw glimpses of the Halaru River and the snowy Forbidden Mountains in the distance. A cool breeze blew from that direction, and he shivered as it hit him.

The Grand Fleet should be arriving on far-away Paradij at any moment, and then victory would be his. Doge Lorenzo asked him about the progress of the assault force each day, since he wanted to stage one of his gala celebrations here on Timian One. Most of the preparations for the festivities had been completed, and the moment he received word of the victory everything would be brought out, including an immense selection of gourmet foods and exotic beverages for the people.

The surprise attack against the Mutati Kingdom had been thirteen years in the making, including the building and manning of the powerful space fleet, and the time to transport it across the galaxy. But General Sajak was a realist, and in any military venture there were risks . . . and unknowns.

He told himself to stop worrying, that everything would go perfectly. Just then, a blast of wind hit him squarely in the face, stinging his skin. He turned to go back inside the apartment.

At his approach, a glax door dilated open. The officer stepped through into a warm parlor that featured shifting electronic paintings on the walls and display cases filled with military memorabilia.

As a result of the anticipated triumph—the biggest in the history of Human-Mutati warfare—General Sajak would gain tremendous prestige. Basking in adulation, he would use his new influence to convince the Doge to stop converting commoners into noblemen, in violation of thousands of years of tradition. Since the days of yore, noblemen had been born into their positions, but under the most recent Doges this had changed drastically. Men were being appointed to high positions based upon a ridiculous premise—their scientific or business acumen—with no consideration given to the purity of their bloodline.

The General watched an electronic painting shift. The stylized image of a podship faded, giving way to a violent depiction of a supernova.

He'd better listen to me.

Having been trained in war college to think in terms of high-stakes games, General Sajak was considering the potential responses he might receive. If Doge Lorenzo chose to disregard the urgent entreaty, a new and drastic course of action would be undertaken.

As the Zultan Abal Meshdi rode a sedan chair across Alliq Plaza, the center of his fabulous city, he was surprised by the sudden coolness of the weather. In the last half hour the temperature had dropped precipitously. Most unusual for this time of year.

On impulse, he ordered the runners to set his chair down near a fountain, and then disembarked onto the flagstones of the plaza. Gazing up at the darkening sky, he didn't think he had ever seen clouds quite like those before, with striations of deep purple against gray that were like arteries about to burst open and rain blood on the planet.

The Mutati homeworld was guarded by a fleet of warships that conducted regular patrols over that galactic sector. On a cosmic scale, this did not comprise much area, but it was substantial in planetary terms. The mounting of such a comprehensive guard force required the allocation of a tremendous amount of personnel and hardware.

The patrol ships, while light, fast, and armed with

heliomagnetic missiles, were not capable of traveling between star systems. To cross deep space, no practical alternative to podships existed. The distances were too great, making the costs involved with traveling by vacuum rocket or other conventional means prohibitive, because of the incredible fuel requirements that would be involved.

Prohibitive for most galactic races, that is. The Merchant Prince Alliance had more money and other resources than anyone else. It was from this seemingly bottomless treasury that General Mah Sajak drew funds to build the Grand Fleet and send it across light years of distance. It was all done with the permission of the Doge and the Council of Forty.

Sajak and his military brain trust knew about the Mutati patrols, and had taken steps to counteract them. For this assault force, timing was everything. At precisely the right moment, the admiral in charge of the fleet would implement the massive destruction plan. It would be horrible, and beautiful at the same moment.

In his mind's eye, the General envisioned the assault force waiting under the cover of an asteroid belt. This part of his imagination was fairly accurate, but beyond that the differences were significant.

When the Mutati patrol moved along to the other side of Paradij, the merchant prince warships made their long-anticipated move. Piercing the upper atmosphere of the Mutati homeworld, the Grand Fleet generated swirls of ionized hydrols around it which looked like large gray-and-white storm clouds, concealing the attackers from the inhabitants of the planet below. Even the sophisticated electronics of the Mutatis could not detect them.

Theoretically.

★ ★ ★ ★ ★

In the sedan chair far below the fleet, a communication transceiver crackled, and the Zultan heard Mutati battle language, chattering frantically. Paradij was under attack! The Humans had generated artificial storm clouds to conceal their forces.

Abal Meshdi stared upward, unmoving, and thought of all the defensive preparations that had been made by the Mutati High Command. They had not known exactly when the attack would occur, but had received a number of clues that it was coming, and—with the approval of the Zultan himself—had made certain clever arrangements.

The Mutati war program, after so many losses to Human forces, was two-pronged. The Zultan's doomsday weapon was undergoing final testing, and barring any unforeseen problems it would soon be launched against enemy planets, annihilating them to the last one.

He also had a shock in store for anyone daring to attack his worlds, as the commander of the enemy fleet was about to discover.

He smiled nervously, and prayed to God-On-High for the defense of sacred Paradij. He hoped that his people had taken adequate steps, because in war, anything could happen.

High in the atmosphere, the clouds roiled.

When Meshdi was a young emir in training for future responsibilities, his grandfather had said to him, "Preparation is the child of necessity." At the time, the boy had not understood the significance of the adage, but later it had become abundantly clear to him.

Thousands of years of hatred and armed conflict against Humans had led to this moment, a stepping stone in what he hoped would ultimately be Mutati dominion. Meshdi felt his pulse accelerate. Since the earliest moments of his recollection he had loathed Humans. Under his leadership, no expense had been spared and important programs had been initiated. Galactic espionage, for one.

Mutatis, by virtue of their ability to shapeshift, could work as spies on Human worlds more easily than the enemy could on Mutati planets . . . provided that Mutatis controlled their strongly allergic reactions in the presence of their arch enemies. Implanted allergy protectors usually worked, but when they failed—as they did occasionally—the consequences could be disastrous. The best solution lay in a small percentage of Mutatis who for unknown reasons did not show any Human aversion—so it was from this group that spies were recruited. There had been a handful of incidents in which even they sometimes developed reactions, but the Zultan played the odds, and thus far his espionage operations had not been compromised.

Humans knew that these enemy incursions were occurring, and had their own safeguards, including regular physical examinations for persons in sensitive positions. Under even a cursory medical examination, a Mutati could be revealed. It just took a needle prick to reveal the color of the blood. But Humans were susceptible to bribes and other deceptions, and Mutati spies continued to ply their artful trade. Secrets were learned, bits and pieces of information that made their way back to Paradij and the Zultan.

In this manner the Mutatis learned—more than a decade ago—that a massive Human fleet was going to be sent against them, but at an unknown time. For years, the Mutatis waited. And waited. They knew . . . or strongly suspected, based upon their knowledge of conventional cross-space transportation technology . . . that a Human fleet could not possibly travel as fast as the mysterious podships.

The sentient pods had never cooperated with any military venture, and in fact had undermined a number of attempts by various races to exploit them for warlike purposes. As a consequence, the Mutatis knew that Humans would need to transport their fleet on their own, without the assistance of podships.

As the clues arrived via their spy network, the Mutati High Command held emergency meetings. They floated an idea that the Humans might move their military hardware and personnel in disguise, a little at a time, using podships. In this manner, they could set up a staging area closer to the core of the Mutati Kingdom, at a place where they could launch their attack more quickly. In an attempt to discover such a location, the Mutatis sent out continual scouting parties in comprehensive, fanning search patterns.

Nothing surfaced. This suggested the probability that the Humans were sending their force en masse from one of their own military bases, which meant time would be needed to make the journey . . . perhaps ten to fifteen years. It also suggested the possibility of obsolescence, since the hardware would be old by the time it arrived at its destination. Maybe the enemy was counting on the element of surprise.

At least we're taking that away from them, the Zultan thought. *But will it be enough?*

From the bridge of his flagship, Admiral Nils Obidos surveyed the protective cloud layer beneath his fleet of ten mother ships that had traveled across space in a bundle of vacuum rockets and were now spread out in attack formation. Minutes ago, each mother ship had disgorged thousands of small fighter-bombers that looked like silver fish flying in the upper atmosphere.

As he watched, the mother ships fired electronic probes into the artificial clouds every few seconds like lightning bolts, checking their thickness and integrity as a shield.

Going well so far, the Admiral thought. This renowned "Mutati-Killer," hero of two big military victories against his arch enemies, stood behind his command chair, with his hands gripping the back. A small man with a jutting jaw, he had a large mole over his left eyebrow.

Moment by moment, inexorably, the masking clouds dropped lower and lower, concealing the advancing fleet like an immense shield. . . .

In order to make the clouds appear authentic, the attackers had initially generated them over a sparsely populated region of the Mutati homeworld, and had then moved them (as if blown by high atmospheric winds) in the direction the Admiral wanted to go, toward the capital city of Jadeen and the surrounding military installations.

A successful strike would be devastating to the Mutatis, cutting the rotten heart out of their entire kingdom.

Looking around the command bridge at the flagship officers who had endured the perils of this long voyage with him, he felt pride in their loyalty and dedication. None of the officers in the fleet had complained about their hardships, nor had the twenty-four thousand fighters under their command.

Jimu, a black, patched-together robot who was Captain of the sentient machines in the fleet, hurried up to Admiral Obidos, and saluted with a short metal arm. In his mechanical voice, the robot gave a concise report. Then, at a nod from his superior, he hurried off, to tend to his duties.

Despite prohibitions against it, a number of women under the Admiral's command had conceived and given birth to children in space—twenty-eight in all—and they were subsequently raised in a community facility. The unauthorized pregnancies had irritated Obidos, but such problems had been minor in comparison with other challenges faced by the task force.

The huge vessel jostled, and the Admiral held onto side bars.

"Just turbulence," one of the officers reported.

Five years into the mission, most of the officers and crew came down with a serious space sickness, including Admiral Obidos. More than three hundred died before the fleet medics came up with a treatment, combining marrow and calcium injections.

After so many years of injections, however, there were side effects. Obidos and the other victims no longer had their own bones, as their entire skeletal structures—even the essential marrow—had dissipated and been replaced by artificial substances. The Admiral had been among those who had suffered the most physical pain—but each day he tried not to think about it.

As the assault force dropped lower and lower in the atmosphere, proceeding slowly and methodically behind the cloud cover, the Admiral felt cold, and shivered. Sliding a forefinger across a touch pad at his belt, he activated a warming mechanism. Within seconds, heat coursed through the artificial marrow cores and calcium deposits of his bones.

Nonetheless, he shivered again.

Obidos could not get warm, no matter how high he turned up the mechanism. There was no remedy for cold fear.

High over the Zultan's head, the storm clouds began to break up, revealing what looked like thousands of silver needles glistening in the sun. Ships . . . and several much larger vessels behind them.

A merchant prince task force!

Abruptly, the flight pattern changed in the sky, and Abal Meshdi thought he detected disarray. He heard confirmation of this over the nearby communication transceiver, as it crackled in Mutati battle language. "We broke the electronic integrity of their shield, and they are attempting to regroup."

Over the open line he heard percussive blasts, and saw distant flashes in the atmosphere. The storm cover had been anticipated, based upon intelligence information that the Mutatis had received.

In short order, the attack turned into an epic debacle, as the Mutatis shot down everything in the merchant prince fleet except for the flagship, which they captured along with the officers and crew. They even took the Admiral prisoner, saved from his intended suicide by a fast-acting Mutati medic.

As he prepared to visit the captured officers in their electronic cells, Abal Meshdi wondered why the merchant princes had undertaken such a risky mission. He was about to board a lift platform, on his way to interrogate and torture the military leaders, when an aide rushed up to him, breathing hard and perspiring.

"Sire, their Admiral is dead!" he reported. He went on to explain that Obidos had taken his own life in a second suicide attempt—after obtaining poison in an unknown way.

Moments later, Meshdi burst into the cell and examined the body himself. There was no sign of life. Off to one side, a dented black mechanical man watched.

"He's the Captain of their machines," the aide said,

pointing. "Calls himself Jimu."

An idea occurred to the Zultan, and he acted on it without delay. Within hours he sent the robot back to Timian One, carrying holos of the humiliating military defeat and of the Admiral's body. Jimu traveled by podship.

But that was only for entertainment, to make Abal Meshdi's prey suffer the most possible agony. Soon he would send them something even bigger, a storm of doomsday weapons.

Demolios.

Chapter Eighteen

> There is a beginning point to everything, and an ending point, but it is not always possible to identify either one.
>
> —Noah Watanabe, *Reflections on my Life*, Guardian Publications

At sunset a brown-and-black catus, one of the thick-furred persinnians that ran wild on the grounds of the Ecological Demonstration Project, stalked a bird. The feline remained low on the dry, yellowing grass, its front paws outstretched, and pulled itself toward a fat pazabird, moving forward only centimeters at a time without making a sound. The white-breasted bird dug around the roots of grass for worms, oblivious to danger.

Thinking he felt movement beneath his feet, Noah got down on all fours and placed an ear to the ground. He heard something, a distant rumbling noise, but could not determine the source. He wondered if it could be a nuisance that had been occurring on Canopa in recent years, groundtruck-sized digging machines that were left behind by mining companies. The "Diggers," with artificial intelligence and the ability to sustain themselves, had been burrowing deep underground and occasionally surfacing like claymoles, tearing up large chunks of real estate and damaging buildings. So far, Noah had been fortunate, but it was an increasingly widespread problem. The Doge himself had ordered their extermination on a variety of merchant prince planets, which amounted to commando raids against the machines in their burrows—going after them like pests.

The rumbling noise subsided, and he felt nothing in the ground. Looking up, he saw the catus pounce, filling the air with feathers. It was an efficient act of predation, with the kill completed in a matter of seconds. Now the catus played with the dead bird, lying on the ground and batting it around like a kittus with a ball.

With the last rays of sunlight kissing his face, he was reminded of an incident from his childhood. No more than seven years old at the time, he had been out in a forest, walking along a path that led from the village to his home. Upon hearing a repetitive thumping sound, he'd noticed a red-crested woodbird pecking away at a rotten log beside the trail. Instinctively, Noah had not moved and was careful not to make a sound. The bird seemed unaware of his presence, and the curious boy stood silently, watching it extract worms from the holes it was making in the soft wood. Presently the bird flew off, into the high branches of a pine tree. Perching there, it fed worms from its beak to hungry chicks that poked their heads out of a hole in the tree trunk.

Afterward, Noah had gone to the rotten log and pulled some of the wood away, enabling him to see many worms writhing around in their moist habitat, trying to burrow deeper into the log to escape him. He had gathered some of the wriggling creatures, taking them home to put in a jar with air holes in the lid. That afternoon, however, his sister Francella stole the worms and chopped them into pieces, just to watch the little segments keep moving. When he found out about this, Noah screamed, but it was too late.

The twins' governess, Ilyana Tinnel, had separated them as they fought. A kindly woman, she showed Noah other worms in the rich soil of her own garden and explained how they enriched the dirt, adding nutrients to it. She told him something that intrigued him, that soil, worms, and birds were all connected and that they worked together, as other life forms did, to enhance the ecology of Canopa. In her world-view, soil was a living organism, part of the vital, breathing planet.

Though his father discounted the concept of complex environmental relationships, it was an astounding revelation to the boy, and proved to be the starting point for his life's work. In his adulthood he extended his study to a number of planets . . . and the roles that Humans and other galactic races played on each of them. Noah learned about incredibly long food chains, all the predators and prey, and marvelous plants that sentient creatures could use for medicines, herbs, and food. For each planet, all of the parts fit together like the pieces of a complicated jigsaw puzzle. . . .

Now the catus, having grown tired of playing with the bird, devoured its prey, bones and all. It was an unpleasant sight for Noah to watch, but entirely necessary in the larger scheme of existence. He would not think of interfering.

His thoughts spun back again, to a time when he began to wonder how life forms survived in hostile environments, such as snow fleas on mountains, lichen on cliff faces, and desert succulents that stored water in their cellular structures. He had also been intrigued by chemical life forms thriving in the deepest ocean trenches where immense pressures would crush other creatures, and by alien races such as Tulyans, that did not need to breathe.

Noah had tried to put things together in new ways. He considered how seeds fell from trees and were carried by winds, so that saplings grew a few meters away, and even farther. It was a continual process of establishing new root systems, growing young plants, and then having seeds carried off again, to someplace new. When he put this information together with what he knew about comets and asteroids—heavenly bodies that carried living seeds around the galaxy in their cellular structures—he found his mind expanding, taking in more and more data. He envisioned fireballs entering atmospheres and spreading seeds . . . not unlike the seeds transported around a planet by its own winds.

Such theoretical linkages had caused him to wonder if planetary ecosystems might possibly extend farther than previously imagined, into the cold vacuum of space. Could each planet, with its seemingly independent environment, actually be linked to others? The seeds carried by comets and asteroids suggested that that this might be possible, as did the gravitational pulls exerted by astronomical bodies on one another, and the fact that the same elements existed in widely-separated locations. It seemed connected, perhaps, to a huge explosion long ago, the legendary "Big Bang" that split an immense mass into the planets, suns, and other components of the universe.

It all boggled Noah's mind, but still another analogy had occurred to him. The galaxy was a sea of stars and planets and other cosmic bodies. A *sea,* with a myriad of mysterious interactions and interdependencies.

Now, thinking back on the events that had turned him into a galactic ecologist, Noah refocused on the grassy spot where the catus had devoured the bird. The feline was gone, and only feathers remained behind. Shadows stretched across the brown-brick and glax buildings of his compound, as if the encroaching night was a predator, sucking away the light. Guardians were leaving the offices, greenhouses, and laboratories on their way home, having completed their work for the day.

Deep in thought, Master Noah left the landscaped area and strode along a path, toward grass- and shrub-covered hills that were beginning to yellow as the summer season established itself. In waning daylight, trail lamps flickered on. He passed half a dozen workers going the other way, and barely noticed them. At the base of the nearest hill he reached a metal gate that covered a vaulted opening cut into the base of the slope. A pool of floodlights illuminated the area. A stocky little guard, armed with a puissant rifle over his shoulder, saluted him.

Passing into a plaxene-lined room beyond the gate, Noah took an *ascensore*—a high-speed lift mechanism—up to a private tram station on top of the hill. He crossed to the other side of a platform, where he boarded a green-and-brown tram car and sat on one of the seats inside the brightly-illuminated passenger compartment. The door slid shut and the vehicle went into motion, leaving the station and accelerating along an unseen electronic wire that transported him out over forested hills and small, shadowy lakes on top of the plateau.

As the car sped into increasing darkness on its invisible wire, Noah felt the buffeting effects of wind gusts. It was unusual for winds to be so strong at this time of year. Only a small event to the untrained eye, but a troubling one to him. Lately things seemed out of balance on Canopa, as if the forces of nature were refusing to continue business as usual. A steady stream of unusual occurrences were being reported by Guardian patrols . . . sudden storms and geological upheavals in remote regions of the planet. One of the Tulyans in his employ, Eshaz, had provided him with some of the information, but he seemed to be holding things back. The Tulyans were a strange breed anyway, but in the years that Eshaz and his companions had worked as

Guardians, Noah had never seen them this way.

Just ahead, bathed in floodlights on a landing pad, he saw the orange shuttle craft that would transport him up to EcoStation, his orbital laboratory and School of Galactic Ecology. He watched a team of Guardians run scanners with lavender lights over the craft to make certain it was safe to ride. In part of Noah's mind the need for such caution seemed preposterous. After all, the merchant princes had permitted him to operate freely for years, having done this out of deference to his powerful father. Now, though, following the attack on CorpOne headquarters, anything was possible. The feisty old Prince had tried to ruin his own son . . . or worse.

Noah could not believe it had all happened. Things were more complicated than ever. Sometimes he wished he was a small boy again, examining flora and fauna with fresh eyes. But the more he learned, the more he realized that he had lost the innocence of youth. His lifelong quest for information, almost desperate because of the finite term of his life, had taken him far away from those early days. Sadness enveloped him now, for it seemed to him that innocence, once lost, could never be regained.

Master Noah boarded the shuttle, and it lifted off. As he looked up at the night sky through the bubble roof of the craft he remembered lying in a meadow one evening long ago, staring in awe and amazement at the stars above him. His life had been a tabula rasa at the time, a white slate extending into the future, waiting for him to make marks upon it.

In the years since that night he had not really learned that much after all, not in the vast scale of the cosmos. Still, as he lifted heavenward, his mind seemed suddenly refreshed and ready to absorb a great deal more, and he felt a new sense of wonder and excitement.

Chapter Nineteen

Sometimes I wish podships had never shown up at all. Our access to them on a limited basis has only whetted our appetites, making us think of astonishing, seemingly unattainable, possibilities. The concept of a *starliner,* for example, a trainlike arrangement of linked podships . . . or a *startruck* in which a podship pulls a long line of container trailers. Alas, such ideas seem destined to remain on the drawing boards.

—Wooton Ichiro, 107th Czar of Commerce for the Merchant Prince Alliance

A dozen workmen slid the immense Aquastar Throne down a roller-ramp from the top of the dais, toward the floor of the elegant chamber. Having been awakened from his bed by the voices and other commotion in there, Doge Lorenzo stood off to one side, watching. He wore a bathrobe with the golden tigerhorse crest of his royal house on the lapel. His thinning gray hair stuck out at the sides.

Noticing him, a small man with a narrow face hurried to his side. "Is there anything you wish, Sire?" the work supervisor asked.

"No, no," Lorenzo said, for he was anxious to get the alterations taken care of, even if these men had made the mistake of beginning work too early in the morning. He didn't feel much like punishing anyone today.

The man bowed and was about to leave when the Doge

said, "Wait. There is something. Have my breakfast tea brought to me here."

"Right away, Sire."

"And send for the Royal Attaché."

"Yes, Your Magnificence."

As his orders were carried out, the Doge's mind spun onto other matters. In his position, he had so much to think about. No other noblemen, not even the princes on the Council of Forty, could fully understand the extent of being a leader in wartime. Foremost in his thoughts, he looked forward to the gala celebration that would occur after the Grand Fleet won its glorious victory against the Mutatis. The announcement was due at any moment, and like a child forced to wait for a present, he was running out of patience.

Although nehrcom transceivers could transmit instantaneously across space, they only operated to and from secure, land-based facilities. With the aid of relay mechanisms, messages could be sent from a planet to nearby ships or space stations, but the reception quality was substantially diminished in the process.

No one except the nehrcom inventor, Prince Jacopo Nehr, knew why such a problem existed, and he was not divulging any secrets. As a consequence, the Grand Fleet had remained out of contact for years as it traveled through enemy star systems and other regions where there were no transceiver units. Some people thought this apparent "Achilles heel" in the communication network had to do with the gravitational or magnetic fields of planets and suns. Others were not so certain, but all agreed on one thing: nehrcoms were almost as mysterious as podships.

Despite the lack of contact, Doge Lorenzo del Velli remained confident of a huge victory over the Mutati Kingdom, and had been receiving nothing but the most glowing assurances to this effect from General Sajak. At the Doge's insistence, concise calculations had been completed by the most advanced Hibbil computers, showing exactly when the Grand Fleet should be filling the skies of Paradij . . . and when the rain of destruction would be complete.

A day ago he had received updated calculations, and had been thinking about them ever since. Unfortunately they included variables and a lot of double-talk from the mathematicians and military advisers who supervised the work. The attack might occur anytime during a thirty day period, beginning with the upcoming weekend.

As he stood there watching the workmen settle his throne onto the floor with a soft thump, he thought back to a decision he had announced the night before, when he notified General Sajak that he was not going to wait for word from the task force before staging the festivities. Instead he wanted them scheduled on the earliest possible day of victory—this Saturday—without revealing in advance the nature of the occasion. Lorenzo was ebullient at the decision, but General Sajak had been oddly silent.

Was the officer worried about something going wrong? Of course not, Lorenzo assured himself. The plan of attack had been worked out in exquisite detail by the best military minds in the realm, and no expense had been spared.

This Saturday the Doge would open his present; the party would be one of the most extravagant celebrations in the history of the Merchant Prince Alliance, overshadowed only by royal coronations and weddings. Covering more than three hundred square blocks of the city of Elysoo, it would be more impressive than the jubilee at the turn of the last century. In fact, as far as anyone could recall, this was slated to be the biggest open-invitation party ever held anywhere. It would be an opportunity for the common people to experience the finest foods, beverages, and entertainment available. As the most successful traders in the galaxy, the merchant princes had everything that the mind could imagine or the heart could want.

The Doge's breakfast tea arrived, and he sat upon his throne to sip it, while the activity continued around him. The workers were cutting open the top of the dais now, to install the lift mechanism that he had specified. Upon learning that an ancient Byzantine Emperor had been in possession of such an apparatus, the Doge vowed to have one, too. He had no idea how the original one operated—probably with slave labor—but he would have a mechanical system for his, and would use it during royal audiences. Up toward the heavens he would go, or down, depending upon his whim and upon the extent of awe and fear he wished to generate.

Pimyt entered the chamber just as the remaining tea was growing cold. Over the noise of ongoing work the two of them discussed the status of preparations for the celebration.

The aging, black-and-white Hibbil seemed more agitated than usual, undoubtedly because of all the arrangements he had been coordinating. His red eyes flashed with intensity. "Despite a high standard of living on Timian One," he said in a squeaky voice, "the event is likely to attract impoverished persons from the back country and a fair share of rowdies who will drink and party to excess."

"Well, take care of it," Lorenzo said, with a dismissive gesture. "Assign my entire special force to work the celebration."

"*All* of your Red Berets? I don't have the authority to do that."

"Stop whining. Prepare the necessary document and I will sign it."

"Yes. Mmmm, a large number of them should be plainclothesmen."

"Attend to it."

"I will, My Lord." The Hibbil concealed a scowl on his furry, graying face. Unknown to the Doge, he would have preferred no festivities at all, since he considered the whole affair a lot of wasted effort when he had more important matters to handle . . . things the Doge didn't know about. Though he concealed it well behind his innocent-looking, bearlike face, Pimyt did not like Humans at all, and he had taken certain steps to make them suffer.

When the Doge had no more orders to issue, the Royal Attaché took his leave.

That afternoon, crews began setting up temporary structures and hanging colorful banners from buildings. Curious crowds gathered in the streets of Elysoo to watch, and heard the scheduling announcement. By tomorrow the people would be jockeying for the best positions to camp, and street musicians, mimes, and jugglers would accelerate their practice sessions, putting the finishing touches on their routines.

And in only a few days, brightly-colored dirigibles would fill the sky, with their telebeam messages proclaiming the epic Human victory.

Chapter Twenty

Do you know what is exciting about the galaxy?
The mystery of it,
for this vast network of star systems, despite its great antiquity,
continually shows us new and unpredictable faces.
—*Scienscroll*, Commentaries 1:29-30

In the bustling main kitchen of the Palazzo Magnifico, seven chefs in white smocks and gold caps hurried from counter to counter, inspecting the decorations on the mini-cakes, fruit biscuits, and other elegant desserts. The five men and two women moved from section to section like wine tasters, sampling the imaginatively-shaped confections and expectorating into buckets on the floor. It was mid-afternoon, a warm day in the city of Elysoo and even warmer in the kitchen, because of the ovens.

A teenage culinary worker, Dux Hannah, wiped perspiration from his brow with a long white sleeve. He noticed a roachrat poking its long black antennae out of a bucket at the exact moment that a female chef was about to spit food into it.

Startled, the chef sprayed her mouthful all over a tray of decorated cookies. "Double damn!" she exclaimed, and swept a thick arm across the contaminated tray, sending it crashing to the floor. Then she gave chase to the fat, beetle-bodied rodent as it ran across the kitchen.

Looking on, the stocky head chef, Verlan Ladoux, flew

into a rage. "Get this kitchen clean!" he shouted. "We feed people, not roachrats!"

Moments later, a team of exterminators appeared with their equipment. Solemnly, they inspected sonic traps under the counters, cleaned dead roachrats out of sealed compartments, and reset the devices.

Dux Hannah and Acey Zelk were members of a Human slave crew. Sixteen-year-old boys, they were first cousins, with no formal education. Acquired on the auction market by Doge del Velli's chief of staff, they had been enslaved because their people—the Barani tribe of Siriki's wild backcountry—had been negligent in paying taxes to the Merchant Prince Alliance. The boys did not look alike at all. Acey had bristly black hair and a wide face, while Dux was taller and thinner, with long blond hair that tended to fall across his eyes.

Owing to his considerable artistic talents, Dux had been ordered to decorate royal cakes and other delicacies, using frosting and sprinkle guns to create swirls, animals, hieroglyphics, and geometric designs. In contrast, Acey had mechanical skills, so he worked with the maintenance staff to keep food-service robots operable.

As the exterminators worked under the counters, slowing the pace of kitchen operations, Chef Ladoux paced about nervously. He was especially agitated today, since food was being prepared for the Doge's elaborate celebration, which had begun that morning. It was early afternoon now, and the kitchen—one of many servicing the festivities—had been operating at peak efficiency for more than a day. Until this interruption.

Acey and Dux exchanged glances, and nodded at each other. This was the moment the boys had long awaited, for they intended to use the confusion to activate their bold plan.

Acey slipped away first and entered a supply room. After shutting and locking the door he reprogrammed one of the robots. The brassex, semi-sentient machine was large and blocky, with a spacious interior where it carried food that it picked up and delivered—enough space for the two young men to hide, if the shelves were removed.

Still in the kitchen, Dux wrote a frosting message on a large ivory-chocolate cake: "I WOULDN'T EAT THIS IF I WERE YOU." He then covered the cake with a silver lid and knocked on the door of the supply room, three taps followed by a pause and then two more taps.

Moments later, the robot marched outside and clanked toward the central market of the city. When out of sight of the palazzo, the machine changed course and took the boys instead to a crowded depot. There they caught a shuttle that took them up to an orbital pod station, high above the atmosphere of the planet. They brought money with them—merchant prince liras—stolen from the chefs' locker room over a period of months.

Presently the boys stood at a broad glax window in a noisy, crowded waiting room, waiting for the next podship to arrive. The pod station was stark and utilitarian, made of unknown, impermeable materials and placed there by unknown methods . . . as others like it had been established in orbital positions around the galaxy.

Below the pod station, through patchy white clouds, Acey and Dux watched early evening shadows creeping across the surface of Timian One as the sun dropped beneath the horizon.

"When do you think the next podship will arrive?" Acey asked.

Looking up at an electronic sign hanging from the ceiling, Dux answered, "Anytime in the next twelve hours."

"I'm not talking about what the podcasters say. Those guys are wrong all the time."

As both teenagers knew, podcasters were expert prognosticators employed by the various galactic races, performing jobs that computers purportedly could not do nearly as well. Working at each pod station, the professionals spent long hours making calculations, figuring podship arrival probabilities based upon past results. The calculations were elaborate, owing to a number of variables and the sometimes unexpected behavior of the podships. The jobs were demanding and required a great deal of education to obtain, including rigid testing procedures. In merchant prince society the positions were considered prestigious for commoners to hold, causing people to compete for entrance into the finest schools.

"Wrong?" Dux said, brushing his long golden hair out of his eyes. "I don't know about that."

"Maybe I've had bad luck, but I've spent days waiting for podships that were supposed to show up and didn't." Acey's chin jutted out stubbornly, as it often did when he debated a point.

"You mean on that cross-space trip you and Grandmamá took?"

"Uh huh, the contest she won."

"I hear there was a big shakeup in the podcaster ranks a couple of years afterward, so hopefully it's better now."

For a long moment, Dux stared at another electronic sign hanging from the ceiling, a display panel that reported information transmitted by "glyphreader" robots from the zero-G docking bays. This one was blank, since there were no podships present at the moment. Had one been docked, the glyphreader would have translated the hieroglyphic destination board on the fuselage and transmitted the results to the various electronic signs around the station. (The alien hieroglyphs were one of the few things that anyone had figured out about the spaceships—a revelation that enabled travelers to know where they were going before boarding one of the vessels.)

When the right opportunity presented itself, Acey and Dux sneaked aboard a podship, without paying any attention to the destination. . . .

Back on Timian One, in the broad *plaza mayore* of the capital city, the citizens went into shock as rumors began to circulate about a catastrophic military loss suffered by the merchant princes at far-away Paradij. It seemed impossible for the Mutatis—who had lost most of the battles fought against the Humans—to have scored such a huge victory. People couldn't believe it. Stunned and fearful, the crowds fell into murmurs. Were Mutati forces on the way here now?

In the throne room of the Palazzo Magnifico, Doge Lorenzo railed at General Sajak, who stood humbly before him in a wrinkled red-and-gold uniform, cap in hand. The furious ruler shouted so loudly that he could be heard all the way out in the corridors and public rooms. It was an embarrassment of epic proportions, the worst military defeat in the history of humanity.

Chapter Twenty-One

Nothing is entirely secure. No matter how many precautions are taken, no matter how much money and manpower are expended, a narrow crack of exposure always remains. Our mortal safety, then, depends upon the inability of an enemy to identify, or capitalize upon, each of his opportunities.

—Admiral Monmouth del Velli,
ancestor of Lorenzo the Magnificent

A slideway took Master Noah from the docked shuttle into EcoStation, an orbital structure that looked like something a child had fitted together with toy parts, but on a very large scale. A round doorway dilated open and Noah stepped through into a vaulted entrance chamber that featured exotic climbing plants visible through glax-plate walls.

He waited while a security officer in a hooded black suit checked him with a scanner beam. The wash of white light felt cool on his skin. Even though Noah suffered this inconvenience every time he came here, it was the result of his own orders, to prevent anyone from pretending to be him. If a saboteur ever got aboard, the entire facility could be destroyed.

Guardian headquarters and this orbiter had state-of-the-art security systems and a private military force, which Noah had ordered on full alert. He'd had nothing to do with the assault on CorpOne, but feared that someone had impersonated his activists in order to make him look bad—

thus paving the way for attacks against his operations.

For a while, he thought his father had laid a trap for him, but he was coming to believe that such a malicious deception was something altogether different from their earlier quarrels, and almost beyond comprehension. The more Noah thought about it, the more he suspected that Francella had masterminded the plan to ruin his reputation at the very least, and quite possibly to kill him. He wondered if his father had participated in such a scheme, perhaps after having been duped and manipulated by his wily daughter. And—plots within plots—had Francella planned to kill both her brother and father in the same incident?

A chill ran down Noah's spine as possibilities curled around him like the tails of demons.

On the other side of a thick glax window, he saw the Adjutant of the Guardians, Subi Danvar, watching the security procedure. Loyal and efficient, he ran the entire Guardian organization whenever Noah was away on business.

Presently the hooded officer nodded stiffly, and on Noah's right the door to a glax-walled booth opened, sliding upward. Stepping inside, Noah waited while an ion mist bathed him and his clothing in a waterless decontamination shower. It only lasted a few seconds, during which he felt a slight warmth, and a tingling sensation. Then an interior door opened.

As the Guardian leader marched into the adjacent room, Subi bowed slightly and said, "I trust you are doing well, Master Noah?"

"Passably, thank you."

After the sound of a musical tone the adjutant said, "Excuse me for a moment, please." From a pocket of his surcoat he removed a headset, and put it on. Telebeam images danced in front of his face, a live connection. He tuned the device so that the color projections grew larger, and filled the air between him and Noah. Two people were shown.

"An urgent transmission from a friend of yours," Subi said. "He is at the entrance gate of the compound." The adjutant was referring to the Ecological Demonstration Project, down on Canopa.

Noah recognized one of the pair, a blond, mustachioed young man standing just outside the guard station. It was Anton Glavine, accompanied by an attractive woman. She had long black hair and a good figure. "You're looking fit, Anton," Noah said, looking away from her.

"I must speak with you."

"This is a busy time, but I can grant you three minutes. Proceed."

"In person. Please."

"I'll return the day after tomorrow. You may await me in one of the guest houses. Make yourself comfortable."

"I must see you now. *Please,* Noah. Allow me to come up there with you. I'd like to bring my girlfriend along, too. This is Tesh Kori."

The woman bowed and smiled. She had emerald green eyes that Noah found striking. But he tried not to look at her, and focused instead on Anton. There were many reasons why Noah would do anything for this young man, reasons that had never been revealed to Anton.

"Very well," Noah said after a long pause, "but I'm about to conduct a class. I will see you afterward."

"All right. Thank you."

Assuming that Anton wanted to express his sympathy over the life-threatening injury to Saito Watanabe, Noah told Subi to telebeam approval to the security people down at the compound, so that the young man and his companion could board a tram car and shuttle.

After Subi took care of this, he put away the headset and said, "Your class awaits you, Master."

The two men walked through a dimly-illuminated corridor. This was a section that had been added to the complex recently. EcoStation, always in geostationary orbit directly above Noah's wildlife preserve and farm, had originally been designed with modular elements. Hence it was easily enlarged with the addition of more units, an ongoing process as the need for more laboratory and classroom space constantly increased. Aside from the benefit of an uncontaminated, off-planet facility for genetic studies on exotic plants and animals, he liked the isolation that the orbiter provided for students, so that they could maximize the learning process. The students lived in dormitories on board.

Soon Noah heard the chattering and giggling of young voices, just ahead. Moments later he and his companion entered the classroom. The students, all new to the school, grew silent.

While the adjutant introduced Noah to thirty men and women dressed in unisex green smocks and trousers, Noah found himself impressed by their erect posture and bright, attentive expressions. They seemed eager to learn and become full-fledged Guardians, and he was just as eager to teach them.

The classroom was surrounded by dwarf oak and blue-bark canopa pines, simulating a forest environment. Birds and small woodland creatures flitted from branch to branch, kept separate from the classroom by an invisible electronic barrier. It was an entirely self-sufficient, small scale environment. Noah had designed it himself, and others that were similar. They doubled as air cleaning facilities for surrounding rooms.

"All of you are volunteers," Noah began, from the lectern, "and you are to be commended for not going to work in a polluting industry, and for instead committing yourselves to the preservation of the galactic environment. The term I have just used—'galactic environment'—is not easily defined, so I will take several moments to explain certain basic concepts to you. . . ."

He gestured with his hands as he spoke, and for almost an hour he went on uninterrupted, while the students listened in fascination, hardly stirring from their seats.

Then he rolled forth a large clearplax box on a cart, and explained that it contained a living organism he had saved from the planet Jaggem while performing ecological recovery operations there. The box held what looked like an amorphous hunk of dark brown flesh, writhing slowly, throbbing and pulsing. But Noah knew it was a lot more than that.

"Meet my friend Lumey," he said. "I named him that because he glows luminescent white when digesting his food."

Noah invited the students to gather around.

"As far as we can tell," he said, "Lumey belongs to a nearly extinct galactic race, and may be the last of his kind. We keep him in a sealed environment, and he might live there for a long time. Or, sadly, he might die before your very eyes. One thing is certain: We could not leave the little fellow on Jaggem, since industrial polluters there destroyed his entire food chain."

"How does he see?" one of the female students asked. "Where are his eyes?"

"According to my biologists, he doesn't have eyes, ears, or a sense of smell. Nonetheless, he uses other senses to get around, and has an innate ability to sense danger, and to survive."

"Is that a face?" one of the young men asked. "He keeps turning a portion of his body toward us." He pointed at a light brown area of flesh. "See. Just a small section that is different in color, and more smoothly textured than the rest of his body."

"Good observation," Noah said. "That seems to be a sensor pad, although we're still not sure what he detects with it. When we found the poor creature in a pile of industrial slag, he was living off his own residual body cells, withering away. We have created a mini environment here where he lives quite well on his own recycled air, and reprocessed waste as well, which exits his body in a mineral-rich condensation and is then scooped up by one of our inventions from eco-recovery. In this case it's a small-scale skyminer, which salvages important elements from the mini-atmosphere and converts them to food for Lumey."

As Noah spoke, he pointed to a miniature skyminer hovering inside the container, and a food processor on one wall. He was about to explain more, when suddenly he stopped in mid-sentence. Startling him, a nehrcom screen on the back wall—which previously had been as black as space—came to life, showing the fuzzy image of a large terramutati. Turning their heads to look back, several students cried out or screamed in horror.

The Mutati was, in its natural state, an almost incomprehensible amalgam of fatty tissue, with bony extrusions for its numerous arms and legs. A tiny head with oversized eyes was barely visible atop folds of fat, like the head of a turtle poking out of its shell. The creature had no mouth, but words came forth in synchronization, as its body quivered and pulsed like gelatin.

"Your security is rather feeble and easy to penetrate," the Mutati said in a crackling, eerie voice. The image on the screen and accompanying sounds, while weak, were the normal quality of a nehrcom transmission that had been relayed from the Canopa ground station. He saw what looked like nehrcom equipment in the background.

"Find out where this is coming from!" Noah barked to Subi. "And evacuate the classroom!" The adjutant ran out into the corridor and shouted for guards. A number of students followed him, but others tarried, staring with transfixed expressions at the screen.

"Get out of here!" Noah shouted at them. "All of you!" He gripped the lectern, and it rocked.

"Out there orbiting Canopa," the electronic intruder said in an irritating, calm tone, "you are not exactly at the center of the galaxy, are you? So I will tell you what has occurred today. A merchant prince assault fleet, sent to Paradij by devious design, has been demolished."

As if to emphasize what the Mutati had just said, a loud static pop sounded, and the last word echoed in the room: ". . . demolished . . . demolished . . . demolished. . . ."

Stunned by the assertion, Noah was not certain if he should believe it. He had heard nothing of a military venture against Paradij. But could this possibly be true?

On the wall screen the Mutati sneezed, coughed, and twitched. The shapeshifter had sneaked onto Timian One, having assumed the identity of a Human and gained access to a nehrcom station while its electronic surveillance system was under repair.

As one of the Mutatis who did not normally show allergic reactions in the proximity of Humans, he had, for a time, experienced no adverse reactions. But eventually the allergies had surfaced and now they were hitting him full force. Even the implanted allergy protector he had as a backup did not work.

* * * * *

As Noah watched the screen, he heard a static hiss, and then saw a gray fog surround the Mutati. Previously Noah had seen captive shapeshifters do this when under stress.

Out of the fog came words. "Abal Meshdi, his Eminence the Zultan of the Mutati Kingdom, has instructed me to present a generous offer to you. We would like to join forces with your Guardians against the evil industrial polluters of the Merchant Prince Alliance. We can provide you with technical advice, even highly portable military hardware to use against the corporations. We have a common enemy."

Unnoticed by Noah, he had been joined in the classroom by two people who entered from a side door, and stood beside him.

"Interesting proposition," one of them said.

Startled, Noah glanced to his left. "Anton!"

"You gave me some kind of high priority clearance to come aboard. Hey, I must be pretty important to you, huh?" He nodded toward his companion. "Meet Tesh Kori."

Noah nodded toward her, but only briefly.

"You're not going to accept that creep's proposal, are you?" Anton asked.

"Of course not. I'd never sell out to the Mutatis."

"I didn't think so." The blond young man looked up at the screen and shouted at it. "He says no! Do you understand?"

"Too bad," the Mutati said. He produced a shiny, metallic device, which he held in front of his face. "I was prepared to offer this to you and your Guardians." Tiny wings popped out of the side of the apparatus. "Stealth bomb. It's undetectable, can fly past any security system and blow up an entire factory. Just think of how much that would help the environment."

"You heard what my friend said," Noah responded.

"Is that your final decision?"

"It is!"

"In that case," the Mutati said, "we wouldn't want this to go to waste." The flying bomb glowed red, and exploded. The transmission flashed bright red and orange, then went dark abruptly, leaving the wall screen black again.

"Did you hear him talking about a Mutati military victory against merchant prince forces?" Noah asked.

"No," Anton said.

Noah went on to relate what he had been told, then said, "Let's hope it isn't true." He paused. "What do you want to see me about?"

"We came to help," Anton replied. "And it looks like you can use it." He put his arm around Tesh. "We want to become Guardians."

"This is not a good time. I thought you were here because of my father's injury."

Anton's face darkened. "I'm sorry that happened, and I hope he gets better. Look, I always told you I wanted to join the Guardians someday, but you gave me a bunch of excuses. You're not going to do that again, are you?"

Noah hesitated. He did not want Anton to do anything dangerous, and was considering how to respond. For years, Noah had concealed from Anton the true identity of the young man's parents . . . that his mother was Noah's sister Francella, making Noah his uncle. The identity of the father was even more shocking.

At that moment, two security men burst into the classroom, apologizing profusely. Seeing the screen dark, one of them said, "We don't know how he got through, sir, but it won't happen again. We'll make sure of it."

Noah didn't see how they would accomplish that if they

didn't know what had happened in the first place. He told the men to have their commander submit a full report to Subi Danver within the hour. Nervously, the pair saluted and hurried away.

Refocusing, Noah saw his nephew standing with Tesh Kori, waiting for a response. He met their hopeful gazes, then looked away for a moment.

Francella had become pregnant after one of her trysts with the Doge Lorenzo himself and had kept the information from him—for reasons that she never revealed. After she gave birth, Noah learned about her indiscretion and insisted upon making certain that the child was cared for properly. Reluctantly, she had given Noah the responsibility of maintaining contact with her son, while she paid the bills for the child's support. It was one of the few things on which she and Noah had ever agreed.

Knowing what he did about his sister's nature, however—her cruelties and selfishness—Noah always wondered why she had not just aborted the fetus. It had given him some hope that she might have a modicum of humanity after all. But Francella always had a way of dashing such sentiments.

Out of concern for the safety of his nephew, Noah had discouraged him from joining the Guardians, and now it was more dangerous than ever. Still, the organization was in desperate need of good people, and Anton certainly qualified. He was a hard worker, honest, and resourceful.

During several moments when Tesh Kori was looking in another direction, Noah studied her exquisite profile, the way she stood tall and proud and beautiful. She glanced at him before he could look away, and he felt drawn into her hypnotic, emerald green eyes.

Finally he looked at Anton, and met the young man's

anxious gaze. With a smile, Noah shook his hand briskly and said, "Welcome to the Guardians." He then shook Tesh's hand. "Both of you. It won't be easy. You'll have to undergo a rigorous training process. Some make it, and some don't."

"We will," Anton said, in a determined voice.

Chapter Twenty-Two

How many aspects of love are there?
How many people have ever lived?
These are the questions, and the answer.

—Princess Meghina of Siriki,
Critiques of a Courtesan

Princess Meghina hardly thought of her magnificent Golden Palace on far-away Siriki. Instead, she spent sixteen hours a day at Prince Saito's bedside in his villa, and took surreptitious steps to obtain the best medical care for him. Inside the elegant, mural-walled reception room that had been converted to a hospital room, two doctors stood behind her, looking at the patient through a clearplax life-support dome and whispering between themselves. In order to avoid a confrontation with Dr. Bichette and Francella, she had identified them as friends, and they were dressed in common daysuits. Now they were alone in the room with Meghina and the ailing Prince.

On the staff of the renowned Nottàmbulo Hospital of Meghina's homeworld, these men were specialists in comas induced by head injuries. The Sirikans had studied the Prince's medical charts that Meghina obtained secretly, and had told her that Bichette, despite bringing in high-priced specialists, had not selected the best people.

One of the Sirikans, Dr. Woods Masin, was a tall black man with a square jaw and gray hair. His companion, Dr. Kydav Uleed, had primitive, rough-boned features like those of a backcountry Human, with a high, sloping forehead and large, protruding cheekbones.

Unable to hear everything they were whispering behind her, the blonde noblewoman stared sadly at the simoil murals on the walls, depicting the fascinating life of the man she loved. A breeze rustled the curtains by an open window, and out beyond the high cliff she saw one of the Prince's flying yachts anchored in the air.

Meghina shifted uneasily on her feet. She wished she had met this great man earlier, and that they might have married. Instead she had been required—for political reasons—to become the wife of Doge Lorenzo del Velli. Her dual life, as royal spouse and courtesan to many of the leading nobles of the realm, was not easy for her. It also made her husband a cuckold, but he didn't seem to mind. He had his own stable of women to satisfy his physical needs, and sometimes he even dangled Meghina's favors in front of influential princes in order to obtain what he wanted from them. It was one of the most unusual marriages anyone had ever heard of, and was conducted without any pretenses.

She gazed at the comatose form of Prince Saito on the bed, which was oversized to accommodate his bulk. It seemed unfair to her that this vital, very *alive* man had been stricken down and reduced to such a sad state, dependent for every breath upon the medical technology that was connected to him. Much, but not all, of the equipment had been provided by the medical division of his own corporation.

At least I've had time with you, my love. For that I shall always be grateful.

"May we open the dome?" It was Dr. Masin, leaning close to her and speaking in a low tone.

"No one is around," Dr. Uleed added.

Nervously, Princess Meghina looked behind her. The main door and a side door were closed. "Be quick about it!" she husked.

The tall, gray-haired Masin swung the life-support dome open and checked the Prince's eyes with a small silvery medical tube, while Uleed held another device on the patient's temple. "He needs to be moved to a hospital," Uleed announced.

"Preferably Nottàmbulo," his companion added.

Suddenly the side door crashed open and Dr. Hurk Bichette burst in. "What is going on here?" he demanded.

"These are specialists from Siriki," Princess Meghina answered, almost shouting at him in return. In a near-breaking voice she introduced them by name, and added that the Prince's condition had worsened. Whereas earlier he had been semi-comatose, with brief periods of enigmatic conversation, now he was trapped in a full coma and had not spoken for more than a week.

"Get away from my patient!" Dr. Bichette roared. He closed the lid of the life-support dome and physically pushed the other doctors away. Bichette's face was flushed, and a large vein throbbed at his temple.

"I want all of you to leave," he insisted. "You are interfering with my medical procedures, and I want this room cleared immediately." He waved his hands at the other doctors and at the Princess.

"How dare you speak to me in that manner?" Meghina exclaimed. "I am of noble blood, the wife of the Doge, and the . . ." Her voice trailed off, since the rest of her résumé could not be put into words that sounded dignified. "I am the . . . favorite . . . of Prince Saito," she added, softly.

For a moment Bichette glared defiantly at her. Then, belatedly, he looked down at the floor and bowed slightly. "I apologize, My Lady. Perhaps the stress of the occasion and the long hours I have devoted to Prince Saito have dulled my manners."

"Step aside, please," Meghina said in a firm tone, "so that my doctors may continue their examination."

With a scowl, Bichette moved away from the bed.

As the Sirikan doctors resumed their work, one on each side of the Prince, Bichette said, "You will find that I have done everything possible."

"You are a general practitioner," Dr. Uleed said, with a quick glance at the target of his words. "This case appears to be beyond the scope of your knowledge."

"A specialist performed the surgery, and I have experts advising me."

"We are familiar with their names . . . and *credentials,*" Uleed snapped. "Let's just say that their reputations are rather limited."

Bichette chewed at his lower lip, and muttered something unintelligible in return.

Hearing a noise behind her, Princess Meghina turned and saw Francella Watanabe standing just inside the main doorway. She appeared to have been observing for a while. Francella's shaved brows had been tinted cherry red, matching her lipstick and her sleeveless damask dress, a garment that featured a plunging neckline, exposing her naval. She wore white gloves that extended to her elbows.

"You should have obtained my permission before bringing these men here," Francella said, locking gazes with Meghina. "In my father's diminished state, I have complete power of attorney to make decisions about his medical care."

"I also have a special relationship with your father," the blonde Princess retorted, "and I have certain rights."

"You are his wife in name only, with limited rights.

Nonetheless, out of courtesy for you, I will not banish you from his presence. You are never again, however, to bring anyone in here to examine my father without my permission. Is that understood?"

In low tones, Meghina conferred with the Sirikan doctors. Wrinkles of concern etched her heart-shaped face. Finally she said to Francella, "Your father needs specialized care at a facility such as the Nottàmbulo Hospital."

"He will not be moved off-world!"

"Don't you want the best for him?"

"I resent your tone."

"This is not a time for petty feelings. We must consider the welfare of Prince Saito."

"It is probable that he will never awaken," Francella said. "Sadly, I must say this."

"You base that statement upon the opinion of a general practitioner."

"And his specialists."

"Who happen to belong to his own drinking club."

"See here," Dr. Bichette interjected. "I will not have my integrity impugned in this manner."

"Be quiet," Francella snapped. "I will take care of this." She pointed at Masin and Uleed. "Leave this room immediately and don't ever come back."

Meghina nodded to them, affirming the command. She would make an attempt to discuss the matter with Francella at a later date, after tempers had calmed.

The Sirikan doctors departed, while Meghina remained behind. She went to the bedside and held Prince Saito's hand. Across the room, beyond her hearing, Francella and Dr. Bichette conferred.

The Prince's hand was cold to the touch, but he clung to life, his chest rising and falling regularly. With a wistful smile Meghina remembered some of their favorite times together, and how startled he'd been upon discovering she was a Mutati. They'd already had sexual relations dozens of times, so he could hardly believe it when she admitted her true physical form to him. She had never, however, shown her Mutati body to him, fearing his revulsion. "I would rather be Human anyway," she had whispered to him.

After that, she had not changed back, and in a matter of weeks, remaining in that state for too long, she no longer had the cellular flexibility to metamorphose at all. She had never felt comfortable as a Mutati anyway, and ever since her childhood had preferred the beauty and functional utility of the Human physical form.

Her decision had not been without its sacrifices. Despite her rank as a Mutati princess, it had rendered her an outcast among her people, preventing her from ever assimilating with them again. In losing her ability to shapeshift, she gave up an act that was extremely pleasurable, even to her. It provided a Mutati with the highest form of bliss—higher even than sex, and left the Mutati in a state of satiated euphoria for an extended period. (A potentially dangerous time, since it made the shapeshifter vulnerable to attack).

Now Meghina looked Human, and would for the rest of her life. She had not contemplated all of the problems that this would entail, such as the signs of aging that had a way of creeping up on this race. Mutatis, in contrast, went at full-vitality through old age, until the moment of their death. In her present form she had to think about face creams and laser treatments in order to remain youthful in appearance, something she would never have bothered to consider in her original bodily structure.

Come back to me, my love, she thought. A tear ran down her cheek as she gazed at the nearly lifeless form of her lover.

Chapter Twenty-Three

Dying is easy. Life is infinitely more difficult.
—Prince Saito Watanabe

As Francella left her father's room and strolled along a loggia, she concealed a smile. The confrontation between Dr. Bichette and the two Sirikan doctors had not disturbed her in the least. Oh, Bichette was upset about his competency being called into question, but that fool didn't matter to her. No criticism could possibly be directed at her for leaving him in charge. After all, he had been Prince Saito's hand-picked personal physician, and an important director of CorpOne's Medical Research Division. On the surface, Francella could not have selected a more appropriate person.

Her father's cliffside villa, with its red tile roof and white stucco walls, overlooked the Valley of the Princes, with the office and industrial complexes of some of the wealthiest corporations in the Alliance. His regal dwelling had been styled in the manner of an ancient Earthian home found in the ruined town of Herculaneum. Roman emperors had enjoyed walkways like this one, with its open-air gallery of imperial statues. The eagle fountain in the terrace courtyard, visible to Francella now through ornate columns lining the loggia, had actually been brought back from Herculaneum, and so had the mosaic tile floor in the opulent private bath building.

As for Meghina, she would bear watching. Hidden

camviewers recorded her every move at the villa, and Francella had been monitoring the medical confrontation from another room, until deciding it was time to intervene.

Noah's fraternal twin waved a hand across a pale yellow identity beam that protected a doorway. After a momentary pause, a heavy alloy door slid open with a smooth click, revealing her father's study—a place he called "the inner sanctum." This room had always been off-limits to Francella and her brother when they were growing up, so it gave her special pleasure to be here now. It was from this study that she had been watching the confrontation in the other room.

No Roman emperor had ever been in possession of the technology that was arrayed on exquisite teakoak and marbelite tables and desks. Tiny computer monitors—each looking like a small electronic eye on the end of a long flexible neck—stood on one side. At a voice command the units were capable of filling the air with holo and telebeam images. This was a data and communications nerve center, not only of this house but also of her father's mega-company, CorpOne. Because of her position as Corporate Security Chief, he had provided her with access codes.

What he'd failed to notice, though, was her dissatisfaction over the way she had been treated in comparison with Noah, and how her resentment had built up over the years into a deep-seated anger. Francella now had an intense and all-consuming need for money, power, and prestige, and wanted to enjoy it all before she grew too old to appreciate such things. In her late thirties, with her vitality enhanced by CorpOne medical products, she was in perfect physical and mental condition to assume control of everything right now—including this study and villa. Her father was too elderly to enjoy such things anyway, so she was doing him a favor by rushing things along. What could be wrong with speeding up the timetable a little?

Glancing at a bank of camviewer screens on the wall, she satisfied herself that Princess Meghina was no longer causing any trouble. Unaware of the surveillance equipment himself, Dr. Bichette sat in a large chair, scowling as he concentrated on the blonde courtesan at the bedside.

Francella sighed. Unfortunately, her father still clung to life like an injured spider on a web, and Dr. Bichette had no idea how long he might continue in that condition. It could go on for years, the nervous doctor had said . . . or the old mogul might just give up and die at any moment. One of Meghina's specialists said that the patient's mind, even in its damaged condition, was making decisions about whether to live or die.

Somewhere in Prince Saito's subconscious he fought on, perhaps out of a powerful desire to be with his courtesan harlot again, or to make decisions about his vast riches. He even had an ultra-high-security treasure room in the villa, where he kept priceless jewels, manuscripts, and artworks. Undoubtedly part of his mind wanted to go in there again, and wallow in his wealth. The way he had it piled up in there, he probably swam in it.

One day the treasure room, like everything else, would belong to her, so she ignored it for the moment. There were easier riches to take. Her father had done exceedingly well as a merchant prince; few had ever done better. Francella only had one regret: she wished she could bottle him up and let him continue making business decisions for her—perhaps as a sentient robot that was completely under her control and had her father's mind. Or a disembodied brain that did what she told it to do and just kept making more and more money for her. Yes, that would be perfect.

Men should do that for women anyway, whether they were fathers, husbands, or lovers: providing money for ladies to spend. Even her brother should get in on the act and send her a steady stream of funds. He was prosperous enough. In fact, it surprised her how he did so well himself; like a junkyard king he made money from dirt, minerals, and plants, performing ecological recovery operations on various worlds and selling environmentally friendly products. In effect, Noah was squeezing money out of nothing.

She had to admire both her father and her brother for their business acumen. They were more alike than either of them realized. And she hated them, with every breath she took.

Keeping them apart for years had been a major victory for her. After the attack on CorpOne headquarters she had leaked phony evidence that it had been committed by Noah and his Guardians, without ever letting anyone know—not even her closest associates—that she was the source of the information, and of the attack itself.

Francella crossed the large study and stood at one of the computers, a segregated unit that kept track of CorpOne's off-planet holdings. Earlier that morning, data in another segregated terminal had referred her to this one, stipulating that it contained information that would enable her to shift assets around. Even with her father's injury, Francella wasn't sure how long he would live, and she wanted to get her hands on as much as she could, as fast as possible. Things could still go wrong, and Noah—against all odds—might still worm his way back into the old man's affections, drastically reducing her share or even cutting her off entirely.

Now she would begin with the saphonium mines of the Veldic Asteroid Belt, where Prince Saito had a subterranean storehouse of uncut gemstones that were among the rarest and most precious in the Merchant Prince Alliance. Delivery of the hoard had been held up by unexplained changes in podship schedules; only recently had the strange vessels resumed calling on that region.

Francella had only to shift the destination codes to her own warehouses on Timian Four, and the treasure-trove would be hers. In anticipation of this (and a lot more), she'd hired private construction crews to work on her property for some time now, putting up more buildings and beefing up the security systems. According to an encrypted nehrcom message she had just received, the job was almost complete.

She kept her plans completely secret, because as far as she was concerned, no one could be trusted. Relationships always had a nasty habit of changing, and if that happened here, if the wrong people learned too much about her operations, she would have to take drastic action. So, by keeping her activities secret and working anonymously through intermediaries, she was actually committing a kindness, making it unnecessary for her to commit violence.

It all made perfect sense to her.

Not that it was unkind to kill. In fact, she would soon do her father a favor by putting him to rest. At his age, it was too difficult for him to control such a huge empire anyway. One or more of his employees—or a corporate competitor—would take advantage of him sooner or later, and that would only upset him. She was avoiding the inevitable unhappiness for him, doing a very nice thing for her aged father.

Without question, it all made perfect sense.

Casually, she nudged the long neck of the computer terminal, and heard the internal whir of the machine. In a moment the eyelike monitor would flash on and project a telebeam, allowing her to review the data as it danced in front of her vision.

At this terminal, however, the tiny screen was illuminated red instead of the normal amber, and did not project at all. Francella caught her breath. None of the other data processors had done this. She took a step back just as the eye changed to bright green and began to project something.

A serpent with glistening fangs lunged at her, coming out of the screen.

Since this had to be an electronic image, Francella felt intuitively that it could not possibly harm her. But she tumbled backward anyway, and scrambled for safety.

The green snake grew longer and chased her, hissing through the air.

She rolled under a table with the mechanical creature right behind her. On the other side she leaped to her feet, changed direction, and tumbled over the top of a desk, scattering a dictocam machine and shiny silver tubes of cartridges that had been stacked there.

The fangs were only centimeters from her. The jaws snapped, but missed.

Desperately, she grabbed one of the tubes, which was heavy from all of the cartridges it contained. Whirling, she slammed it down as hard as she could on the snake-head, expecting her blow to pass through the air without hitting anything. But to her surprise the tube struck something and the creature recoiled, as if in pain.

The serpent turned sickly yellow and crashed noisily onto the tile floor. Tiny metal parts sprayed through the air, and one glanced off Francella's browless forehead, drawing blood. Finally the reptile went silent on the floor. Its shattered carcass did not move.

Confused, Francella went to one of the other computer terminals, and took the tube, now dented, along with her for protection. Carefully, she nudged the neck to turn on the machine. The computer spun through its cycles normally. This time she went through a deep search mechanism, using her passwords to look for all security systems in the room. She should have done so before, but had assumed that her identity would allow her to do anything.

Finally, she set the makeshift weapon aside.

In a few minutes, she found what she was looking for in the database. The snake had been one of several deadly traps in the room, activated under certain circumstances. She shuddered as she looked down at her feet. One of the large tiles to her right was a trap door that would cast her into a drowning pool beneath the villa if she stepped on it. She had narrowly missed it several times.

The tricky old man was even dangerous on his death bed.

Death bed.

She had not used this term previously because of the way her father kept hanging on, but now she did, and liked the sound of it. One way or another, even if it involved additional risk to her, she would finish him off.

With her adrenaline surging from the close escape, Francella spent the rest of the day and night in the study, without eating or drinking anything. After disabling the traps, she used her access codes to divert the Veldic saphonium and rifled his corporate bank accounts, even pilfering tax account funds that had been earmarked for the Doge. She proceeded to steal more assets than the value of an industrialized planet, and covered her trail expertly, so that it looked as if the holdings were still there.

When it was finished, she sat at her father's desk and grinned. He had always encouraged her to excel at data processing.

Her gaze lifted to one of the camviewer screens on the wall. Prince Saito lay alone in the room, sleeping with an almost serene expression on his face. Obviously the old tycoon thought he had taken care of every necessary detail, but he was wrong.

Chapter Twenty-Four

Indecision has killed more people than all the battles of history.

—Supreme General Mah Sajak,
Merchant Prince of Armed Forces

The noble-born princes had been seething for years over their loss of prestige, a trend that began when Lorenzo's father, the Doge Paolantonio IV, began appointing successful businessmen and inventors to princely positions. This policy was amplified under the regime of Lorenzo, causing widespread resentment among the royals.

In the past decade, the disaffected noblemen Prince Giancarlo Paggatini began organizing regular social events for the noble-born princes. These were held at a prestigious resort on Parma, one of the moons of Timian One. In actuality, the gatherings were fronts for meetings, which were attended by a group of malcontents, including General Mah Sajak.

On Parma the most popular attraction was Vius, an immense active volcano with a three hundred kilometer–wide crater. Through a unique network of lava tubes and subterranean currents, Vius circulated the lava so that the caldera was always molten, like a thick, red-hot lake on top of the mountain.

Though nervous about it, General Sajak had been looking forward to this meeting for weeks. He had an agenda in mind, one that he had kept under close wraps. As he passed through airlocks to enter a small terminal building at the edge of the fiery lava cone, he considered what he would say to his comrades, and how he might convince them to take a dangerous step, one that could put all of their lives at risk. He wore his usual baggy red-and-gold uniform and oversized cap, with metallic dress trim on the trousers and on the arms of the jacket.

Behind him, the black, patched-together robot Jimu clanked along . . . the same one that had been in charge of sentient machines in the Grand Fleet, and which was dispatched with evidence of the terrible defeat to the merchant princes. The General, while irritated about the noise Jimu made, had not bothered to have him repaired, since he didn't plan to keep him around for much longer.

Supposedly the terminal building was hermetically sealed in order to keep out toxic gases exuded by the lava, and likewise the gangway that led to a ceramic-hulled luxury yacht that floated on the lake. Still, Sajak smelled fumes as he boarded the craft . . . evidence that there must be a leak somewhere. His nose twitched. Gradually, after walking down a short flight of steps to the spacious dining salon, he no longer noticed the odors, perhaps because they were overridden by mouth-watering cooking aromas from the adjacent galley . . . meat sauces, garlic, exotic spices from all over the galaxy. Through thick-plated windows around the dimly-lit room he saw the red, menacing glow of lava outside, against the starry blackness of night.

The owner of the volcano resort, Prince Giancarlo, rose from the head of a long table as the General strolled in, followed by the clattering robot. Almost all of the seats were filled with noblemen dressed in their silkine and lace finery. They sipped aperitifs from tall, thin goblets, but none of their ladies were present, since the subjects discussed at these meetings were considered private. To the men's way of thinking, women—even those of noble birth—could never occupy the lofty social positions of men.

"Welcome, welcome," Giancarlo Paggatini said, motioning toward a reserved high-back chair on his right. A chubby, rosy-cheeked man, he wore an exquisite platinum-tint shirt with wide, flared sleeves. The consummate host, he always served the finest foods and wines. He grasped the General's hand and shook it energetically.

Trying to conceal his own shaking knees and hands, Sajak instructed the robot to remain off to one side. The officer removed his hat and placed it on a rack under the proffered chair, then sat down quickly. Three little glasses of aperitif were arrayed on the table in front of him, one pink, one green, and one blue.

"You have some catching up to do," the rotund host said.

"With respect, I must decline," the small, bony-featured man said, trying to make his voice sound firm even though his insides churned. "I have important matters to discuss this evening, and do not wish to be impaired."

"You're not going to get serious on us, are you?" protested a prince on the other side of the table. A tall, loose-jowled man with a monocle dangling from his neck, Santino Aggi was already showing the signs of alcohol. He motioned for a waiter to bring him another drink.

"I'm afraid so, my friends," Sajak said. He took a long breath, and waited.

The rest of the noblemen arrived, and finally the boat pulled slowly away from the terminal, out into the cauldron of liquid fire. Within moments the ceramic craft was planing over hot lava and the captain activated its skimmers—temperature-resistant extrusions on the underside of the hull—that caused a kaleidoscope of colors to flash around the boat.

Some of the men on the other end of the table gasped at the spectacular beauty, but those seated nearest to the General remained quiet, as they wondered what he was about to say to them. It disgusted him that some of them didn't want to consider serious political matters, and preferred to just collect earnings that they had inherited. To his credit, Prince Giancarlo was not like that. With a gesture of dismissal and a barked command, the host stopped the waiters from bringing any more drinks and ordered them out of the salon. As they left, they closed all doors.

Conversation ceased around the table as the air of anticipation intensified.

"I'm sorry to dampen the tone of our meeting so early," Sajak said, rising to his feet. "As you know, we normally do little more than commiserate when we get together, sharing tales of woe and our desire for political change."

Two of the princes on the General's side of the table took offense at this remark, and muttered between themselves.

Nervously, the officer fingered a cluster of war medals on his chest, and began. "I presume that all of you have heard of our military defeat at the hands of the Mutatis. Our plan of attack should have succeeded, so the failure had to be due to sabotage, a traitorous act. We are investigating the matter and will take all necessary action."

"One moment, please," Prince Giancarlo said, rising from his chair, his beefy arms extended to reveal shiny rings on his hands.

As he spoke, slots along the center of the long table opened, and dishes of hot, steaming food rotated to the top. Little mechanical robots, dressed like waiters, stood beside each serving dish.

Wielding large utensils, the metal men loaded food onto the diner's plates. However—pursuant to instructions they had received from the host—they did not pour any additional drinks, and only filled water glasses. Some of the princes muttered their displeasure. When their serving tasks were complete, the diminutive robots dropped into the open slots, and the compartments closed behind them.

To the clinking of forksticks—combination eating and cutting implements used by the diners—Sajak continued. "I won't deny it was a personal setback for me . . . I had hoped to gain prestige with a great victory. Nonetheless, I will probably remain Supreme General of the Armed Forces. The Doge has stated openly that he wants me to step down, but I won't do it. I have enough political clout to resist. For awhile, anyway."

"Bravo," Giancarlo Paggatini said, as he stuffed a dripping chunk of Huluvian pheasant into his mouth.

"Times have been changing," the General agreed, ignoring his own food. "Noble birth means much less than ever before. We lost good men and women at Paradij, and a lot of expensive military hardware."

The princes murmured in concurrence.

With a nervous motion, Sajak signaled for the dented, scratched robot to step forward, which it did.

"This is Jimu," the General announced. "I told you about him, but I want you to hear firsthand what he has to say, and what he has to show you."

Dutifully, the robot reported in a hesitating, mechanical voice what he had already told the General, how the Mutatis seemed to be waiting for them and had defeated the attacking fleet at every turn. As he spoke, his artificial eyes glowed yellow, alternately dimming and brightening. Then, opening a compartment in his chest, Jimu projected blue light into the air, the holo evidence that the Mutatis had sent back with him. The images were similar to telebeams, but of an inferior, grainy quality.

When the robot finished and put away the projection mechanism, General Sajak rose and went to him. Jimu, around the height of the small officer, blinked his eyes as he awaited further instructions. Without saying anything, Sajak drew a pearl-handled puissant pistol from a holster at his waist and fired it into the control panel in the center of Jimu's chest.

The robot sputtered a garbled sentence, sparked, and fell with a thud on the deck. He went silent and motionless.

"As you have just seen and heard," Sajak said, holstering his weapon, "the Mutatis have provided information that they could only know if they had actually won the battle. It's obvious how far our Doge has gone to undermine my authority . . . and yours, by association. The Mutatis couldn't have defeated such a force without inside help. I'm sorry to say this, but Lorenzo sacrificed thousands of my people and caused our defeat . . . just to keep me from gaining political influence that might threaten his soft, pampered position."

"What evidence do you have of Lorenzo's involvement?" one of the princes wanted to know.

"The very scale of the debacle proves it, you dolt! We had a perfect mission plan. It couldn't fail. This had to come from the very top."

Taking a deep breath to calm himself, Sajak resumed his seat. He grabbed the blue glass of aperitif in front of him and quaffed the syrupy sweet drink. Thoughtfully, he placed the glass back on the table, while considering how to phrase his comments. "What I am about to propose is risky," he said. "I won't deny that. But I must remind you of the vows we took as members of the Society of Princes, this most secret of organizations."

"Honor to the death!" the men shouted, in unison.

"Every one of us could die for the cause," Sajak said. "I'd hoped it wouldn't come to this, but I'm afraid it's time for us to move against the Doge and his political appointees. Such drastic action has not been necessary for more than a thousand years, so I do not propose it lightly. Lorenzo's attitude, however, leaves us no choice. Each day that we delay, our position erodes."

As he spoke, images appeared on a wall screen behind him. For several moments the nobles watched the Doge at some of his public and private appearances. In each instance he was accompanied by Princess Meghina, or, when she wasn't around, by other women.

"Lorenzo has an open marriage," the officer said. "They both sleep with other people."

"That's nothing new," Santino Aggi said, putting on his monocle. He reached across the table, snared one of the remaining glasses of aperitif in front of the General and sipped it. "I've enjoyed the pleasures of the courtesan myself."

"Don't you see?" Sajak said. "This sort of behavior is a sign of moral decay. It is unseemly for our Doge and his wife to behave as they do, or for us to condone it."

Many of the princes nodded their heads in agreement, and whispered among themselves. Others sat motionless.

The images on the screen shifted, to a scrolling list of names and dates.

"This is the family pedigree claimed by Princess Meghina," the General said, "purportedly all the way back to Ilrac the Conqueror. A close examination of her documentation, however, reveals significant irregularities. We'll have to research it more, including the source of her dowry, but take a look at what I have learned so far. . . . "

For the rest of the evening, as the dinner boat plied the flowing, molten lake, the intense General Sajak presented his information to the assembled lords, and outlined his plan to discredit, and assassinate, the Doge Lorenzo del Velli.

But unknown to any of the noblemen, the robot lying on the floor had not been completely deactivated. Despite his rather rough appearance, Jimu was a sophisticated machine, with a number of customized internal features installed by his Hibbil builders. Silently, his backup brain core heard everything that was said in the dining salon, and recorded it.

Chapter Twenty-Five

Oh, the challenges of leadership!
Can I achieve what God-On-High expects of me?
This I vow: I shall never stop trying.
—Citadel Journals

His Exalted Magnificence the Zultan Abal Meshdi received many messages and reports—from around his realm and from his allies—but never anything like this. With all he had put into the Demolio project—the funds, the manpower, the time, and the angst—this was the most anticipated communication he had ever received.

Everything rode upon the precious research project he had commissioned.

The shapeshifter stared at a purple-and-gold pyramid in the hands of the young royal messenger who fluttered in front of him in the audience hall, his tiny feet not touching the mosaic floor. The slender youth, an aeromutati who had ridden a podship from the Adurian Republic to Paradij, could fly with his short white wings, but not through space. After arriving at the orbital pod station above Paradij, he had taken a shuttle to the ground depot, and from there had flown to the Citadel overlooking the city.

The messenger shivered slightly, perhaps from the chilly air outside, but more likely from fear.

Hesitating, the Zultan did not reach out to accept the communication pyramid. He wondered if there had been unforeseen problems with the Demolio program, or—as he hoped and prayed—had the final testing gone smoothly?

Suddenly, Meshdi grabbed for the pyramid with his middle arm, startling the bearer and causing him to drop it on the hard tile floor with a loud clatter.

Apologizing profusely, the functionary retrieved it. As he fumbled with the device, however, the seal mechanism released and the sides of the pyramid lit up, casting bright light around it.

Disgusted with the ineptitude, the Zultan hand-signaled to a black-uniformed guard in the doorway. The rotund Mutati guard opened fire with his jolong rifle, shooting high-speed projectiles that smashed the aeromutati back against a wall, leaving him a blood-purple mass of torn flesh and broken wings. He slumped to the floor, dead.

As the guard rushed toward the body, the Zultan shouted, "I meant for you to remove him from my sight. It was not necessary to kill him."

"Sorry, Sire. I thought you . . . uh, I . . . misinterpreted your signal."

Abal Meshdi realized that he had himself sent the wrong hand signal. No matter. He would have the guard put to death anyway. The Zultan did not tolerate mistakes. Except his own, of course.

Glaring in feigned disapproval, Meshdi retrieved the communication pyramid and activated it. Through a magnification mechanism on one of the faces of the device, he peered into a deep space sector that he did not recognize . . . a small blue sun, a pink planet, high meteor activity. Something streaked toward the planet from space, and moments later the world detonated, hurtling chunks of debris into the cosmos.

The pyramid glowed brightly for a moment, then went dark.

The audience hall was full of armed guards now, chattering nervously and searching for threats. Calmly, the Zultan again pressed the activation button of the pyramid. The same scene repeated itself, an unknown planet destroyed. No written communication accompanied the display, but under the circumstances he did not need one.

Gazing calmly at the guard who had fired his weapon, Meshdi said sternly, "Beaustan, with your long family history of service to this throne, you should know that it is never good form to kill the bearer of *good* news."

"I'm terribly sorry," the black-uniformed Mutati said. He looked confused, and terrified.

Noting a pool of perspiration forming on the floor beneath his guard, the Zultan smiled. "Well, we can always get new messengers." *And new guards,* he thought. The Zultan pointed a long, bony finger. "Remove the body and bring contractors to repair the damage."

"Immediately, Sire."

As the men worked, Meshdi stood and watched. This was excellent news indeed, and he had worried unnecessarily.

But isn't that the job of a Zultan, he mused, *to worry?* He found himself in a rare, giddy mood.

His secret research program, which had lasted for decades, was about to pay dividends. Finally, Adurian scientists, funded and supervised by Mutatis, had perfected the doomsday weapon. The planet he had just seen explode on the screen had been an uninhabited backwater world, a test case . . . blasted into space trash.

He absolutely *loved* the extrapolation: the entire Merchant Prince Alliance blown to bits and drifting through space like garbage.

Humans are garbage.

Just to play it safe, the detonation of the planet—and its

aftermath—were camouflaged behind a veiling spectral field that made it look as if nothing had occurred at all. It had been an insignificant world in an immense galaxy, but the Zultan did not like to take chances.

Two guards carried the broken body of the royal messenger past him, while others cleaned up blood and feathers from the spot where he fell. A team of contractors—four Mutati females wearing tight coveralls over their lumpy bodies—hurried into the hall carrying tools and equipment.

Now the Zultan of the Mutati Kingdom had only to fund the training of an elite corps of "Mutati outriders" and manufacture enough Demolios to keep them busy—the high-powered torpedo-bombs that were capable of causing so much destruction. Any one of the projectiles could split through the crust and mantle of a planet and penetrate to the molten core within seconds. There it would go nuclear, with catastrophic results.

In this manner, the gleeful Mutati leader would destroy every merchant prince world. Then, to completely eradicate Humans, he would proceed to wipe out even planets that were capable of sustaining their form of life—those having water, the proper atmospheric conditions, and circular orbits that provided them with the most stable environments. By contrast, Mutatis could live on worlds their enemy would find intolerable, where conditions were too hot or too cold, or with atmospheres that were too thin or too thick, and even with gravities that were too heavy or too light. Mutatis—life forms based upon carbon-crystal combinations—were one of the most highly adaptable races in the galaxy. Hence, they could live in many places.

Meshdi, however, had decided to draw a line in space. After having been driven from planet to planet by the aggressive Humans, he would not be pushed back any further.

The successful defense of Paradij had been a warning shot fired across their bow.

The Zultan intended to commence his extermination program with Human fringe worlds, where habitation was low and military defenses were weak, or even nonexistent. Ultimately he planned to strike the key merchant prince planets where hundreds of billions lived, but that would be far more difficult, and would require meticulous planning. Those worlds were on the main podways, and Human agents constantly boarded vessels along the way, searching for dangers with highly effective Mutati-detection equipment.

If he focused on less guarded worlds it would provide the advantage of cutting off escape routes from the more populated planets, leaving the Humans no place to run.

Chapter Twenty-Six

> Sometimes a storm of the heart is more uncomfortable than any other kind.
>
> —Mutati Saying

On a rocky promontory, Noah and Eshaz peered through thin plates of binocular glax that floated in front of their eyes. Automatically, the respective focal points shifted to accommodate their vision, and presently Noah made out the details of an encampment in the canopa pine woods below them. It was early morning on a cloudy day, and thirty Humans were arising in the camp, crawling out of their lean-tos and lighting a community fire to cook breakfast. It had rained heavily the night before, and those who had not constructed adequate shelters looked wet and miserable.

"Anton and the girl are on the right side of the clearing," Noah said, pointing. He had a reddish stubble of beard.

"I see them."

Noah watched as Tesh stood in front of the foliage-roofed, blue-bark structure that she shared with Anton. He was sitting inside on his sleeping mat of soft jalapo leaves, stretching and yawning. He looked dry. Outside, Tesh put on a coat and blew on her hands to warm them. Up on the promontory, Noah was cold himself. If he hadn't known it was midsummer, he might have thought snow was coming.

The rock outcropping on which he stood was five kilometers from his administration building but still on the grounds of the Ecological Demonstration Project. He and

Eshaz had flown a grid-plane there, an aircraft that was parked on a flat area just above them.

Anton and Tesh lived in the primitive encampment with other Guardian trainees, and every day they had to trek back to the administration-education complex for classes. In the evenings they studied under dim lantern lights in their simple structures—a battery of classes that included Outdoor Survival, Cellular Mathematics, and Planetary Ecology. It was a challenging life, a test of the students' endurance and ability to live in harmony with nature. They were provided with only a limited quantity of packaged foods (such as capuchee jerky and puya coffee), and had to forage and hunt for the rest . . . according to instructions they received in class.

So as not to interfere with important ecological relationships, they could only kill certain animals (such as claymoles and abundant birds), and only for food. With respect to the flora, they were also restricted. Monitors in the woods graded their performance.

Through his floating binocular glax Noah saw Tesh carrying a covered bowl over to contribute to the community breakfast. Based upon a report Noah had seen, she planned to prepare a protein paste from wild ingredients: kanoberries, ground grub worms and red ants, and honey. Anton was nursing several bee stings from going after the honey the day before. Tesh had been with him, but according to the report the bees had not bothered her at all.

Now she was urging Anton to get up; he appeared groggy, and kept trying to lie back down. She wouldn't let him, and finally dragged him out of the shelter, half-dressed. Other campers gathered around to watch, and were obviously enjoying the show. Even at this distance Noah could hear them laughing and clapping. But around the perimeter of the group, some people were looking up at the sky instead, which Noah did as well. The clouds were an ominous shade of dark gray, as if they were about to disgorge their heavy, wet contents on the land.

In a few minutes Anton was up and moving around, carrying a big coffee cup. He seemed to have as much energy as most people in the class . . . but nowhere near as much as Tesh. A Human dynamo, she seemed able to call upon some inner reservoir of vitality.

Tesh had a bucket now, and carried it down a steep path to a nearby creek, for water. Noah followed her movements, watching her closely.

"She *is* strikingly beautiful, isn't she?" Eshaz said.

"What?" Noah felt his face flush hot.

"I'm referring to Queen Zilaranda of the Vippandry Protectorate."

"Huh?"

"Just kidding. I mean Tesh Kori."

"Anton's girlfriend? I hadn't noticed."

"Is that so? Then I must have mistaken that gleam in your eyes, my friend."

Noah began to gesture with his hands as he spoke. "Well, she is attractive, but I would never think of showing her any interest—other than professional, of course. She's my . . . friend's . . . girlfriend."

An exceedingly observant sentient, Eshaz had noted with interest Noah's hesitation over the word "friend" . . . but he said nothing of it. Eshaz wondered, though. If young Anton was not a friend, what was he? Certainly not an enemy, or Noah would not have permitted him to train for a position with the Guardians. A rival, perhaps? Had they competed for women in the past? But Noah was at least fifteen years older, and maybe a bit more than that.

A light flashed on in Eshaz's head. At a voice command he increased the power of his binocular glax, which enabled him to study the face of Anton Glavine. To his surprise, the Tulyan noted similarities with the way Noah looked: strong chin, aquiline nose, and wide-spaced hazel eyes.

Could Anton be Noah's son?

As for the young woman, Eshaz found her extraordinary himself, in more than just her beauty, her high energy level, and her resistance to bee stings. The Tulyan had noted in brief conversations with her how quick she was, how obviously intelligent. He could see it in the glint and flash of her emerald green eyes, could hear it in her well-chosen words. In his own intellectual way, Eshaz found her eminently fascinating, but solely for the quality of her mind. Yes, Tesh Kori would make an excellent Guardian one day, and should receive rapid promotions.

Inevitably she might work closely with Noah, perhaps even on his staff. Eshaz envisioned problems between the "friends" if that occurred. In the realm of Human relationships, some things were quite obvious and predictable to the Tulyan.

In the camp below, Tesh brought the bucket of water back . . . while Noah continued to watch her.

Just as the campers finished their breakfast, snow began to fall, only a little at first, and then a blizzard. They ran for cover, while Noah and Eshaz took shelter in their grid-plane and put on warm coats and insulated boots. Hours passed, with no slackening. By mid-afternoon, a meter of white lay on the ground.

During the unexpected snowfall, Noah stayed in touch with his headquarters via the onboard telebeam transmitter. Finally, when the storm let up, he confirmed that a rescue team was about to set out in snow trucks. Concerned that this would take too long, he transmitted back that he and Eshaz were going to inspect the camp, and would meet them there.

Noah and his trusted aide slid open the door of their small aircraft and cleared snow away so that they could get out. With Noah wearing a backpack full of survival gear, the two of them slogged through deep, pristine snow to the edge of the hill. From there, Noah fired a wire at a tree down in the woods and then connected a sling and descent clip to the wire. Glancing back at Eshaz, who held another sling and clip, he said, "Follow me." And he jumped over the edge.

One after the other, the two of them went down the steeply-angled wire. The descent clips had braking mechanisms that squeaked, but they worked properly, enabling the pair to proceed at a controlled rate of speed.

When they descended as far as they could on the wire, they switched on motors to lower their slings to the ground. Reaching the camp a short while later, Noah feared the worst. Heavy snow had caved in many of the roofs, and the air was still. He detected no signs of life.

Then he heard something, and looked to the right. On the creek side of the camp, snow shifted, breaking away with soft thumps, and he heard voices from that direction. "It's about time you got here!" a woman shouted, cheerily. Noah recognized Tesh. As she stepped out from what looked like a snow cave, he counted four others behind her, including Anton.

Eshaz got to them first, and looked into the opening. Moments later, he reported, "They're all here . . . and all are smiling."

"We're OK, except one of the boys has a broken wrist," Tesh said to Noah. She wore a sweater and jeans, and with a bare hand brushed snow from her shoulders and arms. Then, while Eshaz tended to the injured student, Tesh told Noah that the entire class had been caught unawares, but had pooled their resources, especially when some of the lean-to structures failed. As snow pummeled them, they had built a larger shelter, and huddled together inside.

"Do we all get A's?" Anton asked, with a wide grin.

"You can count on it," Noah promised. "But this is crazy. It never snows around here in the summer."

As if to show him how wrong he was, a howling arctic wind blasted through the trees, and the temperature dropped precipitously. Noah and Eshaz joined the others inside the makeshift shelter. This further delayed the rescuers in their snow machines, but they finally rolled noisily into the camp. . . .

At well past midnight, Noah and Eshaz stood in the large lobby of the Guardian administration building, wearing dry clothes and drinking hot chocolate. Around them their companions chattered excitedly about the unexpected adventure. Curiously, the temperature had been rising quickly in the last few hours, and snow was melting outside, with water running off the rooftop and overflowing the gutters.

Standing nearby, Tesh and Anton had been bundled up in warm coats, but heat coming in from outside forced them to remove them. Others were doing the same, and no one understood what was occurring. With one exception.

"Canopa is not healthy," Eshaz murmured, as he gazed into the distance.

By the following morning, even with the sun shining, the temperature began to drop once more, and snow accompanied the plunge, although considerably less than before. By evening the temperature rose and melted away the blanket of white, but it did not get as warm as the first night. Another day and night of this ensued—three in all—with the odd reversal of expected patterns repeating themselves, but in diminishing form.

On the third night, Noah and Eshaz stood outside the main building, gazing up at a starry sky. To a certain extent Noah understood the Tulyan's remark about Canopa. Both of them believed that planets were vital organisms, and that the galaxy was populated by living, Gaea-type worlds. They had discussed this subject in the past, but only in general terms that never quite satisfied Noah's desire for information.

It always seemed to him that Eshaz knew more than he was revealing about the subject. Even though Noah had coined the phrase "galactic ecology," he did not really feel like an expert on the subject. He was only a student himself, with a great deal to learn.

"Perhaps one day you will decide to tell me more," Noah said.

"Perhaps," came the response.

Chapter Twenty-Seven

The wise merchant prince emulates the predator.
—"Discourses on Power,"
confidential memo from Doge Lorenzo

For weeks Prince Saito had clung to life, sustained by the life-support dome over him and the auxiliary medical equipment connected to his failing body. Since the injury he had lost more than forty kilograms, and looked pale. Princess Meghina felt as if she was caught in a nightmare, unable to save the man she loved. Each day was like the one before it and the one that followed, and she fell into a dismal routine.

She had been staying at an elegant hotel, only a short distance away by groundjet. In view of her high social status and special relationship with the Prince she might have stayed in his villa, but Francella had proffered no invitation and Meghina had too much pride to push the issue. Hence, the Princess had decided to go somewhere else, where she could have a little breathing room.

Each morning at eight o'clock, her groundjet left the hotel and took her to the Prince's villa high on the cliff, a short ride. She then remained at his side until late evening, talking to him, holding his hand, massaging his shoulders . . . and never giving up hope that he might regain consciousness. Sometimes she sustained herself by dipping into her memory vault and reliving wonderful moments the two of them had shared.

"Remember that time we went on a sand-skiing holiday to

Lost Lake Desert, and I tumbled down a huge dune and disappeared? You rushed down to rescue me, my gallant knight. I'll never forget how you cleared away the sand so that I could breathe, and then you kissed me. I carry that kiss with me every day, and so many others, my darling. . . ."

While recounting the anecdote for him she held his hand, and thought she felt his pulse quicken for a moment.

A fast learner, Meghina had developed an understanding of the cell meters, immuno monitors, and other machines connected to his body. She began to memorize the results and compare them with prior outcomes, while asking a lot of questions of any doctor or nurse who happened to be in her proximity.

Late one night, after staying with the Prince all day, she kissed him gently and felt the coldness of his lips, so cruelly different from the passion they had shared not so long ago. During the groundjet ride back afterward, she'd cried, afraid that he would never recover. But it had been only a short trip and only a short cry. By the time she arrived at her hotel suite she reminded herself that she needed to be strong for him, and she prepared for the next day.

Upon returning to the villa the following morning, however, she walked into the sick room and found the life-support dome sitting on the floor by the bed, with a blanket over the Prince, including his face.

No one else was in the room; just the two of them.

"My love. No! Please, no, not you. . . ."

Gasping in shock and disbelief, she removed the blanket from his head and kissed him one last time, dropping Mutati tears on his lifeless face. He looked so small and fragile, where once he had been such a powerhouse of a man. She glanced around, but saw no one.

Prince Saito was gone, leaving the courtesan with only her memories.

A short while later, Dr. Bichette marched into the room, followed by two large men in black tunics, capes, and fez hats. *Undertakers,* Meghina thought, unable to stop the flow of tears. A motorized gurney rolled behind them, controlled by a transmitter held by one of the men. Bichette looked stern and impatient, as if other matters were more important to him than this one, and he had been delayed by the inconvenience of Prince Saito's injury.

Despite her abiding sadness and the tears that continued to flow, Princess Meghina thought of Saito's daughter, and how she must be hurting. Presumably Francella was in the house, and had been with her father earlier in the morning, perhaps before he died. Meghina hoped that he had felt the warmth of his daughter's touch during his final moments.

Resolving to offer her condolences to Francella, despite the past animosity between them, Meghina walked out to the loggia and peered into room after room. She took several deep breaths. This was not an easy thing for her to do. But she lifted her head high and continued looking. Her noble prince would have wanted her to rise above personal conflict, and she would make every effort to do exactly that.

At the far end of the loggia she passed a hand through the pale yellow identity beam that protected the Prince's study. Presently the heavy alloy door slid open with a smooth click, and she stepped through.

"What are you doing here?" It was Francella, looking up from a long-necked computer terminal just inside the doorway. Her face was filled with rage and hatred.

"I . . . I just wanted to offer my condolences for your loss."

Unaffected by the deep sadness on the face of the blonde

woman, Francella shouted at her, "You were his whore, but I am his heir. Now get out!"

Maintaining her composure, Meghina gazed down the bridge of her nose and retorted, "I am a *courtesan*. There is a difference." Not wishing to get into an emotional argument so soon after a death, she whirled smoothly and left. . . .

A short while later, Francella went to the local nehrcom transmitting station and sent a message to Doge del Velli, requesting an audience with him, so that they might discuss their new working relationship. Actually, she had forged important documents that she wanted him to sign, and she knew exactly how to gain his cooperation. It was the sort of behavior that the merchant princes liked and expected anyway, and no one enjoyed this sort of interaction more than Lorenzo, even if he had to give something up in the process.

Chapter Twenty-Eight

Sometimes when you want to think big, it is necessary to begin with the very small.

—*Scienscroll,* Commentaries 8:55

After completing their outdoor survival training and a battery of preliminary classes, Tesh Kori and Anton Glavine were promoted to the School of Galactic Ecology on the orbital EcoStation. There they began more advanced studies, including Correlated Astronomy, Planetary Reclamation, and Eco-Activism. Tesh excelled in her studies, while Anton did acceptable, but not outstanding, work. Both of them were still only probationary Guardians, and could not become full-fledged members until they graduated.

During a lunch break inside EcoStation's crowded automatic cafeteria, they sat at a small table by a window that afforded a distant view of Canopa, beyond wind-sculpted clouds below them. One of the cloud formations made Tesh giggle, since it resembled a corpulent Mutati, with a small head and a lumpy body.

Upon hearing her, Anton looked up from an electronic book that he had been reading. His eyes were bloodshot from staying up late the night before, studying for his first examination in Eco-Activism. He had been pushing himself, trying to prove to Tesh that he could keep up with her. She smiled gently at the thought of this mere *humanus ordinaire* trying to match her own performance levels, an utter and complete impossibility. Perhaps she should diminish her accomplishments, as a kindness to him. Human males, so competitive with everyone in their spheres, didn't like to be shown up by females, and especially not by females with whom they were having relationships.

Several tables away, the scaly-skinned, reptilian Eshaz was deep in conversation with Noah Watanabe. On a cart beside them, Noah had brought along the nearly extinct alien he had rescued from Jaggem, the amorphous creature he called Lumey. Surprising everyone, and Noah more than anyone, Lumey no longer needed to be kept inside the sealed container. Perhaps in response to Noah's loving attention, the creature had healed, and was now living off a variety of foods. At the moment, Noah had the case open, and was tossing occasional scraps of food inside. As each morsel arrived, Lumey slithered his body over it and absorbed it into his skin, glowing luminescent white for a few moments at a time during the digestive process. But Tesh was more interested in another, much larger creature. Eshaz.

The Tulyan, while an ancient rival of her own Parvii race, had not appeared to recognize her true self . . . the tiny person hiding inside. She had never heard of a Tulyan seeing through a Parvii magnification system, but it was said that they knew such devices existed. Although Tesh did not go out of her way to talk with Eshaz, she did not attempt to avoid him, either. She was not overly worried, since the energy field around her worked to conceal her identity from all galactic races, even defeating the most sophisticated scanners.

As she gazed at him now, he glanced suddenly in her direction, but only for a moment before continuing his discussion. He placed a hand gently on Noah's shoulder, leading her to believe that he might be expressing his condolences to the Guardian leader over the death of his father.

This Tulyan was unlike others that Tesh had observed in her seven hundred years of life, in that he socialized easily with Humans and even ate their food in large portions. Normally Tulyans were insular, sticking to their own kind and the ways of their own people. Considering the cuisine of alien races far inferior to their own, they were fussy about what they ate and drank, too. Curiously, though, Eshaz seemed to actually *prefer* Human food—even the barely adequate fare of this school cafeteria. As for Tesh, she didn't concern herself with taste in the least; she was capable of experiencing it, but enjoyed other senses more. She simply ate what was nutritious.

Based upon her miniature racial physique, one might think that she could only consume half a thimbleful of lunch. But this was not the case at all: she ate (or seemed to eat) as much as any other woman. In reality, however, almost all of her food was being diverted by the magnification system into a concealed food chamber that she could dump later, at her convenience. The chamber was much larger than she was in her natural Parvii state, and it occupied a space below the location of her true form.

Unknown to anyone gazing upon her, Tesh (like any magnified Parvii) floated inside the brain section of the image, with the shimmering light of the enlargement mechanism all around her. The secret, comparatively immense food chamber became only a sac with the thinnest of membranes after she emptied it—so that whenever she wished to return to her normal size, the sac compressed to an object as small as a Parvii marble, which she could carry about in a pocket. Thus she could easily exist in two realms, and was able to shift quickly between them.

In recent days she and Anton had begun to make love

again. After their passionate first encounter, he had refused to do it again for a time, telling her that they should develop their relationship more first. Assuming it was some misguided Human sense of guilt combined with gallantry, she had not argued. Gradually her seductive methods worked anyway, and his resistance melted away like an ice sculpture in the tropics. Human men, even if they tried, could not resist a beautiful woman forever. He had been a challenge—she had to admit that—but only for awhile.

Thinking of this, and of the sexuality of Human men in general, her gaze wandered over to the table where Noah Watanabe sat with the Tulyan. Engrossed in conversation, the Guardian leader didn't appear to notice her at all. In fact, whenever they encountered one another in the corridors or classrooms of the space station he seemed to make a point of avoiding her. It was not simply disinterest on his part, either. To her it looked like considerably more than that, as if he had a strong emotional feeling about her—either attraction or loathing—which he tried to manifest as detachment. Whatever he felt toward her, he was not concealing it entirely, though, and she intended to pursue the matter further.

Another challenge. . . .

Chapter Twenty-Nine

> Danger: Never tamper with the inner workings of a sentient machine. For service, contact one of our factory-trained technicians.
>
> —Hibbil product statement,
> sent out with each AI robot

After General Sajak shot Jimu, the robot had been left for the mechanical equivalent of dead. Servants on the dinner boat had been told to toss him into the molten lava lake of the volcano, but in private they had attempted to reactivate him instead, thinking he might perform some of their more menial chores. It was a risky enterprise, but with the noblemen gone they thought they could get away with it—while taking care to keep the robot hidden whenever the wrong people were around.

Operating on one of his backup systems, Jimu had heard every word spoken at the clandestine meeting of the nobleborn princes, and had recorded all of it into his core processing unit. He was conscious now, as the servants worked on his mechanisms in an attempt to resuscitate him. He could not see anything, but based upon the position of his body and the sounds around him Jimu guessed that he was on a table or a counter, in a small room. Detecting the odors of grime and decaying food, he thought it might be a lunchroom.

One of the men had experience with robots, but not enough to understand the sophisticated internal workings of this one. Jimu could tell what they were doing at every moment, as they attempted to rebuild and reconnect fiber optics, trillian capacitors, and data transmission zips, but these guys were not that smart and were doing it all wrong, causing more damage than good.

In fact, the way these servants were going they wouldn't get anything working, and might give up. Most of all, Jimu didn't want them to throw him in the hot lava. If they did that, he might not ever recover.

He checked data in his systems. The central core with which he was thinking at this very moment—in essence the soul of the machine—was protected by a ten-centimeter thick shell, designed to withstand the impact of falling from great heights or being hit by a groundtruck. Constructed of ascarb fiber materials, the box was resistant to fire as well, up to twelve hundred and fifty degrees Celsius for a ten hour period. He paused and asked himself a question: What was the temperature of molten lava? His data banks provided the answer: a little less than twelve hundred degrees.

As Jimu thought more about it, he realized that this was not a margin of comfort for him. Within a few minutes of immersion in the lava, every part in his body with the exception of the core shell would melt away. He would be left with ten final hours to think, followed by the disintegration of the central shell itself. That might take another thirty minutes at most before molten material started leaking in.

His survival depended upon staying out of the lava lake.

But he was helpless to act. While he had a self-functioning repair system, it only worked with raw materials provided by the Hibbils under factory conditions.

He could only wait, and hope. . . .

Agonizing hours went by, during which time Jimu began to despair. The Humans kept doing the wrong things, making incorrect connections. It would never work. Then, he sensed something strange.

"Look!" one of the Humans exclaimed. "His arm just moved!"

"I didn't see it."

Jimu hesitated. Then, ever so slightly, he moved the arm again . . . no more than a twitch.

How can this possibly be happening? he wondered.

Jimu analyzed the repairs, and confirmed that they were not done properly. Then he examined them more carefully, and was astounded. The Humans had found an alternative way of making his arm operate, but without its full range of movement.

Excited Human: "There! Did you see it?"

"Yeah."

"I saw it, too," another voice said.

Feverishly, they continued working on the control panel, and soon both of the mechanical arms were moving, and the fists were flexing open and closed. The Humans brought his legs to life next, and the components of his metal face. All functioned in only a very limited fashion, without the capabilities he'd had before.

Finally, peering through narrowly open eyes, Jimu took a playful swing at one of the servants, and narrowly missed his jaw.

"Whoa!" the man exclaimed, as he easily dodged the blow.

"Do you think he's dangerous?" another asked.

You bet I am, Jimu thought. He opened his glowing yellow eyes all the way and sat up, causing quite a start from the servants. There were four Humans in the room, staring wide-eyed at him as if he were the ancient Frankenstein monster of Earthlore, come back to life.

Chapter Thirty

> The concept of a soul is one of the pillars of fear-based religions, suggesting that there is no escape from the wrath of the Supreme Being, even after death. This is a clever deceit, designed to control followers. We can do as we please.
>
> —Halama Erstad,
> Chairman of Merchant Priests

Noah stood with a crowd inside the gated hillside necropolis, squinting in afternoon sunlight that flashed through puffy clouds. He could see the Valley of the Princes below, and the inverted pyramid of the CorpOne headquarters building, with bolts of lightning flashing across the sky beyond. It was warm and he felt no breeze, a respite from the freak weather of recent days that had postponed the funeral of Prince Saito Watanabe. Now nine days after his death, it was finally taking place.

But the funeral procession seemed like too much of a festive parade, and Noah detested every moment of it. On one level, he fully understood the concept of celebrating the life of a prominent man. Certainly Prince Saito Watanabe had been one of the most admired noblemen in the entire Merchant Prince Alliance. No one had more business acumen than he; no one possessed more ability to generate immense profits. But at what cost? As Master of the Guardians, Noah understood only too well the wholesale destruction of galactic environments by CorpOne and its competitors, and he could never forgive his father for his part in that. Not even now.

On no account did he feel like honoring the life of such a man. The old mogul had not been a good person by any definition. Noah was simply paying his respects. He stood on a grassy elevation beside a narrow one-way road, with his adjutant Subi Danvar and a squad of armed Guardian security men keeping vigilance nearby. Eshaz had come along as well, but he remained a little downhill from Noah, saying he did not wish to intrude.

In a display of great pageantry and fanfare—with trumpets, court jugglers, drummers, and scantily-clad female dancers—a noisy procession made its way past the onlookers and began to ascend the steepest portion of the road. A jeweled monolith crowned the top of the hill, a magnificent mausoleum that Prince Saito had commissioned for his final resting place. But it was like no other funerary structure that had ever been built.

Across the road from Noah and his small entourage the Doge Lorenzo del Velli wore a golden surcoat and matching liripipe hat. A large group surrounded him, including his blonde wife, the Princess Meghina, in a spectacular gown of golden leaves and a rubyesque tiara. The most famous courtesan in the galaxy and the lover of many a nobleman, she stood proudly with her chin uplifted, and seemed out of place in the company around her, as if they were rabble and she their queen.

This enigmatic woman had been the paramour of Prince Saito, and everyone knew it, even her own powerful husband. Noah had never met her himself, since she had begun her relationship with his father after the blowup that sent Noah off on his own. She looked so elegant over there, so proud and haughty.

Near the Doge, Francella Watanabe wore a tight, shimmering red dress with a low neckline and a tall red hat. She had no eyebrows at all, not even her customary painted ones, and above the long slope of her forehead the red hat had twin antennae, so that she looked like an insect in Human skin. She smoked a long fumestik while chattering incessantly and smiling, as if she were attending a gay soiree.

Francella and Noah gave each other periodic dirty looks across the roadway, but had not spoken to one another today. Noah had separated himself from her intentionally in order to avoid a scene, even though he knew she was working her manipulative, seductive wiles with Lorenzo and his sycophants. She had publicly accused Noah of murder, and he had denied it. A full-scale investigation—ordered by the Doge—was underway, but thus far Noah had not followed the advice of his aides, and had not hired his own legal team to defend himself. He thought that would only make him look guilty and worried, when he was neither.

Someone had hired phony Guardian soldiers to attack CorpOne headquarters, and Noah's loathsome sister undoubtedly played a key role in the planning and financing. Conceivably, Francella may have even suggested the staged event to the old man, twisting facts to get him involved in it. Noah conjectured as well on what part, if any, Princess Meghina may have had in the conspiracy. He had a lot of questions, and no answers.

Behind the procession of entertainers, twenty hoverfloats moved slowly uphill, providing garish displays of CorpOne products. Right after them came a black, robot-operated hearse, with the blue-and-silver elephant-design banners of CorpOne fluttering on the fenders. The great man lay inside, on his way to his final destination. Noah felt a wave of bereavement over the loss, but tried to suppress it with righteous anger.

As the hearse passed a high jadeglax structure by the roadway, a white-robed Merchant Priest on a high platform scattered holy water, and read passages from the *Scienscroll* over a blaring loudspeaker system. Noah could not make out the words, but didn't care.

A small number of noblemen and ladies stood on Noah's side of the roadway, but maintained their distance from him. One was Jacopo Nehr, accompanied by his brother Giovanni and by Jacopo's unmarried, fortyish daughter Nirella. A reserve colonel in the Doge's paramilitary Red Berets, Jacopo Nehr wore a red-and-gold uniform decked with medals and ribbons, while his brother had on a blue tunic, leggings, and a surcoat.

Gazing at the chisel-featured brothers, Noah envied their close relationship and wished that he and his twin sister might have gotten along, and even been close. But it was too late for such sentiments. Far too late.

Despite his efforts to feel otherwise, Noah could not help grieving for his father, and thought back to better times they shared, especially when Noah's mother was alive. Noah, working for CorpOne at the time, had been trying unsuccessfully to get his father to change his business practices. After Noah's mother died in that grid-plane crash, the two men no longer had a buffer between them, and the inevitable explosion occurred. Francella had reveled in the breakup, not concealing her glee in the least, and not even showing much emotion over the death of their mother.

Noah hated to think about his own family relationships, as they made him sick to his stomach. But here, under the solemn circumstances, he couldn't help himself.

With the sun warming his face and shoulders, it almost

seemed like a normal summer day to him. He felt anything but normal, though. Things seemed horribly out of balance.

The entertainers and corporate floats at the head of the procession split off onto side roads, while the robot-operated hearse continued uphill, to the jeweled mausoleum on top. Wide, diamonix-faceted doors slid open on the structure, and the hearse entered. Not long afterward Noah heard a small explosion, and the building turned fiery red as Prince Saito Watanabe—one of the greatest industrialists in history—was cremated inside the very building that would become his tomb. The unusual funerary arrangement had been specified in his will, and reportedly had been carried out with considerable difficulty.

Just then the ground rumbled and shook beneath Noah's feet, nearly causing him to fall over. A huge bolt of lightning accompanied by a thunderous explosion struck near the monolith. The ground rumbled and broke away, and the ornate structure tilted, then tumbled with a tremendous crash onto its side, still glowing red.

The mourners panicked and ran in all directions, but Noah remained in place, watching the others scatter. A short distance downhill, Eshaz stayed where he was, too.

The shaking of the ground ceased, and the sky began to clear. . . .

"This planet is dying," Eshaz murmured to himself. "And the web as well."

He sensed forces at work that could not be controlled by any galactic race, and which he might not even be able to identify.

A shudder passed through his body.

In a very real sense it seemed to Eshaz that the Great Unknown was a black box filled with nasty surprises, and something was opening the container a little at a time, permitting the contents to escape. It was an enormous cosmic mystery, and he feared it. But he also felt like a detective, with an immense and intriguing enigma to solve.

He saw Noah studying him, perhaps guessing at his thoughts. This remarkable man, so advanced in his thinking, had asked for more information. And Eshaz, while he had lived for almost a million years and knew much more than he had revealed to his friend, did not possess nearly all of the answers himself.

The Elders would not want Eshaz to discuss such matters with a mere Human, but for such an extraordinary example of the race he thought an exception might be in order.

Over the better part of a week, Jimu worked in secrecy for the servants of the Parma dining salon, performing menial chores when management was not around. At night the conspirators locked their prized robot in a storage room and went home to small cabins that were provided for them a short distance away.

One evening when all was quiet, Jimu broke out and fled into the surreal, red-glowing darkness of the volcanic moon. By the following day he reached a depot, where he mingled with the robots of a work crew and boarded a shuttle with them.

He soon discovered that they were headed for Canopa, where laborers were needed to work on a damaged mausoleum. . . .

Chapter Thirty-One

> A secret within a secret. This is the most difficult to unravel.
>
> —Anonymous

At the conclusion of the horrendous funeral, the Nehr brothers took a shuttle to the nearest pod station, and from there caught a podship to Timian One, the breathtaking capital world of the Merchant Prince Alliance.

Now, as the pair rode a ground-jet back to the headquarters of Nehrcom Industries, Giovanni Nehr considered how to say something important. He was slumped into one of the soft, deep seats in the passenger cabin, while Jacopo sat across from him, studying an electronic copy of the quasi-religious *Scienscroll.*

The Great Inventor, Gio thought bitterly. It was a title commonly applied to his graying older brother, for developing the nehrcom cross-galaxy transceiver.

His big secret.

Gio touched a combination of toggles on a small vending machine between the seats, causing the Hibbil device to manufacture a pill according to his specifications. A bright red capsule tumbled into a receptacle. With a shaking hand he grabbed the narcotic and gulped it, and seconds later felt it take effect on his mind. He inhaled several deep breaths, and tried to maintain control over his emotions. The drug only helped a little, but he didn't want to consume more right away, since he had such a sensitive constitution.

For the past two generations, secrets had been the economic life blood of the Nehr family. His parents had made a fortune by sending hunters out into the galaxy to capture Mutatis, which were subsequently used—under extreme secrecy—as biological factories, processing foreign substances in their bodies and metamorphosing them into hallucinogenic drugs.

On Forzin, a remote moon of the Canopa Star System, the family had kept Mutatis penned up like farm animals for the production of the drugs. The prisoners were force fed carefully-selected substances such as ravenflower hips, bacchanal barley, and toxilia, powerful agents that overwhelmed Mutati immune systems and tapped into their shapeshifting cores. In this manner the transformative powers of the Mutatis were rerouted, causing the creatures to change the extrinsic substances into exotic hallucinogens instead of metamorphosing their own flesh.

Each captive Mutati created a different narcotic, which was extracted from his blood. The Nehrs called their products "powerdrugs," since the procedure always resulted in something highly potent. The wide variation and unpredictability made the substances extremely exciting . . . and expensive.

The drugs, as individual as each Mutati, all bore letter and numerical code names, from P-1 through P-1725 . . . meaning that a total of one thousand, seven hundred twenty-five of the creatures had been captured and forced to produce. Some of the narcotics were more popular than others, such as P-918, which simulated Human flight when the user took it. But when the Mutati producing that variation finally died, the drug was gone forever . . . with the exception of any that might have been stockpiled. Like rare vintages of wine, preferred varieties went up in value, and people could make money by trading them on galactic commodities markets.

The business all came to a sudden, violent end when the last Mutati broke free, killed Gio's parents, and destroyed the manufactory. Jacopo had been fifteen at the time, and Gio barely three.

As Gio grew up he followed a different course from his famous sibling, and became something of a ne'er-do-well, failing in a number of risky business ventures. Two years ago, Jacopo rescued him from a bad drug overdose and gave him a job in administration with Nehrcom Industries.

Gio, however, was less than appreciative, as he did not like Jacopo's condescending attitude toward him. The younger Nehr also felt extreme jealousy toward his brother . . . and while he fought to suppress it, he rarely succeeded. Like a toxic leak that could not be sealed, the feelings continued to seep into his mind, poisoning it.

Although the pair resembled one another in their chiseled facial features, the similarity ended there. Gio was taller and heavier, with a muscular physique that he had developed with sterisone drugs and regular visits to Hibbil body-enhancement facilities. If he wanted to, he could break his brother's body in half with his bare hands, and sometimes thought about doing exactly that. Jacopo often wore a reserve military officer's uniform, but that was just for show; he was not tough at all.

Across the passenger cabin, Jacopo continued to read his electronic copy of the *Scienscroll.*

Gio glared at him and thought, smugly, *I have secrets too, Big Brother. And you're not going to like them.* He bit his lower lip. *OK, let's start with this one.*

In the most pleasant of tones, Gio announced, "I will be resigning soon."

The great man looked up from his reading and lifted an eyebrow in surprise, but only a little. "To do what?"

"I don't know. I need to try something new."

Jacopo showed little reaction. It was exactly as Gio expected, and made him doubly glad that he was about to steal something important—the secret of his brother's nehrcom transceiver. For some unknown reason, Jacopo fully trusted only one person, his own daughter Nirella, and had given her responsibility for protecting information about the invention.

But Nirella had made a mistake, and her opportunistic uncle was about to capitalize upon it.

Chapter Thirty-Two

What is the origin of the pods? If we could answer that, it might reveal much about the nature and purpose of our galaxy.

—"Great Questions"
(Mutati Royal Astronomical Society)

The podship emerged from space in a burst of green luminescence, having traveled the arcane, faster-than-light pathways known only to these sentient spacecraft. With glowing green particles clinging to the mottled, blimp-shaped hull and dissipating around it, the vessel approached a pod station that flickered in and out of view. The arrival seemed like tens of thousands that had preceded it, and even more that were expected to follow.

The intelligent ship carried a small red-and-gold vessel in its hold, ostensibly one of the Doge's merchant schooners on a trading mission. Purportedly it was filled with wondrous products from exotic ports near and far, such as Churian teas, Kazupan silkine gowns, Hibbil machines, Adurian organics, glax lenses, and pearlian spices.

But inside the faux schooner sat a Mutati outrider disguised as a Human. In a trance, he quoted aloud from *The Holy Writ* of his people, the purity-extolling religious text that was the doctrinal basis for the annihilation of unclean Humans throughout the galaxy.

The podship docked at a zero-G berth inside the orbital station. Momentarily, without a creak or a squeak, doors opened in the vessel's gray-and-black, living tissue underbelly.

The disguised Mutati craft inside the cargo hold dropped like a child from a cosmic womb. The engines of the fake schooner surged on, and the pilot guided it past loading docks and walkways. All pod stations were built essentially the same, and so were the interrelated podships, so the pilot—even though he had never been to this particular station before—knew his way around.

As the outrider taxied, he passed a "glyphreader" robot patrolling the sealed walkways, one of the sentient machines that scanned and translated the pinkish-red geometric designs on arriving podships, which indicated their routes. It was one of the few mysteries about podships that the galactic races had been able to figure out—the way the markings changed constantly, like destination screens on jetbuses. The robot had an electronic sign atop its head, a small version of larger display panels that hung from ceilings. All were written in Galeng, the common language of the galactic races.

Smoothly, engines purring, the Mutati guided his little ship out of the station and dropped down into weightless space, with a blue-green planet visible far below. Twin jets of white-hot exhaust shot out of the double tail of the clandestine schooner, and the craft accelerated downward. Within seconds, instruments told the pilot he was inside the atmospheric envelope of the planet, and he saw ionized orange sparks from the friction of the hull as it skimmed the air.

The Mutati, his senses deadened by focal drugs, had no ancillary thoughts in his mind. He recalled nothing of his life or family or career, none of which existed for him anymore. His entire *raison d'être,* everything he had done in his life up to this point, culminated in this one task. The assignment had come directly from the Zultan Abal Meshdi himself.

I cannot fail.

He studied his console of instruments and electronic charts. The globe below had a crust of thirty-three kilometers in thickness, with sedimentary materials and an upper shell of granite. Basalt, gabbro, and other rock types were beneath that . . . then the mantle, and the molten core.

Switching on a prismatic timer, the outrider set the torpedo, which in reality was his entire schooner. The doomsday device . . . a Demolio . . . screamed down toward the ice-covered southern continent of the planet.

Thousands of years ago this had been an important world to the Humans, where billions of people lived. Stripped bare by endless wars and the insatiable appetites of Human industry, it now contained a mere thirty million inhabitants.

"Earth," the Mutati muttered as his suicide torpedo penetrated the crust. Seconds later, it reached the fiery core and went nuclear. The planet was obliterated in an explosion, so sudden and immense that it consumed the pod station and the podship as well, before it could set course for a new star system.

Chapter Thirty-Three

> Reputedly, Doge Lorenzo del Velli is the greatest patron of business and science in history . . . but this is his own propaganda, cleverly disguised as fact.
>
> —*Succession: a Concise History of the Doges* (one of the banned books)

On distant Canopa, Francella Watanabe rode a slideway from a shuttle depot to a white, bubble-shaped nehrcom transmitting station. In a hurry, she wore a simple black dress and no makeup, so that her bald eyebrows and forehead glistened in bright morning sunlight.

The cross-space transmission facility sat in a hollow at the perimeter of the Valley of Princes, and was protected from attack by an implosive energy shield that encircled it, both above and below ground. It was a new structure, replacing one that had been blown up by a Mutati suicide bomber. The landscaping and other finishing touches were still under construction.

As she stepped off the sliding walkway and climbed wide marble steps Francella felt the invisible electronic field all around her, and experienced a shortness of breath from the anxiety this always gave her. The system read her identity at every imaginable level, and she wondered if it would make a mistake and not recognize her. These highly sensitive security units required a great deal of maintenance; they were always breaking down and under repair. During one of the down-times at the former station, a disguised Mutati sneaked in and sent messages, before destroying the facility.

Because of the high degree of concern over security, there were stories of mistaken arrest, and even one instance where a noble-born prince was misidentified and died from the stress of it. Francella felt strong enough to endure any rigid, probing procedures that the mechanism might put her through, but she hated the thought of wasted time. She had so many important things to do, secret things, and hardly enough time to complete them.

The electronic system emitted a friendly beep, allowing her to pass. The rooms inside the building were a brilliant, almost blinding white, with complex geometric ceilings but few furnishings, as if the contents had not arrived yet, or as if the designer expected to receive additional objects at some later date. But she knew the interior was complete. All of the stations were like this.

In an immense room beneath a glax dome stood one of the ultra-secret, platinum-cased nehrcom transceivers, with chromatic surveillance beams darting in all directions around it. For a few seconds, a rainbow of color washed across her, then moved on. Reportedly Jacopo Nehr, ever paranoid about keeping his priceless business secrets, continually rotated his security systems, to keep potential thieves off balance. This particular apparatus looked the same as the last time she had been here, but she suspected subtle differences.

The platform on which the nehrcom sat resembled a religious shrine, and not by accident, some people asserted, considering the reverence with which the instantaneous communication device was held. Arguably the greatest feat of technology ever conceived by the galactic races, it was second in its impact only to a concoction that was generally attributed to the Supreme Being himself . . . an entire race of sentient podships.

Under a new security procedure, users of the transceiver were not permitted to touch it or even to go near it, and instead had to remain behind a glowing blue railing that encircled the center of the room. Francella stepped up to the electronic barrier and tapped one of the buttons on a panel, indicating that she wanted to pick up a message.

Presently a hatch opened in the floor on the other side of the railing and a platform rose, bearing a nehrcom operator dressed in a black robe with a nebula swirl on the chest. When the mechanism came to a rest he stepped off and approached Francella.

"Here is your message, Lady Watanabe," he said.

As she accepted a folded sheet of brown parchment it irritated her that she had been required to come here personally to pick it up, but the Doge sometimes made this a requirement when he sent transmittals, even the most innocuous of them. As a rule, nehrcoms were entrusted for delivery to *messagèros,* the bonded couriers who worked for the Merchant Prince Alliance.

While the operator waited, Francella read the Doge's brief communication. He had consented to the audience that she had requested, and told her what time to appear for it.

"Please inform the Doge I will be there," she said.

The operator nodded.

As she left and descended the steps outside, one of the CorpOne vice-presidents stopped her, a toothy man with a bald head. "Did you hear about the catastrophe?" he asked.

When she gazed at him blankly, he told her that Earth had been destroyed. "It's gone," he said, "with only space debris left."

"What happened?"

"No one knows. A huge comet, maybe."

"No matter," Francella said. "It was only a backwater planet, of little concern to the Alliance."

With that she hurried away, to complete her scheming tasks.

Chapter Thirty-Four

I care nothing if my people love me.
The primary emotion I wish to elicit is *fear*.

—Doge Lorenzo del Velli,
as told by the Hibbil Pimyt

Princess Meghina strolled along a narrow path that overlooked the grounds of the Palazzo Magnifico and its fabulous orange-and-yellow Daedalian Labyrinth. A mini-forest formed in an intricate web of natural mazes around a Minotaur statue, it was a great delight to members of the royal court and to scientists as well, who frequently came to study the plants and take samples of them. The only such forest in existence, it was of unknown origin, and resisted all efforts to transplant it.

Meghina had been on Timian One for two weeks following the disastrous funeral on Canopa. Even though she and the Doge had the most famous open marriage in the Merchant Prince Alliance, there had been tension between them over her long-standing relationship with Prince Saito, and even jealousy on the day of the tycoon's ceremony. Afterward, the Doge had insisted that she come to the capital for an indeterminate period, and he had been displaying her at state functions, making her remain at his side like a living, ornamental doll. It was childish on his part, but no one could defy him when he really wanted something.

Doge Lorenzo had respected Prince Saito, even revered him for his business acumen. As long as the Prince was alive, the Doge looked the other way and said little about the relationship with Meghina. There were important professional connections between the men, and noble princes never let women come between them. Now that Saito was gone, however, the situation was different.

At dinner each evening, with only Lorenzo and his pretty blonde wife seated at an immense table in the Grand Banquet Hall, he continually harped at her, demanding to know personal details about her affair with the dead man. She tried to answer his questions, but no response seemed sufficient, and he kept snapping at her and digging deeper, asking additional questions.

The Doge had been watching her every move, mostly through his agents but often on his own. At the moment he was attempting to conceal himself on the pathway behind her, thinking she would not notice him if he dressed in the garb of an ordinary court noble . . . royal blue surcoat, leggings, and liripipe hat. She smiled to herself, but it was more a grimace than anything else.

He could behave so immaturely at times. She didn't understand the double standard involved here. Well, actually, she did *understand* it as the chauvinistic manner of the merchant princes, but it was not fair. Her husband performed sexual acts with more than a hundred women a year, while her tally was a scant tenth of that, and only with noblemen of the highest stations. The sin she had committed in Lorenzo's eyes, however, had been to care deeply about one of them without making any attempt to camouflage her feelings.

She missed Saito so much that it hurt, and her husband knew it.

Pausing to catch her breath, she pretended to examine a poppy garden, while actually looking peripherally at her husband, at least fifty meters down trail. He had stopped, and was acting as if he was cleaning something off his shoes with a stick.

Part of her wanted to go back there and confront him, shouting her feelings at the top of her voice. But a proper lady would never conduct herself in that manner. The noblewomen of the Merchant Prince Alliance were all trained in civilized behavior . . . making them what was known as *urbanitas* . . . from an early age. She needed to comport herself at all times as if she was actually one of those ladies. An uncultured, or *rusticitas* person, was not welcome in court society.

All of her life, going back to the early years in which she had grown up as a Mutati princess on Paradij, she had longed to be a beautiful, elegantly-dressed Human lady, socializing with handsome Human men. The princess had always considered Mutatis ugly in their natural state, with their rolling mounds of fat, tiny heads, and oversized eyes. She had run away from the Mutati Kingdom in order to live out her fantasy, and for years it had gone well. Meghina achieved all of the wealth and social position that a woman could want, and had enjoyed the affections of a man she loved. But after the death of Prince Saito her fantasy seemed to burst. Everything looked dark and dismal to her now, and she wondered if she had made a terrible mistake when she abandoned her roots.

With a deep and abiding sadness, she picked a bright yellow pollenflower to remind her of her lost love, and continued along the path, away from her observer.

At dinner that evening, as expected, Lorenzo lay in waiting for her. A valet reported to the Princess that the aged Doge had been sitting at the table for more than an hour, drinking wine and getting meaner by the minute. He had thrown crystal glasses and candlesticks at servants, shouted epithets at them, and even threatened to kill one on the spot and use his body as a centerpiece for the table.

His behavior hardly qualified as civilized, but in his position he could do anything he pleased.

As Meghina swept into the Grand Banquet Hall she wore a shimmering gown of metallic blue Sirikan cloth, with golden lace at the bodice that revealed her ample breasts. Above her heart-shaped face, her blonde hair rose in an elaborate structure, with wings at the sides and a ruby tiara gracing the front.

Her husband did not rise for her, and hardly looked in her direction when a servant helped her onto a high-backed chair. She sat on the Doge's right, not a safe distance away.

"Good evening, Your Magnificence," she said in a melodic tone. Meghina wore a subtle floral perfume that she knew he liked.

Lorenzo gulped a glass of red wine and glared at her with dark, watery eyes that suggested things he did to Mutati prisoners in one of the gaol's torture chambers. If he ever discovered her true identity, she had no doubt of her fate.

"Are you my wife or aren't you?" he demanded. His gaze focused on the scant lace over her bosom.

"I am your wife, Sire . . . and more. I serve nobility." It was a rather open-ended response, but one that presented her position to him clearly—she had informed him in the very beginning that she wished to be a courtesan and not merely a wife.

A servant came to pour more wine, but had to duck and run for cover when the old man pummeled him with tableware that crashed and broke on the floor.

"Get out!" Lorenzo thundered to the hapless fellow. "Can't you see I want peace and quiet?"

When they were alone in the great hall, Lorenzo gripped Meghina's wrist on top of the table and rasped, "After your lover's funeral, you ordered the restoration of his mausoleum, didn't you?"

"Yes," she admitted, "but I thought you would want that. He was your friend and an important prince."

"It is unseemly for you to arrange for the work personally." He squeezed her wrist tightly. "You see that, don't you?"

"I had hoped to remove the worry from you, Sire, since you are so busy." *Busy following me around,* she thought.

A cruel smile cut the features of his leathery face, with a bit of drool sliding from one side of his mouth. "How thoughtful of you," he said in a low, menacing tone, "toward me and my late friend."

"I had hoped to be," she said. Tugging slightly at her wrist, she protested, "You're hurting me."

"What?" He looked down, saw his own knuckles white from squeezing, and let go.

She rubbed her reddened wrist to get circulation going again. If she had known how violent Human noblemen could be, she might have taken steps to safeguard herself more after shapeshifting into Human form. Certain protective features could have been concealed in the flesh. As it was now, she could never change back again and was as vulnerable to injury or death as any Human female.

"Is work on the mausoleum finished?" he asked in an annoyed tone. He glanced around, as if looking for an inattentive servant to attack.

"They should be lifting it back onto its foundation about now."

"And the contractor's invoices?" He raised his voice. "You aren't paying them personally, are you?"

"I advanced some funds in order to get things going. I was only trying to remove the burden from you."

"All costs must be born by the state, and not by the wife of the Doge. Have the bills sent to me!"

"As you wish, My Lord. Shall we dine now?" Noting his continued interest in her bosom, she smiled sweetly and asked, "Or would you prefer your dessert first?"

His face provided the answer. Human men were so transparent when they wished to have intercourse. But she would tease this one first, with a sexually-charged dance of bewitchment.

On Canopa, Jimu had been one of hundreds of robots assigned to lift and repair the damaged mausoleum of Prince Saito Watanabe. The mechanical man melted into the background and did as he was told by the Human work bosses.

The structure rested in its proper position now, but the jeweled walls had been fractured, and were undergoing repair by a team of specialists who worked on low scaffolds. The work bosses had described the powerful lightning strike and ground tremor that caused all this damage as a freak act of nature. Jimu didn't know anything about that. He focused on his assignment, retrieving and listing the priceless gems that were scattered around the site.

At the top of the hill, he added a bucketful of jewels to a growing pile. Security was everywhere, with armed soldiers watching every move that he and his companions made, like the guards for a prison work crew. After a while Jimu peered through a broken wall in the mausoleum. Inside stood a glassy statue of the dead prince, with both arms broken off. Workers were repairing them.

Despite high security, Jimu had the intelligence to circumvent it, and he sneaked away, this time making his way onto a podship bound for the Inn of the White Sun. He had heard about a group of sentient robots that operated a way station there, and wanted to see what it was like for machines to control their own destinies. . . .

Chapter Thirty-Five

Is there anything larger than the galaxy?
And even if there is, what difference does it make?
—Anonymous note, found inside a piece
of malfunctioning Hibbil machinery

When Jimu arrived at the Inn of the White Sun, he was astounded by the ingenious architecture of this hivelike way station that had been constructed in an orbital ring. The views of the planet Ignem, far below, were spectacular through bubble windows, and unlike anything he had ever seen before. The world looked like the largest gemstone in the galaxy, and it changed moment by moment, displaying different color combinations in shifting light.

"So you've heard of us, eh?" a flat-bodied robot said, as they stood on an observation deck. Within an hour of his arrival, Jimu had been introduced to Thinker, the leader of the mechanical colony. Narrowing his metal-lidded eyes, Thinker added, "What is it you've heard?"

"That you control your own destinies." With one hand, Jimu rubbed a small dent on his own torso. He rather liked the feeling, for it made him think of the adversities he had overcome.

"I mean, what is it you've been told we do here?"

"That you run this inn, and make a great deal of money at it. Robots all over the galaxy speak of this place with affection and admiration."

"Anything else?"

"No, nothing."

"That is good, very good."

Not wishing to conceal anything from this important robot, Jimu said, "I was Captain of the sentient machines on the Human Grand Fleet. You may have heard of it . . . the force that attacked the Mutati Kingdom and lost."

"Yes," Thinker said, staring at Jimu's dented, scratched body. "And a military disaster does not look good on your résumé."

"I wasn't to blame for it, but listen to this." In his concise, mechanical voice Jimu described General Sajak's suspicion that Doge Lorenzo had sabotaged the fleet.

"Preposterous," Thinker said. "The Doge would never do that."

"Nonetheless, General Sajak is convinced of it, and is conspiring to assassinate Lorenzo."

Without warning, Thinker inserted a flexible probe into Jimu's control panel. Jimu went numb, like a patient under anesthetic.

"You are telling me the truth," Thinker announced presently, in a flat voice. He withdrew the probe, then asked, "Who set up your control box? I've never seen connections like this."

"A Human food-service worker. He had only a little experience with machines, I'm afraid."

"You don't have full range of movement do you? I noticed considerable stiffness as you walked."

"You're right." Jimu lifted an arm, but not very high, then showed how the elbow didn't bend as far as it should. He demonstrated similar problems with other joints.

"We'll have to get you into the shop. But first, I want to show you our operation here. As a military robot, you will appreciate it." The cerebral leader paused. "In fact, with your credentials, you deserve to be an officer again. Let's make it Captain, all right?"

"In what force?" Jimu's glowing yellow eyes opened wide.

He pointed a steely finger at Ignem. "We are building an army down there."

"And you've already decided to make me a part of it?"

"I make quick decisions," Thinker said. "That's why I'm in charge here. Besides, nothing eludes my interface probe. In only a few seconds, I learned all about you."

Later that day, Thinker escorted Jimu down to the surface of Ignem, to a camouflaged headquarters building that had been made to look like no more than a high spot on the surrounding black obsidian plain. There the newcomer was introduced to five other officers, all matching his own rank. One, a tall machine named Gearjok, had served as a technical robot on a Merchant Prince warship, responsible for maintaining mechanical systems. The other captains—Whee, Nouter, Fivvul, and Qarmax—had all worked in various machine supervisory roles for the armed forces of the Humans. In each case the robots had been discarded at the end of their useful lives, and had been salvaged by Thinker.

After a while, Gearjok slapped Jimu on his metal backside and said, "Enough of this. Now let's introduce you to the others."

As the mechanical men strolled outside, it pleased Jimu that none of his new comrades seemed to envy him for his quick promotion to their own level. He had seen such feelings of animosity in machine groups before, metastasizing like cancers and destroying the ability of the robots to work together. It was one of the undesirable traits of Humans that some mechanicals had acquired, but here it seemed to have been programmed out.

Jimu followed the others into a vacuum tube, which transported them with whooshes and thumps up to the roof of the headquarters, which they called the Command Center. From the top, he saw volcanoes in the distance, suddenly active and spewing fire and smoke into the atmosphere. Overhead, through the increasingly murky sky, he barely made out the orbital ring of the Inn of the White Sun.

Hearing a rumbling noise, he lowered his gaze and saw black plates slide open on the floor of the obsidian plain. Thousands of machines poured out, like fat, oddly-shaped insects from a burrow. He gaped in disbelief.

The robots began to form into ranks, but a number of them had problems and bumped into each other or stopped functioning. One, a round-backed mechanism who resembled a silver beetle, fell onto his back at the front of the ranks and could not right himself. Very few of them were shiny; most had unsightly dents and patch marks.

"As you can see, we still have some kinks to work out," Thinker said. "But believe me, we've made a lot of progress."

The worst robots were taken away for more repairs, and soon the remaining machines—around three thousand of them—were arrayed in neat infantry formations, identifiable to Jimu as the boxy ranks of ancient Earthian legions. He had mixed feelings about what he was seeing. In one respect, this was not a very impressive display. But in another, at least it existed.

A machine army!

He noted that only a small number of the troops carried weapons, and those were mostly outdated pelleteers and slingknives, along with a few modern puissant rifles. Some of the robots seemed to know how to handle their implements of war, while others did not. This certainly was a motley gathering of individuals and equipment.

"We'll have to send them back to barracks shortly," Thinker said. "We keep maneuvers out here to a minimum, to avoid detection by enemies."

"And who are our enemies?" Jimu inquired.

"There are always enemies. The trick is to identify them in time and take appropriate action."

"I see." Jimu nodded, but made a creaking sound as he did so. One more thing to fix.

With a sudden clatter of metal, Thinker folded closed, so that he looked like a dull-gray metal box.

"He does that sometimes," Gearjok said, "when he needs to consider something really important. It gives him absolute darkness and silence. The trouble is, when he thinks about deep philosophical matters he tends to fall asleep in the quiet darkness, with all of his senses blocked or shut off. Whenever that happens, we reactivate him by shaking him gently."

Moments later, Thinker opened back up, and said, "I've been meaning to offer our services to mankind one day, in repayment for inventing sentient machines in the first place."

"But Humans discarded these machines," Jimu said.

"We still owe them some loyalty for creating us. Never forget that, Jimu. You and I would not be having this conversation at all if not for Humans. I think they threw us away in error, and I've been looking for an opportunity to prove it. I assure you, that despite the fumbling appearance of my troops, it is a skillful deception." He touched a long scratch on his own torso. "Conventional wisdom holds that a well-run military force should be spotless and polished, thus instilling a sense of pride and personal self-worth into the organization. But there are distinct advantages to a less-than-perfect appearance. It can cause an opponent to underestimate your abilities."

"That makes sense," Jimu admitted. "Do you mean to tell me that even those machines that stopped functioning out on the parade ground did so by design?"

Thinker cut a jagged grin across his metal face. "Not exactly, but things *are* getting better."

"The robots here are independently self-replicating," Gearjok said to Jimu, "and you can be, too, with a little updating."

Thinker explained that he had developed a sentient machine manufacturing process that did not exist anywhere else in the galaxy. His metal men were able to make copies of themselves by finding their own raw materials and making their own parts, even recycling old items as necessary. He mentioned what Jimu already knew, that there were other machines that could self-replicate (such as those of the Hibbils), but only in regimented factories, with raw materials provided for them under assembly line conditions.

"Is that why the robots are not uniform?" Jimu asked.

"Precisely. They use whatever materials are available to them."

"With my own scrapes and dents, I should fit in nicely around here."

"You'll get a lot more before you're through," Thinker said. He paused, and added, "I am troubled about the assassination plot against Doge Lorenzo. It seems to me that this is the opportunity we've been looking for."

Solemnly, Thinker placed a metal hand on Jimu's shoulder and said, "I want you to lead a small force of our best fighting robots to Timian One and inform the Doge that he is in danger."

"Me?"

"I like what I see in you, Jimu. You have experience, but even more importantly you have special qualities of leadership . . . your own way of solving problems. And you heard the conspirators yourself."

"I'm honored, but . . ."

"You will inform him of the danger, and come right back. I need you here, to assist with the army we are forming."

"I don't feel ready for such an important assignment."

"Nonsense. We just need to update your operating systems and data banks, clean you up a bit, and you'll be ready to go. Another advantage that we have over Humans. With us, the learning curve is almost immediate."

"You're going to intervene in Human politics?"

"Doge Lorenzo is in danger, and we must do something!"

"Then I'm your robot. But first I must confess, anxiety is heating up my circuits. Could you ask the programmers to take care of that too, please?"

"Don't worry. We'll get you in shape for the assignment." Exuberantly, Thinker slapped his new comrade on the back, leaving one more dent, a little one.

Chapter Thirty-Six

The soil beneath your feet is never as solid as it looks. You must continually probe and turn over rocks, never letting your guard down.

—From *The Tulyan Compendium*

Noah led Tesh along a path that skirted his own home, with its gray shingle walls and white columns, matching the main administration building and complex of buildings that were partially visible downhill, through a stand of canopa oaks. Focused on the ecological training he was giving to her, he hardly noticed where they were. For the past three days, he had been spending private time with this intellectually gifted young woman, the top student in his school, sharing his personal insights with her, grooming her for the important position he hoped she would hold one day with the Guardians.

He had another matter on his mind as well. Word had reached him that Earth had been destroyed in a sudden, mysterious explosion that left the original home of humanity a debris field, floating in space. The most widely accepted theory was that a comet had hit the sparsely-populated planet, or a meteor, but astronomers had not seen anything unusual in that sector prior to the detonation. Another theory held that it might have been a huge volcanic chain reaction, and still another suggested that the Mutatis had done it. Every one of those ideas seemed far-fetched to the experts, and Noah wasn't sure himself.

As an ecologist, he would be analyzing all available data as it came in. Under the circumstances, though, with the death of his father and the suspicions that had been cast in his direction about that incident, he didn't want to go anywhere near the remains of Earth, or engage any of his own investigators. His own advisers suggested that he maintain a low profile, or his enemies would find a way to blame Earth on him, too. He and Subi were convinced that Noah's enemies—undoubtedly including Francella—wanted to discredit him and his planetary recovery operations. Many of the corporate princes were opposed to his environmental policies and recommendations, and considered him a thorn in their collective side. Now, with the influential Saito Watanabe out of the way, the son had become an even easier target.

Bending down, Noah selected a large oak leaf and held it up, so that midday sunlight revealed the gold-and-brown details of its pattern. "Look at the perfect symmetry of these lines," he said, passing a finger over the leaf. "Amazing, isn't it? I've seen such perfection all over the galaxy, in leaves, seashells, spider webs, and in so many other amazing objects of nature. It shows an interconnectedness, that planets are linked to one another."

"Your concept of galactic ecology," she said, "the interconnectedness of life in remote star systems."

He nodded. "A controversial concept, but I've never shied away from controversy. I think life sprouted in similar forms all over the galaxy, and probably all over the universe."

"Like the theory of parallel evolution," she observed, "but bigger than the similar life forms found on the continents or islands of one planet. You're talking about each planet as an island in a cosmic sea, with parallel life forms sprouting all over the place."

"That's correct," he said, beaming at her.

"I've been wondering about something," she said, looking at him intently with her bright green eyes. "Your writings are silent on this point, but do you think a cosmic wind carries seeds and cells from planet to planet?"

He tried not to think about the physical attraction he felt for her, and as before he set it aside. "Perhaps, and perhaps not. I've never been able to prove it one way or another."

"Doesn't all this prove the existence of a higher power, holding sway over everything, creating perfect beauty? Doesn't it prove that there really is a God?"

"It doesn't prove anything of the kind, only that there is an interconnectedness."

"I see. You're a scientist, not a religious scholar."

He smiled. "The universe is an incredible mystery. We see what we want to see in it, and delight in its boundless wonders." Noah let the leaf go, and a gust of wind picked it up, lifting it gracefully out through an opening in the trees, toward his headquarters on the land below. He watched the leaf until it eventually drifted down, out of view.

Placing a hand on his arm, Tesh said, "Perhaps I shouldn't say this, but I feel something between us." Slowly, hesitantly, he looked at her, and she moved around in front of him, so that he could not avoid her easily.

"I don't know what you mean," he said, lying. The wind whipped his curly, reddish hair.

Abruptly, she stretched up and kissed him on the mouth, so passionately that he had difficulty pulling away, but finally did so.

Folding her arms across her chest, she said, "I suppose you have this problem with many of your female students, and I'm sorry if I make you uncomfortable, but I've always been direct."

"I'm your professor, that's all." Noah was not entirely surprised by her forwardness, having noticed the way she looked at him seductively with her emerald eyes, and the gentle, alluring tones of her voice whenever she spoke to him. He had been trying to maintain his distance from her, but she must have noticed something in his demeanor, a weakness that she could exploit. He didn't entirely trust her, or any women who used their looks and wiles to lure men. Too many were like Sirens, he thought, enticing men onto dangerous shoals.

His eyes flashed as he looked at her. Despite his misgivings, Noah longed for a closer relationship with her, but fought his emotions, trying to retain his professional demeanor. Other female students had made overtures toward him, and he had always taken the high road, never succumbing to the desires he had felt for them. By avoiding embarrassing and compromising entanglements, he had remained proud of himself. But now, more than ever before, he felt vulnerable.

"You're Anton's girlfriend," Noah said, flatly. He looked away, at the sun dappled trees on the slope below them. "He's like a . . . younger brother . . . to me, and I could never consider betraying him."

"I've made no promises to him," she said.

"But I've made promises to myself."

"And I respect that." She moved away a little. "Look, I've always been a flirt. I've dated men of many galactic races, have always been a traveler. Maybe you're better off avoiding me."

As Noah led the way on a trail back downhill, he had no inkling of the extent of her travels, that she could actually guide podships on fantastic journeys across the galaxy, that she had already lived for more than seven centuries, and that she was not at all what she appeared to be.

"Are you going to kick me out of school for this?" she asked.

"Of course not. You're an exceptional student. You just need to understand that I have boundaries."

"At least you know I wasn't doing anything to influence my grades," she said with a laugh. "I already have the highest test scores."

He laughed with her, but didn't like what he was feeling. Aside from the professional distance he wanted from his students, he felt what could only be described as a prurient desire for her, and it wasn't right. He was not that sort of a person . . . at least, he didn't think he was.

As they reached the glax-walled main entrance of the administration building, his adjutant Subi Danvar rushed up, wearing the green-and-brown uniform of the Guardians. "We have a problem," the rotund man said, wiping perspiration from his brow. "Diggers."

"They're on our property?" he asked.

"Southwest corner of the compound," Danvar said. "They came up underneath a maintenance building and tore up the floor pretty bad before diving back into the ground. We lost a lot of equipment. Some of it damaged, and some just disappeared into the hole with them."

"More than one Digger?"

"Three of the mechanical pests. Two big ones and a little one. Like a small family of them."

Nodding, Noah said, "Form an extermination squad to go after them in their burrows."

"It will be done, sir. We have a man who served on one of the Doge's extermination squads before joining us. I'll get his advice."

"Good."

"Can I join the squad?" Tesh asked.

"What?" Noah said. "But you have no experience."

"I'm a fast learner, and it sounds like important work to me."

"What about your studies?" Noah asked.

"To tell you the truth, it's become too easy for me. I need a change of pace, if it's all right with you, sir. Call it penance."

Not understanding what she meant, the adjutant crinkled his brow.

"Just a private joke," Noah said to him. Glancing at the young woman, he told her, "All right. We'll give you extracurricular credit for the work. The machines are tearing up the environment, after all, so it is related to your studies."

The following morning, Anton Glavine was waiting at Noah's office when he arrived for work. With an infusercup of strong coffee in his hand, Noah greeted him, and let him in.

"I want to join the extermination squad, too," Anton announced, as Noah went around and sat at his desk.

"Out of the question. You need to complete your studies."

"So does Tesh. She says you're giving her extracurricular credit for Digger duty."

"That's true, but she's way ahead of you in her lessons, and can afford to take time away from the classroom. You don't have that luxury."

The young man chewed at the blond mustache on his upper lip. "I need to watch out for her, make sure she's safe."

"Tesh can take care of herself."

"I don't agree. This is a new operation." His hazel eyes

narrowed. "It's really important to me, Noah. I won't be any good in class at all if you don't let me go."

Noah still had not told Anton who his parents were—Doge Lorenzo and Noah's own sister Francella—but he knew he could not keep the secret forever. Anton was no longer a child, and had a right to know. He was behaving like a man right now, taking responsibility for the woman he cared about, the woman Noah couldn't help caring about himself.

A long period of silence ensued between the men. Finally, Noah said to his nephew, "All right."

Shortly after Anton left his office, Noah received encouraging news from Subi Danvar. The extermination squads used by Doge Lorenzo had developed relatively safe, efficient means of combating the mechanical pests, and had designed their own remote-controlled probes and tunneling machines . . . equipment that Subi Danvar was purchasing. The adjutant had also been able to hire more experienced men and women to join the squad, and was referring to them as commandos.

"It'll be safer than riding up to EcoStation," Subi assured him.

"I hope you're right," Noah said.

Chapter Thirty-Seven

It is said that God made the Tulyan Starcloud in the image of heaven.

—From *The Book of Tulyan Lore*

On an orbital pod station, Eshaz stood at the end of a line of passengers, waiting to board a mottled gray-and-black spacecraft. He was returning to the starcloud for a regularly scheduled session of the Council of Elders, to report to them on his travels and activities . . . a requirement for all of his people who spent time away from home. The passengers included scores of other Tulyans—web caretakers like himself—along with a colorful assortment of galactic races.

Eshaz touched the side of the large, bulging vessel, felt the slight warmth and barely discernible pulse of living tissue. "Hello, old friend," he whispered, thinking back to a halcyon time long ago when Tulyans held dominion over this podship and its brethren.

Now, in direct contact with the creature, Eshaz felt his own thoughts trying to penetrate and read the ancient mind of the podship, in a way that Tulyans could do with members of their own race, and with other galactic races. But this podship was not amenable to having its thoughts read. It was under the control of another entity, another galactic race.

The throb on the thick skin quickened just a little, and then slowed as the podship's tiny but powerful Parvii pilot detected the alien intrusion and warded it off.

Feeling a deep sadness for millions of years past and what could never be recaptured, Eshaz withdrew his hand and moved closer to the stout Huluvian man ahead of him in line. Others joined the queue behind Eshaz. His joints and muscles were aching again, the condition that seemed to run parallel with the decline of Timeweb.

The old Tulyan set his personal discomfort aside. His thoughts drifted off.

Contrary to popular belief, the Mutatis were not the most important shapeshifters in the galaxy. Certainly, they were the most numerous and caused the most trouble, especially for the Humans who were their mortal enemies. But they had a rival in the magical art of appearance modification, a race that was the glue of the galaxy, the podships that provided faster-than-light space travel to everyone at no charge.

Widely considered the greatest mystery in the cosmos, the pods were of uncertain origin and purpose. Even Tulyans, who knew the migration patterns of the whale-like creatures and had the ability to pilot them in ancient times, never discovered the spacefarers' deepest, most profound secrets. Eshaz's people were well aware of their shapeshifting abilities, however, the way the living, sentient Aopoddae were all of a similar blimp shape, but morphed the cellular structures of their interior spaces to provide compartments for passengers, complete with portholes, and even destination boards on the outsides of the hulls. The Tulyans knew, as well, how to reach the sectoid chamber at the core of each podship, where Eshaz's kinsmen used to navigate the spacecraft, but which was now blocked to them by the superior powers of the Parviis.

A hatch opened in the hull of the podship, like a mouth on the side. The line began to move forward, and moments later Eshaz stepped aboard and took a seat on one of the utilitarian dark-gray benches. Looking around, he noted the features of the passenger compartment, the similarities and subtle differences in comparison with other pods . . . the patterns of gray-and-black streaks and pale yellow veins.

Passengers did not need any form of breathing apparatus, since the interior of the podship had an oxygen and nutrient-rich life support system generated by the mysterious biological workings of the creature—enabling different types of life forms to survive in their confines.

Most of the benches accommodated three passengers, but Eshaz was so large that there was only enough space for one tall, slender Vandurian to sit beside him. The two of them exchanged stiff glances, without words. Strangers usually didn't talk at all during these voyages, and not just because of the shortness of the trips—only a few minutes to traverse vast distances of space. Instead, they were silent to a great extent because of the sense of awe and infinite, cosmic serenity that the podships inspired in their passengers. Some races revered the podships as godlike creatures, or as messengers of the Supreme Being, or even as incarnations of the Supreme Being.

From his seat Eshaz noticed a slight pulsing of the interior wall beside him, and he touched it gently with a bronze, scaly hand, feeling the warm skin of the sentient creature. Again, the vibration quickened when he touched it, but only for a moment. Eshaz liked to think that the podship was trying to reach out to him, longing for the ancient times as much as he was himself.

"So long, old friend," the Tulyan said, withdrawing his hand.

Beside him, the Vandurian scowled and blinked his oversized eyes, but said nothing.

According to Tulyan legend, one day the podships would transport their passengers to an ethereal realm, a place so enchanted that it was beyond words. Eshaz had always tried to visualize what that magical province might look like, and how it would engage his seven senses, but always he returned to the same conundrum. How could that ultimate realm be any more impressive than his own solar system, the Tulyan Starcloud? The possibility seemed unimaginable.

He felt the sentient spacecraft engage with one podway and then another in rapid succession, making course changes in seconds and fractions of seconds. In what seemed like the blink of an eye, Eshaz had traversed a million star systems, and he stepped off onto the pod station orbiting Tulé, the largest planet in his beloved Tulyan Starcloud.

Far below the pod station he saw the immense Council Chamber, an inverted dome that floated above the planet in a hazy, milky sky, illuminated by a pair of weak suns. From the soft golden glow of the chamber, he knew that the Elders were inside, awaiting him. But the news he brought for them was not good this time.

Timeweb—the connective tissue of the entire galaxy—was showing further, ominous signs of disintegration.

Chapter Thirty-Eight

> Your enemy is not really defeated as long as he still exists. He can always regroup, gain strength and strike a lethal blow.
>
> —Mutati Saying

In a foul mood, the Zultan Abal Meshdi strolled along an arcade, a circle of arches and columns around the Citadel's grandest, most famous fountain. Morning sunlight played off the cascading water, but even the beauty and serenity of this special place did not calm him. He had affairs of state on his mind, matters to consider away from the clatter and clutter of advisers and attendants.

Inside the deep, aquamarine water of the fountain's pond, twenty hydromutatis swam energetically, whirling and swooping in a traditional water dance while metamorphosing from exotic sea creatures to asexual humanoids with fins and tails. As they concluded the performance, the hydromutatis merged into one large gargantufish—an ancient, exotic life form—and leaped over the fountain with elegant power, landing in water on the other side with hardly a splash.

The Zultan was a terramutati himself, the most common form of his species. This gave him some advantages, but also presented him with a number of challenges. He was not telepathic like hydromutatis, and could not fly like aeromutatis. The three groups were essentially political factions, cooperating as they needed to while constantly competing for business advantages and political offices.

Feeling sudden heat from a medallion that hung around his neck, the Zultan knew that an important message had arrived for him. Since he was not in his throne room, and had prohibited anyone from calling upon him out here where he liked to relax, he knew it had to be something critical. During this time of war, the news could be really bad. It probably was, he decided gloomily, as he watched the gargantufish swim around the pond.

Transmitting a thought signal, he felt the information materialize in his brain, just five concise words:

Earth destroyed by our Demolio

Summoning additional details, a holovideo appeared in the air before the Zultan's eyes, with three-dimensional color and percussive sound. Taken by the heroic Mutati outrider who piloted the doomsday weapon into the planet, cracking it open, the holovideo survived because he transmitted a signal to a Mutati deep-space observation post.

Elation filled Abal Meshdi. Here at last was proof positive that his gallant outriders could get past Human security and destroy one of their most beloved planets, the ancient cradle of their despicable civilization. Prior to its destruction Earth had not sustained much population, having declined over the centuries as people emigrated to other worlds. It had retained symbolic value to the Merchant Prince Alliance, however, and its loss was sure to inflict serious emotional distress on them.

Tears of joy formed in his eyes. He was so proud of the brave Mutati outrider who had completed this suicide mission, submitting to the will of God On-High and permitting himself to be consumed in the detonation of the planet.

We will build a monument to him in this Citadel, the Zultan thought, *a fine statue showing him riding the Demolio into the heart of Earth, and the planet shattering.*

The image pleased him immensely.

Heroes had stepped forth from the very beginning of the doomsday program, even in the years of the testing process. The outriders—all volunteers from the three factions of Mutati society—understood their collective fate clearly, and it served to energize them, the opportunity to take the ultimate trip to eternal glory. From the outset, the Zultan had received more volunteers than he needed, enabling his officers to select only the best candidates, improving the odds of success.

Many of the volunteers wore Adurian minigyros, which the Zultan distributed in large numbers to the populace, so that they would better understand the decisions he made. The devices made them closer to God On-High, a benefit that the Zultan had thus far concealed from the Adurians, to keep them from raising the price.

The telepathic hydromutatis, who were prohibited from intruding on the Zultan's inner thoughts, seemed to have done so anyway, because they divided again and began to perform a celebratory dance, skimming along the surface of the pond like race boats, then diving and soaring up out of the water into the air and diving back down, in perfect synchronization. Abal Meshdi was actually pleased that they had violated a rule this time, since they were making him feel even better. Perhaps he would not punish them much for their infraction.

Presently, the twenty hydromutatis assumed their natural appearance structures, masses of swimming, fatty tissue with tiny heads. They formed a circle in the water and spun faster and faster until they were a blur and the water churned like a large blender. They were the fastest, most impressive swimmers he had ever seen. But they seemed agitated, undoubtedly because they knew what the Zultan had in mind. They were telepaths after all, and continued their unlawful acts, using their powers to violate the serenity and privacy of his royal thoughts.

From a fatty fold of his body, Abal Meshdi brought forth a black jolong rifle and fired it into the pond, causing the water to run purple. He peppered the fountain with projectiles, then paused. One hydromutati continued to move. It twitched and writhed, and tried to make its way to an edge of the pond.

Meshdi pressed the firing button, but his weapon jammed. With a curse, he attempted to hurl the rifle like a spear, but it flipped over and over in the air. His aim was fortunate, though, because the butt of the rifle hit the hydromutati squarely on the head, knocking brain matter loose and causing the creature to stop moving entirely.

Twenty bodies floated on top of the purple pond now, with fountain spray misting over them. Meshdi thought it was a surprisingly pretty sight, despite the unfortunate circumstances.

The Zultan shook his head in dismay. He didn't like to kill such beautiful, perfect organisms, but they had violated his rules and he could not tolerate that, no matter their intention to help him.

He accepted no excuses from anyone, even if this resulted in political repercussions, the inevitable complaints from hydromutati leaders. Rules were rules, after all.

With that matter resolved for the moment, Meshdi thought about beautiful Mutati planets that had been overrun by aggressive Humans over the centuries, worlds that had ample water, breathable atmospheres, and stable, circular orbits. Aside from their constant business pursuits, the merchant princes invariably targeted the most scenic planets for takeover. In this regard, Humans and Mutatis were similar—they enjoyed picturesque landscapes, seascapes, and mountainscapes.

While Mutatis could adapt to virtually any environment or climate, Abal Meshdi resented having to retreat. Centuries ago, the two races had tried to live side by side, but problems soon ensued. Humans were exceedingly combative, belligerent, and offensive. Even with the aid of antiallergenic implants, Mutati revulsion against disgusting Humans could not be overcome. There had been numerous battles and wars for control of particular planets and star systems. With inferior technology, the Mutatis were usually beaten back and driven out, and finally sought refuge on planets that were of little interest to Humans.

It had been a long, humiliating journey, harmful to the pride of the Mutati people, but that was about to change. Earth was a first step, and there would be many more.

The Demolio—his doomsday weapon—made that possible. Payback time.

While the Zultan had been thinking of annihilating the Humans, he had wavered a bit recently, since his own son Hari'Adab disagreed with his aggressive approach. Perhaps Meshdi would simply teach the Humans a lesson by killing only a few hundred billion of them and wiping out half their planets.

God On-High will guide me.

Chapter Thirty-Nine

> All documents are rooted in falsehood anyway. I only filed my papers that way to protect myself.
>
> —Francella Watanabe, journal notes

On the morning of her scheduled audience with the glorious Doge Lorenzo del Velli, Francella entered the Audience Hall of the Palazzo Magnifico. The tall, redheaded woman carried a sheath of documents under one arm, and found a place to stand in the designated waiting area of the immense marble floor.

It was an intimidating chamber, as large as a prince's villa, with a platinum filigree ceiling towering seven stories overhead. On the walls and ceiling were frescoes depicting Human technology, trade, religion, and science, along with heroic portrayals of the most famous doges in history. At the center of the great room, Lorenzo sat upon a throne carved in the shape of a merchant schooner, typical of the commercial vessels that carried his goods to the farthest reaches of the galaxy, inside the bellies of podships.

For a moment she caught his gaze, but he didn't smile, as he normally did upon seeing her. He seemed preoccupied, agitated, and looked away. . . .

The peculiar and as yet unexplained destruction of Earth two weeks ago had unsettled Lorenzo's mind, and he really didn't know if he could ever recover from the shock. As a boy, he and his family had gone there on pilgrimages and vacations, and he had always felt roots on that world, strong connections that were unseen but nevertheless existed. Everywhere he went in those days, he learned the ancient histories of the armies and passions that had flowed across the landscapes, the hopes and dreams of mankind that had eventually spread into the rest of the galaxy as they reached for the stars and built spaceships to take them there. In the centuries before the appearance of podships, Humans had settled a dozen solar systems—and had expanded from there with the sudden and mysterious gift of faster-than-light travel.

The podships had been such an unexplained boon to mankind's desires to spread throughout the galaxy. But were they really a boon, after all? Hadn't they brought severe problems as well as benefits? The terrible, never-ending war against the Mutati Kingdom, for one thing, a conflict that had undoubtedly caused the demise of Earth. Humans and Mutatis hadn't even known one another existed until the strange, sentient spaceships brought them together. Was that done by design, to cause a war that would result in the destruction of two civilizations?

Or only one? he thought nervously. *If our enemies were responsible for what happened to Earth, there may be no safe refuge from them in the entire galaxy. How could the Mutatis possibly have accomplished such a terrible thing?*

It galled the greatest prince in the realm that he had to be dependent upon the mute podships, which showed up regularly and performed their tasks day after day, year after year, at no charge. Aside from his suspicions about their intent, it was a failure of Human technology, and a big one, that the mysterious system of space travel could not be figured out and duplicated—or exceeded.

Unaware of the fact that Tulyans controlled podships in ancient times, and Parviis did in modern times, Lorenzo thought that all attempts to capture podships were doomed to failure. He knew of examples in which Humans—and other races that used these creatures for transport—got too aggressive, causing the large pods to react forcefully, shutting their transport systems down and disappearing into space. A decade ago, a squad of Vandurian troops had tried to commandeer one of the podships by force of arms, while riding inside as passengers. None of them survived the attempt, or at least they were never seen again. For a year afterward, the podships refused to provide any transport service to or from Vandurian planets, and then, as if lifting the suspension, the services resumed. All without any explanation or communication of any sort. Just ships showing up or not showing up.

It was all very unsettling, and he wished that the princes and their allies had not grown so dependent on such strange, uncommunicative creatures.

Podships were, without question, *living* organisms. Anyone traveling aboard one sensed a strong presence around him, and felt a faint pulse within the walls. Some passengers even claimed to have seen the vessels change their appearances in small degrees, slight adjustments in the cabins or basic amenities. The process by which the creatures fashioned themselves into spacecraft was not at all understood, nor was it known from where they came. One theory, among many, held that they were cosmic chunks of space debris, each bearing a speck of the soul of God. . . .

With such far-reaching issues on his mind, the gray-haired Doge raised a jeweled tigerhorse scepter to begin the audience session. His attaché, the furry Hibbil Pimyt, guided an old woman to the base of the dais, and then whispered, seemingly to himself. In reality, he was speaking into a comm-unit, transmitting to a receiver implanted in Lorenzo's ear.

"She was your mother's most trusted housekeeper, Takla Shoshobi."

"Nice to see you again, Takla," Lorenzo said, although he didn't recognize her at all, or recall the name.

"I don't wish to waste your valuable time," the crone said in a croaking voice, "I just wanted to thank you for everything you've done for my family."

"Yes, yes, of course. I am pleased that you are here." With a broad smile, he looked around the audience chamber, as if she was just one of many examples of his magnanimity.

"I am the last of my family," she said. "All of the others died in the war, in your prisons, or of starvation in one of your roachrat-infested ghettos."

"My ghettos? I have no *ghettos!*"

"Then why are they called 'lorenzos'?"

The Doge caught Pimyt's gaze. Looking suddenly alarmed, the Hibbil grabbed her by the arm and dragged her away.

"Thanks for nothing!" she shouted. "All of our allegiance to you, all of our sacrifices, and what do you give us in return? Nothing!"

Guards took charge of the struggling, ranting old woman and escorted her out of the chamber.

"That was all staged for your entertainment," Lorenzo exclaimed to the men and women in the chamber, with a twisted smile. "Just a little change of pace to get things going."

Uneasy laughter carried through the great room.

"I'm very sorry," Pimyt whispered over the private communications link. "So terribly sorry. She said she wanted to give you a blessing, and since her credentials were above suspicion, I thought it would be all right. Of course, I should have known that no one is above suspicion. It won't happen again, Sire."

Lorenzo the Magnificent rolled his eyes, but actually felt pleased with himself for the way he had handled the situation. Leadership was like that. He had to respond to unexpected problems, always maintaining his composure and never allowing the bubble to burst, never permitting his subjects to see through the barriers he had set up.

For the rest of the morning, he conducted a typical audience session, responding to commoners and dignitaries as they come to him with requests. He granted and denied favors with a wave of his tigerhorse scepter, and finally gazed down upon the last person—Francella Watanabe. According to her appointment summary, she had estate documents for his review and approval. She handed them to Pimyt, and he scurried up the stairs of the dais with them.

Looking over the estate papers, Lorenzo said, "I'm very sorry about the death of your father, the eminent Prince Saito. He was a great man, one of the beacons of the Alliance."

Murmurings of concurrence passed through the chamber.

"Thank you, My Lord," Francella said, with a pretty smile.

The Doge pretended to read the papers in detail, although he had already reviewed them beforehand. A commoner by birth, she was applying to be made a Princess of the Realm, which the Doge could grant to important families. With her father gone, as she stated in the papers, she was the logical person to be elevated in status. To support her case, she included a certified copy of Prince Saito's will, which had already been filed and probated. He had bequeathed everything to her and nothing to her twin brother. Additional documents showed that he had formally disinherited Noah.

Asking her a few official-sounding questions, Lorenzo nodded solemnly at her answers. The two of them had known each other for years, on the most intimate basis. She was an attractive, statuesque woman, and as she addressed him, the womanizing Doge found himself increasingly captivated by the comeliness of her figure and her dark brown eyes.

For several minutes, they engaged in a formal discussion for the sake of the onlookers, but her submission was a fait accompli. Finally, waving aside the whispered concerns of his attaché, Pimyt, he openly invited her to his private chamber to discuss the matter further. There, they pulled one another's clothes off and made love, as they had done so many times before.

Then, while the scheming woman was dressing, Lorenzo summoned Pimyt, and formally approved her documents, making her a Princess of the Realm.

In reality, even though Saito Watanabe told many people that he had disowned his son, he had never actually completed the necessary documents, hoping that he and Noah would reconcile one day. Without the Doge's knowledge, Francella had brought forged estate papers with her.

In the actual documents, which she had destroyed, Prince Saito had left half of his estate to his son.

Chapter Forty

A secret is never meant to be kept. It is always trying to break out of the box confining it.

—Graffiti, Gaol of Brimrock

The shuttle trip down to the surface of the Mutati homeworld would take longer than his entire cross-space journey to the Paradij pod station, covering millions of parsecs. This seemed incongruous to Giovanni Nehr, but it was the reality nonetheless. Hyper-fast podships were one of the greatest mysteries in the universe, but he had another one with him, in the heavy parcel he carried under his arm.

Boarding the shuttle, he was confronted by two Mutati guards, their large, pulpy bodies draped in black uniforms. They ran the yellow beam of a scanner over his body and the package, to make certain he wasn't carrying anything dangerous.

During the procedure, Gio smiled confidently. In reality, he *was* carrying something explosive—but not in the usual sense of the word. Speaking to them in common Galeng, he provided his name and demanded to see the Zultan Abal Meshdi himself.

Surprised, the guards laughed, a peculiar squeaky sound. "Our Zultan?" one of them said. "Don't you know he hunts down your kind and tortures them?"

"Tell him I am Giovanni Nehr, brother of Jacopo Nehr, inventor of the nehrcom. You are familiar with that device?"

The guards looked at him stupidly.

"Just tell him I'm a very important person," Gio added.

"Our scanner shows you are carrying rocks," the shorter of the guards said. "Are they pretty stones?"

"Oh yes, pretty stones for your Zultan. He will like them."

The taller guard reached out and was about to touch the parcel, when he started to sneeze and sniffle. His companion's eyes began to water, and he coughed.

In proximity to the Human, both guards were becoming uncomfortable, not having bothered to wear implanted allergy protectors near their own homeworld. Their small fleshy faces reddened and they stepped back, taking seats on the shuttle as far away from Gio as possible. There were no other passengers.

"What sort of a fool are you?" the taller of the guards asked, eyeing him with contempt. His large eyes had become purple-veined and watery.

"A *Human* fool," his companion answered. He sniffled and laughed, then sneezed.

After the shuttle landed, four guards replaced the initial pair. Staying as far away from Giovanni as possible, they took him by groundjet to the imposing Citadel.

After a careful security screening and a check of his identity documents, the visitor was escorted through a long portico and then into a maze of interior corridors and lifts that took them to one of the upper levels of the Citadel. The parcel was carried by a guard, who put gloves on before touching it. As Gio's escort of Mutati men sniffled, sneezed, and wiped tears from their eyes, they spoke to him in Galeng.

"Are you brave or just crazy?" one asked.

"Perhaps both," came the reply.

"You are fortunate that the Zultan has consented to see

you. As the brother of the nehrcom inventor, you are an important person in the Merchant Prince Alliance."

"Ah, so you know what a nehrcom is?" Gio asked.

"I've heard of it," the guard said, although he did not elaborate.

Ahead of them, two immense doors carved with space battle scenes swung open, revealing a glittering audience hall beyond. An immense Mutati in a jeweled golden robe sat in the center, on a high throne. Curiously, he had some sort of a blue bubble attached to his forehead, a device with internal workings that bathed his face in spinning circles of multicolored light.

Gio took a deep breath, for this had to be the Zultan Abal Meshdi himself. As Gio approached, the Mutati removed the bubble device and handed it to an attendant. With a scowl on his face, the Zultan stared down silently at his visitor as if observing every detail, absorbing information without words.

The hall was nearly empty, except for a few attendants around the perimeter. Gio noticed a hairless alien standing off to one side as well, and judged him to be an Adurian, a race that was said to be allied with the Mutatis. This one wore a black suit and a white cape, and he had a number of colorful caste markings on his face and forearms.

"Greetings, bold Human," the Zultan said. "You have a gift for me? I like gifts."

The guards halted Gio at the base of the throne. He felt very small in this immense chamber, like a tiny child in the midst of the oversized Mutatis and furnishings.

Looking up, he bowed and said, "Your Eminence, I bring a gift for all of your people, not just for you personally."

"What?" He looked displeased. "Not for me personally, you say?"

"Of course, you don't have to share it if you don't want to," Gio added hastily. He glanced sidelong at the parcel held by one of the guards.

"What sort of strange offering do you bring?" Meshdi demanded.

"Unlike anything you have ever seen. It will enable your great kingdom to compete with the Merchant Prince Alliance."

From his quivering, pulsating mound of fat, the Zultan sneezed and then responded huffily. "What makes you think we wish to *compete* with our inferiors?" Surveying the fearless Human, he added, "Nonetheless, what is your gift? If it is a good one, I will be pleased."

At a signal from the Zultan, the guard stepped up to the throne, and handed him the parcel.

Meshdi examined the package, turning it over and over without opening it. "The scanner report says that there are rocks inside," he said, with a sly expression. "I think you have rocks in your head, too."

The Adurian, having moved closer for a better view, snickered.

"I have not brought you common rocks, Your Eminence." Gio motioned. "Please, open your gift."

Beaming like a fat child, the Zultan tore off the plaxene wrapping, then lifted the lid of a box inside. A wash of green light startled him, and he almost dropped everything.

The guards clicked their weapons, but Meshdi waved them off.

"Jewels?" he exclaimed, looking at them with his eyes wide. "These glitter in ways I have never seen before." He selected one of the small green gems and held it up to the light. A peculiar fascination filled his face.

"You hold in your hand a great military secret," Gio

said, "the secret of the nehrcom transceiver, sometimes referred to as the Nehr Cannon."

With a perplexed expression, the Mutati asked, "Instantaneous communication across space? This is the secret?"

"It is."

He looked confused, but his dark eyes glinted with pleasure. "But how does it work?" He put the gem back in the box, picked up another.

Having penetrated his brother's computer system to learn the secret of the cross-space transmission device, Gio began to spew forth information, telling how to cut the rare stones and align them for perfect transmission, holding nothing back. He knew it was foolhardy to do this, and perhaps even suicidal, but he didn't care. After working closely with his brother, and seeing the decadence and debauchery of the merchant princes, Gio had decided it was only a matter of time before the determined Mutatis defeated them, and he wanted to be on the winning side. Even if he never saw that day and these shapeshifters put him to death, he would go to his grave knowing he had knocked the arrogant Jacopo Nehr off his pedestal.

The transmitter wasn't really a cannon at all, Gio announced. The term "Nehr Cannon" was merely selected to confuse and misdirect the curious. He even told the Zultan how to mine for the deep-shaft piezoelectric emeralds, and that they could be found on a number of planets around the galaxy, including some that had no military defenses. He provided a list.

Finally, Giovanni Nehr fell silent.

"Is that all you know?" the Zultan inquired.

"It is, Majesty."

"Then of what use are you to me anymore?"

"I assumed you would be grateful." Feeling a surge of

unexpected panic, he added a lie: "Besides, my expertise will still be needed to perfect your own galactic communication system, to work out any problems that you are bound to encounter."

"But if you betrayed your own people—including your own brother—we cannot trust you, either. Your disloyalty marks you as dangerous and unreliable. If what you have said is true—and we recorded all of it—we have scientists capable of replicating the nehrcom transceiver and dealing with problems. We don't need you."

"But I brought you a gift! You should be grateful!"

"You said yourself that it was not for me personally, that it was for my people. Thus, you committed a social gaffe, an unforgivable faux pas in our culture." His large eyes narrowed. "You should have researched more carefully."

With a cruel smile, Abal Meshdi motioned for the guards to take the sputtering, suddenly terrified man away. "Foolish Human, you will not live long enough to learn how to bargain."

Under tight security, Gio was taken to a prison moon orbiting the planet Dij. He recognized the name the moment he heard it. This was one of the worlds stripped of all resources and abandoned by the Merchant Prince Alliance.

He did not know, however, that on the surface of Dij, under the direction of Hari'Adab Meshdi—the Emir and eldest son of the Zultan—planet-busting Demolio torpedoes were being constructed.

Chapter Forty-One

> Disaster—and salvation—usually come from unexpected sources.
>
> —Data Banks, sentient machine repository

A polyglax bubble stood in the middle of a circle of standing noblemen, all dressed in jerkins, capes, and liripipe hats. Inside the clear enclosure—a combat rink—a pair of crimson eagles fluttered and ripped at each other with beaks and talons, powerful birds shrieking and tearing one another to shreds, spattering blood on the bubble's interior. Their wings had been cropped, so that they could not fly.

"Kill him!" one of the men shouted, his voice hardly rising above the noise of the birds.

"Rip his heart out!" another shouted.

As the birds gouged each other, making feathers fly, spectators threw merchant prince liras and platinum coins in a wide dish on top of the bubble, making bets and raising them or dropping out of the game, depending on the progress of their feathered champions.

Lorenzo del Velli had placed a wager on the larger bird, but it was losing to its smaller, faster, competitor. The Doge was not pleased, but still was not ready to give up yet. With a scowl, he threw more money on the pile. It was late evening, and he was in the illuminated courtyard of his Palazzo Magnifico, with young members of his royal court. Around them, most of the lights in the palace were out.

He liked to associate with people much younger than he was. They gave him energy, almost making him forget what an old man he was becoming. Even with all of his wealth—no prince had more money—he could not slow the advances of age. Time was like a thief, and a sneaky one at that, taking what rightfully belonged to him when he was unaware, moment by moment.

And unknown to him, another time thief lurked in the shadows behind shrubbery, looking on. . . .

In all of the realm of the merchant princes, there was perhaps no more loyal robot than Jimu. This had something to do with his original programming, since all MPA robots were programmed to be loyal to their Human creators. But it had even more to do with his sentient character, which he had developed on his own, through devotion and hard work.

As a robot, Jimu had been maltreated by Humans for decades. They had always overworked him and kept him going with whatever parts they could lay their hands on, no matter how that decreased his operating abilities. His Human masters could have installed new program modules in him, or the latest grappling arms, but had not bothered to do so. They just kept cobbling him together while awaiting new automaton models, always intending to replace him. But Jimu fooled them.

By the force of his personality, his dogged determination and will to survive, he had basically maintained himself, locating or rebuilding his own parts, always remaining cheerful and making himself useful. In his machine unit he had risen to the rank of a noncommissioned officer—a duty sergeant—but still people spoke constantly of getting rid of him in favor of a newer, more efficient model.

On a number of occasions Jimu had felt the end was near, especially during the Battle of Irriga years ago, when his undercarriage was shot out from under him. Thinking he was useless, soldiers dumped his mangled metal body in a pile of scraps and forgot about him. But he still had his upper body and backup battery pack, and managed to pull himself around until he found another machine with the parts he needed. Within hours, he put himself back together and reported for duty.

That created quite a stir in the ranks of Humans, and the soldiers took him on as a mascot, symbolizing the fighting spirit of their unit. They promoted him to Captain of Machines—a rank that put him in charge of six thousand other robots. For a while, Jimu felt basically invulnerable, as the soldiers maintained him passably well, even knocking out some of his dents and polishing him up. But personalities changed around him as his military friends moved on to other assignments, and one day Jimu again felt forgotten, and had to fend for himself with new troops, who didn't know his personal story or care about him.

But he hadn't blamed them for that. Humans were Humans and machines were only machines, even with the enhancement of sentient programming. Machines would not exist at all if not for the inventive, godlike spark of the Human minds that designed and built them in the first place.

Of all living Humans, Jimu felt that the Doge Lorenzo most deserved his loyalty and dedication, since that nobleman was the titular head of the revered Humans, the prince who was so admired by his peers that they elevated him to the highest station in the galaxy.

So it was that Jimu and his force of twenty fighting robots, having come all the way from the Inn of the White

Sun to serve the Doge, found themselves watching the eagles fight, or more precisely, watching over Lorenzo to make certain he was safe.

Several days ago, Jimu had marched up to one of the palazzo guard stations and stated his business to the Red Beret soldier on duty there. "I'm here to warn the Doge that people intend to harm him," Jimu had said.

The soldier had taken one look at him, at his dented, scraped body and glowing yellow eyes, and he cut loose with a belly laugh. Then, looking closely at the rest of the patched-up robots who had accompanied Jimu, he laughed even more.

Jimu had not taken offense, for he'd seen Humans like this before, the shallow types who made judgments based upon appearances. It was one of the biggest weaknesses of human nature, their inability to avoid superficiality, but he forgave them for it.

"The Doge is in great danger," Jimu said.

"And I suppose you're here to protect him?"

"If necessary, yes."

More guards came over, weapons at the ready. They stood around, smirking, laughing, and hurling insults at the visitor. "You and your pals look like zombie robots," one said. "Who dug you up?"

"Zombiebots," another said. And they laughed uproariously.

Jimu didn't respond to any of those insults, for they had nothing to do with his mission. He and his companions concealed their own weaponry within compartments on their metal bodies, and he knew he could easily overwhelm these fools and enter the palazzo. But that would only cause more Red Berets to come, and a wild battle would ensue. No, that would never do.

"I can see you do not understand," Jimu finally said. "There is nothing more for me to do here." With that, he turned and departed, and took his odd little squadron with him.

But the following morning, Jimu and his robots got into the palazzo anyway. Having put the royal home under observation, he knew that household robots ran errands, getting food and other supplies. In an alley behind one of the markets, Jimu had cornered one of the robots and then interfaced with it, programming it to open a servant's door later that night.

Normally this would not have been possible, since all of the Doge's robots had built-in security measures that prevented tampering. After General Sajak shot Jimu, however, the servants who reactivated him accidentally tapped into a deep data transmission zip that had been installed by the Hibbils. This opened up programs to Jimu that he had not previously realized he had. Later, after Thinker had him overhauled, Jimu found that he functioned with new mental acuity, beyond any of the programs installed in ordinary robots. That superior knowledge had enabled him to easily bypass the security barriers of the Doge's household robot.

Thus the entire squadron got in, and they set up clandestine positions around the palazzo. . . .

For days and nights afterward, without any break, Jimu and his squad concealed themselves carefully around the royal palazzo, their powerful puissant rifles at the ready, weapons that had been hidden inside their motley assortment of mechanical bodies. . . .

Now they stood on balconies and rooftops, looking down on the courtyard, at the boisterous activities of the Doge and his royal companions. The Humans were getting louder as they gambled and drank.

Suddenly, in the shadows below, Jimu saw a hunched-over man run between bushes, moving from the concealment of one to another. Then he saw three more hunched-over shapes, doing the same.

He sent an electronic signal to his companions, cocked his own rifle. Around him, he heard the faint buzzing of their activated weapons.

The robots fired in synchronization, lighting the shrubbery on fire with powerful blasts, making flares out of all of the bushes around the perimeter of the courtyard. Simultaneously, half of the robot force surged into the courtyard from the lower level.

Men shouted and scattered on the flagstones. The fighting eagles got loose, but with their cropped wings they could only fly a few feet off the ground before crashing into someone and flopping onto the courtyard. Blood and feathers filled the air.

In the melee, four hooded, black figures emerged from their hiding places and tried to flee, firing handguns at robots that pursued them. But the robots were not deterred, and knocked them onto the flagstones, then snapped restraint cables on them.

Jimu hurried down to the courtyard, which was illuminated by the crackling, burning bushes. The palace staff rushed forward to douse water on the flames, keeping them from catching the buildings on fire. Under Jimu's watchful gaze, the robots removed hoods from the captives. He recognized one of them, and so did the noblemen gathering around.

"You!" Doge Lorenzo shouted. "General Sajak, why are you dressed like that?"

"Some things are best not delegated," Sajak said, with a sneer. "I wanted to do this job myself."

Dragging the small, slender man to his feet, Jimu said, "He intended to assassinate you."

"Is that true?" Lorenzo asked.

The General smiled. His eyes burned with hatred.

Searching his data banks, Jimu said, "He doesn't like your politics, Doge Lorenzo, and feels that only noble-born princes should hold high office—not entrepreneurs and inventors."

Moments later, Lorenzo was surrounded by his special police, the Red Berets. They were heavily armed men in red uniforms and floppy caps.

"And where were you when I needed you?" the Doge asked, of the squad leader.

The uniformed man looked embarrassed.

"These robots saved my hide," Lorenzo said, patting Jimu on his metal backside. "Maybe you should give them your uniforms."

"I'm sorry, sir," the squad leader said. "We didn't expect any problems from your royal court, and General Sajak must have used his security clearance to get through. This was totally unexpected."

"Then why were these robots on alert? Are they smarter than you?"

"I'm sorry, Doge Lorenzo. It won't happen again."

"With all due respect, Sire," Jimu said, "your household security could use considerable improvement." He told how he had waylaid a household robot and reprogrammed it to allow him to gain access to the palazzo, and how he had originally learned of the assassination plot at the lava lake on one of the moons of Timian One. He provided as many names as he knew, including that of Prince Giancarlo Paggatini, the nobleman who organized the secret meetings of General Sajak and his conspirators.

"The way you got in here is very interesting," Lorenzo said. "And quite disturbing. Fortunately for me, you're not one of their agents."

With a gesture at the Red Beret squad leader, the Doge barked, "Go! Get out of my sight, all of you! Take Sajak and his goons with you. The arrogant fool! He wanted to kill me himself. You are to interrogate them, and I mean *interrogate*. Find out everything. See who's involved in the conspiracy. I want every name."

"It will be done, sir."

Like whipped daggs, the Red Berets left, handling the men in black roughly. Despite their shortcomings, Jimu knew that the special police were a fierce bunch, highly motivated and dedicated in their own way. An ancient law enforcement group, they had their own secret rituals, language, and symbols. If anyone could get the answers Lorenzo wanted, they could.

"Come with me, robots," Lorenzo said. "I'm going to show you how to bet on an eagle fight." With that, he put his arm around Jimu's rounded shoulders, and led him back to the bubble enclosure. Fresh eagles were brought in, and the entertainment resumed.

Chapter Forty-Two

Infinity beckons.

—Parvii Inspiration

Perched inside the core of the most unusual biological organism in the galaxy, the tiny man noticed a hesitation in the sentient spacecraft. He had just established a course, but the podship had not yet responded.

Seconds passed. This had never happened to him before. By now, they should be speeding along the podways, racing past star systems, bound for the farthest regions of the galaxy.

The diminutive Parvii pilot required no food or water for sustenance, and none of the other nutrients commonly needed by the galactic races. And, while the various chambers of the large podship contained an ample supply of oxygen, the pilot didn't require any. He could fly free in the vacuum of space, and in a swarm with other members of his race could reach tremendous speeds.

Until moments ago, Woldn had been in total control of the podship, having captured and tamed it with millions of his miniature followers, who subsequently departed for other duties. They were like wranglers of wild tigerhorses, and Woldn was the most skilled of them all. He was the Eye of the Swarm, commanding decillions of Parviis, an entire galactic race. Now he was performing a task he normally delegated, in order to keep his piloting and navigation skills sharp.

Finally, Woldn felt the great ship shudder into motion and accelerate.

In its wordless way, the podship was communicating with him, sending a stream of messages that filled Woldn's brain. Through the sentient creature's far-reaching eyes—indiscernible cells all over the outside of its body—Woldn peered deep with the podship, into the curving green webs of time and space.

Way off in the distance and directly ahead, an orange light flashed.

The blimp-shaped podship—carrying a variety of galactic races in its passenger compartment and cargo hold—accelerated onto the web on a new course, wrenching command away from the Parvii leader, though he struggled mightily, invoking the most severe guidance-and-control words in his repertoire. Mysteriously, his efforts were to no avail.

Within minutes, the spacecraft slowed near a debris field and circled it at a safe distance. Through the mind he shared with the pod, Woldn felt a tremendous sense of loss. A podship had just died here, along with its Parvii pilot.

Most unusual, a Parvii death here, and he'd received no signal of distress along the telepathic connections he maintained with all of his people, stretching across the entire galaxy. This suggested to him that there had either been a psychic breakdown, which occurred occasionally, or that the violent event had been so sudden and unexpected that the pilot had not had time to send a signal.

Woldn got his bearings and figured out where he was . . . and what was missing. A planet had exploded, a world the Humans called Mars. Within moments, he saw other podships approach and circle nearby, with Parviis inside their sectoid control chambers, helpless to control the spacecraft, trying to comprehend. This was the same solar system where an earlier explosion had occurred, the one that took Earth with it.

Both planets and their inhabitants had been dispatched to oblivion, their remnants scattered in space.

Was something wrong in this sector, causing natural disasters—or could there be another explanation? Woldn would return to his people, and order a full investigation. . . .

Chapter Forty-Three

Our young must always learn the most important lessons of life firsthand. It has been this way since time immemorial.

—Mutati Observation

Two of the passengers on board Woldn's podship were Acey Zelk and Dux Hannah, the teenage Humans who had escaped from Timian One. Crowded with others at the membranous portholes, they saw a large debris field outside.

"Where are we?" Acey asked, as he and Dux tried to maintain their spot by a porthole, while an assortment of creatures pushed for better views.

"I have no idea," Dux said.

With difficulty the boys held their position. Only a small percentage of the passengers were Human, or even humanoid. In close proximity to so many different races, Dux picked up odors he'd never experienced before. Not all of the smells were unpleasant, though some certainly were. He also picked up a musk odor from the skin of the podship.

A pale-skinned Kichi woman beside them gasped as body parts floated by, most of them Human . . . arms, legs, and heads with crusts of blood frozen on them. One completely intact body drifted into view, a young woman fully clothed in layers of unsoiled skirts, her face frozen in a broad smile, as if someone had pulled her picture out of a photo album and put a three-dimensional form to it. She showed no signs of trauma, which seemed remarkable to

Dux in view of the obvious violence that had occurred here. He wondered what could possibly have caused such a catastrophe.

"Might have been a merchant prince planet," a man said.

"It was," another said. Dux saw a Jimlat man standing taller than the throng, his blockish head shaved. Blinking his tiny gray eyes, the Jimlat studied a handheld instrument. "They called it Mars."

"Mars?" Dux said. "Then it's completely gone, destroyed?"

"That'd be my bet. Course, some of it remains." With a facetious smile, he nodded toward the nearest porthole. "Out there."

"Maybe you'd like me to climb up there and rearrange your ugly face," Acey said, making a move toward him.

Dux grabbed his cousin's arm to restrain him. "What are his fighting capabilities?" Dux asked in a low tone.

"If you let go of me, I'll find out."

"Don't chance it. We don't need to look for trouble." He looked around, at the hostile gazes of some of the aliens, and their gleaming eyes. Obviously, they wanted to see a fight, and probably didn't care if Acey got hurt . . . or worse. A number of races around the galaxy resented Humans for the financial and military successes of the merchant princes, so the young men had to be on constant alert for potential trouble. Acey lost his temper too much, didn't always think through the consequences of his actions.

Hearing a thump beside him, Dux looked at the porthole, and recoiled in horror. A little Huluvian girl screamed, and was consoled by her mother. The bloody face of a man bobbed against the outside of the window, seeming to stare into the passenger compartment. The face, and its torn body, drifted away.

The podship, still moving slowly, proceeded through the shocking milieu, passing floating fragments of what had once been a vibrant world on one of the main merchant prince trading routes. Machine parts, building fragments, and many shredded body parts, some of them so small that they must have belonged to children. Dux could hardly bear to look any more but did nonetheless, in horrified fascination. Around him, hardly anyone spoke anymore. Most of the noises were sobbing sounds, and whimpering cries of disbelief, even from non-Humans. An alien in a business suit said the planet must have been hit by a meteor, and several onlookers agreed.

After only a few minutes that seemed like an eternity, the podship changed course. It headed away from the debris field and picked up speed. Soon they flashed by star systems, spiral nebulas, and glowing asteroid belts. For a fraction of a second, a comet seemed to try to keep up with them, then fell back.

The podship resumed a normal route, making its regular stops, as shown on route boards at both ends of the passenger compartment. Some of the passengers moved away from the windows, but many remained standing, numb with shock. Along the way, the various races disembarked, and others got aboard. Odors changed. Dialects drifted through the cabin. New passengers heard the terrible news about Mars, and no one understood what could have happened.

Finally the boys disembarked at Nui-Lin in a remote sector of the galaxy, an exotic world they had heard about in their travels, where they hoped to secure jobs. They had with them the address of a residential construction project where the pay was said to be excellent, and the name of a man who had put out a call for workers.

The shuttle was unlike any they had seen before, resembling a broad green leaf with a tiny bubble of a cabin on the underside. The craft descended, and when it reached the atmosphere the engines shut off and it drifted down, landing gently on the black pavement of a spaceport.

The terminal building abutted a thick jungle, draped with vines. They caught a jitney driven by a long-eared Cogg, one of the natives of this world. They told him where they wanted to go, as did many of the other passengers as they boarded, and he promised to let the new riders know when he reached their various destinations.

He was not a very good driver, though, or didn't seem able to talk and drive at the same time, as he insisted on delivering a monologue about the various types of flora and fauna as he sped past them. Some of them he scraped with the vehicle, and once he very nearly drove off a precipice into a tree-choked ravine. Those passengers who were Coggs didn't show any fear, but other races were on the edges of their seats, and some demanded to get off. Ignoring their pleas, the driver refused to stop. In some places a thick canopy of trees overhung the road, creating a tunnel effect that required him to turn on a bright headlamp.

They passed through a town that looked like a village in a fairy tale, with narrow cobblestone streets and quaint homes that were not constructed entirely straight, or which had fallen into a pattern of leaning to one side or the other for what might have been centuries. The majority of the Coggs and the most fearful foreigners got out in the town, and then the jitney continued on its way, along a narrow highway that skirted a silvery sea. Immense birds soared out over the water, with sunlight glinting off their golden wings, making the birds look as if they were really built out of gold, and should be too heavy to fly.

The driver kept chattering, babbling like a tour guide. Then he began talking about galactic politics, and his comments about the Merchant Prince Alliance were less than complimentary. This surprised Dux, since Coggs were supposedly neutral. He shrugged. This must be an oddball, an eccentric fellow who was out of step with his people.

"This is it," the driver announced, as he pulled levers on the dashboard to squeak the bus to a stop. Carrying their bags, Acey and Dux stepped off at a narrow path, which the driver told them to take. "The construction site is just a short distance," he said, pointing toward a cluster of one-story buildings in a clearing.

The boys found signs written in the common galactic language of Galeng, telling them where to report for work. Inside a large, open-walled hut, they located the very Cogg whose name they had been given far across the galaxy, Bibby Greer. As the long-eared work supervisor introduced himself to them and shook their hands, he smiled in such a friendly fashion that Dux thought he would be the best boss they ever had. He could not have been more wrong. The experience would, in fact, be exactly the opposite.

Suddenly the tentacles of a plant darted in through the open walls and wrapped themselves around the boys, so that they could not escape. Before their eyes, the Cogg metamorphosed into a tremulous mound of fat, with a tiny head and oversized eyes. A Mutati!

Dux felt a sinking sensation.

"Welcome to our fly trap," Bibby Greer announced with a nasty grin.

Chapter Forty-Four

It is as if the entire galaxy is being sucked downward, into the black void of the undergalaxy. Is there life in that Stygian realm? I shudder to imagine it.

—Eshaz, Remarks to the Council

The green-and-brown groundjet sped across a broad meadow of flowers, passing over the plants like a windless whisper, not disturbing them at all. This was a specially modified craft that Noah had ordered, with hover capabilities that could be activated when going over sensitive environmental areas.

"It is good to see you back," Noah said to Eshaz, who sat beside him in the passenger seat, his large body overflowing the chair and draping off the sides. Noah piloted the machine. "I trust you had a pleasant visit with your Elders?"

"Oh, the Tulyan Starcloud is the most wondrous place in all of creation," he replied, "and my people are the most pleasant to be around. No offense to present company, of course."

"I understand. There's no place like home, the old saying goes."

"How true it is."

"Your people are pacifists, aren't they?"

"We pride ourselves on non-violence, but I would not go so far as to say that we are complete pacifists. We do not claim to be perfect, only that we strive to be so. We are not political in any way. Tulyans try to go about their daily lives peacefully while contributing to their environs, instead of detracting from them."

"The peaceful nature of Tulyans explains why it must be so nice to be with them on the Starcloud. I can't visualize a single argument there. It must be total bliss, almost a fantasy land."

"Well, we do have rather heated discussions, but for the most part you're not far off." Eshaz smiled, but to Noah it seemed forced.

Noah steered toward a maintenance building at the southwest corner of his compound. Diggers had torn through the floor of the building, creating a lot of damage. Subi Danvar and the commando team he had organized were using this as a staging area to launch extermination efforts, and over the weeks they had experienced some success against the renegade machines.

"I would like to see the Tulyan Starcloud someday," Noah said, as he had on occasion before. "I know, you said how rare it is for outsiders to be permitted there, but perhaps you could mention my name to the Elders as a possibility."

"I already have," Eshaz said with a decidedly pained expression. "Perhaps someday we can do it, my friend."

It seemed to Noah that his trusted companion was sadder than he should be, that his demeanor did not match his words. Perhaps he was just tired. This Tulyan was quite an old fellow, after all. Noah wasn't certain exactly how old, and Eshaz always shunted such questions aside, but he thought it might be around a hundred or more standard years of age. With no idea how much of a colossal underestimation this was, Noah worried about the health of the old fellow.

Eshaz was a valued contributor to the Ecological Demonstration Project on Canopa and had helped with a number of planetary recovery operations around the galaxy. He always seemed to know more about local environments than anyone, and gave advice about exactly what would work best—from flora to fauna to geology. But he was also a man of secrets, as were the other Tulyans who worked for Noah. They liked to spend a lot of time by themselves, wandering around planets and communing with nature in their arcane ways.

As Noah drew near the maintenance building, he noticed new holes in the ground beyond the structure, gaping excavations that he was certain his own people had not made. "Looks like more trouble here," he said, as he brought the groundjet to a stop near a team of his uniformed Guardians. He recognized Subi Danvar, Tesh Kori, and Anton Glavine.

"There is trouble everywhere," Eshaz said.

With a nod, but not totally understanding what he meant, Noah stepped out. The two of them went their separate ways.

Taking a walk through the nearby woods, Eshaz contemplated the troubles he had seen, and the troubles that he saw coming.

The meeting with the Council of Elders had gone much more poorly than he had anticipated, even considering the bad news that he brought to them. As it turned out, he was not the only caretaker of Timeweb to report an acceleration of problems they had noticed earlier, an increasingly serious deterioration of the vital strands holding the galaxy together. The situation had, in fact, reached crisis proportions.

Upon entering the inverted dome of the Council Chamber for the regularly scheduled meeting, Eshaz had found himself in a raucous throng of his peers, all clamoring to tell their stories. While he had observed serious galactic damage himself, the most grave report of all came from Ildawk, who described a complete web collapse in the Huluvian Sector, and the disappearance of two entire solar systems with it, decimating the Huluvian race.

Listening solemnly, the Elders had absorbed the information and conferred among themselves. First Elder Kre'n, a broad-necked female who was the head of the Council, then made a solemn pronouncement:

"All of you must redouble your efforts, or soon the galaxy will reach a state of critical mass, where the deterioration cannot be reversed."

Turning to Eshaz, who stood at the front of the throng of caretakers, Kre'n then said, "Tell us what you see."

Most Tulyans were prescient, with an ability to peer into paranormal realms, even into other time periods—and Eshaz was among the best with this ability. It gave him special value, but he didn't like to use the talent. Often, it upset him too much.

Feeling exasperated, he closed his heavy-lidded eyes and peered into the time continuum of the cosmos, but saw nothing this time, not even a flicker of activity. Was that a foretelling in itself, an indication of what was to come? Utter, motionless blackness?

With a shudder, Eshaz opened his eyes. Standing before his superiors, he shook his bronze-scaled head and said, "I see nothing, First Elder. There is too much disturbance in the galaxy. It is blocking me."

In a sense, this excuse was true, but not completely. He strongly suspected something else was interfering, a personal failure.

Kre'n nodded. "So it is. So it must be."

The other Elders nodded, and whispered among themselves. Normally stoic, they were showing signs of emotion this time. He heard a sad edge to Kre'n's voice, as if in realization that the end of the galaxy might be approaching. He saw worried glints in the eyes of these ancients, slight frowns on their faces.

In the past Eshaz had predicted the emergence of black holes, of suns going nova, and of gas giant planets erupting. Now, however, he felt useless, and angry with himself. He was beginning to wonder if it was not a cosmic disturbance at all, but was instead his own increasing stress, causing him to lose his timeseeing ability at a moment when he—and his people—most needed it. He felt as if he was letting them down, as if he was letting all of the galactic races down. Life . . . so fragile, and his own abilities were disintegrating. Almost everywhere, Timeweb was crumbling.

A possibility occurred to him. There had been no signs of web deterioration anywhere near his beloved Tulyan Starcloud, so he wondered if that sector of the galaxy could possibly be spared.

What will become of my people? he wondered, *if our sector is spared and we have nothing left to caretake?*

The twenty old women and men of the Council were the foremost web masters in the galaxy, Tulyans who were ancient and sagacious when Eshaz was born almost a million standard years ago. The Elders knew so much more than he did about the galaxy—it was like his own knowledge in comparison with that of the most enlightened Human . . . Noah Watanabe, for example. The differences were so great that there was no fair comparison, and in his own limited state Eshaz could only defer to these ancient Tulyans, and hope he would himself become as wise and revered one day.

For that to happen, though, the galaxy needed to survive. And at the moment, the prospects for that did not look good at all. . . .

Having made his report to the wise old Tulyans, Eshaz was back on Canopa now, working with Noah and his Guardians. The Council of Elders had ordered Eshaz and all other web caretakers to amplify their ecological preservation efforts, and now they were to report more frequently than before. Because of the ominous signs noted by Eshaz and his peers in the field, the Council had also decided to dispatch more caretaker observers around the galaxy. They would serve under various guises, because Tulyans were not permitted to tell other races what they were doing, not even ecologically conscious individuals such as Noah Watanabe. No one but a Tulyan could possibly understand the enormity of the responsibilities they had.

"We are a race of givers," Kre'n said once, "while the other races are takers, users, destroyers."

It was true, so tragically true. And now all of the abuses of civilization were taking their terrible toll.

To aid in their caretaking efforts, the Tulyans did have a few podships that had been captured in the wild reaches of space, from intercepting the ancient migration routes of the creatures. But the pods had to be hidden carefully in order to avoid having them taken by Parvii swarms . . . or by the ravenous demons of the undergalaxy. With only limited resources, the dedicated Tulyans could not do much . . . nowhere near what they achieved in ancient, bygone times.

Emerging from his walk in the woods, Eshaz stared for a long while at the Humans bustling around the new Digger holes. The exterminators were dropping probes into the openings, to search for the malfunctioning machines.

Eshaz rather liked these Humans, especially Noah, who had more upstanding qualities than any other alien he'd ever encountered. In his long life, Eshaz had known many persons of various races, and some of them were extraordinary historical figures, males and females who were much honored by their people. Always, though, the Tulyan had tried to maintain his distance from aliens he admired. In large part this was to preserve his own emotional balance, since it was too difficult to get attached to sentients who had such short life spans in comparison with his own.

But now, for the first time, Eshaz was breaking that hard-and-fast rule. No matter how much he had tried to avoid it, he could not help feeling tremendous esteem for Noah Watanabe . . . and a strong bond of affection. While some of the reasons for this were obvious to Eshaz, he also felt something ineffable toward the Human, an almost instinctual sensation that was as inexplicable to him as his inability to peer through the veils of time.

Chapter Forty-Five

I only collect on promises. I don't fulfill them.
—Doge Lorenzo del Velli

The Doge Lorenzo del Velli prided himself on his nefarious plots and schemes. He liked to do things behind the scenes to effect important changes, so that the persons targeted were blind-sided, and never figured out what happened to them. It was a game he liked to play. In his position, of course, he didn't have to do that, because he was the most powerful man in the galaxy. But he preferred subtle methods rather than using hammers. He liked to compare his "little tricks," as he called them, to a whispering wind that slipped up behind the victim unawares and suddenly transformed itself into a hurricane.

Several years ago, a warlord prince had been openly critical of Lorenzo's administration, making the ridiculous assertion that the Doge was doing such a terrible job that he should relinquish his throne to the first person who asked for it—since anyone could do better. It was such an absurd idea that it didn't deserve a response, at least not a direct one.

So, after considering the matter at length, Lorenzo and his Royal Attaché came up with a way to silence the outspoken critic. Pimyt spread a convincing rumor, complete with falsified evidence, that the grumbling Prince was having an affair with General Mah Sajak's attractive, flirtatious wife. The General, who was often away from home in battles against the Mutatis, became so convinced of the story that he hired assassins to go after the Prince.

It all went perfectly, and when Lorenzo received confirmation of the killing, Pimyt could hardly control his elation, for he claimed that he had come up with the plan. The furry little Hibbil did four back flips and half a dozen spinning rolls, landing on his feet at the base of the Doge's throne.

"Whatever do you think you're doing?" Lorenzo had asked. "It was my idea, not yours." This was not entirely true, and the Doge knew it. But he also knew he could win any argument with the Hibbil.

"Oh, my mistake," Pimyt said, in a tone that bordered on the sarcastic. Then, as if to sublimate any anger he could not express, he did the reverse of the gymnastics he had just accomplished, with six reverse spinning rolls followed by four front flips.

"There," Pimyt said. "That neutralizes my little celebration, as if it never happened."

Now the Doge had another serious problem, one that his lover Francella Watanabe wanted taken care of. She had told him about it in bed, asserting what a terrible, deceptive man her own brother was. Of course, Lorenzo was not foolish enough to believe all of those distortions, for he knew Noah personally and also knew how to spin his own tales. But he let on that he believed her, and she was most grateful for the sympathy he expressed, just one of his many skills.

That night—in return for his promise to have Noah killed at the first opportunity—Francella bestowed her generous personal favors on him. Just this morning, Lorenzo had set in motion his own plan to accomplish the assassination. After all, he had plenty of excellent ideas himself, and didn't need to always rely upon that fur-ball Pimyt to solve every problem.

Having solved that for the moment, Lorenzo turned to other matters, and conferred with his royal astronomers over the Earth-Mars disasters. They cited examples of other odd events occurring around the galaxy . . . ground giving way underneath people, exposing immense, seemingly bottomless sinkholes, and large chunks of planets (or entire small planets) disappearing into voids. Survivors told harrowing tales, and investigators were working on the problem, but thus far had not come up with any solutions.

"How could entire planets disappear?" Lorenzo asked them.

"If it were only Earth and Mars, we might think it was a problem with the yellow sun in that solar system," the lead astronomer said, a grizzled old man who dressed impeccably. "We've seen at least one example of a sun giving off destructive solar energy that destroyed all of the planets orbiting it, one by one. But that can't be the case here. The problem is too widespread, and the results differ. Sometimes we find space debris, and other times there's nothing left . . . a complete vanishing act."

"My grandfather used to tell me about Earth and Mars," Lorenzo said. "He said that Human migrations departed from them thousands of years ago, spreading the seeds of our race across hundreds of star systems."

"It's a big loss," the old astronomer said, shaking his head sadly.

Afterward, when he had time to think by himself, the Doge was left with an unsettled feeling. What if something terrible were to happen to Canopa or Siriki . . . or even worse, to Timian One? He could hardly imagine such events, and yet, something told him they were entirely possible.

Chapter Forty-Six

> Thanks to medical technology, the average lifespan of a human being has risen steadily in modern times. It now stands at 106.4 years for women, and 94.1 years for men . . . with men lagging in large part because of war deaths.
>
> —MPA Actuarial Office

On the grounds of his Ecological Demonstration Project, Noah Watanabe stood inside an energy production chamber, surrounded by crystalglax tanks and tubes. Checking gauges and meters, he monitored the progress of one of the experiments. This particular test system was the brainchild of a team of his brightest students. Designed to harness and amplify energy generated by thousands of green plants, it had sounded far-fetched to him at first, but just might work after all. Using collection units that floated over the plants, from field to field, they collected energy from various botanical species, for the purpose of observing differences between them and optimizing future Human exploitation of the technology.

Speaking into a computer, Noah instructed it to provide day by day comparisons for the past six months. Long charts scrolled down the monitor, providing field by field and species by species analyses. Curiously, imported Sirikan sporeweeds were beginning to outperform the other plants, whereas initially they had not done well at all. In recent days the technicians had found a way of tweaking the sensitive organisms, irritating them to create more oxygen and other cellular exhalants, for transfer to the EDP's energy production chamber.

Subi Danvar opened the chamber door and entered, but it closed so hard behind him that the images on the screen jiggled. "Master Noah, you don't need to perform these tasks," the heavyset man said as he lumbered across the floor. "We have people to do them for you."

"This is turning into an important test program," Noah said. "I want to check it firsthand."

"You have thousands of employees, so that you can free yourself from such responsibilities." His tone became acidic. "It's called delegation."

"Are you saying I don't know how to manage people?" Noah asked, with a twinkle in his eye.

"Well," Subi said, with his own blue-eyed sparkle, "you've never figured out how to keep *me* in line, have you?"

"I'll grant you that, old friend." He paused. "Of course, I could fire you."

"Then who would protect your well-exposed backside?" Subi rubbed the purple birthmark on his own chin, and it seemed to brighten.

"Is that all you are, Subi, padding for my derriere?"

"I could say something to devastate you now," he countered, "but I'll give you a break this time."

"Sure, sure."

They exchanged mock scowls.

The two men were not angry with each other, not in the least. It was just a typical bantering session between them, with each trying to gain a verbal leg up on the other. A mental wrestling match. It didn't keep either of them from focusing on their work, and had actually proved to be a way of reducing the natural stresses of their jobs. They always took great care not to exchange sharp repartees in front of other employees, however, not wishing to give anyone the impression that the men did not respect one another.

Noah ordered a printout, then had to grab hold of a thick vertical tube when the chamber started to shake, accompanied by a loud rumbling noise.

"Uh oh," Subi said. "I hope it's not what I think it is."

They hurried to leave, but stumbled and fell together when the konker floor buckled and cracked beneath them. Struggling back to their feet, they made it to the door, but it was stuck and would not open. Behind them, the floor was breaking apart, and the noise had become deafening. Cracking, roaring sounds, and loud engine noises.

"Diggers!" Noah shouted, as he and Subi pulled with all of their strength at the door. It budged, just a little.

The floor of the chamber erupted, with a deafening roar.

Noah and Subi got the door open and ran outside. Moments later, the walls and ceiling of the chamber collapsed and fell into a newly made hole. Noah barely got a glimpse of the tail end of a Digger as it dove back into the ground with the debris. The elongated, silvery machine was covered in dirt; it had huge treads, and large, spinning drill bits on its body. Anyone coming close to one would be torn apart, but Noah's extermination squads had modern, remote controlled boring machines of their own to chase down the pesky, mole-like Diggers and wipe them out.

The most danger occurred if people were inside a building, because it often took so long to get outside, and damage to the structure could prevent escape—as had almost happened to Noah and Subi. If people were outside, however, they could usually escape from the errant machines without harm, since the contraptions made so much noise when they were coming that people had time to get out of the way.

But the renegade machines seemed to get irritated whenever they were attacked, and might even be self-replicating. For each one that was destroyed, two more seemed to pop out of the ground. The very act of chasing the Diggers down seemed to trigger a survival instinct in them. Still, reports reaching Noah showed that the population of the machines on Canopa was actually dwindling. Their behavior was decidedly curious.

Under Subi Danvar's command, Anton Glavine and Tesh Kori, along with other anti-Digger commandos, dropped explosive depth-probes into the hole. Moments later, detonations sounded, and the ground shook.

"We've got 'em on the run now," Subi said. He started to grin, but Noah saw it fade suddenly, and heard more machinery noises, and gunfire.

On a handheld surveillance monitor, Noah saw silver vehicles approaching along the main road into the compound, and uniformed men running beside them. He recognized blue-and-silver CorpOne banners fluttering over the military squadron. His own sister Francella was in control of the family corporation now, and Noah was certain that this was no welcoming party. Not content to acquire all of the wealth of their father, she had apparently decided to go on the offensive against her twin.

As Noah and his adjutant ran for shelter and shouted commands into transmitters, his mind whirled. Did she hope to capture or kill him? There had been rumors that she wanted to make Noah the scapegoat for the death of Prince Saito Watanabe, and perhaps they were true after all.

Blue tracer fire hissed over their heads. Noah and Subi ducked into a bolt-hole that they had opened with an electronic signal, and the hatch closed behind them. They joined hundreds of green-and-brown uniformed Guardians running for emergency stations. Everyone had done this drill before, and knew the priorities.

Noah continued to wonder. He had expected Francella's attempt to blame him for the death of their father, but had not anticipated a military onslaught from her. That was far too brash, so she must have the backing of Doge Lorenzo for something like this. Yes, that was undoubtedly it. They were lovers, after all.

Guardians cleared the way for Noah and Subi, and the two of them boarded a grid-plane. Just as they jumped aboard, Noah noticed Tesh and Anton with a group of other Digger exterminators, all of them covered in dirt from the recent attack.

"Bring those two with us," Noah ordered, "and as many others as we can. Tell everyone possible to take off for EcoStation. Priority One. From there we might have time to figure out what to do."

He knew that his Guardian Security Force was defending against the attack. He'd seen them beginning to fight back just before he and Subi made it into the bolthole. But he also knew what CorpOne could throw against them, and worried about whether they had the firepower to defend the compound. He would stay there and man the guns himself, but Subi had developed contingency plans to keep enemies from getting to Noah, and Noah knew that his followers needed him for inspiration.

"You're the soul of this organization," the loyal adjutant had said to him on more than one occasion.

Now Noah nodded to Anton and Tesh as they boarded with him. Moments later, the grid-plane rocketed out of its underground bunker, followed by other green-and-brown escape aircraft, at irregular intervals.

On board EcoStation, high in orbit over the planet, Noah reviewed security procedures with Subi and three Guardian officers. After they left his office, he stood at a wide window, gazing down at Canopa below, at the continents and oceans that looked so calm from this distance. Touching a transmitter on his wrist, he activated the magnaview feature of the glax, and it zoomed in on his Ecological Demonstration Project compound. The resolution was so clear that he could see uniformed soldiers hurrying in and out of the vehicles and structures.

His blood boiled, as he thought of all the ecological work that those idiots would trample on, desecrating years of effort. It looked like a military base down there now, with vehicles and aircraft pouring in. And not just those of CorpOne, either, he noticed with a sinking feeling. Doge Lorenzo's forces were there as well, in their cardinal red uniforms.

Atop the administration building, his green-and-brown flag still fluttered defiantly in a slight breeze. Then he saw it being lowered.

"You asked to see me?" a man said.

Turning, Noah saw the mustachioed Anton Glavine enter the office and stand by the desk, looking nervous and upset. His black trousers were torn, and one of his knees was bloodied.

Noah switched off the viewer. "I have something to say to you," he began. At a wave of his hand, the office door closed, and he blocked all intercom systems.

"Tesh and I appreciate what you've done for us," Anton said. "OK if I sit down? I injured my leg in a fall."

"Sure. Go ahead."

Anton slid into one of three chairs that fronted the desk.

Too agitated to sit, Noah paced back and forth by the window. "I should have told you this earlier," he said, "but for your sake I thought it was best to hold back the information. I hope you're not angry with me, because I always had your welfare in mind."

"I would never question that." The younger man appeared to be perplexed. His hazel eyes looked straight at Noah.

"I've always acted like a big brother to you," Noah said. "You thought I started out as a friend of your parents, but that isn't the whole story." He took a deep breath. "They weren't really your parents, not birth parents anyway."

Sitting straight up, Anton said, "What?"

"You and I are related by blood."

"You're not my . . . father? We are only seventeen years apart."

He shook his head. "I'm your uncle."

Stopping the pacing, Noah could see Anton's mind churning through the possibilities, behind the gaze of his eyes.

"My uncle?" His face contorted. "My mother isn't Francella? God, I hope not!"

"She is, unfortunately." Noah folded his arms across his chest. "After you were born, she paid for your care, but never bothered to see you again or even ask about you. I doubt if she even remembers the name of the family that took you in, or your own given name that they provided for you. I'm really sorry, Anton."

Anger filled the young man's face. "You should have told me. I'm twenty years old, not a baby."

"It never seemed like a good time. I wanted to spare you. Now isn't the greatest time, either, but I don't feel I can wait any longer. We're all in danger, and in case something more happens. . . ." Noah's eyes misted over, and he choked up.

"OK," Anton said. He went to his newly discovered uncle, half-smiled. "I know you mean the best."

"Don't be too quick to forgive me. I have something more to tell you."

"Worse than what you already told me?"

"It depends on how you look at it."

"Well?" Anton stood up, went over to the window by Noah.

"Doge Lorenzo is your father."

"Now I know you're kidding."

"Look at me, boy. Do I look like I'm kidding?" Noah stared hard at him, unblinking.

"Is that all you have to tell me? Or does it get even worse?"

"Lorenzo doesn't know about you. My sister didn't want him to know she was pregnant, so she stayed away from him until after you were born, and then said she had been tending to family business matters."

He looked numb. "I need time to absorb this."

Noah went on to tell Anton about the military insignias he had seen through the magnaviewer, that Francella and Lorenzo appeared to have combined their forces to attack the compound. They might even be down there together right now.

"I wish they were," Anton replied, "and that we could drop a bomb on them." He sulked toward the door, opened it.

Just before he left, Noah said, "Be cautious with the information. Revealing it to anyone could put you at more risk."

"Everything's dangerous nowadays," Anton said, and he closed the door behind him.

Chapter Forty-Seven

No one is ever totally free. Everyone is confined by his own mortality.

—Jacopo Nehr

On the Mutati prison moon of Omo, Giovanni Nehr lamented his situation. He had hoped to get rich by turning the nehrcom secret over to the shapeshifters, but it had not worked out that way at all. In the process, he had also hoped to avenge himself against his smug, overbearing brother Jacopo, but he might never learn if that happened. Gio should not have proceeded without knowing the outcome in advance. In retrospect, he realized that he should have envisioned the possibilities better before committing himself.

Now he toiled in white-hot sunlight, carrying stones from one side of a field to another. Obviously, the work had no purpose whatsoever except to occupy and annoy the prisoners, because there were other men like him moving the stones again, to another place. Back and forth and around and around hundreds of Human men in checkered prison garb went, only occasionally getting water breaks, and then only to drink a brackish, green liquid that looked positively lethal. He swallowed as little of the slimy fluid as possible.

During one of the breaks, he sat cross-legged on a flat rock and struck up a conversation with two young men standing nearby, who identified themselves as Acey Zelk and Dux Hannah. The pair had been discussing the destruction of the planet Mars, wondering how it could have happened. Upon hearing the boys say they'd seen the debris field, Gio asked for more information. They described the horrors of the aftermath, and said some of the onlookers theorized a meteor may have hit the planet.

"Must have been quite a blast," Gio said.

To Dux, the man didn't seem very sympathetic. The teenager had heard that Mars was only lightly populated and not on any important commercial routes, but that still meant the loss of hundreds of thousands of people.

For several moments, the three of them gazed off into the distance at shimmering bubbles of air that floated between the moon and the planet Dij, a large ball that looked like it was below the moon.

"Those bubbles are strangely beautiful," Dux said.

The others agreed, and then Gio expressed his opinion about the uselessness of their labor, just carrying rocks around.

Grinning in a disarming way, Acey said, "Try to see the positive side, friend. We're getting a good workout, keeping our bodies in shape."

"Unless this green water gets us," Dux added, spitting it out and making a face.

"Where are you from?" Gio asked.

"Siriki," Acey said.

"Ah yes, the world of Princess Meghina. Do you know her?"

"Do we look like her social set?" Acey asked.

"I guess not. I'm from Canopa myself, the most beautiful planet in the galaxy."

"We've seen a lot of worlds," Dux said to the older man. "Canopa is nice, but not exotic enough for me."

"Yeah," Acey agreed. "Too civilized." He paused, and asked the Canopan, "How did the Mutatis get you?"

Gio grimaced, shook his head. "I'd rather not say. Something dumb I did, dumb and embarrassing."

"Could say the same for us," Dux admitted. "We were snared on a Mutati-controlled vacation planet, like insects in a fly trap, they said to us."

Into the throng of prisoners strutted six guards, fleshy creatures who moved with remarkable speed despite their great girths. The shapeshifters stood in the center, each of them looking in a different direction at the relaxing men.

Without warning, lances of orange fire shot from weapons attached to their wrists, hitting many of the prisoners. "Back to work, you slackers!" they shouted with cruel glee, as the captives cried out in pain and surprise, and jumped in attempts to get out of the way.

On a second burst of fire, Dux was struck in the shoulder, burning through his thin shirt to the skin. Acey was hit on one arm—but both boys refused to cry out. They just moved back into the work detail and did as they were told.

These guards were bored, Dux realized. They had rousted the prisoners from breaks before, but never like this. Previously it had been with shouts, threats, and strange curses, and once they had hurled small, stinging stones at the men. On rare occasions, the Mutati overseers were even pleasant, but Dux came to realize that this was just a sadistic game with them, as they easily shifted back to cruel behavior.

The next time they had a chance to talk, following an evening meal, the two young prisoners and their new friend discussed an escape plan. The moon on which they were incarcerated, in low orbit over Dij, was connected to the Mutati-controlled world by airvators, shimmering capsules of air that rose and descended with passengers inside. From air pressure, they had firm interior walls, floors, and ceilings, but they had no real substance. To observers looking upward, it seemed like the passengers were floating on air bubbles . . . which, in fact, they were doing. Each airvator was controlled by an operator inside who wore a pressure-regulator, strapped around his torso.

Pursuant to a plan that Dux developed, Acey—who was mechanically inclined—stole one of the regulators and put it on, then generated a pale yellow bubble around them.

"It's easy to operate," Acey said. The mechanism made a soft hiss. "Hang on," he said. "Here we go!"

Looking around, Dux grabbed a railing as they lifted into the air. His companions did the same, and barely in the nick of time, because the capsule flipped over, tossing them around.

"Sorry," Acey said. He righted the airvator, increased the power, and they went higher into the air.

Dux felt lightness in his feet, the gravity field weakening as they moved farther from the moon.

"I'm turning on artificial gravity now," Acey said.

Dux felt it kick on, as his feet settled firmly to the deck of the airvator.

"Beyond the moon's atmosphere now," Acey reported. "We're in a narrow band of space between Omo and Dij. In a few moments, we'll enter the stratosphere of the planet."

But as they descended toward Dij, Mutati guards in another airvator spotted them and opened fire.

Acey changed course, and inside the enclosure the three of them tried to duck. Projectiles hit their airvator, puncturing the seal and damaging the pressure mechanism.

Acey tried to re-inflate, but they began to lose pressure and tumbled rapidly. Dux saw a gaping hole on one side of the bubble, an opening that shifted when Gio moved around.

"Stay away from the hole!" Acey yelled. "Watch out!"

Gio lunged at Dux and said, "Careful! You could fall a long way!" He gave Dux a hard push toward the cavity.

Dux was nearly as tall as his attacker, but thinner and less muscular. The older man was stronger, and had the added element of surprise. Still, the youth had wiry strength, and fought desperately to avoid falling to his certain death. He lost his grip on the railing, but tumbled to the other side of the capsule and grabbed hold again.

"Just a mistake," Gio said. "It wasn't what it must have looked like. I was just trying to keep my balance, didn't mean to push you."

"Like hell," Dux said.

Acey struggled with the regulator and managed to increase the air pressure, but only a little.

The airvator hurtled downward, spinning.

Suddenly an emergency system went on, and the hole sealed over. The airvator began to descend at a normal speed until it settled onto the ground. As it landed, the mechanism shut down, and the shimmering bubble disappeared entirely, leaving only a wisp of color behind that soon dissipated in the air. The three of them ran from the guards, whose airvator landed moments later. Gio ran in a separate direction from the boys.

Acey and Dux scampered across a storage compound enclosed by energy-field fences. They hurried by a faceless servobot and boarded a small gray ship, slipping into the cargo hold amidst large crates, bags, and barrels. The pair were barely inside when the hatch slid shut behind them, and the craft lifted off.

Peering through a porthole, Dux saw the vessel speeding toward the setting sun on the horizon, skimming over grassy hills and treetops. Acey showed interest in something else, an arched doorway in the forward bulkhead of the hold. He strode through, and disappeared for several moments.

When Dux followed, he found his cousin standing at a control panel on the bridge of the ship, examining the instruments. Glancing back, Acey said, "This thing's on automatic, a programmed route."

"To where?"

"Can't tell." He tapped a light green screen, said, "This is the destination board, full of numbers and letters. We're on course for Destination 1-A, wherever that is. My guess is this is a supply ship, and after we deliver cargo there, it keeps going on its route, to other destinations."

"Too bad we're so low to the ground," Dux said. "I'd give *your* right arm for a pod station right now."

"And I'd give your right eye," said the other, with a wink and a grin. He glanced out the front window. "Whoa, what's that?"

Ahead, Dux saw a building that at first appeared to be one-story. As they neared the structure—which was constructed of patterned geometric blocks—he realized it was at least ten stories in height, with huge open doorways and ships inside that look like merchant schooners, even painted the red-and-gold of the Merchant Prince Alliance. Lights began to flicker on as the sun dipped below the horizon.

"Something doesn't look right here," Dux said. "Our princes would never buy ships from the Mutatis, or sell anything to them."

Inside the facility, he identified the lumpy shapes of Mutati workmen, fitting some sort of hardware into one of the vessels. A complex of smaller buildings was adjacent, surrounded by a high fence. He saw hundreds of blue-uniformed shapeshifters on the grounds, and more of the schooner-like vessels.

"What is this place?" Dux asked.

"Looks like a manufacturing facility," Acey said. "Military, from the look of it, and the level of security."

"Something to do with fake merchant prince schooners," Dux said.

"That'd be my bet."

Their ship set down a short distance away on a shadowy landing field, where only servobots awaited them, simpleton machines that were programmed to perform a limited number of tasks, repetitively. Moments later, a hatch opened in the floor of the cargo hold, and a ramp extended down to the pavement. On-board systems began sliding items down the ramp, where the bots loaded them onto a groundtruck.

In the cargo hold, Acey used a strip of metal to pry open a crate. "Just food," he said, peering inside. While the unloading operation continued, he avoided the flexing servo-arms of the bots and broke into another crate, followed by another.

"I know what this is," he said, pulling out a black field gun. Rummaging around in the crate, he found ammunition, which he began loading into the weapon.

"What are you doing?" Dux asked.

"You want to join the fun, or are you just going to watch?"

"Uh, I don't . . ."

Acey grabbed another gun and more ammunition from the crate just before a servomechanism grabbed the open container and slid it down the ramp, followed by the others he had opened. Finally the hatch closed, and the ship began to lift off. Acey handed the first weapon to Dux, then loaded the second one and fired it at a porthole, blasting it open. Hefting the heavy gun and touching the firing pad, Dux blew open another porthole.

The boys exchanged quick glances, and grinned at each other. Mutatis were the mortal enemies of all Humans, and these two had been indoctrinated in this belief system from an early age.

Without another word, they fired into the building with the powerful field guns, hitting the schooners and barrels of chemicals, which exploded into flames. In a matter of seconds the entire facility was ablaze and alarm klaxons were sounding. Like ants in a frenzy, uniformed Mutatis scurried around, trying to figure out what had happened. The boys emptied their guns into the soldiers, dropping many of them and sending others scrambling for cover.

The cargo ship flew on its programmed course past the flames, while the teenagers shouted in glee at the unexpected bonus, and reloaded their weapons. At last they were getting even for what the Mutatis had done to them, and in the process had undoubtedly saved the lives of Humans who might have been the victims of whatever weapons systems they were constructing inside that building.

Acey ran back onto the bridge, and smashed something. "They're coming after us!" he shouted. "I see two blips on the scanscreen."

Dux hurried to the back of the hold and blasted open another porthole. He saw a pair of fighter ships speeding after them, with the factory burning behind them. Dux opened fire on them, and they fired back.

Just then, the cargo vessel banked left and surged upward, in a burst of acceleration. Dux held on and kept firing the field gun. He hit the short wing of one of the pursuit ships, and the craft spun out of control.

"I overrode the program!" Acey shouted. "This baby really has power!"

"I got one of them!" Dux yelled. His field gun was more powerful than the armaments of the fighter ships, and had a longer range. One ship slammed into the ground and exploded in a fireball, and then he hit the other one, which blew up in midair.

The cargo vessel, lifting higher and higher into the sky, had proven to be more versatile than Acey or Dux could have possibly imagined. They flew to a pod station, jumped onto a deck and used the field guns to shoot their way past any Mutatis they encountered.

Boarding a podship that arrived a few minutes later, they left chaos in their wake. The sentient spacecraft departed for deep space. . . .

When they were safely off-planet, Acey and Dux talked about what they would like to do to that slimy Canopan—Giovanni Nehr—if they ever saw him again.

Chapter Forty-Eight

> Opportunities are all around you, waiting to be plucked like gemstones from a jeweler's tray.
>
> —Malbert Nehr, to his sons

Giovanni Nehr was not as skilled as the boys in getting away from the Mutati world. He hid in the marshland for two days, drinking rainwater and not eating anything. Seeing shuttles lift off regularly in the distance, he made his way through swamp and jungle to the edge of the transport station. For most of a day he watched the shuttles taking off and landing. Early that evening, in geostationary orbit high overhead, he saw a bright light, which he judged must be a pod station.

Darkness dropped like a thick black blanket over the land. It was a moonless, starless night, illuminated only by the pod station and the landing lights of the shuttles. Gradually, he built up his courage, and crept across the landing field.

Concealing himself behind a stack of shipping crates, he watched Mutati soldiers supervise robots that were loading a shuttle, using heavy equipment. On occasion the Mutatis came close to Gio, only a couple of meters away, without seeing him in the shadows.

As he watched, he discovered something very interesting. Even when he was relatively near the shapeshifters, they showed no signs of anti-Human, allergic reactions . . . apparently as long as they could not see him, as long as they were unaware of his presence.

Gio learned something else as well, of even greater significance. From his place of concealment, waiting for an opportunity to sneak aboard a shuttle, he overheard two Mutati officers supervising the loading operation, giving the robots voice commands in Galeng. The pair also talked between themselves about impending military missions against the Humans . . . stepped-up attacks.

"It's nothing like the merchant princes have ever seen before," one of the Mutatis said. "They can't defend against it."

"The Demolio program is brilliant, isn't it?" said the other. "This will be the deciding factor in the war."

The voices drifted off as the Mutatis moved farther away. When they returned, they were discussing the same subject, but there were no specifics. They kept referring to something called "Demolio."

Demolio?

Whatever it was, it sounded big to Gio, and he wondered if he could get a reward for tipping off the merchant princes about it. But for his next venture he vowed to do more research in advance, so that he didn't get into trouble again, the way he did with the Mutatis. Always the opportunist, Gio knew there was a great potential for profit during wartime. If he could only escape and take advantage of the situation. . . .

The loading took the better part of an hour, after which the Mutatis and robots boarded a motocart and sped away across the landing field.

With the shuttle unattended, Gio made his way to a loading hatch and sneaked aboard the craft. Hours passed while he waited inside in the darkness of a cargo hold.

He drifted off to sleep on the hard deck, then awoke hours later at the sound of voices, and the rumble of an engine as it surged on and vibrated the vessel. He hoped the interior air would be breathable when they reached orbital space. Dim light filtered into the hold, making him think it might be dawn.

Gio yawned and stretched. His muscles were sore, and hunger gnawed at his stomach, like a creature consuming his body from the inside out. He felt air circulating in the hold, and heard the whir of fans. The ship lifted off.

In only a few minutes, he felt weightless, and then the craft's gravitational system kicked on. Presently, he heard what he judged to be the sound of a docking mechanism engaging, perhaps at a pod station or space station.

Soon he heard voices again, an angry confrontation outside. Peeking around the edge of an open hatchway, he saw the Mutatis on the loading platform of a pod station, arguing with a pair of pale-skinned Kichi men. The Kichis claimed that the Mutatis had taken their docking berth, and they were quite upset.

"Take another berth," one of the Mutati officers said. He pointed the forefingers of his three hands to another docking spot, a short distance away.

"No," the tallest Kichi said. "We reserved this one for a freighter arriving in the next half hour."

"What difference does it make which berth you get?" the Mutati asked. "They're all the same, just holding spots until a pod takes us aboard."

"It makes a lot of difference, you fat pile of ugly. You have five minutes to get out of here, or we're going to cut your piece of junk loose." He spit on the Mutati vessel.

Enraged Mutatis surrounded them. But the Kichis activated a long, high-pitched signal, and moments later a throng of them came running toward the platform.

During the wild melee, Gio saw a podship arrive in one

of the zero-g docking berths at the center of the station, where passengers were already lined up to board. On impulse, he ran for the ship, but had to pass the fighting aliens to get there.

A Mutati guard spotted him as he crept out of the shuttle, and opened fire with a jolong rifle. Sparkling blue projectiles whizzed by his head, and thumped into the thick gray-and-black skin of the podship. The vessel shuddered.

Gio ran to the front of the line and pushed his way on, out of turn.

"Who do you think you are?" a Jimlat dwarf shouted, after Gio shoved him aside and he fell to the dock.

Ignoring him, Gio found a seat on a bench at the rear of the passenger compartment. A handful of additional passengers boarded, but not the dwarf. Without warning, before the normal amount of time allowed for boarding, the podship hatch closed, and the large sentient vessel got underway.

The cabin wasn't even half full, but apparently the podship had been agitated by the projectiles hitting its side, even though it would take more firepower than that to harm one of the creatures. Some of the passengers glared back at Gio, but he ignored them.

Noticing a stinging on his left arm, he examined it. Just a flesh wound visible through the torn sleeve of his shirt, with a little trickle of blood. Nothing to dampen the ebullience he was feeling. He had gotten away from the Mutatis, and was free now.

Chapter Forty-Nine

My mind cuts in many directions.
The gyrodome makes the blades sharper.
—Zultan Abal Meshdi

It was difficult to imagine that anyone could be unhappy living in the magnificent Citadel of Paradij. As the Zultan of the Mutati Kingdom, Abal Meshdi possessed everything a shapeshifter could desire, including a harem of the most stunning and sensual Mutati women in all of creation, each of them rounded heaps of rolling fat. On a terraced hillside, his private baths offered a broad selection of mineral and spirit waters from all over the galaxy, for soothing his tired bones and renewing his energy, which had been sapped by endless affairs of state. Tens of thousands of Mutatis, robots, and the slaves of various races (other than allergy-producing Humans) worked for him in the Citadel, a virtual city within the capital city, attending to his every need, his every whim.

Originally, Paradij had not been a world that appealed to any galactic race for habitation, since it was covered with arid deserts and vast salt flats. But the planet featured deep aquifers, essentially subterranean seas. The Mutatis—driven there by Human attacks against their other planets—had set up a massive hydraulic engineering project to bring the water to the surface, which they then used to create rivers, lakes, and irrigation canals for crops and forests. The costs in money and the expenditure of time had been enormous, but the marvelous result had been a source of inspiration to all Mutatis. It showed what they could do in even the most difficult environments, and that the greedy, aggressive Humans could not take everything away from them.

He lived in such exquisite luxury that he didn't really need to go to war against the merchant princes. But they had insulted him and his people, driving them from one world to the next, never letting up.

And Mutatis did not take insults lightly.

With many important matters weighing heavily on his mind, the big shapeshifter shuffled toward the clearglax bubble of his gyrodome, which he'd had moved to one of the highest rooms in the Citadel, where he could be closer to God-on-High. The platform inside the dome spun slowly now as it awaited him, making a faint, inviting hum. Pursuant to his instructions, the mind-enhancing unit was in its simplest, most basic configuration, without the customized compartments that could be fitted on the outside to contain aeromutatis and hydromutatis. Sometimes he did not want such distractions.

Just then an aide interrupted him and said, "Pardon me, Your Eminence, but there is a messenger to see you. He says it is important."

Shaking his tiny head in dismay, since he really needed what he had come to call his "morning gyro treatment," the Zultan said, "Very well, send him in."

Moments later a uniformed aeromutati flew into the chamber, and hovered in the air. It was one of the small, speedy flyers who were best suited for such tasks. "There are two messages, Sire. I carry one"—he held a small communication pyramid in one hand—"and the other is outside."

"Outside?" Abal Meshdi said.

"Look over there, My Zultan," the messenger said. He pointed to a small window on the narrow north end of the chamber.

Hurrying to the window, Meshdi beheld a sight that surprised him, and filled him with patriotic pride. He counted ten outrider schooners flying in formation over the capital city, swooping this way and that.

"They are performing for you, Sire, in honor of the glory they will achieve when you send them into battle."

"But I thought there was a delay in production," the Zultan said. "I was told that the vessels would not be ready for another month."

"Apparently they solved the problem," the messenger said, with a shrug of his narrow shoulders. "Look, Sire, the outriders have come to receive your blessing before departing on their holy missions and giving up their lives."

Filled with pride, the Zultan watched the bomb-laden schooners, each a beautiful doomsday machine capable of annihilating an entire enemy planet. Such a magnificent, perfect design. Truly, his researchers were inspired by God-on-High when they developed this most perfect and deadly of all weapons!

The Zultan felt tremendously humbled by all of this. As the leader of trillions of Mutatis, he was still only a tool of the Almighty, put here on Paradij to further the hallowed Mutati mission. Today, his sacred duty was to dispatch these outriders.

Already two fringe planets under enemy control—Earth and Mars—had fallen victim to his deadly design. And one additional outrider had been sent as well, with orders to strike against a third planet in the future at a predetermined time, on a Mutati holy day. Now—glory of glories!—ten more magnificent weapons were ready to go, and only needed his blessing before surging off into space.

The opening salvos of the Demolio program were all according to a precise, sacred pattern of numerology, following mathematical formulas laid out in *The Holy Writ* of his people. Two, one, and ten were sacred numbers, referring to a sequence of events that occurred long ago in Mutati history, leading to the most celebrated of military victories.

Until now.

It was not necessary to wait for confirmation of the third kill—the outrider who was still out there—before sending more of his brethren into the fray. The excited Zultan knew nothing could go wrong with any of the attacks, and that the third one would go off without a hitch, scattering another merchant prince planet to the cosmic winds. Then there would be ten more.

And many more after that.

"Everything is predetermined," he thought, quoting from the ancient sacred text of *The Holy Writ.*

The Zultan felt euphoria sweeping over him, and then noticed the aeromutati fluttering its short wings, still waiting to deliver the second message. "Oh yes," Meshdi said, extending a hand, palm up.

The messenger placed the gleaming communication pyramid on his palm. Afterward, the aeromutati tried to leave, but Abal Meshdi shouted after him, "Wait! I might send a response."

The Zultan didn't want to believe the message.

Angrily, he hurled the communication pyramid at the aeromutati and hit him square in the head, dropping him out of the air, where he had been hovering. The flying Mutati thudded heavily to the floor, didn't even twitch. He was dead, but this didn't make the Zultan feel any better.

"It's not possible!" he bellowed.

According to the missive, his son Hari'Adab had barely escaped with his life when enemy commandos destroyed the Demolio manufacturing plant, along with the adjacent outrider training facility. The ten planet-busting schooners now at Paradij had been dispatched shortly before the disaster, and—for reasons of military security—had flown across the solar system by conventional hydion propulsion.

Two attendants ran into the chamber. "Your Eminence?" one of them said. "Is everything all right?"

Reaching into the pockets of his robe with his two outer hands, Meshdi brought out a pair of long knives. Thunk. Thunk. The motions were smooth as he hurled the blades expertly at the terramutatis, hitting each of them in their torsos. The attendants dropped into piles of pulpy, bleeding flesh, beside the messenger.

For months, the Zultan had been practicing with his knives, throwing them at target boards. Fortunately for his aim, the attendants had been wide, easy targets. But he still didn't feel any better.

I need to kill Humans, not my own people.

Extremely agitated, he entered the gyrodome and stood on the whirling floor. Closing his eyes, he felt the mechanism probing his overburdened mind, trying to purge it of the weight of vital duties and decisions. But it only made him feel worse.

When he finally stepped out of the gyrodome, the Zultan felt confused and uncertain. Now he would need to wait for instructions from God-on-High before proceeding. Clearly, it was not enough to only destroy ten merchant prince planets, since the enemy had hundreds, and military-industrial facilities on many of them. With only a limited number of doomsday weapons and no manufacturing facility to replace them, Abal Meshdi needed to rework his war plan.

As he watched the gyrodome stop spinning and shut down, he made a new vow. The destruction of his Demolio facility would slow the Zultan down, but he would resume operations as quickly as possible at another location, diverting all possible resources to the project.

And next time there would be no security breach.

Chapter Fifty

> There are so many ways to kill a prisoner, and so many ways to make it entertaining.
>
> —Supreme General Mah Sajak

Princess Meghina sat beside her husband in the royal box, with immense red-and-gold banners fluttering overhead, each emblazoned with the golden tigerhorse crest of the House of del Velli. They gazed down on the broad central square of the capital city, thronged with people who came to see the public executions. It was a cloudy afternoon, and she shivered as a breeze picked up from the west.

At the near end of the square, a platform had been constructed with a simple-looking chair mounted atop it . . . a device that her husband had said was actually a newly-designed execution machine. Perhaps a meter away, and around the same height as the empty chair, stood an alloy framework with a black tube on top of it. Wishing to spare herself some of the horror of whatever they had in mind for the prisoner, she had not asked him for details, and had silenced him when he tried to tell her. But in her high station, she still had to attend the event.

Now she gasped as a blue flame surged straight in the air from the top of the alloy stand, coming from the tube. The crowd roared its mindless approval, and then grew even louder when four guards escorted the condemned man toward the platform. Sajak wore a red hood over his head, and a simple red smock; without his uniform he looked very small and thin. Onlookers moved aside as the guards pressed their way through.

Meghina, the most famous noblewoman in the Merchant Prince Alliance, loathed these macabre spectacles that Lorenzo staged too frequently, and disliked the way he made her observe them whenever they were together. She and the Doge could not be more different, but eighteen years ago she had consented to marry him for the sake of her own House of Siriki, to give her people enhanced military protection and commercial benefits.

Over the time that they had been married—living much of the time on different worlds—she had tried to see good things in him, and on occasion his small kindnesses surfaced. But she felt no passion for the nobleman, no spark, not the way she had cherished Prince Saito. Such a distinguished old gentleman the industrialist had been, and what a terrible loss when he didn't come out of his coma. She wondered if the rumors were true, that his own son had attacked CorpOne, leading to his death. If so, she hoped he got what he deserved.

In front of the Doge and his lady, entertainers wandered through the crowd, playing music, singing songs, and juggling, throwing glimmerballs high in the air. Hawkers worked the perimeter, selling gourmet foods to the excited people who had come to see fifteen traitors die.

How ironic this whole scenario was, Meghina thought, as she watched two black-robed men take custody of the hooded prisoner and lead him up the steps of the platform. General Mah Sajak had been a renowned torturer of Mutatis, and now Lorenzo promised he was going to die as horribly as he always gave it out himself. Fittingly, according to her husband, today's means of execution was a device of Sajak's own invention, a machine that he had been developing, and which no one had ever put to use. Until now.

Atop the platform, one of the robed men removed Sajak's hood with a flourish, which seemed odd to Meghina. Normally it was the other way around; they put a hood on a victim just before executing him, a gesture of compassion at the end. But there was nothing normal about today's event. General Sajak had been the most trusted military officer in the entire Merchant Prince Alliance, and had committed the ultimate betrayal.

Seeing the chair and the blue flame beside it, Sajak began to scream in terror, and tried unsuccessfully to free himself. The crowd grew quiet, except for the call of a food hawker, an odd sound drowned out by the General's panicked shrieks.

"No, no!" he pleaded. "Not this! Please, not this! I'll give you more names, people who conspire against the Doge!" Even from her distance of perhaps thirty meters away, Meghina saw the terror on the disgraced officer's gaunt face, the way his eyes seemed twice their normal size.

Doge Lorenzo waved one hand, and a holo-image appeared in the air over the execution machine, a three-dimensional schematic drawing of the device.

"General Mah Sajak invented this machine himself!" a mechanical voice proclaimed over the loudspeaker system. "These are his own drawings!"

The image spun slowly, so that all could see it.

The elegant Princess didn't want to watch this terrible event, but knew she had no choice. Her husband and the crowd would expect it, and she could not lose face by disappointing them.

"No!" Sajak screamed. He tried to kick one of the robed men in the groin, but a thick garment prevented this. In response, the man backhanded the prisoner, sending him sprawling. Forcefully, the ominously-attired pair then dragged Sajak to the chair and strapped him to it, while he continued to scream and shout his promises to reveal new information.

It did him no good, for his fate had been sealed. A black, rather dented robot climbed the platform, and removed the tube that was shooting the blue flame, so that it was now a mobile torch.

Pointing it toward the sky, the robot turned the flame up, to double its previous size. The crowd thundered its approval.

Even over that noise, Meghina heard Sajak's screams.

"Louder," Doge Lorenzo said, to an aide.

Moments later, someone turned up the volume on a fireproof microphone that Sajak wore on his person. His shuddering screams reverberated across the square, sending the crowd into a frenzy of pleasure.

Holding the torch, the sentient robot activated a laser eye on it, and directed a bright red light at the prisoner's booted left foot. Jimu moved closer, and a metallic strap shot out of the device in his hand, wrapping itself around Sajak's lower left leg, just above his ankle.

"No!" he screamed. "Don't do this to me!"

The blue flame darted forward hungrily, and consumed the boot and the General's foot. His screams intensified, but the robot paid no attention. This evil man had tried to assassinate the Doge, the greatest Human in the galaxy.

Where there had been a foot only moments before, nothing but a charred, cauterized stump remained now.

Moments later, Jimu burned the right foot off. The robot expected Sajak to pass out from the pain, but he didn't, and kept wailing and crying for mercy. An expert at torture himself, the General was suffering indignity on top of indignity at the hands of the robot. The lower legs followed, then the thighs. Piece by piece, Jimu melted the body from the feet up. When he got to the lower torso, Sajak finally grew quiet and motionless.

The crowd cheered and clapped. Children giggled and played. Musicians struck up joyous tunes, and acrobats performed.

In a cruel spectacle, other robots under Jimu's command then executed General Sajak's co-conspirators the same way, one by one and piece by piece. Princess Meghina nearly gagged at the odor of charred flesh. Admittedly, these were all bad people, but she couldn't avoid her feelings of intense sadness. Faking a little sneeze, she leaned forward and wiped tears from her eyes, not wanting anyone to see.

Through it all, she sat silently beside Lorenzo, showing the Doge and the public one face, while concealing another one.

Following the executions, Doge Lorenzo appointed the famed inventor Jacopo Nehr to a new position, surprising many people. Nehr—previously only a reserve colonel—became Supreme General of the Merchant Prince Armed Forces, taking control away from the noble-born princes, whose champion had been Sajak. The new military commander owned several machine manufacturing plants on Hibbil worlds, and preferred the uniformity of those new machines to Jimu and his motley bunch. Still, Nehr could not deny their loyalty or accomplishments, so he rewarded them by commissioning all of them Red Beret officers.

In the process, Jimu was initiated into the rituals and secrets of the elite paramilitary organization, whose primary mission was to protect the Doge. This pleased the robot immensely, but he found himself troubled by the memory of the terrible defeat suffered by the Grand Fleet at Paradij . . . the biggest military loss in merchant prince history. Sadness and guilt permeated his mechanical brain, but his logical circuitry told him that he had not been at fault, and that he had done his best possible job as Captain of the sentient machines.

Even so, he felt an inexplicable need to make up for the loss, in some manner. The loyal robot vowed to work even harder on behalf of Doge Lorenzo.

Chapter Fifty-One

We have been taught from birth to never trust any member of another race, not even those who profess to be our greatest, most virtuous friends.

—Hibbil Instruction

He knew he must be a comical sight this morning, a furry little Hibbil in the saddle of an immense tigerhorse, but Pimyt didn't care.

Far ahead, at the edge of a clearing, the Royal Attaché heard barking hounds and the shouts of other riders, who were barely visible to him as they hunted an elusive ivix. Pimyt sat sidesaddle on a magnificent bay steed at the rear of the pack, thinking about how much he hated having to get up so early, without time for a civilized breakfast. Hunger pangs gnawed at his stomach.

He tried to put such thoughts aside, knowing that his opportunity to get even for such discomforts would come. Very soon.

An ivix? Who cared about running one of those tiny horned creatures to ground and taking it home to stuff as a trophy? Pimyt had much more important prey in mind.

Purportedly, his own people were to Humans what Adurians were to Mutatis—allies, advisers, and legitimate business associates. But none of that was really true. It was all a deadly ruse. The extent of the treachery was immense and so cleverly fabricated that it spanned an entire galaxy.

The web of deceit permeated both Human and Mutati

society at the highest levels.

As the Doge Lorenzo del Velli's most trusted associate, Pimyt exerted a great deal of influence over affairs of the realm. In the past, the furry, innocent-looking little fellow had even been appointed temporary Regent of the entire Merchant Prince Alliance, until the princes decided upon a new leader.

But Hibbils had never been loyal to Humans, nor had Adurians ever been allegiant to Mutatis. The Hibbils and Adurians were, in fact, secretly allied with one another in what they called the HibAdu Coalition, and for centuries had developed a diabolical scheme to overthrow both the Merchant Prince Alliance and the Mutati Kingdom.

Lorenzo was somewhere up ahead with most of the other riders, on the heels of the barking hounds and the little ivix that they all sought. It hardly seemed worth the effort to Pimyt. But he participated anyway, as he was expected to do. Not being of noble blood himself, some of the riders resented his presence, but he didn't care about any of that, the petty politics of Human society.

To his credit, Doge Lorenzo didn't care much about the pedigree of noble blood, even though it coursed through his own veins. Rather, he preferred to promote people on the basis of merit, regardless of the circumstances of birth. But that was not enough to redeem himself in the eyes of Pimyt or his Hibbil brethren. No Human could ever do that, and especially not the leader of their damnable kind.

In his years as a trusted confidant of Doge Lorenzo, Pimyt had accomplished a great deal, and in the process he had learned not to trust anyone. The downside of a lapse or oversight was too great. Better not to rely on anyone except his own people. Promises made between races were notoriously unreliable. Even the alliance between the Hibbils and the Adurians had its dangers, which his people were monitoring carefully.

Abruptly, Pimyt noticed that the hounds were running toward him, barking loudly, and the rest of the hunters were following them. Then he noticed something running low to the ground just ahead of the daggs, a little horned creature with fur that glinted gold when morning sunlight hit it.

Concealing himself and his mount in a thicket of leyland maples, he waited until the ivix ran by, then fired a shot from his vest-pocket gun at it, hitting the animal square in the side of its body. This was not a proper thing to do, so he quickly rode away through the trees, to avoid detection. Coming around behind the hunters again, he sat atop his tigerhorse, looking down at the fallen ivex.

"Looks like it's been shot," said a fop from the royal court.

"Who would do such an unsportsmanlike thing?" Lorenzo asked, looking from face to face. Since he trusted Pimyt explicitly, however, his gaze hardly touched the Hibbil.

No one seemed to know the answer.

As they rode back to the stables together, Pimyt felt very pleased. Now that this consummate waste of time was over, he could sit down for a decent meal. Despite his small stature, he had a voracious appetite. All of his people were this way, so it was a wonder that they didn't grow any larger.

That evening at his private apartment in the capital city, Pimyt received a coded message chip, containing very interesting information from his Adurian co-conspirators. With information from an unlikely source—Jacopo Nehr's own brother Giovanni—the Mutatis now had the secret of the nehrcom cross-space communication system. This was highly useful information to Pimyt. Not for the technology, but for the *lack of it* . . . and the leverage this gave him. Jacopo Nehr had always been so secretive about the workings of the device, and now it turned out that it was not so complicated after all. With the message, Pimyt received a holo replica of the entire nehrcom transceiver, showing its simple inner workings.

The following afternoon, Pimyt plodded into Jacopo Nehr's private offices for an appointment he had requested, ostensibly to discuss details of their new working relationship. Behind his gleaming sirikan teak desk, Nehr looked more rested than usual, perhaps reflecting his contentment at having been selected as the top military officer in the Alliance.

"Congratulations on your appointment, General Nehr."

"Thank you."

"I would have thought you'd be out drilling your officers on your new programs," Pimyt said, as he climbed onto a chair that was too large for him and plopped himself down.

Nehr beamed. "As a businessman, I've learned how to delegate."

"I see. And how to manage crises, I presume?"

The man's eyes narrowed, just a little. "Of course. That comes with the territory."

"We'll see how good you are at it, then."

Leaning forward nervously, Nehr asked, "What do you mean?"

At a snap of his fingers, Pimyt produced a holo-image of the nehrcom transceiver, showing all of its inner workings. Like a bubble, it floated in front of the startled inventor, whose eyes looked more like an owl's now than those of a Human. The Hibbil suppressed a smile.

"W-where did you g-get this?" he stammered.

Ignoring the question, Pimyt said, "So, your famous transceiver is only a box of piezoelectric emeralds cut precisely and then arranged and linked in a specific way to open up the cross-galactic transmission lines. Interesting, isn't it, how the most important ideas are often so simple?"

"But h-how?. . . . w-where did you . . . ?" Undoubtedly envisioning his galactic corporation crumbling around him, Nehr could hardly complete a sentence.

"I have my sources, shall we say? Let me caution you, before we go any farther, that I have given copies of this holo to certain key . . . associates for safekeeping. And if anything were to happen to me . . ." He smiled. "I need not go into detail, do I?"

Astounded, Nehr stared at the holo of precisely-arranged gems inside its box.

The Royal Attaché smiled, and said, "*Great* inventor! What a joke that is. As a Hibbil, with a long tradition of innovative manufacturing and development techniques, I know the difference."

"I've had my suspicions about you for a long time," Nehr muttered.

"And you consider yourself a fine judge of character, I presume?"

"What are you driving at?"

Rubbing his furry chin, Pimyt decided not to reveal what was on the verge of passing across his lips, that Nehr's own brother had betrayed him. No need to reveal that yet. There might be an opportunity to gain an advantage over the brother, too.

"Well?"

Delaying his response, Pimyt studied his new captive, considering how best to leash him and prevent him from biting. Nehr was red-faced. Perspiration trickled down his brow, into his eyes.

"If you don't cooperate with me," Pimyt said, "I'm in a position to ruin you. If I reveal your nehrcom secrets, you will no longer have a monopoly on instantaneous communication across the galaxy. There's also the little matter of your machine-manufacturing plants on Hibbil worlds. They could easily be nationalized, taken away from you."

"Get to the point. What is it you want?"

"Not so much. Just a little arrangement." Again, he hesitated, this time for dramatic effect. Nehr was getting more red-faced, sweating more.

"Here is what you will do," Pimyt finally said. "Periodically, I will give you communiqués, which you are to transmit to all planets in the Merchant Prince Alliance."

"Concerning what?"

"You are in no position to ask questions. And do not discuss this with anyone but me, in private. Not even Doge Lorenzo. Understood?"

The inventor nodded, reluctantly. He looked displeased and trapped.

Pimyt smiled. Unrevealed to Jacopo or any other Human, the Hibbils and Adurians had a military agenda of their own, and were now in a position to influence the placement and strength of Human forces. Some of the messages, in the midst of innocuous ones, would involve military matters. . . .

Chapter Fifty-Two

People change, and so do worlds. The universe remains constant.

—Saying of the Sirikan Hill People

Inside an oval chamber on the lowest level of EcoStation, Noah stood at the most powerful magnaviewer window aboard, providing him with a high-resolution picture of the planet below the geostationary orbiter. Once, Canopa had been his world. He had known it well, and especially his beloved Ecological Demonstration Project there.

Subi Danvar wanted him to leave the orbital platform and seek refuge on some distant planet. But that was against Noah's nature. He didn't like to run away from anything, no matter how much sense it made to do so. Earlier, when he'd been caught in the surprise attack on CorpOne headquarters, he'd only been accompanied by a small entourage, and it had seemed prudent to escape quickly and analyze the situation. Now he hesitated, searching for alternatives.

Having received telebeam reports from the ground, and having watched through his magnaviewer, he knew that his security force had fought valiantly, and still held tenuous control over the southwest corner of the compound. But they had been unable to defend the main buildings, which had fallen to superior Red Beret and CorpOne forces. Such a disturbing alliance between his own sister Francella and Doge Lorenzo, and Subi had intercepted reports that more of their forces were on the way. It was only a matter of time until the brave Guardian defenders lost what little ground they still held.

And EcoStation would be next. The orbital platform had armoring and other defensive features, but could never hold out against a full-scale onslaught.

Several days ago, Noah had relayed an urgent nehrcom message directly to the Palazzo Magnifico, demanding an explanation for the attack and an emergency meeting with the Doge. So far there had been no response, but he continued to hold out hope.

He had not anticipated his sister's military aggression, nor her devious strategy of aligning herself with the man whom Noah had thought was no longer her lover. Those assumptions seemed to have been entirely wrong, and were costly mistakes. She might have stepped up the Lorenzo relationship with her lies and tricks, falsely accusing Noah of killing their father. Or perhaps she and the Doge had collaborated from the very beginning in the murder of Prince Saito, to take control of his business empire and blame the death on Noah.

He wanted to believe the best about Lorenzo del Velli, that the powerful leader had only been duped after the CorpOne attack, and that he and Francella had not collaborated in the murder. Lorenzo had been a patron to both Saito Watanabe and Jacopo Nehr, neither of whom had been noble born but whose careers had been advanced because of the support of the Doge.

Gazing down through the magnification window at his besieged compound, Noah felt rage and confusion, seeing the Doge's elite Red Beret soldiers setting up their own military installations. Some of the Doge's long-range artillery pieces were pointed up, aimed ominously at the orbiter. Nonetheless, Noah did not order an emergency change in the orbital path.

No matter the lies Francella told him, he couldn't believe that Lorenzo would try to blow him out of space. Not after what the Watanabe family had done for the Merchant Prince Alliance, far beyond the munitions plants that were part of Prince Saito's diverse corporate empire. Noah himself had contributed substantially to the war effort, restoring the ecology of the formerly worthless planet of Jaggem, so that it could be used as a key military outpost by the Alliance. The Doge had even visited Jaggem during the final stages of the reconstruction, to commend Noah and his Guardians for their excellent work. Noah always wanted to believe the best about people.

Suddenly, he saw a flash on the ground. One of the artillery pieces!

Then a flash from another gun, and an explosion in midair.

Having gotten into bed with Francella Watanabe in more ways than one, Doge Lorenzo del Velli had ordered the stationing of his elite Red Beret troops at her brother's ecological demonstration compound. Military personnel worked all around him now, setting up a command center in Noah Watanabe's former office. Lorenzo had stopped by to inspect the facility.

He had been frustrated by the holdouts in the southwest corner of the compound. Noah's security forces still held onto the maintenance and warehouse building there, but they wouldn't last long. He had more troops and weapons on the way.

As for EcoStation orbiting high overhead, the Doge had initially ordered its destruction, as Francella had demanded. She wanted him to "blast it out of orbit" with one of the big artillery pieces, and the final countdown had been initiated.

At the last possible moment, he had received an intelligence report that contained startling information. Lorenzo had shouted to stop the firing of the weapon, but he had been too late, and it had gone off. Thinking quickly, he had ordered an immediate intercepting shot, which followed in seconds, at an even higher velocity. The two projectiles had exploded in midair.

Now, breathing a heavy sigh of relief, the Doge reread the report. So perplexing. Supposedly his illegitimate son, Anton Glavine, was on board EcoStation . . . a son he didn't even know he had, and Francella Watanabe was the mother. The report contained purported evidence of the parentage, which would still require confirmation. If accurate, though, Francella would have a lot of explaining to do.

Could it possibly be true? Lorenzo had been told by a doctor that he could not father any more children, and had given up hope. But somehow, miraculously. . . .

He caught himself, didn't dare hope, not without confirmation. But if the young man really was the only male child sired by Lorenzo the Magnificent, that was not something to be destroyed easily.

The Doge would have to take other measures to kill Noah Watanabe, no matter what Francella wanted.

Chapter Fifty-Three

It is said of Francella Watanabe that she should have been born a man, and that she has spent her life trying to make up for this affront.

—From *Red Rage*, the unauthorized biography

It had not been their typical bedroom encounter. Usually the passion of the two lovers was physical, but now it filled the air. They had been about to make love and had taken off their clothes in a frenzy, throwing them in all directions, hardly able to wait. Then he told her.

"You spared EcoStation?" Francella screamed, rolling away from Lorenzo and sitting up on the bed. "Even though you knew my brother was up there, a sitting duck? How could you, after what he did to my father?" Furious, she pulled a long chartreuse blouse over her nakedness and clasped one of the buttons.

"You haven't been entirely truthful with me, have you?" he shouted back at her, only inches from her face. He grabbed the blouse and ripped it open.

She slapped him across the face. "I told you everything, the way Noah had my father killed, and all the other terrible things he did."

With a curse, Lorenzo held her wrists, preventing her from striking him again. "I'm not talking about Noah, although perhaps I should. As for your father, there are other more likely suspects."

"Which means?"

He smiled savagely. "For another time, my sweet. We want to save things to argue about later." Then, holding both of her hands with one, he used his other to smooth her long red hair. "I so enjoy it when we make up."

Glaring, Francella tried to pull away, but he held her tightly.

"You are a woman of secrets, aren't you?"

"Every woman has her secrets, you fool."

"But not nearly as interesting as yours. Would you like to tell me about our love child?"

He saw her face tighten, the knotting of muscles on her cheeks. "What do you mean?" she asked.

"The boy you concealed from me. My own *son,* damn you!"

She reddened. He saw the guilt all over her, didn't need any other confirmation.

"After he was born, I sent him away," she admitted, unable to hold gazes with him.

"And had your evil brother take care of him."

"No, I put the boy with a foster family."

Letting her go, Lorenzo pushed her away, against the headboard of the bed. "From what I hear, Noah has been monitoring his care for years, and recently made the boy one of his Guardians."

"One of his Guardians?"

"Our son is on EcoStation with Noah."

"So what? Kill them both, for all I care."

"But I have no other sons, don't you see? Princess Meghina has born only daughters for me. My love child with you, it seems, is the rightful heir to my legacy. Assuming the Council of Forty proclaims him Doge, that is. Just think of it, Francella, history will call him The Bastard Doge."

"That wouldn't be any different from now," she snapped. "We already have a bastard in that position."

After a look of shock and anger, he let loose a deep, resounding guffaw, and said, "You're only saying that because you mean it." Laughing, he chased her around the bedroom, not letting her get to the door. Finally, exhausted and furious, she tumbled to the floor.

He took her in his arms, and finished ripping off her blouse.

Chapter Fifty-Four

The Human mind contains a universe of secrets.
—Noah Watanabe

An electronic field veiled the assault ship, making it invisible to the security force on the space station. This was accomplished with a stealth skin that projected images from one side of the large vessel's skin to the other, shifting seamlessly as the craft moved. The noise and heat signatures had been masked as well, and like a ghost the craft docked, undetected, on the underside of the immense orbiter.

A hatch door slid open on the vessel, followed by a large circular hatch on the space station, activated by a signal that kept the alarm system from going off. Hundreds of men in red uniforms slipped into a shadowy corridor, each of them made invisible by computerized images projected from one side of each body to the other, as if the person was not there at all.

All were Red Berets, the Doge's elite, fiercely loyal fighting force.

Through visors on their helmets, the men saw their companions, all dressed in red uniforms with caps. Heavily armed, they rushed through one corridor and another, using silencers on their handguns to kill any green-and-brown Guardians they encountered. With holo-schematics of the orbiter, images that danced on the visors in front of their eyes, they thought they knew the proper route. The route program had not been updated for all of the changes that had been made to the modular station, however, and the squad ran right past an entrance hatch to the classroom section. They then took a high-speed elevator to a lower level, the wrong one.

The Red had also failed to take precautions to bring weapons whose projectiles would not penetrate the skin of the space station. Errant shots went through exterior walls, activating the orbiter's emergency systems, which closed bulkhead doors and sealed holes to prevent catastrophic depressurization.

Alarm systems went off, and something in the jangle of electronics shut down their computerized image projectors. Suddenly the intruders were visible to guards, who fired stunner pellets at them, hitting one of the men and dropping him to the metal deck. The others ran on, leaving him behind.

Earlier, Noah had seen the artillery flashes, and his security advisers had confirmed to him that the second flash had been an intercepting shot. This had given him some measure of reassurance that Doge Lorenzo was not going to do anything rash. The first shot appeared to have been an equipment malfunction, which they had corrected immediately.

Now, as the alarms went off Noah stood in the school module, having just conducted a meeting with a number of his Guardians, trying to answer their questions and allay their fears. He had spoken truthfully to his loyal followers, not wishing to conceal anything from them.

None of his people had expressed any desire to abandon EcoStation, but he thought that might change when they were alone and not under the attentive eyes of their peers, not trying to prove anything to anyone or show courage they didn't really feel. They were all brave enough, Noah realized, but few of them were trained fighters. Only the security personnel. The rest were students, and support staff for the orbital platform.

The meeting had just ended, and he had been conferring with Tesh and Anton, considering what to do next. In a few minutes, Noah was scheduled for a one-on-one conference with Subi Danvar to consider alternatives.

Just then, the three of them heard the screaming wail of alarm klaxons. On a wall-mounted security screen, they saw Red Beret soldiers running through the corridors, firing weapons. Activating sound, Noah heard the squadron leader shouting to his companions.

"We're on the wrong level!" he shouted. "Glavine has classes on Level Four!"

"They're looking for me!" Anton said. "Why?"

"Your father's special forces," Tesh said. "And they don't look friendly."

"Somehow they know your schedule," Noah said, wondering how they had gotten the information, and what they hoped to do with it.

"My father either wants to kill me or kidnap me," Anton said.

Noah took a deep, agitated breath. He remembered what his adjutant Subi Danvar always told him, that he was the soul of the Guardians and needed to survive for the sake of the organization and all they stood for. In his desire to fight back against his sister and the Doge, Noah had not wanted to follow the advice for his own welfare, and had only gone along with it reluctantly. Now he needed to survive and fight another day, for his vital cause and for the people who believed in him.

Some time ago he had asked the Doge for an emergency meeting to explain the attack against the ecology compound, and at last he had his answer. Noah saw no advantage in being taken to any meeting by force, or in dying here.

Speaking sharply into a lapel microphone, he told Subi to broadcast a general evacuation order to everyone on the station, readying ships that would disperse his people to predetermined locations on Canopa. Then he commanded the adjutant to prepare a grid-plane for him, and provided a short list of passengers he wanted to accompany him. Over the communication link, Danvar confirmed receiving the message, and said he would take care of it all right away.

"Hurry!" Noah urged, leading the way through a door at the rear of the classroom. The trio ran through a narrow corridor to a spiral stairway and bounded up four levels, taking two steps at a time.

They reached the top and ran through a wide doorway onto a metalloy platform. Grid-planes were tethered on the other side of a bubble window, their green-and-brown hulls floating in zero gravity. Guardians ran toward the three people on the platform, their boots making echoing sounds. Subi Danvar, moving quickly despite his broad girth, led them.

"I issued your evacuation order, Master Noah," Subi reported, "and all ships are ready."

Seeing Eshaz reach the platform, which was on his short list of priority passengers, Noah motioned for him to join them.

The group hurried through an airlock and boarded one of the grid-planes. Subi Danvar took the controls, and powered up the engines. The sleek craft surged out of the docking bay into orbital space.

Through a porthole, Noah saw two red gunships, more of the Doge's force. One of them opened fire with automatic weapons, ripping holes through the cabin. Noah heard the hiss of escaping air, and the whistle of repair systems going on, sealing the holes in the hull.

"Get this crate going!" he shouted to Subi. "We're faster than they are!"

"I'm trying!" Subi shouted. "Hold on. Here we go!"

The supercharged grid-plane picked up speed, and the passengers found things to hold onto: seat backs, bulkheads, railings. Through a porthole, Noah saw other escape ships scattering away from the station, using their superior speed and on-board scanning equipment to elude the Doge's electronic grids. Noah knew that some of his followers would still be captured or killed, but all of them had the same opportunity to get away that he did.

"We need to get to a podship," Noah said. "There's a planet we can go where our environmental activists have a clandestine support network. I've told some of you about it . . . Plevin Four."

"I'll do the best I can," Subi said, "but the Doge may already have gunships around the pod station."

Anton asked a question about Plevin Four, said he was unfamiliar with it. Tesh told him it was an abandoned world, that it had a history alternating between Mutati and MPA control.

Just as Noah started to tell his nephew more about Plevin Four, projectiles ripped through the passenger compartment. He felt something sting his arm, and the side of his head. Then something tore into his left foot. Terrible pain, and dizziness. He lost consciousness and fell in a bloody heap on the carpeted deck. . . .

Sitting by Noah, Tesh held his bleeding head on her lap, as the grid-plane accelerated and automatic systems repaired the hull damage. A wall and ceiling of the cabin had been torn up. Anton popped open a first-aid kit, began applying gauze bandages on the wounds. Eshaz came over and stood silently, looking down at the fallen Master of the Guardians.

Tesh had never understood Tulyans, the way they kept their emotions bottled up, never revealing their inner thoughts. She knew that Noah thought highly of this one, so she tried to show him respect. But it was not easy. Her own Parvii people and the Tulyans were natural enemies, ancient competitors for dominion over the galactic herds of podships. So far Eshaz had shown no indication of recognizing her—the Parvii magnification system was a closely guarded secret—but she didn't trust him.

"We're beginning to outdistance them!" Subi shouted. "Almost out of range now."

Looking up, Tesh saw blue tracers zip by a porthole, but nothing more hit them. She heard Subi say the vessel's onboard repair systems were continuing to seal the holes.

"Noah needs medical attention," Tesh said. "His head is bleeding, and his foot is torn up bad." She checked the bandages, and it occurred to her how Human bodies, like this ship, had automatic repair systems—but how much better it would be if people were capable of healing themselves from even the most serious wounds. She worried about Noah, having grown to admire him, and hoped for more between them.

"I'll see what I can find," Subi said, "but we need to leave Canopa as soon as possible. It's too hot for us here." He steered down into the atmosphere of Canopa, causing sparks to fly off the underside of the hull during reentry. When they were a couple of thousand meters above the planet, he leveled out and slowed.

Going over to a porthole, Tesh surveyed the trees and

farms of the countryside below, then pointed and said, "Head that way: northeast, I think. I know a doctor." She glanced at her wristchron, which had adjusted itself to their locale, and saw that it was late afternoon. "He should be home now, too."

A few minutes later, they set down on a wide parking area between the sprawling main house and the tigerhorse stables. Half a dozen men emerged from the front of the house, dressed in cloaks and brocaded surcoats. Ladies in shimmering evening gowns stood on the broad porch behind them, some holding drinks.

One of the men, square-jawed, went down the steps and strode toward the grid-plane. Tesh recognized Dr. Hurk Bichette, her former lover. The two of them exchanged glares.

She led Subi and Anton, and introduced them. "Sorry to interrupt your dinner party," Tesh said, "but we have an emergency. Noah Watanabe is on board, and he's seriously injured."

"Head wound," Subi said. "But that looks like a glancing blow. His left foot might be the worst of it. He passed out after he got hit there."

"I'll get my bag," Bichette said, in his deep voice. He ran inside the house, and emerged moments later, carrying a black bag and a large packet with a clear covering, showing a variety of healing pads inside, of varying sizes.

"Let me help you with that," Tesh said, taking the packet from him and then following him aboard the grid-plane.

While Bichette kneeled over Noah and tended to him on the deck, Tesh helped. Looking up, she saw Subi step forward with a handgun. "I'm afraid we'll have to borrow you for a while," he told the doctor. "We'll send apology cards to your dinner guests."

"What do you mean?" Bichette asked.

"It's no longer safe for us on Canopa," Anton said, accepting the gun as Subi handed it to him. "We have another planet in mind, and you're going with us."

She looked over at Eshaz. The large, bronze-scaled Tulyan stood silently, watching with a dismal, deeply concerned expression.

"But I can't!" Bichette protested. "This isn't an ordinary dinner party. It's an important business meeting. My guests are wealthy investors, considering a business proposition I made to them."

"Business can wait," Subi said, as he slipped into the command chair. Safety restraints snapped automatically into place around him, but he shoved them away. "Lives can't."

"Listen to me. Noah needs a hospital. We can't have him bouncing around in a grid-plane." The vein on Bichette's temple throbbed.

"I'll take off smoothly," Subi said. "We don't have any way of securing him, of strapping him down."

"Stop thinking about yourself," Tesh said to Bichette, "and tend to your patient."

The doctor glowered at her, but did as she demanded.

Tesh felt the grid-plane's rocket system kick on, but as promised they made a smooth ascent. In a matter of minutes, they reached the upper atmosphere, then surged into orbital space, with the vessel's gravitational system on.

"Where are we going?" Tesh asked.

"Plevin Four," Subi said. "That's where Noah told me to go."

"But he's been injured, needs a hospital."

"They have a medical facility on Plevin Four," Subi said.

Through the wide front window, Tesh saw the globular pod station ahead, floating. Subi drew near, then circled the station twice, without entering any of the docking bays. "Keep your eyes open for bad guys," he said, looking at the ships that were lined up inside. Tesh only saw two, and neither of them was emblazoned with the Doge's or CorpOne's colors.

Warily, Subi guided the vessel into one of the docking bays and found a berth. "We got here fast," he said, "but our pursuers aren't far behind us."

Just then, Tesh felt a pressure change inside the cabin, and heard a faint, familiar pop. Looking out a side windowport, she saw green luminescence around a podship as it floated toward the main docking bay of the station. As seconds passed, the luminescence dissipated, leaving the mottled gray-and-black exterior of the vessel. All of the sentient spacecraft looked essentially the same to the untrained eye, but Tesh recognized the characteristic streaks and other markings on this one. She had been in the Parvii swarm that originally captured it in deep space, more than five centuries ago. While the Parviis had taken control of the vast majority of podships long before that, there were always wild pods wandering through the cosmos, strays to be rounded up.

Presently, a wide door opened on the side of the podship. All three of the waiting vessels floated aboard into the cavernous cargo hold, and their crews secured them to tethers.

They got underway quickly, engaging with the podways of deep space, connective fibers so fine that they could not be seen by anyone except the podships, and a handful of other races. Parviis were among the select few, but in their case it was only while at the helms of podships. Tesh was not certain who the pilot of this craft was, since assignments changed regularly. She could go into the sectoid chamber and find out—perhaps it was an old friend—but it was risky to do so, since she might be observed while changing her personal magnification system, getting smaller and later getting larger again. Usually, she did not take the chance, and certainly not this time, when she wanted to be near Noah and do whatever she could to keep him alive.

At least he was breathing regularly, and from the expression on his face he did not appear to be in any pain. Such an attractive man, she thought, with his freckles and curly red hair. He was the strong, take-charge type, so certain of his purpose in life and able to inspire others around him. *You certainly inspired me,* she thought. Gently, she touched his temple on the uninjured side of his head, and felt the reassuring pulse of his heartbeat.

She caught a hard gaze from Anton, who sat by a porthole, intermittently looking out into the cargo hold or at her. Since picking up Dr. Bichette, Tesh had noticed Anton acting irritably, as if jealous of her former lover. She felt nothing for Bichette anymore, not for months now. That relationship was over.

Or was Anton jealous of Noah instead? While expressing concern for his injured uncle, Anton might actually resent the attention she was giving him herself. And she really did care about him. Maybe Anton had noticed something. She didn't care. In her long lifetime, Tesh had been with many men, and always knew that she would have to end each relationship one day. Her lifespan was much longer than theirs, after all, and she didn't want to stay with a person who was going to die. She didn't think it was cruel on her part. In reality, she was overly sensitive and always tried to keep from getting too close to anyone, since that only made it more difficult. Her feelings for Noah were developing, but different from anything she had experienced before. She felt excitement at this, and fear.

The podship made only two brief stops along the way, at pod stations in remote sectors where there was not much activity. On board the grid-plane, Tesh and Dr. Bichette rounded up pillows, blankets, and anything else they could find to make the patient more comfortable. Once, Noah had moved his hands, as if gesturing with them while he talked, and his lips moved, without making any sounds. Then he became motionless again, except for his regular breathing and pulse.

Through it all, Eshaz said nothing, did nothing. To Tesh, it was very strange. She thought he should be doing something to help.

Only a few minutes after leaving Canopa and journeying far across the galaxy, the sentient spacecraft arrived at a pod station orbiting the planet of Plevin Four, in a belt of dead galactic stars. Subi provided details as he guided the grid-plane out of the cargo hold, then through a docking bay of the pod station, and out into orbital space. He shifted the propulsion system to conventional hydion, since they were away from the grid-system of Canopa.

"This world was stripped of its natural resources long ago by CorpOne mining operations," he said. "PF—its common name—is technically still owned by the corporation but is valued on their balance sheets at virtually nothing. We Guardians have been 'squatting' here for years without detection, using it as a training station and bolt-hole."

"Doesn't look like much," Anton said, studying a report on the ship's computer. "Hardly any natural beauty, bad weather, irritable natives. I see why you weren't noticed here."

"It's a good training ground," Subi said.

The craft headed down through a hazy atmosphere, toward the surface of the planet, with its gray-and-yellow hills, rivers, and lakes. "We do terraforming experiments here, practicing our ecological engineering methods for use elsewhere."

Through the front window of the grid-plane, Tesh saw a deep scar running for perhaps a thousand kilometers on the surface of PF. She asked about it, and when the adjutant did not reply Anton checked the on-board computer terminal.

"CorpOne leased it out to a strip mining operation," he said. "Doesn't say here what they took out, but whatever it was, they must have gotten all that was worth getting. Looks dead down there now."

The grid-plane flew low over the terrain. In six hours they reached the dark side of the planet, and Tesh made out a dark, serpentine river below. They flew over it for a distance, then slowed and hovered in front of a high embankment, illuminated by spotlights from the aircraft. Two big doors yawned open in the riverbank, revealing a large, dark chamber beyond. With the aircraft's spotlights probing ahead, making fingers of illumination, they flew into the chamber. Looking back, Tesh saw the cliff doors close.

As Subi landed and shut down the engines, he said, "Centuries ago, PF was under Mutati control. How the MPA took it away from them, I don't know. This is a military bunker originally built by Mutati civil engineers. A short ways downriver, it empties into a swirling, pale yellow sea."

"Sounds picturesque," Anton said, his voice caustic. "Can't wait to see it tomorrow." He caught a sharp glance of displeasure from Tesh, who then went to check on Noah.

She watched Dr. Bichette replace the healing pads on his patient's injured foot.

"Head's OK but his foot doesn't look any better," Bichette said. "It's badly mangled and in need of more than these pads."

Tesh felt tears welling in her eyes. She looked away. Through the portholes and front window, she saw that they had landed below the level of the river. Murky water could be seen through thick glax viewing plates and airlocks.

"Wonder where everyone is," Subi said. He stood at the open hatch of the grid-plane, gazing out into the cavern. Behind him, a heavy plate slid over the control panel of the aircraft, apparently preventing anyone from stealing it. Tesh noticed him slip something into his pocket.

Deep in thought, the big adjutant bounded down the steps to the rock floor of the chamber, then ducked around the tail of the aircraft to the other side. She saw him open a heavy metal door and stride through, into what looked like a room, or perhaps a corridor. A while later, he returned. By then, Tesh and Anton were outside the grid-plane, looking around themselves. Dr. Bichette and Eshaz were still inside with Noah.

Subi said, "Hundreds of Guardians are supposed to be here, but it doesn't look like anyone's been here for months."

"What do we do now?" Tesh asked. "This doesn't look like any place to stay, especially with Noah's condition. You said it had a medical facility."

"That wasn't entirely true," Subi admitted, rubbing the purple birthmark on his face. "They used to have a small clinic here, but I was hoping that Master Noah would come back to consciousness, especially after we got the doctor. Noah wanted to come here, so I thought I should do what he wanted."

She frowned. "But you've been to other planets with him, all the ecological reconstruction projects around the galaxy. Surely one of them is better than this place?"

He shook his head. "They're all well known, so the Doge probably sent forces to them, taking control of the projects. In fact, any of the main merchant princes' worlds are a problem now, because of the dragnet that's out for us."

"I see." Tesh felt frustrated, and angry that Noah wasn't getting the care he needed.

She heard what sounded like an anguished cry, coming from the grid-plane. Worried, she ran up the steps into the passenger cabin.

Dr. Bichette held a bloody white cloth, wrapped around something.

"One of Noah's feet was so badly shot up that I had to amputate it," he said, in an emotionless voice.

Horrified, Tesh looked down at the unfortunate Noah, who lay on the deck, face up. His head rested on a pillow, and he had a thin blanket over him. Another bloody white cloth was wrapped around the stump where his foot used to be. He slept, as before, except now his face was a mask of anguish.

"You fool!" Tesh screamed. "Why did you do that?"

"I did what I had to do. It was either that, or infection would have set in and he would have lost his entire leg. Or his life."

"But the healing pads . . ."

He shook his head. "They don't solve everything. I had no choice."

"Why didn't you consult with the rest of us? Maybe we could have figured out another place to go, where they have medical facilities. Damn you, Hurk!

"And you, Eshaz!" she howled, glaring at the motionless

Tulyan. "Why didn't you stop him?"

"I'm not a doctor, madam."

Turning back to Bichette, she started beating on his chest. The doctor backed up, looking surprised and shocked.

Anton pulled her off him, and forced her to sit on the deck, where he knelt beside her. "You need to calm down," he said. "The doctor only did what he thought was best. He couldn't consult with us. As Eshaz said, we aren't doctors. The decision was Dr. Bichette's alone."

"Let go of me," she demanded, trying to pull free of his strong grip.

But he held on. "Not until you promise to calm down."

Stubbornly, she shook her head, and Anton held tight. . . .

The surgical procedure had been a traumatic event for his uncle, but Anton couldn't suppress feeling envy, having noticed that Tesh was overly interested in Noah.

It was driving the young man crazy.

Chapter Fifty-Five

A thought has no dimensions, no weight, no color, no texture, no way to look at it, touch it, or hold it in your hands. And yet, it has substance. It is the spark of every galactic race, the flame of their hopes and dreams. It is the spark of the robot race.

—Thinker, *Contemplations*

It looked like no more than a dull gray metal box, sitting on an observation deck at the Inn of the White Sun. Inside, a sentient robot was in deep contemplation, having folded himself inward to avoid distractions and interruptions.

In the decades since Hibbils had manufactured him on their Cluster Worlds, Thinker had interacted with countless Humans. Some he liked and some he did not, but always he treated them with deference and respect, since Humans had designed him and paid for his manufacture and he was honor-bound to serve their needs. Even now, after they discarded him in a trash heap, and he and others like him had to regenerate themselves, he bore no feelings of malice toward the people who threw him away.

That may, in fact, have been a blessing to him.

By virtue of his own ingenuity and perseverance, Thinker had developed a considerable degree of independence from Humans. Certainly, he did not serve them on a daily basis anymore, and saw far fewer of them than he used to. In addition, he had discovered new abilities that he didn't know he had, and which he didn't think had ever been programmed into him.

He had thought up the idea of creating a machine army out of discarded robots, and for more than a year they had been training down on the surface of Ignem. Not so long ago, Jimu led a squad of his soldiers on a mission to save Doge Lorenzo from an assassination attempt, and they were so gloriously successful that the Doge had invited them to join his special force, the prestigious Red Berets.

Sensing something, Thinker unfolded himself into the familiar form of a flat-bodied robot, the way he had looked when Humans first designed him, before he later added the folding feature himself.

Out in space not far from the inn, he saw a burst of green luminescence as a podship arrived, seeming to pop out of another dimension into this one. The gray-and-black vessel, making one of the stops on its route, proceeded to the pod station.

Thinker hurried to the lobby of the inn, to see if there were any guest arrivals. He was not the innkeeper; other robots did that for him. But as one of the machines who founded the inn, he liked to break his intense contemplation routines on occasion to see the colorful galactic races and robots that stopped off here on their various personal, business, and government missions.

Ten minutes later, only one passenger stepped into the lobby of the machine-run lodge in the orbital ring, having taken a shuttle from the pod station. Carrying no luggage, he strode to the registration desk, and spoke to the robot clerk. Curious, Thinker eavesdropped from a short distance away.

"My name is Giovanni Nehr," the man said. "I'm on my way to Timian One, but first I need a little R and R."

Searching his data banks, Thinker found entries about

this tall, sharp-featured man, and visuals to confirm the identity. This was the younger brother of the famous nehrcom inventor, Jacopo Nehr. He had a healing pad on his left arm, over the bicep.

"Seven nights, please," the visitor said. Reaching into his pocket, he dumped a handful of lira chips into a hopper. The alloy pieces rattled around, and the machine dropped his change into a tray. Nehr stuffed the smaller denominations into his pocket.

"I see you are hurt," Thinker said, stepping closer with a clatter.

After looking him over, Nehr said, "It's nothing. Just a nick."

"Would you like us to look at it?"

"No, thank you." The smile was stiff, making Thinker suspicious, as if he might be hiding something.

"That looks like a Mutati healing pad," the robot observed. "It has a distinctive fold and color."

"Oh? I wasn't aware of that. A passenger on the podship handed it to me."

"A *Mutati* passenger?"

The man reddened. "If so, I wasn't aware of it. He looked Human to me. He seemed kind enough, and wouldn't have cared about me if he really was a Mutati. Would he?"

"You wouldn't think so. Unless he was trying to get information out of you. Did he ask a lot of questions?"

"Like you, you mean?" Nehr smiled stiffly.

"Yes."

"Well, come to think of it, he was rather curious."

"And what did you tell him?"

"Mmmm, not much. The cross-space journey was brief, only a few minutes."

"Forgive my questions, but we are very security conscious here, and our data banks require information."

"I am quite tired," Nehr said, "so if you will forgive me, I'd like to go to my room now."

But Thinker took a step closer, and his voice intensified, since he always worried about what Mutatis were up to, and the harm they constantly inflicted on Humans. "Did you see any Mutatis that were recognizable?"

"By name, you mean? I'm not personally acquainted with their kind."

"By *race,* Mr. Nehr. Did you see any shapeshifters in their natural, fleshy form, perhaps in the neutral confines of the podship?"

"Yes. They travel, as all of the races do."

"I'm sensing something more. Forgive me, Mr. Nehr, but I am very perceptive. I have developed my mind and senses to very high levels. Sometimes I wonder if I have what you Humans refer to as a sixth sense. Am I mistaken about you?"

Chewing at the inside of his mouth, Nehr said, "Not exactly." He paused, and leaned back against the registration desk. "I went to a planet called Nui-Lin for a vacation, and found out it was a Mutati front. They took me prisoner and put me on a prison moon. I barely escaped with my life." He touched his injured arm.

Thinker detected a mélange of truth and fiction, but didn't press any more, and bade the man good day. As Nehr followed a bellhop robot to his room, Thinker sorted through what he had just heard, and combined it with what he had been learning from other travelers. The Mutatis were more active along the space corridors than they had been in many years. Historically, this meant they were up to something big, perhaps a surprise military attack. They were a race of devious tricksters, able to assume many guises and sneak behind enemy lines to learn information.

Quickly, Thinker dictated a letter into his internal word processor and transferred it to a disk cylinder, for delivery to the Doge Lorenzo del Velli. With no nehrcom transmitter available at the Inn of the White Sun, the missive would go out on the next podship, carried to the merchant prince capital by Agar, a repaired messenger robot.

Unfortunately, due to a programming glitch, Agar would become lost in deep space and never make it to his destination. No one ever would ever hear from him again.

Chapter Fifty-Six

Dreams are the products of imagination, and the fuel of civilization.

—Chia, a merchant prince poet

Back when they were small boys, Dux Hannah and his cousin Acey Zelk used to dream of running away to space together and sharing grand adventures, of meeting beautiful girls and getting richer than the grandest princes in the realm.

Living in the wild back country of Siriki, their plans had been vague in those days, more the fantasies of fanciful children than reality. Then they were enslaved, first by merchant princes and later by Mutatis, before using their wiles to escape from both. Thus, before their seventeenth birthdays, they had been abused by both sides of the ongoing galactic war. This might have left them feeling put upon and filled with hatred toward their captors, but it had done nothing of the kind. On the contrary, they remained upbeat, and harkened back to the "old days" when they planned to share fabulous journeys together.

Through all that they had shared, the boys had forged a bond between them, a friendship that extended far beyond the familial blood they shared. Their camaraderie had been forged in a crucible of perilous escapades, when any moment might have been their last. But they persevered through what they called "misadventures," and lived to look back on the experiences, and even to laugh about them.

After escaping from the Mutati prison moon, Dux and

Acey stowed away on conventional spacecraft and podships, vagabonding from one star system to another, from one pod station to another. If a place interested them, perhaps after talking with strangers along the way, they went down to the planet and investigated it.

Now they were on the third such world they had visited in the past few weeks, each time having to panhandle for shuttle fares, since they had no money. While podship trips were free of charge—on routes developed by the mysterious, sentient pods—shuttle trips usually were not. This could have left the boys stranded in space if they had not been able to figure out ways to get down to the planets.

It was risky leaving the pod stations and venturing down, so before venturing to the surface, they developed the habit of asking as many questions as they could. If they didn't like the answers, or if they could not get enough information to make them feel comfortable, they remained in space and caught the next podship, bound for unknown sectors. This caused them to avoid both MPA and Mutati worlds, and to shun planets controlled by the allies of both sides as well, principally those of the Hibbils and the Adurians.

Such caution did not restrict their movements that much. The galaxy was a vast place, filled with colorful races and exotic worlds. In spite of their youth, Dux and Acey became good judges of character. That didn't mean someone couldn't slip something by them, but they did work hard at it, and they were both quite intelligent, despite having no formal education. . . .

On Vippandry, their shuttle descended past the Floating Airgardens, one of the Wonders of the Galaxy. The gardens, circular tiers of flowers and lawns that floated in the lower atmosphere, rose more than seven kilometers into the air and covered many cubic meters. They looked to the naked eye like holo projections, but were real, kept aloft by exotic, lighter-than-air plants from all over the galaxy, selected by master gardeners.

The shuttle pilot, a Vippandry with billowing white hair, acted like a tour guide for the trip down from the pod station. "You're lucky," he said. "The gardeners are at work now." He laughed. "I should have charged you more."

The passengers—an assortment of shapes and races—thronged to the windows, pushing for better views. They oohed and awed in their native languages, while gardeners wearing jet packs pruned the plants and added aerosol nutrients to the lighter-than-air soils. Dux thought they looked like bees or hummingbirds tending flowers, nurturing them.

At the Airgarden Gift Shop, Dux and Acey read a computerized bulletin board, looking for jobs. They paused to peruse enlistment ads for Noah Watanabe's Guardians, and learned of the ecological engineering work they performed on several planets. The work sounded interesting to the young men, and they liked a good cause, but they had something more adventurous in mind.

They spent more than a day panhandling around the shuttleport, and on the narrow, cobblestone streets of the nearby old city. The following day they made it back to the orbital pod station.

While waiting for the next podship into space, they wandered along the sealed walkways of the station. Looking through plax viewing windows at the ships out in the zero-g docking bays, they watched the crews as they performed various tasks or just stood around chatting. One mixed group of aliens and Humans had a mechanical problem with their spaceclipper. Wearing breather suits, they had one of the engine compartments open, with parts scattered on the adhesive surface of a work platform. An old vessel, it had maroon-and-vermillion swirls on the sides, and the graceful structural lines of a bygone era. Somehow its crew had managed to keep it going this long, but to Dux it looked like the end of the line. The name of the vessel was emblazoned on its side in golden letters, "*Avelo.*"

As the two teenagers looked on, a Hibbil crewman stepped through an airlock and approached them, a rugged-looking little fellow dressed in black. He wore an eye patch, and a sword in a scabbard.

"Where you boys headed?" he asked in a squeaky voice.

"Deep space," Acey said.

"That covers a lot of territory, doesn't it?" He rubbed his furry chin. "Any place in particular?"

They shook their heads.

"We're a treasure ship," the Hibbil said, gripping the handle of his sword. "I'm Mac Golden, official purser on the voyage. I keep track of everything important for the captain." The little fellow beamed proudly. "He considers me the most trustworthy person on the crew."

"Your ship is full of treasure?"

"Sometimes it is, sometimes it isn't. On this run, we've had a streak of bad luck, more trouble than you could. . . ." He paused, and stared at a podship as it entered the docking bay. Simultaneously, the crew of the treasure ship stopped working, to look.

The podship swung wildly and bumped into the Hibbil's vessel, almost jerking it free of its moorings. Then the podship continued on its way, to the main docking bay at the center of the pod station. When it was safe, the crew returned to their work on the engine.

"That's the third time one of those pods has nudged us," Mac Golden said. "They seem impatient to get us out of here, but we can't leave yet."

"C'mon," Dux said to Acey. "Let's go catch our ride."

But Acey hesitated. He watched the crew at work, then went over and spoke to them through a wall speaker. "These hydion drives can be temperamental, eh?" Acey said.

"You know anything about them?" one of the crew asked from out in the docking bay, a tall, black-bearded Ordian.

"Yeah, a little."

A short while later the podship left, again bumping into the *Avelo*, and then continuing on its way.

Saying he might be able to help, Acey talked them into loaning him a breather suit. He went out and immersed himself in the engine work, examining the pieces carefully, discussing them with the crew, asking questions like a doctor diagnosing the symptoms of a patient. One of the men took an interest in Acey, a gray-beard who wore a dirty white shirt and a red sash around his waist.

"That's Wimm Yuell," Mac said. "Our captain."

Dux nodded. A while later, a dark-skinned alien—small and swarthy, with a pointed snout—emerged from the ship and passed food bars around to the crew as they worked. He didn't wear a breather, making Dux wonder where he was from. Dux got one of the bars from Mac. He found it delicious, but with fruity flavors that he couldn't identify.

Acey kept working with the captain and the others, and they seemed to be following his advice. The crew was putting the engine back together, while Acey used diagnostic devices to test the components.

Bored and wanting to leave, Dux strolled down the walkway. He learned from a glyphreader panel hanging from the ceiling that the next podship wasn't due for a couple of days.

Dux took his time, exploring the walkways and the waiting room, looking at reading material that had been left behind. He spent some time chatting with an old man who called himself the manager of the pod station, though Dux didn't think any such position existed. He seemed a little touched in the head, but harmless enough.

By the time Dux returned, the crew was excited and smiling. They had the engine running, and were patting Acey on the back.

Coming over to Dux, Mac Golden said, "Your cousin asked just the right questions to get the mechanics thinking along the proper lines."

"I was afraid he'd ruin something," Dux said, glancing at the tough-looking little Hibbil.

"Welcome to the *Avelo*," Mac said, reaching up and shaking Dux's hand energetically.

When they were underway in space, Dux and Acey met the whole crew, an eclectic group of androids, Humans, and aliens who followed treasure maps, tips, and hunches all over the galaxy. They looked like a rough-and-tumble bunch, but took a liking to the young men.

Captain Yuell said to them, "You each get half shares to start, with the opportunity of working your way up."

"That's great, sir," Acey said. "You can count on us. We can do men's work, you'll see."

"We specialize in searching for merchant shipwrecks," the captain said. "But it takes more than maps."

"Well if you're looking for luck," Acey said, "I can provide that."

"Luck has a way of changing around here," Mac Golden said. "Don't get too full of yourself. Not yet."

Acey's face reddened, and he said, "Yes, sir. Sorry. . . ."

The young men found themselves on a voyage unlike anything they had ever imagined, bound for unknown parts, with undiscovered adventures and treasures awaiting them.

Chapter Fifty-Seven

If not for the magic of perception,
nothing would exist.
It is the spark of the universe.
—Parvii Inspiration

Like a visitor to a municipal aquarium, the woman stood in front of a large clearglax plate, gazing out at the marine shapes swimming in the water, but it was murky out there and she was having some difficulty discerning what she was seeing.

Nothing was as it seemed here. This was not an aquarium, and she was not a full-sized human. Tesh Kori felt dampness in the air, and pulled her coat tighter around her shivering body. Back at the grid-plane, Noah still had not returned to consciousness after almost two days. She'd been worrying about him when she went to the window wall, and had tried to calm herself by looking out into the flowing river. But it was having the opposite, disturbing effect on her. She tried to peer deeper into the water.

On her right, she heard her companions working to open a stone door that none of them had noticed before, in what had appeared to be a solid rock wall. That morning, Anton had discovered the almost undetectable door, and now they were using cutting tools on it.

Standing at what looked like a wall of water, she'd been thinking about perception, and the old Parvii saying about it being the spark of the universe. She wondered, as she had before, what the architect of that aphorism had in mind when he or she came up with it. Didn't perception extend to all of the senses, and not just to what you could see? Yes, of course, and at the moment she considered her various known senses and one that was not so easy to identify, lying just beneath the surface of her consciousness. Humans and their tiny Parvii cousins called it the sixth sense, but other races had a different number for it, since they had more or less senses. But the various sentient races were in universal agreement: this level of awareness existed.

Through the clear plates, Tesh saw frothing out in the river, and large, blurry shapes swimming toward her and then veering off to one side or the other, getting enticingly close to the glax without allowing her to see what they were. She touched the thick window wall, the coolness of it, and frowned.

There is danger here, she thought. And she was about to call for her companions when she heard Anton shout.

"Tesh! Get over here!" He stood in an open doorway, where there had been none before. The others were behind him, moving around inside another chamber. Their voices were murmurous, agitated.

Hurrying over there, she saw an additional chamber fronting the river. While smaller than the main chamber, it had a window wall as high as the other one. She went inside, and her nostrils wrinkled as she picked up a revolting stench.

Death.

In one corner, she saw the blackened, charred bodies of Humans jammed up against the rock wall—men and women who seemed to have been trying to escape but had no way out. She noted burned, bloody Guardian uniforms on some of them, while the clothing of others, and most of their skin, had been burned off. The victims had pitted eye sockets, seared-off hair, and scorch marks on their melted, horribly burned faces.

"This explains where thirty of the missing Guardians are," Dr. Bichette said.

Anton shone a flashbeam on the walls, went around and rubbed his hands over the surfaces, checking them. "But what could have killed these people?" he asked. "We came through the only door, and it was sealed from the inside."

"A locked-door mystery," Eshaz said. His bronze-scaled face, usually taciturn, showed concern now, in the downturn of the reptilian snout and the nervous gaze of the slitted eyes. "I don't like it in here."

"This was supposed to be a safe room," Anton said, "where they could get away from attackers. I suspect the other Guardians are around here somewhere, too, in additional safe rooms, or maybe up on the surface. They were trying to get away from something."

"And it got them anyway," Bichette said. "I think Eshaz is right. This place gives me the creeps. Let's go."

"I was just about to call for all of you," Tesh said, as the group moved toward the door. She pointed at the window wall and the blurry, swimming shapes out in the current. They had moved over to this chamber now and were continuing their strange water dance, getting closer and closer without revealing details of their features. They were large, the size of canopan sharks or dolphins.

Something flashed in the water, but for only a second, a glint of color. Red.

"Hurry," Eshaz said, pushing his Human companions toward the door. "Those are hydromutatis, swimming shapeshifters. They're still here from the time when this planet was controlled by the Mutati Kingdom."

As they reached the grid plane and boarded, Eshaz added, "I have heard of worlds with large bodies of water, where all of the hydromutatis could not be killed off by the Humans who took over."

"I've heard the same," Tesh said. "Hydromutatis are much more elusive than terramutatis or aeromutatis, and are very difficult to hunt down."

Eshaz nodded his scaly bronze head. The grid-plane shook as he boarded, from his great weight.

"But the hydromutatis are sealed off from the chambers," Anton said. "They couldn't have killed the Guardians."

"The creatures are rumored to have telepathic powers," Eshaz said. "They are also called Seatels."

As Tesh took a seat and watched Subi Danvar work the controls, she felt a tingle in her mind, and heard what sounded like pounding against the walls of the bunker, like a heavy surf slamming into a bulkhead. Or like Diggers burrowing their way through rock and dirt.

She heard a mechanical whine as Subi tried to start the engines. But they didn't catch. At the window wall, she saw scores of Seatels, their features clearly visible now, with smoldering red eyes and undersized heads.

Suddenly, a lance of light from one of the Seatels hit the grid-plane and fried the engines, so that they would not start. . . .

Chapter Fifty-Eight

From birth to death, life is a game of chance.
—Old Sirikan Saying

Even Doge Lorenzo del Velli, the richest and most powerful Human in the galaxy, liked to keep a little extra spending money around. He was not certain exactly why he felt the need to carry liras around with him in the pockets of his royal robe, but he did anyway. Perhaps it was just to reassure himself that the assets were available if he ever needed them, an eventuality that would require catastrophic changes in his life. He would have to lose his magnificent palazzo, all of his corporate holdings, and find himself tossed out in the street. All utterly impossible, but he felt helpless to avoid the feelings, the chronic fear.

This theory carried through the rest of his life. In secret places all over the galaxy, he had stashed his treasures, culled from the legitimate and illegitimate profits of his business and governmental enterprises. This went far beyond liras, although he had plenty of those in various places. Of critical importance, he didn't want to depend on the solvency of the merchant prince economy. To protect against that, he owned, among other things, some of the largest and most valuable gemstones in all of creation. This included the famous Veldic Saphostone, which disappeared from the Intergalactic Museum one day and found its way—through a circuitous path—to him.

The men who had taken it for him had been put to

death. Now no one knew his little secret.

Each morning, as he was doing now, Lorenzo strolled through his ornamental Galeng gardens, passed a guard station, and entered a scaled-down version of his Palazzo Magnifico that had the same number of rooms and the same configuration, but with much smaller dimensions. He rather liked his "Palazzito" for its coziness, but it was not a suitable place for contemplation, or a place to be alone. It was, instead, where he practiced what he most enjoyed doing.

Gambling at the most sophisticated gaming tables in the galaxy.

The first to arrive in his private casino, the Doge went from machine to machine in the Blue Chamber, activating the programs, seeing how well he could do at the mechanical games of chance. His favorite, where he stood the longest this morning, was a simulated suicide machine, called Spheres. He didn't have to put money or chips in it, because he owned the establishment. After a scanner identified him, he could play it to his heart's content.

By voice command, he selected the means of "death" that he preferred, and instantly the ominous hologram of a Mutati with a huge handgun appeared on one side of him, with the weapon pointed at his head.

Next he specified the amount of his wager, which in reality wasn't anything at all. But he provided a number anyway, and the screen in front of him filled with hundreds of tiny spheres, each with a different color and number on them. He had only two minutes. With a foot pedal, he directed the motion of the balls, trying to balance them on a narrow bar.

In only a minute, he had seven spheres lined up, and his score appeared on the screen: 17,252. It had to be higher than the last time he played the game, or the holo shapeshifter would fire, and a holo of blood would be all over his head and clothing.

The last time he played, his score was 17,251, and he liked to cut it close, only increasing by one point at a time. This was the most risky way to play, dancing on the edge of the proverbial sword, but it energized him.

Game after game, he increased by one point, without fail. He became aware of a crowd of men and women streaming into the chamber around him, the royal court. They cheered him on and chanted his name. He liked that, playing the hero. One day, he might even use the threat of a real Mutati with a weapon, instead of a hologram.

Presently, Francella came in and sat by him. She wore a low-cut black lace dress, with a long red fall of hair cascading over her shoulders.

Only she and Lorenzo knew that he could not lose here, not in his own casino. If he didn't measure up at any game that involved skill or if a game of chance did not go his way, the machine compensated, and he won anyway. It did not work that way for the other players, and they lost a lot of money on a regular basis. But as members of the Doge's royal court, they had no choice. If they wanted to remain in his favor, they needed to participate in what Lorenzo called "friendly exchanges."

Actually, this meant transferring their funds to the casino, and ultimately into one of the Doge's secret stashes. It was an additional source of income for him, one of many.

And he needed all he could get, he thought, as he looked into Francella's dark brown eyes. She was an expensive mistress.

Chapter Fifty-Nine

For as long as there has been warfare, there has been subterfuge. It can be the key to victory.

—Mutati military handbook

Just above the hazy atmospheric envelope of Plevin Four, a podship emerged from space in a burst of translucent green light, having traveled the faster-than-light podways known to the sentient space travelers. It settled into a docking station at the little-used pod station.

A cargo hold opened like a mouth in the side of the podship, and a long black transport ship slipped out into the docking bay, followed by what looked like a red-and-gold merchant schooner.

But this vessel was not that at all.

The Mutati outrider at the controls taxied out into space, and went through the detailed checklist he had learned at the training camp on Dij, just prior to its destruction. He had prepared carefully for this moment, and would only get one opportunity to make good.

Today my life and death meet, he thought, feeling supreme joy at the prospect of his final journey to heaven.

This Demolio suicide mission had been dispatched prior to the attack against the factory by a pair of Human escapees from a Mutati prison moon. The vessel had no long-range communication device aboard, so the pilot didn't know what had happened. He also could not be called back by the Zultan and diverted to a more significant planet. The timing of the attack had been predetermined, and he had waited in deep space for the moment to arrive.

The pilot looked forward to his own glorious death, and to his ascension into heaven. It would be wonderful, but in a way he wished he might have gone on the Demolio mission later. In recent weeks he'd been hearing intriguing rumors of an instantaneous cross-galactic communication system under development by the Mutati Kingdom. Everyone was curious about how it worked, and how it would enhance the war effort.

But it all seemed like another universe to him, another life. The fate of the galactic communication system was just one of many loose ends he had left behind, along with family, friends, and his career as a construction superintendent.

He would never know that the Mutatis were investigating the Human's own cross-space nehrcom system, based upon information secretly provided by Jacopo Nehr's brother. Through their own experiments the Mutatis had confirmed what they were told by the turncoat Human, that nehrcoms only operated between land-based, planetary installations. The only exceptions to this were the lower quality relay transmissions that could be made to and from space stations or spaceships that were near nehrcom planets. At that very moment, the Mutatis were building nehrcom stations on distant star systems, to conduct their initial tests.

Nor would the pilot ever learn the strategy behind his own demise. The Mutati High Command was willing to sacrifice not only terramutati outriders such as himself, but any Mutatis, such as Seatels, who might still reside on Human-controlled planets. He only had a narrow view of his mission, the scant but focused information that had been drilled into his mind by his trainers.

All thoughts faded now. The shapeshifter had completed his final checklist, making all of the necessary settings. The kamikaze torpedo was heading for its target, accelerating. . . .

From somewhere, Tesh Kori heard a piercing, high-pitched whine that hurt her ears, followed by a rumbling sound, and a huge explosion.

Chapter Sixty

I cannot bear the thought of my own death. If only there were a way to prevent it, I would give anything. Well, *almost* anything. I'd have to keep something to sustain me in my long life, after all.

—Doge Lorenzo del Velli, private notes

The elegant nobleman hated "up-shuttles." Even when he ordered the pilots to ascend as slowly as possible through the atmosphere, the Doge Lorenzo del Velli always got nosebleeds. They were more of an irritation and an embarrassment than anything else, since trillions of his followers in the Alliance gave him superhuman, almost godlike attributes. But inside shuttles, doing something commonplace, just going from planet to pod station, Lorenzo had to sit with a white handkerchief over his nose, glaring around to make sure that no one was staring at him.

At mid-morning, he rode with a handful of military officers, bureaucrats, and his usual entourage of personal attendants. None of them seemed to pay any attention to his condition, and certainly none dared mention it to him. From experience, they knew he snapped back whenever that particular subject came up.

For this up-shuttle ride, he was not, however, going to a pod station. Instead, he was making his first inspection trip to EcoStation, having received confirmation from his officers that they had taken control of it away from the remnants of Noah Watanabe's defenders. He wanted to see the famous orbital facility firsthand and make decisions about the future of the asset. His first inclination had been to destroy it, now that his son was not there, but his bankers had told him he could make money with the operation, just as Noah did. This intrigued the Doge.

The southwest corner of the Ecological Demonstration Project compound had not been so easy to take over, but that morning the Guardians had finally fallen there, too. His troops had captured some of them, but most had disappeared into the surrounding forests and hills, melting away with high efficiency. His Red Berets had searched for them and had found a few. They were living off the land, surviving like animals in the wild. Noah Watanabe, the master ecologist, must have taught them how to do that.

The Doge smiled bitterly as he dabbed at his nose. Those forest rats were more trouble than they were worth. He had called off the search operations, since they were too costly and not worth the effort. Noah's Guardians were useless as a fighting force now. Lorenzo didn't worry about them anymore.

Still, he had a certain amount of grudging respect for them.

Of course, he could throw mininukes or pulse bombs into the woods, but he didn't want the political fallout that would certainly result from the use of such controversial weapons. No, it wasn't worth it at all.

Doge Lorenzo had not taken a complete inventory, but it seemed to him that every bone in his body ached from the night of ardor he'd spent with Francella. They had made love in virtually every room of her brother's house, which was on the grounds of the Ecological Demonstration Project that the Guardians had abandoned. For days, the woman had been in a frenzy that alternated between rage and passion. One moment she would tear apart Noah's offices or the parlor of his home, and the next she would want Lorenzo to make love to her, right in the middle of the rubble.

The Doge had not participated in the destruction himself, except as an observer, but he had found the violence tremendously exciting, and stimulating. Francella's emotions and sexuality were raw and almost primal, although she was also highly intelligent, with a wide knowledge of business and cultural matters. She could speak at length about virtually any subject. Then, in the privacy of a bedroom (or any other room for that matter), she might become someone entirely different, as if a switch had been activated.

He sighed. Lorenzo had never met anyone like her, and didn't expect that he ever would.

Only the day before, he had received a paternity report that he had requested. His investigators had confirmed to him that Anton Glavine really was his son, and Francella was the mother.

Initially, Lorenzo had been angry at her for concealing such an important matter from him for all of these years. In the face of his rage she finally apologized in tears, and insisted that she'd only done it for his own good, since she hadn't thought that he wanted a bastard child to interfere with any sons he might have sired through marriage. With years passing, and the Doge having only daughters, Francella had claimed she'd wanted to tell him the truth, but had never found the right opportunity to do so. She also admitted not feeling comfortable as a parent herself, and hoping against hope that Lorenzo would one day father a son by legitimate means, thus creating an untainted noble heir.

Eventually Lorenzo had told her he forgave her, and this was true for the most part, since he had never been able to stay angry with Francella for any reason during the more than two decades of their relationship. On a certain level, just below his full consciousness, he had always known that he was a slave to his passion for her. He always tried not to dwell on any negative thoughts about Prince Saito's daughter, or the way he felt for her. He only knew for certain that he could not live without her, despite her selfish ways. . . .

The shuttle floated into a docking berth on the space station, and airlocks clicked into place. Lorenzo sniffled blood up his nostrils, trying not to be too loud. Gradually, as he stepped into the corridors of the space station with his officers, his nose stopped bleeding and he began to feel better.

Robots wearing red caps stood guard at doorways along the way. Some of the sentient machines were black, and others silver. Many had dents and metal patches. Lorenzo liked this group despite their appearance, and had rewarded them for saving his life by making them full-fledged Red Berets. They looked particularly proud this morning. As he rounded a corner, he saw their leader Jimu using a probe to interface with another machine.

Jimu had been expanding the number of machines under Doge Lorenzo's command, cleverly replicating them without the need for Human intervention. They recycled old parts, found their own raw materials, and fabricated replacement parts. The machines were loyal, efficient, and cost him very little, since they took care of themselves. It was an ideal situation.

But as he looked around at the green-and-brown walls and peered into empty classrooms and offices, knowing his son Anton had been there before him, his mood darkened.

He worried over the young man's welfare. Both anxious and furious at the situation, he swung an arm at a hanging plant in one of the lunchrooms, and became entangled in it. The whole thing ripped loose from its ceiling hooks, and he fell with it over a table, cursing.

"Are you all right, Sire?" one of his aides said, running over to free him from the snarl of vines and leaves. "Oh Sire, you're injured."

"It's only a little nosebleed, you fool! I'm fine, fine. Now, get away from me."

Pushing the man out of the way and nearly tripping as he stepped away from the plant, the Doge issued a stream of expletives.

"Sorry, Sire, sorry," the hapless man said as he tripped and fell himself.

"How am I supposed to run the Alliance when I'm surrounded by idiots?" Lorenzo, asked, as he returned to the corridor and rejoined the officers who were showing him around.

The Doge was extremely worried about his newly-discovered son, and suspected that Noah was trying to maintain control over him as a means of leverage, for his own selfish ends. Francella had said that Noah knew all along about the real parentage of Anton, and that he had assumed the role of an attentive family friend when he knew all along that he was really the young man's genetic uncle.

It enraged Lorenzo how Noah was putting Anton in danger to further his own schemes. The Doge was even beginning to believe Francella's claim that Noah had been responsible for the death of his own father and for other crimes, while putting up the public persona of the great galactic ecologist.

As far as Lorenzo was concerned, the meeting that Noah

had demanded with him must have only been a stalling technique, to give him more time to escape, undoubtedly with treasures he had stolen from Canopa. Noah Watanabe had proven himself to be anything but a man of high morals.

The inspection tour took until early afternoon, after which Lorenzo caught a shuttle back to Canopa. He was especially looking forward to another tryst with Francella, which should put him in a better mood than he was in now.

His attaché Pimyt met him at the shuttle station. The furry little Hibbil strutted up and asked, "Any sign of Noah or your son?"

"Nothing."

The Hibbil spoke nervously as he walked beside his much taller superior. "I have a groundjet waiting to take you to the pod station, Sire, for your trip back to Elysoo."

"I'm going back to the compound first," Lorenzo said.

"But you've conquered it, and the space station, too. What more do you need to do?"

"Since when do you question me, or direct my actions? I will notify you when I am ready to return."

"But much important business needs your attention, Sire. Diplomats and other dignitaries are at the palazzo, anxious to speak with you."

Stopping, Lorenzo confronted the little alien. "I don't answer to you," he said, "or to any of the *dignitaries,* as you call them."

"It's that CorpOne woman, isn't it, Sire? Pardon me for saying so, but she's dangerous. I hear she holds aspirations of becoming Doge herself."

"Preposterous! There has never been a female Doge, and there never will be!"

"I'm sure you're right, Sire. I'm just providing you with

the information, for you to handle as you see fit."

"As for 'that CorpOne woman,' I'll spend as much time with her as I please, whenever I please."

"Of course. My apologies, Doge Lorenzo. I only have your welfare in mind."

"As soon as you get back to the palazzo, send for my wife. Have her waiting for me when I return."

"When will that be?"

"Just get her there. And say nothing to her of my whereabouts, or the military operation we conducted against Noah Watanabe."

The furry little attaché bowed very low to the ground, and hurried off to do as he was told.

Priding himself on his ability to manage relationships with several women at once, Lorenzo intended to make love to both Meghina and Francella in the next few days, but would keep them far apart because of the loathing the women felt toward each other.

Chapter Sixty-One

In sentient machines, as in biological creatures, allegiance is always emotion-based. And that makes it notoriously unreliable.

—Thinker, internal observation

On the planet Ignem, far beneath the orbital ring containing the Inn of the White Sun, the flat-bodied robot moved with uncharacteristic vigor, examining each mechanical soldier in the parade formation, using his interface probe to check their operating programs.

Thinker had to move quickly. There wasn't much time to get the army ready. Beyond the formation, he saw smoke drifting over a volcano. But that was normal for Ignem, and certainly not the problem that had him so very, very concerned.

The robot's sensor probe darted out of one hand and snapped into a port on the side of the robot in front of him, making its interface connection.

Data poured into Thinker's analytical brain. After only a few seconds, he shook his head. Another defective machine. Too many of them. Simultaneously, his officer robots moved along the ranks, checking the battle fitness of other soldiers.

"Remove this robot from the ranks," Thinker said to an aide behind him, "and take him in for servicing." Thinker downloaded a list of needed repairs into the robot, disconnected his probe, and moved on to the next one.

The next in line was not really a robot at all. Giovanni Nehr stood ramrod straight, wearing machinelike armor that he had received after volunteering to serve the mechanical army. Gio's request had been unusual, and totally unanticipated by the robot leader. At first, Thinker had resisted.

"I'll be the best fighter in the army, sir," he had promised. "Just give me the chance to prove myself, please." He went on to admit that he'd had a falling out with his famous brother, and would prefer to follow an entirely new career.

"Well, this would certainly qualify as that," Thinker had said.

The two of them had laughed and clasped hands, metal against flesh.

Now, Thinker thought the new recruit looked quite good despite the dents in his armor. It occurred to the robot leader, though, that he could not interface with this Human to download the contents of his mind, the way he could with the mechanical soldiers. How useful it would be, Thinker realized, if he had that ability, since he still had questions about Giovanni Nehr.

For several seconds, Thinker paused and allowed his internal programming to search through the various data banks, determining if a complete machine to Human interface was possible. The data revealed a number of obstacles, but he thought it just might be possible. At the first opportunity he would perform a deeper analysis, and see if the technology could be developed.

Saying nothing to Nehr, Thinker moved on down the line.

The recycled fighting robots looked at their commander with sensor-blinking surprise as he hurried among them, inspecting components and issuing terse commands. In the past he had moved slowly and deliberately, a robot of thought, not of action. But he always knew he could get around quicker if he had to; it had only been necessary to activate one of the backup programs he had for emergencies.

The situation he faced at this time was exactly that. . . .

In the afternoon, Thinker inspected his manufacturing and assembly plants, a hive of buildings constructed at the jewel-like base of a volcano. Like the robots under his command, and like himself for that matter, the structures and machinery inside were all cobbled together from whatever parts the enterprising robots could locate, scavenged from dump heaps all over the galaxy and brought here.

He could order replacement parts from the Hibbils, but that would be prohibitively expensive. Besides, he didn't trust those deceptive little fur balls, having discovered some of the insidious programs they had installed in sentient machines. Thinker preferred to make his own new parts, or rebuild old ones. Here on Ignem, his blast furnaces heated up metals, plax, and other materials for re-use. He had assembly lines in which mobile and fixed robots worked on old bodies and interior components.

Deep in thought, Thinker strutted down the main aisle of his largest assembly plant. For a moment he paused to watch the blue light of a laser soldering machine as it fused the sealing strip on a synaptic board, one of the brain components of a Series 1405 automaton. He hated using such old machines, since they didn't have nearly as many features as the newer ones, but at least this series had always been reliable.

Yet, his thoughts were elsewhere.

Jimu and his squad were supposed to have returned by now. Instead, Thinker had learned they were staying with the Doge, as members of his elite Red Beret corps. From the reports reaching Thinker, he knew that the initial mission had been successful, as Jimu had saved the Doge's life. But in doing so, the infernal robot had ingratiated himself so much to Lorenzo that the nobleman had praised Jimu and offered him a career in the Red Berets . . . an offer that was accepted.

Jimu is no longer under my command, Thinker thought. He had sent numerous messages to Jimu by courier, but had received no response. Still, Thinker had obtained a great deal of information about his activities.

At this very moment, the wayward robot was doing something very, very troubling. On the resource-rich planet of Canopa, under the auspices of the powerful Doge, he was increasing the number of fighting robots under his own command. The original squadron of twenty had multiplied, and at last report comprised more than four hundred. Jimu was highly intelligent, with fine internal programming. On more than one occasion, he had proven his survival abilities, and Thinker, recognizing talent, had promoted him.

But perhaps the promotion had been premature. In retrospect, it seemed to him that Jimu had been exceedingly emotional by robotic standards, overzealous and too dedicated to Humans. It was a fine line, but clearly Jimu had gone too far. He should have completed his mission, saving the Doge's life, and returned. Now he was something of a loose cannon.

This concerned Thinker greatly, but not for selfish reasons, not because Jimu was in a position of high influence and becoming well-known in his own right. To the contrary, Thinker's motivations were pure, and he honestly believed that Jimu needed guidance. A sentient robot couldn't just go off half-cocked and start building an army. He needed extensive education and preparation before taking that step. He needed a great deal of wisdom and moral instruction, and a huge amount of specific knowledge in his data banks. Otherwise, the army would not receive the proper programming, and could become a liability instead of an asset.

In particular, without the fail-safe mechanisms that Thinker always installed in the programming of sentient machines who followed him, they could go out of control and cause a lot of damage. Thinker had seen it happen before. It was called a robotic chain reaction. After one machine went bad it infected others, and they all went bad. Like a mob or a wolf pack, they took on new and menacing personalities, wreaking havoc against any biological organism unfortunate enough to cross their path.

Jimu had the fail-safe in his own programming. Thinker had installed it himself when he interfaced with him. But Jimu still didn't know how to build an army; he didn't know how to reprogram other robots to keep them from breaking down, and perhaps going berserk.

Thinker had no personal concerns, no petty jealousies. If Jimu had expressed a desire to build an army himself, and if it made sense to do so, Thinker would have set him on a training course to make it possible. But that had never occurred. The proper procedures had not been followed.

I should have handled him more carefully, he thought glumly, *given him a tight internal program that compelled him to complete the one mission only. I'm no perfect army builder myself.*

Hearing a machine voice, Thinker swiveled his head and looked around. The plant superintendent, Saccary, stood behind him. A small robot with an unusual porcelain-like face containing synthetic Human features, Saccary asked,

"I have a hundred more of these automatons backed up for repairs, with worn out synaptic board sealing strips, but I'm running out of parts."

"I'll see what I can do."

"Thank you, sir. May I give you a list of other parts we need?"

Thinker nodded stiffly and then moved on, accompanied by the superintendent.

With the Jimu matter dominating his concerns, Thinker slipped into a deep mental state in which he split his exterior self away from the inner core of his consciousness. The exterior self continued to interact with Saccary, accessing data banks for information and conversing with him, but at the core of his conscience Thinker didn't hear or sense any of that. A volcano could erupt, sending everything flying and tumbling, and if his brain survived he might go on with his line of deep, uninterrupted thought.

In all of the galaxy, no robot was more altruistic or loyal to Humans than Thinker, more totally selfless. He knew this to be so with an almost absolute certainty, since he had downloaded the programs of thousands of robots into his own circuitry, and had analyzed them. Thinker did not consider himself morally superior out of any sense of pride; rather, he knew it to be the simple, unadorned truth.

Now he needed to deal with the crisis quickly, before Jimu built a force that was too large. At the pace the rogue robot had been increasing his numbers, he would one day exceed Thinker's own army, which had slowed its growth rate due to a limited availability of key raw materials. Jimu, with his central location and the blessing of Doge Lorenzo del Velli, had no such limitations.

And Thinker had another reason in mind, a very deep and specific worry, beyond any general concern about robotic breakdowns and chain reactions. Thinker had heard about the Doge's attacks on Noah Watanabe, and was horrified by them. As far as Thinker was concerned, Noah was the machine leader's own Human equivalent, the most altruistic and untainted of his kind. From the reports of travelers stopping at the Inn of the White Sun, Thinker had been inspired by stories of Noah Watanabe and the idealistic mission of the Guardians. He had always hoped to meet the man one day, and perhaps that day was coming.

Noah was the most indispensable member of his race, just as Thinker himself was to his own. Even robots, in Thinker's alternate but highly informed way of looking at things, constituted a racial type. The mechanicals were sentient, after all, and had emotions and desires, just like biologicals. Intelligent machines were born in a sense, could reproduce themselves, and could die. Just because they had no flesh or cellular structures meant nothing. Thinker had his own definitions.

Of supreme importance, Thinker did not want Jimu's force to contribute to the annihilation of Noah Watanabe . . . and he intended to counter that. He would still make efforts to contact Jimu and talk sense into him, but didn't hold out much hope for that.

Like a sleepwalker, Thinker strutted across a landing field toward a gleaming white shuttle. With only a surface awareness of his surroundings, he boarded the craft for the ride up to the Inn of the White Sun.

During the few minutes required for the trip, Thinker searched his data banks for important information. With all of the facts that he collected around the galaxy, constantly interfacing with thousands of robots, he had the equivalent of an intelligence operation—a spy network—within his own internal circuitry. Noting that Noah Watanabe and his grid-plane had been spotted on podships and in pod stations in recent weeks, Thinker made a chart of the Guardian leader's travels around the galaxy.

In actuality, the robot was going through a probability program. There were gaps in the information, but he had enough to determine that Noah was no longer on Canopa, and no longer on board his orbital station high over the planet, either.

The fugitive and a small entourage had—with near statistical certainty—escaped to a remote planet in the Plevin Star System.

Chapter Sixty-Two

> We Parviis are greatly advantaged by our size, or lack of it, depending upon your perspective. With the enhancement of our magnification systems we can appear to be what we are not, while still retaining what Humans are not.
>
> —The Parvii View of Evolution

In the thunder and blur of the mysterious explosion, Tesh, Anton and their companions felt an emptiness in the pits of their stomachs, and a sensation of extreme speed. Subi shouted that stabilizers had automatically extruded from the undercarriage of the grid-plane, attaching the craft to the floor of the bunker. Inside the cabin of the plane, objects were flying around and things were slamming into the outside of the fuselage.

Everyone held on, and they made heroic efforts to protect the still-unconscious Noah. After attempts by the others, Eshaz was able to reach Noah and wedge himself in a corner by the command console, while keeping a powerful, protective grip on the Human.

The movement settled down, and as Tesh looked at Eshaz, who was shifting his hold on Noah, she thought the Tulyan looked almost maternal, the way he cradled the unconscious man's head and kept a blanket over him. It seemed incongruous for her to be feeling positive thoughts about one of her mortal enemies, but she couldn't avoid the feelings.

As if he were a doctor himself, Eshaz checked the healing pad on one side of Noah's head, satisfying himself that it was still secure and pumping nutrients into the wound. The reptilian Tulyan looked up. For a moment he exchanged glances with Tesh, and she saw kindness in his slitted, pale gray eyes. Then Eshaz again focused his attention on Noah, and whispered something to him.

Through the thick windowglax of the bunker, Tesh saw that the river was no longer visible. Instead it looked like they were in outer space, with blackness and flickering dots of light marking distant suns.

She heard Anton and Subi wondering if the cosmic view might be caused by some sort of a projection mechanism, but suddenly she had an entirely different, much more startling idea. Could it possibly be?

Abruptly, she ran to the exit hatch and touched a button to open it. Without waiting for the automatic stairway to descend and lock into place, she jumped out of the gridplane and landed on the floor of the bunker.

"I'll be right back!" she shouted. "Everyone wait here."

Before anyone could react, she ran for a passageway.

She heard shouts of confusion and concern behind her, with Anton running after her with the others, calling her name. "Tesh! Tesh! Where are you going? Come back!"

But none of them could keep up with her, or begin to imagine where she had gone. . . .

Tesh did something only a Parvii could do. To anyone observing her, she seemed to disappear. She was miniature now, having switched off the magnification system that made her look as large as the giant Humans. She ran with a blur of speed, much faster than she could have moved in her magnified state, which interfered with her natural abilities. Like most Parviis, Tesh preferred her normal size. It provided her with so many more intriguing options, involving speed, access, and personal safety.

She stood in what looked like a rocky passageway now. She touched the walls around her, felt the cold hardness. And knew something with absolute certainty.

This is not rock.

Finding the subtle but telltale burrowing marks she was looking for, she entered a minuscule opening in the stony surface, like a bee going into a hive hole. Once inside, she followed the traditional maze of passageways and now-dormant signal scramblers, designed to keep intruders and probing electronics out. She knew the way well. It was essentially the same in every podship.

Within moments, she located the large sectoid chamber, the nerve center of the pod, still glowing with a faint green luminescence and humming in a barely audible tone. This surprised her, and gave her hope. But the walls were hard, as if fossilized. Could the creature regenerate itself, coming back from its long dormancy? She had heard of cases where this had actually occurred, and of others in which the sectoid chamber was the last portion of the creature to die, like a heart that continued to beat but no longer had the strength to sustain the rest of the body.

Tesh's own metabolism had been going at full speed, driving her forward. Suddenly it slowed, and she moved ahead cautiously. In shock, she stared at the unmistakable remains of a skeleton lying on the floor ahead of her, a humanoid like herself and around the same diminutive size, with streaks of dark green and black on the bones.

A long-dead Parvii, one of her own people.

She murmured an ancient, silent prayer over the body, felt an immense welling of emotion. Even though her kinsmen were numerous, she had always been taught that even one death was significant, since it was a loss suffered by the swarm.

If uninterrupted by calamity, Parviis lived comparatively long lives, substantially more than her own seven hundred twelve years, but they were still mortal. They could be killed in accidents, or could fall victim to specific, odious diseases.

While this one lay on its side now, it appeared to have died and rigidified in a crouching position, as if it had wanted to spring out into space and rejoin a swarm, but perhaps had been too injured to do so. Crouching for a time after death, the Parvii's flesh and internal organs had fallen away, and sometime afterward the bones fell over.

It was as Tesh had suspected. Their grid-plane had not landed in an abandoned Mutati military bunker at all. Rather, they had entered the cargo hold of what had originally been a podship that crashed into the riverbank centuries ago—and which was subsequently found by Mutatis and converted to their purposes. Hence the thick glax windows, ceramic airlocks, and added rooms. The Mutatis must have had some means of communicating with their hydromutati cousins from there, the Seatels, perhaps through some sort of technology that interacted with the telepathy of the Seatels.

Later, perhaps from an adverse military operation, or a disease, the Mutatis no longer occupied the bunker. For some reason, the Seatels were left behind. Then, when Noah's Guardians arrived, the hydromutati telepaths killed them . . . and were about to kill Noah, Tesh, and the rest of their group when the planet exploded.

But why had the podship crashed on Plevin Four in the first place? Something must have gone wrong with the Parvii pilot . . . an illness, a misjudgment? Or some failure by the podship itself. Such events were rare, but over the course of millenniums did occur.

Another realization hit her.

We are no longer on Plevin Four. It doesn't exist anymore.

The cosmic blackness and flickering, distant suns were stark confirmation, seen around drifting chunks of the dead world. The podship, even with improvised Mutati window walls, had survived the explosion. In its present state, with the body as cold and hard as stone, the podship had effectively armored itself against the explosion, and this had not been compromised by the Mutati alterations.

The planet is gone, and we are drifting in space. What happened?

She could not imagine. An entire planet! She had been in the midst of a huge explosion.

Above all, Tesh could not shake the intense sadness over her lost comrade, even though she had never known him personally. But she had no time for emotion.

Podships were hardy creatures, and it might just be possible to revive this one. She had to hurry. The bunker was tightly sealed, but soon her companions could run out of air. She did not have that problem. It was one of the principle advantages of Parvii evolution.

Chapter Sixty-Three

The Eye of the Swarm is in telepathic contact with his Parvii swarms, all over the galaxy. It is a vast morphic field, but has been subject to increasing problems, running parallel with the disintegration of the cosmic web.

—Thinker's data bank: *Galactic Leaders*

They were as thick as locusts, but did not fly over hills and crops, looking for plants to ravage. Instead, they journeyed from one star system to another on a mission that was nearly as old as the galaxy itself. A distant observer might have wondered what was moving so rapidly through the heavens, and would have undoubtedly guessed wrong.

At Woldn's command, the swarm appeared to take the shape of a comet, then an asteroid belt, and then a string of planets flung out of orbit by God. These were shapeshifters on an immense scale, a malleable multitude that covered much of a galactic sector at a time . . . and even more, if they switched on their personal magnification systems simultaneously. But individually, they were exceedingly small, like tiny pixies or fairies.

For more than a thousand years, Woldn had been the Eye of the Swarm, the leader of the entire Parvii race. At the center of the formation, he flew with them now, speeding past brilliant suns and multicolored nebulas, swooping, diving, circling, going faster than podships or as slow as a Human walking through space. At times, Woldn felt like an artist of movement, the conductor of a great galactic symphony.

Some of his followers rose through the ranks because they displayed special talents, the most gifted of whom were wranglers who specialized in the capture of wild, migrating podships, and pilots who could guide the mysterious sentient spacecraft on long journeys.

Periodically, the wranglers and pilots were given rest between assignments, time on their own that could last for years in succession. In the typical lifetime of a Parvii, that was not very long at all. Woldn himself had lived for nearly two millennia.

I am the Eye of the Swarm.

At will, Woldn's thoughts expanded and contracted as he guided his beloved throng, directing their movements telepathically, knowing their collective and individual thoughts as if they were part of his own body. He made them curve upward and then down, like a rollercoaster in space, and then formed them into a twisting Mobius strip that looked like a contorted conveyor belt.

He was in fact the eye of many, many Parvii swarms in all sectors of the galaxy, controlling them with his powerful beaming thoughts, keeping track of them at all times, no matter how far away they were. His minions had telepathic powers as well, but on nowhere near the scale of his. Woldn's abilities—while still subject to the limitations of psychic breakdowns that affected all members of his race, and inhibited by an increasing number of telepathic dead zones in the galaxy—were historically unparalleled. He was the chosen one, the most gifted of the gifted, capable of wrangling and piloting podships, capable of stretching his thoughts, and his swarms, across vast distances.

It was his raison d'être to capture and control every

podship possible. His swarms were relentless, and he would send millions of the tiny breed on a mission to capture just a few podships, or only one. That's how valuable the sentient Aopoddae were to them, for they were the best means by which the various galactic races could travel across vast distances of space at hyper speeds.

Had they been savvy businessmen, with avaricious hearts like those of the merchant princes, the Parviis could have turned this monopoly into huge profits and used the funds to build an empire. But they had no use for money; it was not the currency of their existence. They did not live on planets or have any desire for worldly things. Beautiful objects meant nothing to them. They did not even need the oxygen of a planet, and traveled through space without any sort of breathing apparatus.

Parviis measured their accomplishments in terms of the success of their race. In the overall perspective, the individual was of little consequence to them, for he could do almost nothing without the collective strength of his companions.

Even so, one Parvii inside the sectoid chamber of a podship—when trained and entrusted with that position—could control that marvelous creature, guiding it though the treacherous pathways of space. But as many podships as they controlled, there were always wild pods out in the far reaches. Though some of their migration patterns were known, no one knew where the Aopoddae came from originally, whether they were generated through some sexual liaison or just appeared out of the ether.

Woldn led his swarm to the dark side of the Tulyan Starcloud, a region where the sun never shone. He had received intelligence reports from Parvii operatives that this was where the bronze, scaly Tulyans were hiding podships, reports that he had picked up telepathically. They told him exactly where to look.

But the ships were not there anymore. Were they all out on the podways, transporting Tulyans to unknown regions?

Stretching his swarm out and using all of the eyes of its members, Woldn picked up their thoughts, and beheld a region of space as large as four ordinary solar systems. Though he usually paid little attention to beauty, here he felt truly stirred to the depths of his soul. This was one of the most spectacular regions he had ever seen, very nearly as lovely as the Parvii Fold, that sacred galactic region where his people bred, and where they went to die when their long lifetimes wound down.

Cosmic mists floated through the starcloud, a rainbow of swirling gas that at times seemed to take on magical shapes. He'd heard a legend that the mists conformed to the vivid, collective imaginations of the Tulyans themselves, and that the entire region, with its islands of land, were products of their minds.

Woldn doubted if that could be true. The Tulyans had not been powerful enough to defeat his people, so he did not see how such an extrasensory feat could be possible. After all, if they were that powerful they could just visualize weapons to defeat the Parviis, something customized to block the telepathic signals that controlled the swarms. He and his minions had been here before, and occasionally made captures of hidden podships in this region. But the Tulyans were clever, with a variety of tricks in their repertoire.

He steered the swarm through a thick mist that grew intensely red as he got into it, and then became darker and completely encompassed the multitude of Parviis. Soon Woldn could see nothing at all. He sensed the fear and mounting panic of his people around him, but ordered them to change the configuration of the formation and continue on, which they did, in the shape of a wide, spinning fan blade.

Faster and faster they spun as they flew, in an effort to dissipate the mist by sweeping it out of position, but Woldn felt something resisting his efforts, as if the legend was true and the Tulyans really were holding the mist in place through the collective power of their minds.

Then he felt something give way. The mist separated, and Woldn saw dozens of podships floating in the vacuum of space, tethered together. For a moment, he hesitated, as this was more than they usually had at one time. In the clearing, shuttles approached the podships, and Woldn saw Tulyans inside the shuttles, peering out of the portholes with their slitted gray eyes. They were so peculiar in appearance, looking in his direction, seeing their Parvii enemies.

He felt his swarm wanting to surge forward, but he held them back, and watched as the shuttles moved between the gray-and-black pods, depositing Tulyans into each spaceship. Woldn was amused by their pathetic effort to escape.

As the Tulyan pilots took control of the podships, the vessel hulls metamorphosed, taking on scaly, reptilian skin and Tulyan facial features. The podships got underway, and accelerated. But as fast as they were, they could not escape, not even on the podways. The pursuing swarm split into as many segments as there were pods and ran each of them down. Woldn remained behind, but experienced the simultaneous captures telepathically.

In short order the Parviis took control of the small fleet, and as their pilots went to work the podships changed back to their original blimp-like appearances. The Eye of the Swarm had all of the sentient spacecraft brought to him, and ordered his people to imprison the Tulyans inside the shuttles. He didn't kill his enemies, but refused to listen when they protested that they needed the podships to perform important ecological work on a galactic scale.

"I sentence all of you to retirement!" Woldn shouted. As he spoke, his people uttered the words simultaneously to the Tulyans inside the shuttles, producing an eerie synchronized voice.

Muttering with displeasure, the bronze-scaled aliens did not fight back. As big as they were, Tulyans had traditionally been a non-violent race. They also knew they were powerless against such a formidable enemy.

In short order Woldn led his swarm, the captured podships, and the imprisoned Tulyans to a region of deep space, where he assigned a pilot to each craft and turned them loose on the podways, increasing the galactic transport fleet under his command.

This had all happened before, an eternal cycle of dispute between the two races. The Tulyans, no matter their losses and inadequacies, continually tried to regain control of podships and hide them from their unrelenting Parvii competitors, using different methods of concealment.

And these newly captured Tulyans, like others before them, would be used as bargaining chips for timeseeing services the Parviis wanted from those few Tulyans who had such abilities, so that the Parviis could obtain reports on events a short distance in the future. While the most gifted timeseers had only imperfect abilities, it was, nonetheless, a highly-desired service to the tiny, swarming creatures.

Chapter Sixty-Four

> In a special corner of my imagination there is no distinction between thought and reality, as one melds gently into the other, along a vast continuum. There, perception takes on substance, and thoughts are as tangible as anything perceived with the known senses.
>
> —Noah Watanabe,
> *Drifting in the Ether* (unpublished notes)

A short while ago, the dreaming man had been immersed in a cacophony of chaos.

In the din and violence of his physical awareness, he had tried to prepare himself for a realm where he would have no more need for thoughts, no worries or desires to clutter his mind. He had been wondering what sort of reality that might be, and if, on some level, he would still be conscious of it. The answer to these questions meant a great deal to him.

But clarity was elusive.

For some time now, Noah Watanabe had been seeking doorways out of the darkness that encompassed him. He had been sending mental probes in various directions, searching for escape from the barless prison of his comatose mind.

His mind was the key to his body, for his physical form could not function without mental impulses. But he sensed that his intellect was also the key to something far greater than one mortal body and all of the trivial details that made up its daily routines. He felt a tremendous frustration as he realized this with absolute certainty, while his brain was completely locked up and unable to attain its potential.

Once more he tried to escape, and again he failed. Unable to come out of the coma, Noah's thoughts focused on a prison within a prison. He re-experienced the onslaught against EcoStation by Red Beret forces, saw them running through the corridors, shouting commands. In painstaking detail he relived the attack, and his escape in the grid-plane.

Through the porthole, he saw the Doge's red gunships again, firing at the escaping vessel, tearing through the hull just as Subi was increasing the acceleration. Only moments away from freedom.

In the void between the spacecraft, Noah saw the path of enemy projectiles as they sped toward him. As yet, nothing had hit Noah or any of his companions.

For a long, lingering moment, Noah awaited the inevitable, knowing there was no escape from that fate, or the one that held him tightly now. Silence encased him, the eerie stillness of impending death.

The grid-plane was not going fast enough!

The projectiles drew closer. They were right outside the porthole now, only a fraction of a second from impact. He flinched, then felt searing pain. He tried to scream, but in the vault of darkness he had no voice.

Chapter Sixty-Five

Visual observation is not the same as confirmation.
—Sulu Granby, Philosopher of Old Mars

Resembling a small, bronze-scaled dragon, Eshaz knelt beside the comatose form of Noah, who lay on the carpeted deck of the grid-plane, with a blanket over him and a pillow beneath his head. His Human friend had not been doing well; the vital signs had declined precipitously to a dangerous level. In addition, the Tulyan's own bodily aches and pains had been worsening of late—the apparent link with the decline in Timeweb—but he tried not to think about all those things.

Instead, he gazed off into the distance, seeing through the walls of the grid-plane and the damaged, stranded podship that encompassed it and floated in space. Debris from the planetary explosion bobbed near them like flotsam on the sea, great chunks of rock and turf. But none of that inhibited his vision in the least. He saw through it all, to the other side.

With slitted gray eyes, Eshaz peered far into the galaxy, as if through a child's looking glass. But this was no juvenile activity. Nothing had ever been easy for him, since he had always taken his responsibilities seriously. His ancient ability permitted him to gaze far across the galaxy, to stars and planets and his own starcloud, floating like an oasis in a vast wasteland, most of which was entirely devoid of life.

Home.

Whenever he peered into the galaxy, he always liked to start out this way, making certain the sacred Tulyan homeland was still intact, that the Council Chamber was lit, and everything was all right. Considering the tenuous state of the galaxy, this was not always a certainty. There were no distance or time factors diminishing the sighting. He was peering into the present, not the past. Like using a super zoom lens that spanned the curvatures, folds, and distances of time and space.

A tear of relief ran down the bronze, scaly skin of his face. The legendary Tulyan Starcloud floated serenely in space, looking no different from this distant vantage than it had long ago. He knew, because he had lived for nearly a million standard years.

The visual confirmation gave him great comfort, but on this occasion he took only a moment to look in that direction, because of a pressing matter that required his attention. Sadly, there were so many of them nowadays, an acceleration of bad events.

Refocusing, he saw a tiny Parvii woman exploring the hidden passageways and chambers of the stranded podship that contained his grid-plane. As was the case with all Tulyans, Eshaz's ability to see Parviis in this paranormal manner was limited: for unknown reasons, he and his comrades could not see their tiny enemies in swarms, but occasionally they could see individuals, especially when the individual was far from the center of a swarm.

With a start, Eshaz recognized the Parvii woman.

Tesh!

He'd thought something was strange about her, but had been unable to determine what. Though he knew Parviis could alter their size, he hadn't suspected her of being one of them. But he had no time for personal reproach. Something was far more important than that, or than the control of a single sentient pod.

Eshaz, like all Tulyans, could see Timeweb, the exceedingly strong, hidden strands that connected an entire galaxy. He saw that this podship was hung up on one of the strands, and that it had been propelled into that position by the explosion on Plevin Four. What caused such a catastrophe? He had no idea.

He spotted a tiny rip in the web adjacent to the podship—a defect just starting to form in the fabric of space. It was an early stage timehole, barely discernible to his trained eye, and not visible to other galactic races at all. If left unchecked, it would grow in severity, eventually reaching a dangerous advanced stage, when it was visible to Humans and other races. The most severe timeholes, if they occurred in proximity to planets, could rip portions of earth and rock away, sucking them into bottomless holes in the cosmos.

It was frustrating to him. Wherever he went in the galaxy he fixed these web defects, or thought he did, but frequently another one appeared only a short distance away. He had hoped that these ominous signs of galactic disintegration would reverse and either heal themselves or stop appearing, but that had not been the case at all.

This one, while small, was in a bad location, out in the middle of space by a vital, structural fold in the galaxy, where it could easily enlarge and cause serious havoc in an entire sector.

But he wasn't thinking so much about that. He had another thought in mind. Still kneeling by Noah, but not looking at him, he placed a scaly hand over the man's forehead, and felt the life ebbing away.

I must move quickly.

On impulse, Eshaz was about to attempt something he should not do without approval from the Council of Elders. But Noah Watanabe was a rare person, one who behaved more like a Tulyan than a Human. He truly cared about the environment, and for more than just one planet. Noah saw—or *sensed*—an interconnectedness spanning the galaxy, and galaxies linked with other galaxies.

But is he the one spoken of in our legends?

So many important questions, and so little time. Eshaz only knew one thing for certain, a visceral sense that saving Noah was far more important than trying to gain control of this podship, or even repairing the rip in Timeweb.

Using his free hand, the Tulyan reached overhead, and onlookers were startled to see him and Noah flicker in and out of view. Unknown to them, Eshaz had his scaly hand pressed against a torn spot on the web just above him.

With a shudder, he felt energy flowing from the rift, coursing through his body into Noah Watanabe. . . .

Chapter Sixty-Six

How do we measure the accomplishments of our lives? By this do we measure our happiness, or our despair.

—Anton Glavine, *Reflections*

The crew of the *Avelo*, following one of Captain Yuell's rare and prized treasure maps, made several passes around Wuxx Reef, in a blue binary star system. The yellowing parchment, which he had spread open on the bridge of the ship, described fully laden merchant prince schooners that were missing in that sector, but without precise information on the exact location of the wrecks.

In only a few hours, the adventurers struck pay dirt, locating a spice schooner that had crashed into a cave within the floating rock formation, so that it was not visible from the outside. They only found it by sending a scouting party into the cave in a speedplane, with the red-sashed captain at the controls.

The wreck contained a cargo of exotic Old Earth spices, in sealed, largely undamaged containers. Captain Yuell, with a wide-ranging knowledge of commodities and values, said that he would investigate before selling the salvaged goods, since some of the spices might be irreplaceable, now that Earth was destroyed.

"This cargo might even be needed by scientists to regenerate seeds," he theorized as Acey, Dux, and other crewmen loaded bags, chests, and barrels into the *Avelo*. "In fact, even without knowing what we can get for the haul, I'm going to award all of you a bonus. We're overdue for a celebration."

When the loading was completed, he patted Acey on the back, and added, "You and your cousin have done fine work for our little enterprise, and now you'll learn how we let our hair down." Ever since helping with the repair of the hydion engine, Acey had become one of his favorites, almost like a son. . . .

The following day, Captain Yuell took his treasure ship crew to the dusty planet of Adurian for a celebration. As the men strutted into a dimly-lit saloon they wore their finest clothes, with eye patches, bandanas, baggy trousers, and gleaming knives at their waists. Captain Yuell and the little Hibbil Mac Golden wore ceremonial swords.

"Stick with me, lads," the captain said to Acey and Dux, "and I'll teach you how to have a good time."

Most of the patrons in the crowded tavern were Adurians, looking like humanoids with small, antlike heads and bulbous, oversized eyes. But there were a handful of other races as well, chubby Kichis, tall Vandurians, and bearded Ordians. As the treasure crew entered, conversation halted, but resumed soon afterward when the visitors glared around.

"They don't want trouble with us," Mac Golden said, keeping his hand near his sword.

A curvaceous Jimlat woman, with a pretty but blockish face, smiled at Dux, causing the young man to blush.

"You like that one?" Yuell asked.

"Uh, I have a girlfriend waiting for me at home," Dux said, lying.

"Well, this is where we keep ourselves tuned up in the love department," Yuell said, with a wide grin. "Don't want to get rusty on these long voyages." He and the men laughed.

Like ancient Earth cowboys after a cattle drive, the crew drank heavily and gambled in the smoky main room. More Jimlat women emerged from back rooms, and mingled with the men. Even Acey had one on his lap, but Dux, being more shy, kept his distance. For a while, Dux even tried to avoid gambling, since he and Acey had already lost so much. But after a couple of "high-du" drink injections, he joined his friends in a card game.

By the time Dux slipped into one of the high-backed chairs, the game was getting boisterous, with the participants shouting at each other, and not always good-naturedly. As Mac Golden explained in his squeaky little voice, this was Endo, the favorite pastime of the hairless, homopod Adurians—a fast moving competition in which electronic cards changed their faces and numbers in the blink of an eye, reducing or increasing their values.

Each player had an electronic screen on the table in front of him, with cards flashing across the surface. If certain card combinations showed up, the player had to press a button quickly to select it, or lose the hand. Acey had the best luck with the cards that came up, and the quickest reactions of anyone at the table. No one, not even Dux, could even come close.

"Time to quit!" Captain Yuell exclaimed finally, as he rose to his feet. "We better get Acey out of here before he ruins the whole Adurian economy."

But just as he said this, Dux got his own winning hand on the screen, and he pressed the button. The screen locked in place, showing the faces of six Adurian women, side by side, each of them wearing matching sunbonnets. The word "WINNER" appeared on his screen in Galeng.

"Hey, look at this!" one of the treasure hunters exclaimed. "We've got another big winner here!"

But before Dux could celebrate, the faces on his screen changed, to pictures of Acey Zelk and Dux Hannah at the center, along with four blank faces, two on each side.

"What the. . . ." Unable to comprehend what he was seeing, Dux leaned close to the screen, and blinked his eyes in disbelief. The blank cards changed, to four uniformed men wearing hats marked "POLICE."

Dux's companions all said they had the same screens.

"Let's get outta here," Captain Yuell said, leading the way to the exit.

Just then, the front door of the saloon burst open, and white-uniformed Adurian police officers swarmed in. Yuell and Golden charged into their midst with swords drawn, scattering the officers with the aggressive attack. The rest of the treasure ship crew waded in behind them, swinging chairs, clubs, bottles, and anything else they could get their hands on. Acey got on top of the bar and leaped down on two officers, smashing both of them to the floor hard. This knocked one unconscious, and Acey head-butted the other one into a similar state, then jumped over the motionless Adurians and attacked others.

Dux did what he could himself, but he wasn't the fighter the others were. An Adurian officer hit him in the side of the face with a stun club, sending him reeling and tumbling back under a table. Dux tried to sit up, but felt a little dizzy. Nonetheless, he climbed out and hurtled himself against the police, swinging his fists and screaming obscenities at them.

The police officers had apparently expected their numerical superiority to be enough to take the motley treasure ship crew into custody, but soon discovered how wrong they were. The Adurians tried to draw their pistols from holsters, but only one of them pulled a gun free, and he didn't get an opportunity to use it, because Mac Golden severed his arm at the elbow with a swish of his sword. The injured Adurian ran from the saloon into the street, screaming and spurting gouts of blood. Other officers ran after him in terror, and most of those remaining in the saloon were on the floor, either unconscious or dead.

Just as Dux was fighting another, having punched him in the face, he heard someone shout, "Duck, Dux!"

Without delaying to consider why, Dux did as he was told. A fraction of a second later Captain Yuell fired one of the officers' own guns, a thunderous blast that blew the alien's head off only inches away from a startled Dux.

The captain then led a retreat. They made it to a shuttle and lifted off just before the shuttleport filled with police vehicles. As they rocketed upward, Dux saw police aircraft arrive and circle the landing field below.

"I didn't see any other shuttles down there," Mac Golden said, as he wiped his bloody sword on a cloth. "It'll take 'em awhile to mount a pursuit, and by then we should be long gone."

"But they can still catch us at the pod station," Acey said, "while we're waiting for a podship."

"Not so," the Hibbil said. "I checked the glyphreader before we went down to the surface. We'll have a wait of maybe fifteen minutes after arriving at the station, and then we're off on our next adventure."

The furry ship's purser, who prided himself on keeping track of important matters for the captain, proved to be correct.

When the entire crew was safely in outer space aboard their treasure ship, everyone surrounded Dux and Acey.

"What did you do to the Adurians?" Captain Yuell asked. "You guys are on their most wanted list."

"We didn't do much," Acey said.

"Aw, come on," Yuell said. "They had pictures of both of you."

"Well," Dux said, looking at Acey and then the captain, "maybe we should have told you this before, but we didn't think you would care."

"This sounds serious," Mac Golden said, moving close and staring up at Dux.

The teenagers went on to describe how they had destroyed the Mutati manufacturing facility on Dij, and how they had barely escaped with their lives.

"You should have told us that earlier," Captain Yuell said, scowling. "You put my entire crew at peril."

"We didn't think it would hurt going to an Adurian world," Acey said.

"Oh you didn't, did you?" Mac Golden said. The little Hibbil stomped his foot angrily. "Don't you boys know anything about politics?"

"Uh, we grew up in the backwoods of Siriki," Dux said. "We don't know much about stuff like that."

"Don't you know that the Mutatis and Adurians are allies?" Golden shouted.

Dux felt a flush of hotness in his face, and caught the nervous gaze of Acey. The two of them shrugged. . . .

Captain Yuell did not kick the boys off the ship. He said that they had learned their lesson, but obtained their promises not to keep any more important secrets from their crewmates. "We're your family now," he said. "I'm your Dad and Golden here is your Mom."

"Hey!" the Hibbil said. "I don't like the sound of that." He and the captain sparred playfully with swords, while the boys and the rest of the crew laughed and shouted insults. . . .

But none of them, with the exception of Mac Golden, knew that the Hibbils and Adurians were secretly allied with each other, and intended to destroy both the Humans and the Mutatis. The HibAdu Coalition had placed sleeper agents all over the galaxy, with standing orders to await further instructions. Golden was one of those agents himself, but he had recently decided not to follow activation orders, if he ever got them.

Like Acey and Dux, the furry little Hibbil had found a new family. He liked these Humans, and would never consider betraying them. But he fell short of revealing what he knew about the HibAdu Coalition's scheme, and the danger it presented to the entire Human race.

Golden didn't want to think about all of that, and hoped the whole situation would just go away, without harming any of the people who had grown close to him.

Chapter Sixty-Seven

No one can ever see all of the interesting places in this galaxy. At least, I used to think that way.

—Noah Watanabe

His friends who attended to him would have confirmed that Noah did not leave the deck of the grid-plane, where he lay in deep sleep, not having awakened or even moved for days. Untended, his reddish beard had been growing. But his mind was more active than ever, and—unknown to the Guardians around him—he was about to take a fantastic mental journey.

Sitting on the carpeted deck beside Noah's supine form, Eshaz talked soothingly to him, massaging the man's forehead as gently as he could with one scaly hand.

On the surface of his consciousness, Noah was aware of his alien friend, and of a mysterious healing treatment he had administered. But Noah made no effort to respond to the Tulyan, or to communicate with him in any manner. His attentions were focused elsewhere.

He heard Tesh say, excitedly, "Look, his eyelids are fluttering!"

And he heard a murmuring of conversation around him, as the others came over to see if Noah was coming back to consciousness. It almost seemed to him that he could if he really wanted to, but something much more important drew him away from them . . . and he felt his mind expanding, questing outward.

Noah felt drawn by something momentous he needed to discover. Instinct told him it would most certainly be dangerous, and that if he went too deeply into his subconscious, he might never be able to wake up. The experience might kill him, but he had to take it anyway.

He felt a beckoning, something tugging at his mind, teasing it, promising unknown delights. In his mind's eye, he saw a dark cloud in space, with a faint illumination beyond, delineating the shape of the mass. Every few seconds, something flashed behind the cloud, making its outline sharper. It was like a lightning storm, but that did not seem possible, since he was in deep space, far beyond any atmospheric envelope.

Earlier, Noah had heard Tesh and Eshaz discussing the explosion of Plevin Four, and it occurred to him that a chunk of atmosphere might have lifted into space and sealed inexplicably, and that it was now beyond a cloud of space dust, flashing. The wild beauty could be like a last hurrah before the pocket of air disappeared forever, along with the planet.

Of course, none of that seemed possible. But still, he wondered. The visual effect was compelling.

As if released from his body, Noah's mind felt like it was floating in space, similar to the atmosphere that appeared to have broken away from the dead planet. His consciousness drifted on an empyrean current, taking him past blindingly spectacular sights. A massive yellow sun went nova in an awe-inspiring burst of destructive beauty, and in the next star system an even larger sun, a red giant, dropped into a black hole and then faded abruptly, like a dramatic sunset with all of its light suddenly sucked away.

He felt a mental click, and the scene before his inner eye shifted. Noah was no longer floating, no longer just observing. He found himself spread-eagled, connected to an immense gossamer web, but he was not a prisoner of it. This was the most marvelous sensation!

To his astonishment he was able to flip from one section of the pale green web to another—left, right, up, down, forward, and backward. Awkwardly, he went in several directions, one after the other, and then found he could gain better control over his movements. On impulse, he accelerated into deep space and spun through the cosmos, passing by asteroids, worlds, star systems, and even passing completely *through* other ghostly, acrobatic figures like him, of various recognizable races.

But there were other phantom creatures out there as well, some spinning, some darting, and others seeming to run in space, their appendages dancing along the webbing. Some were humanoid, while others looked like mythological animals, such as he had never seen before.

One with a lion head and serpentine body approached and kept pace beside him, staring at him as if trying to decide whether to devour him or not. Concerned, Noah tried to go faster than before, but the ghostly creature stayed with him.

Unable to get away, Noah wanted to cry out in terror, but knew his voice would make no sound in the airless void of space. Like a man in the wilderness facing a ferocious beast, he attempted to show no fear, and made a defiant, aggressive face at the would-be predator, along with wildly dramatic hand gestures.

Finally, apparently bored, the beast drifted off into the tail of a passing comet, and disappeared entirely.

Noah went on to cartwheel across the galaxy, a cosmic voyager in a realm he had never known existed. He was a mote in the heavens. With surprising ease, he gained new skills flying in this realm, and was able to increase his speed and maneuverability. He kept up with other creatures, following them for a while and then breaking off to go his own way. There seemed no limit to the places he could go, but none of them seemed tangible. It was all dreamlike, as if he was peering into a dimension that did not really exist.

And a disturbing thought intruded: *The Doge tried to kill me, and my sister put him up to it. Has she succeeded? Am I dead, or dying? Is that true of the others out here, too?*

He thought back on the near-death stories he had heard—of a person's life flashing in front of his eyes in seconds or fractions of seconds, and of a light at the end of a tunnel, beckoning him to go through and discover the light, beckoning him to . . .

For the first time, Noah wasn't certain if passing through meant dying or living. In the past he'd always thought if he went to the other side of the tunnel he would die, and that the light was heaven, drawing him like a magnet. But now he wasn't so certain. Couldn't the light represent life instead, pulling him out of the darkness of death?

He saw no tunnel at all now, though it seemed appropriate to him that he should. After all, wasn't he on the brink of death? Hadn't he chosen not to swim to the top of his consciousness where his friends were? Instead, he'd gone in a different, very dangerous direction. But a fascinating direction, where he had so much to learn, so much to experience.

Somehow, through everything, his personal fate seemed of little importance.

He was out in the middle of the vast galaxy where the lifetime of a human being was so infinitesimal in the scale of time that it hardly mattered at all. But could a life form that had only been alive briefly still accomplish something meaningful? The common fruit fly lived but a few hours, and some organisms even less than that. Could the death of that fly affect events on the other side of the universe?

Noah thought it was possible, an extrapolation of a "butterfly flapping its wings" theory his mother had once told him, how that seemingly inconsequential occurrence could affect events on the other side of a planet.

He thought of the theories of relativity, of quantum mechanics, and of macro systems—of worlds orbiting stars, of entire galaxies hurtling through the cosmos, and of the all-encompassing universe expanding, fleeing from the singularity where the Big Bang was supposed to have occurred.

But his lingering physical reality interfered rudely with the serenity of such ruminations.

My sister tried to kill me!

The galactic images faded, and his eyes fluttered open. For an instant, he saw the scaly, reptilian face of Eshaz and his gray-slitted alien eyes, peering hard at him. A universe of caring in those eyes. The Tulyan had always been a giver, quick to do whatever he could for his friends, and for the environment.

But those eyes harbored a universe of secrets.

Abruptly, of his own volition, Noah found himself back in the strange cosmic realm again, spread-eagled on the gossamer web, spinning, cartwheeling across the galaxy. He peered into places where Humans could not look, and not knowing what he saw, he failed to comprehend.

Noah's mind filled to bursting. He wanted to come back again some other time and re-experience this . . . if the opportunity ever presented itself to him. Logically, it seemed to him that he must be going stark, raving mad, but he felt the opposite, that he was more focused than ever before in his life. In the spaceship of his mind he journeyed far from anyplace he had ever been before, on an expedition that his physical body, subject to its corporeal limitations, could not possibly undertake.

With his new awareness, he didn't see how the concept of a physical form fit into a realm that seemed to be constructed of something else entirely, and where the spiritual meant more than anything he could touch. His eyes were transmitting extraordinary images to him.

The faint green webbing curved and stretched off into infinity, surrounding and penetrating him, connecting him with all that had ever been and all that ever would be. He could not comprehend how he knew this, only that he did, and that he had always known it, and always would, since he would never die as long as he remained connected to this marvelous galactic structure. He felt it giving him life, renewing and enhancing his energy, and that this was one of the secrets in Eshaz's eyes.

But there were more, many more.

As Noah spun away into this alternate dimension, he saw his friend's eyes superimposed over the cosmic tableau, and felt the Tulyan's presence with him, sharing the connection the two of them had with the webbing. Eshaz was making this experience available for him; Eshaz was saving his life by showing him . . . what? Heaven?

Most astonishing. The slenderest threads connected Noah to a hidden network that spanned everything in existence, a godlike web that gave life and took it away. Despite the guidance of his friend, Noah feared that he would lose contact and never find his way back to this realm again. What a tragedy that would be, what a fathomless loss. He realized with a start that he hadn't been moving at all, that he had been connected to one strand, and that the web had been folding and refolding and unfolding around him, in a magical display of empyrean origami.

Such beauty he had never before beheld or even imagined possible, as he saw sunlight glistening off the green webbing in star system after star system. Exquisitely perfect in its design, this galactic mesh appeared to be an extrapolation of elegant patterns seen on planets . . . of the designs in spider webs, leaves, and seashells. It all seemed linked to him, and all of it had to be the achievement of a remarkable higher power.

There could be no other possible explanation.

For a moment his vision shifted, and he saw green-and-brown skymining ships floating over the surface of a planet, scooping air and processing important elements out of it. On a plateau below the ships he saw his company's base of operations for that world, which he recognized as Jaggem. It gave him reassurance to see the important work continuing, despite his own absence. He had left good people in charge.

Then he saw a contingent of red-uniformed men supervising the operations, and his spirits dropped. The Doge's Red Berets.

Presently the images faded, replaced by the twinkling void of deep space and the pale green filigree. Ahead, he saw chunks of matter hurtling through the cosmos, some pieces without apparent direction, while others . . . *podships!* . . . were racing along the gossamer web strands. Appearing Lilliputian in comparison with the immensity of his own form, they sped right through him without apparent harm. Such a peculiar sensation. He felt as if he was stretched across a vast distance. A mental stretch, he believed, and not a physical one, but the mind had brought along an enlarged ghost of its body.

The folding images seemed to fade away now, although Noah beheld a curvature of webbing stretched to infinity, faintly fluttering on a cosmic wind. Again he had the illusion of whirling and spinning along the strands himself, and he saw once more that the web was really doing tricks around him, creating the most wondrous of all illusions.

On impulse, Noah thought of grabbing the podships as they sped around him and through him. How incredible that would be, if he could only stop one and examine it closely, without harming anything. But as he considered this more it didn't seem wise, even if he could accomplish it. Noah did not want to interfere in natural processes, didn't want to disturb the exquisite perfection of the heavens. He didn't think it was possible anyway; it would be like trying to reach from one dimension into another one.

Again, his brain clicked, and the focus of his inner eye shifted.

Eshaz felt Noah pulling away from him, and he tried to prevent it. But this Human had grown too strong for even a large Tulyan to keep under control. He pushed Eshaz away with surprising strength, and the bronze-scaled creature tumbled backward, onto the deck of the grid-plane.

Timeweb's healing powers had worked. But spiders of worry scuttled through the Tulyan's thoughts.

What have I done?

As the podships continued to speed by, Noah discovered that he could make mental linkages with them one at a time, only for a few moments in each case, but enough for him to obtain information. He saw inside the living, spacefaring vessels and understood how they operated. Everyone knew that the podships were living organisms, but their inner workings had always been mysterious. He learned for the first time that they were piloted by tiny humanoid creatures, who guided the ships across the far reaches of space. Two very different organisms were working together . . . perhaps the strangest of all symbiotic relationships, it seemed to Noah.

The images were clear at times but kept slipping in and out of focus and blurring.

Some podships carried a number of merchant ships in their cargo holds—typically fifteen or twenty—while others had a wild assortment of passengers on board: Humans, Mutatis, machines, various aliens. One pod was transporting the Doge Lorenzo del Velli and Noah's twin sister toward Canopa. He heard them in the grand salon of their private yacht, talking about most of Noah's Guardians having scattered into the woods and hills, where they were living off the land.

"They're not worth going after," Francella said to the Doge in an eerie, distant voice. "We need to focus our forces on finding Noah and killing him. Only then will I be satisfied."

Lorenzo nodded, and said something unintelligible. He seemed to be in acquiescence.

From afar, Noah felt a chill as he stared at his fraternal twin's hardened face, with her treacherous dark eyes and bald eyebrows. She had become his bête noire, or perhaps she always had been, and he hadn't paid enough attention to the danger. Her image grew fuzzy and then sharpened again.

First she kills our father and cleverly blames me. Now she seeks to assassinate me, and the manipulated Doge thinks she is justified.

Noah tried not to hate her, not wanting to carry such a burden in his heart. But it was not easy to fight the strong feelings.

Abruptly and without his impetus, the images of Francella and Lorenzo, and of the podship carrying their yacht, vanished.

Inside the cargo hold of another sentient pod, a motley assortment of sentient machines from the White Sun star system were aboard at least a dozen battered transport ships, also bound for Canopa. While most of the robots were silent and packed in close quarters, Noah determined their origin and destination from a conversation that their leader, a flat-bodied machine, was having with a subordinate. But the cosmic eavesdropper could not determine why they were en route.

In the hold of yet another podship, he saw a peculiar pilot at the controls of a spacecraft that looked exactly like a merchant prince schooner, including the red-and-gold colors on the hull. Visible through the thick plax of the front window, the pilot had shapeshifted to make himself look Human. But Noah—he wasn't sure how—could tell that he wasn't Human at all.

What is a Mutati doing with one of our ships?

Our ships? The thought stuck in his throat, because he and Doge Lorenzo were mortal enemies now. Noah wasn't certain where his own home was any more, but his allegiance to humankind had never faltered.

Gazing past the Mutati, he scanned the schooner's interior and saw a strange array of gleaming tubes built into the hull, an arrangement he could not identify. He tried to see more, but the image faded and disappeared. Moments later it flickered back, and he saw the podship arrive at the orbital station over Ilbao, one of the Mutati worlds. The pilot offloaded his schooner and took it out into orbital space, perhaps fifty kilometers away. There, he held a geostationary position.

With new eyes, Noah scanned the podways. Images blurred and clarified, shifted out of focus and grew sharper. Floating near various pod stations around the galaxy, he saw a total of ten matching schooners, each with a solitary Mutati aboard, and each with the odd, unidentifiable tubes inside the vessels. It was extremely peculiar, but undoubtedly the Merchant Prince Alliance had already sighted the vessels, and would take action against them.

Or had they? Looking back, he realized that all of the strange schooners were stationed over Mutati worlds, inside enemy territory. Perhaps they were listening posts, part of a defensive network. But why were they all merchant prince schooners, or made to look like them? Most perplexing.

His focus shifted, and Noah saw something he hadn't noticed before. A podship lay motionless in space, and he sensed difficulty there, that the spacecraft was marooned and in need of assistance. If he could help, it would not be interfering; he would be going to the aid of a stranded traveler.

But can I do anything?

Zooming in, he absorbed a vision of the vessel into his mind, and saw a green-and-brown grid-plane in the cargo hold, and—to his amazement—his own Human form lying comatose inside the plane, with Eshaz tending to him.

We're on board a podship? But how? The answer eluded him.

Letting his mind permeate the rest of the podship, Noah focused on a green, glowing chamber at the core, and he seeped inside. Touching the core with his probing thoughts, he suddenly felt the craft lurch into motion, which at first surprised him. Then, as he thought about it, the experience seemed oddly familiar, though he could not determine why. He only knew one thing for certain, that the sentient podship was responding to his mental commands, leaping onto a different cosmic strand than the one it had been on before, a different podway headed in a different direction.

Gaining control was a fantastic sensation, and Noah Watanabe had a destination in mind.

Canopa.

He had decided to return home, and saw clearly how to get there. He gave instructions to the podship, through the mental linkage they shared.

Then Noah sensed another entity in the navigation chamber with him, and saw a tiny, barely discernible creature clinging to one of the walls. Incredibly, it was struggling to take command of the pod away from him. . . .

Chapter Sixty-Eight

We are taught from birth to never let our guard down, and how to protect ourselves against mortal enemies. But this aggression, I never anticipated.

—Tesh Kori

Tesh had been stunned to find another entity—one she saw as a looming, shadowy form—take control of the podship away from her and send it in wild, spinning dives through space, finally locking onto a course for Canopa. It had been a surprise takeover.

Now Tesh went through the ritualistic steps involved with occupying this sacred chamber, this womb within a womb, and she uttered a litany of ancient *benedictios,* the guidance-and-control phrases her people had employed for millions of years.

The podship quivered, and started to respond to her commands, but only for a few seconds before it stopped, as the intruder fought for control.

This was unlike any battle Tesh had ever experienced, as she faced a specter that kept coming at her and neutralizing her strength. She never felt her foe touch her, only the numbing effects of its ghostly power.

Normally, when a Parvii entered a sectoid chamber, that was enough to control the creature, using ancient words and a gentle touch anyplace on a sectoid wall. Now, however, the podship was confused, as it was receiving conflicting orders from different entities, different galactic races. Her opponent was not a Parvii. She knew that for certain, but little else. She didn't think it was a Tulyan, either, for she had never known one to behave this way.

The powerful phantom stood inside the sectoid chamber, but details of its body were not discernible. Only a distorted shadow of whatever it was. It almost looked Human in shape, but with gross distortions on the head and appendages, as if something had pulled it, stretching it out.

Scurrying along the wall in front of the shadow, Tesh gained access to the core of the creature's body by pressing her hands hard on a small, bright green wall section of the sectoid chamber, which was the nerve center of the creature. This technique, known as the "Parvii Hold," was used by the wranglers of wild Aopoddae out in the galaxy, to tame particularly rebellious pods. She'd learned it from an old veteran. On the downside, the trick would only work for a few minutes before the pod shifted the location of its nerve center, moving the bright patch of color to another place.

But that might just be enough time.

As she pressed against the tough flesh with both hands, pushing this way and that to steer and send acceleration signals, the pod finally began to follow her commands.

Tesh needed to focus all of her considerable powers, not letting up for even a fraction of a second. By means of her connection, she saw through the visual sensors of the pod creature. Ahead, the faint green strands of the web seemed limitless, although an ancient legend said they did stop somewhere, at the end of the galaxy.

She saw the intruder's shadow move. Focusing, she tried again to see bodily and facial features, but none were apparent. Her adversary—she couldn't determine the gender—seemed much larger than she was, but she could not even tell if it had a face, in the common sense. From the humanoid shadow, she wondered if it might be a rogue Parvii using some sort of modified magnification mechanism. Looking around carefully, she saw no evidence of this. But her opponent continued to cause her trouble.

Receiving mental impulses from Tesh's mysterious opponent, the pod began to slow. She pressed even harder on the green nerve center, which had not shifted position yet. The podship shuddered, and resumed the speed she wanted.

Tesh felt no more opposition, and she saw no sign of the shadowy form. She hoped it was gone, but kept her guard up. It took only a few minutes for her to cross space, but seemed like much longer.

Feeling uneasy, she guided the craft to a remote pod station, not on the busiest podways. As she pulled into the main docking bay of the station, she saw no other spacecraft at all, exactly as she had anticipated. Tesh needed to keep control of this pod, and did not want any distractions.

The podship seemed edgy. It didn't shift its nerve center, but if it did she vowed to locate it again, doing whatever was necessary to maintain the upper hand.

The pod station orbited over a world that had not been inhabited in more than three hundred years. It no longer had shuttle service, so anyone wishing to go down to the surface needed to bring their own landing craft, which she didn't have. She just wanted to focus on the podship, keeping it from breaking free of her, or from falling under the control of her unseen competitor.

Where was that shadowy form now? She saw no sign of it. Perhaps on the journey across space it had fallen away, and would no longer be any trouble to her. Either that, or it had died in the struggle to oppose her superior powers.

Looking through the visual sensors of the agitated podship, Tesh saw that the station was as she recalled it from earlier in her life, an unadorned structure orbiting over the tundra of a small, icy planet.

Chapter Sixty-Nine

Each life is a journey, from birth to death, from wake to slumber.

—Parvii Inspiration

After searching the sectoid chamber carefully and finding nothing out of the ordinary, Tesh became convinced that her mysterious adversary had departed. It had been the strangest experience of her life.

Playing it safe, upon leaving the core chamber she sealed it with her own private command signal to the podship, making it impossible for anyone to gain access without her permission. No one, not even Woldn himself, the Eye of the Swarm, could override a Parvii command signal to a podship. The bond between pilot and beast was too strong.

In a shadowy corridor of the spacecraft, Tesh then enlarged herself by switching on her personal magnification system. She felt the energy field crackle on the surface of her skin.

After waiting a few seconds for the familiar but uncomfortable sensation to pass, she hurried back through the maze of passageways. Rounding a turn, she encountered a worried Anton Glavine.

"Where have you been?" he demanded.

"You wouldn't believe me if I told you," she said with an enigmatic smile.

"Try me."

"Perhaps another time."

Though he tried to block her way while demanding answers, she pushed past him and climbed the short stairway into the passenger cabin of the grid-plane, which was still inside the podship's cargo hold.

There she saw Noah lying comatose on the deck, as before, with a blanket over him and the healing pad bulging on one side of his head. His body jerked and he flailed his arms for several seconds, before going motionless again.

Dr. Bichette sat on a pillow beside him, tending to him, while Eshaz loomed over both of them, looking on. . . .

Moments before, Noah had felt the podship settle into a docking berth. He had almost, but not quite, been able to pilot the sentient vessel. Most remarkable. But something . . . or someone . . . had overridden him. During the cross-space journey, the spacecraft had stopped complying with his commands. It all seemed like a dream.

Previously, Noah had been content to remain physically unconscious, so that he could journey in his mind. But now he struggled to awaken. He heard Dr. Bichette's excited voice, then felt the rough, scaly touch of Eshaz on his hand. And he heard other voices.

Like a diver short on air, swimming frantically toward a luminous surface, he struggled with all of his strength, pulling upward, using his arms. The voices became a little louder. In addition to the doctor, he recognized Tesh, Anton, and Subi.

Must reach them. Must see them.

Heavy. Too heavy. He felt himself sinking, and the voices fading.

Swim harder.

Just when he thought he would never make it, and would fade away to oblivion, he finally reached the surface and gasped for air. He felt an odd sensation in his left foot, but tried to put it out of his mind.

"We cannot remain here!" Noah shouted, flailing his arms and struggling to fill his lungs with air. "I tried to go to Canopa, but the podship wouldn't cooperate."

He opened his eyes, blinked, and saw Tesh staring at him. She looked stunned.

"He's babbling something about the podship," Bichette said.

"I'm not babbling, you fool!" Noah snapped. "I was in the navigation chamber, don't you understand? For a few moments, I had the podship under control! It was an incredible feeling!"

"He's delusional," the doctor said. "Must be the anesthesia I had to give him. Poor fellow. I wish I could have saved the foot."

Foot? With the blanket gone, Noah looked down. A thick white healing pad was on the bottom of his left leg, where his foot should be.

I'm not awake yet.

But he felt Tesh's hand on his, the gentle caress of her touch. He tried to stand up, but could not support himself on one foot. Eshaz kept him from falling, and eased him back down. Bewildered, Noah looked around.

His gaze met Dr. Bichette's. Sadness there, and guilt. "I'm sorry," he said. "I had to amputate."

Again, Noah felt Tesh's touch, this time on his forearm. "We're so sorry," she whispered.

He looked at her, and saw that she still appeared to be stunned, presumably over his tragic operation. Bichette was spouting medical details, but Noah tuned him out. His foot was gone, and nothing could be done about that now, since he had moral objections to the cloning of Human body parts. Somehow, as sad as he was, and as angry as he was at the doctor, Noah felt great comfort from Tesh. He could not take his eyes off her.

But something seemed different about her. He couldn't quite tell what, but he was sure of it.

Chapter Seventy

The proper course of honor is not always clear. Is it more honorable to follow a family tradition, or to follow what is in your heart?

—Emir Hari'Adab

A tall metalloy platform stood at the center of the construction site, with a bubble cab atop the platform and eight crane booms extending from the core, like the legs of an immense spider. Eight robots inside the high cab operated the system, and with them stood a young Mutati in a purple-and-gold robe, watching the progress.

Hari'Adab Meshdi—son of the Zultan—could just as easily have supervised from the ground, but this high perch gave him a better vantage point. Besides, he felt dismal about the project, and wouldn't mind too much if the whole rig toppled over and took him with it.

A gust of wind buffeted the cab, but the Emir didn't bother to hold on. Dejectedly, he bumped against a window and leaned there for a moment before straightening himself.

The explosives belt under his robe felt uncomfortable against the soft flesh of his Mutati belly, and reaching under his clothing he loosened it a little.

One of the robots, a ball of rivets with red eyes, turned toward him without comprehension, then looked away and resumed its work. The cranes moved in synchronization, sliding mezzanine floor pieces into slots in vertical posts, and then snapping on the interior walls.

In only a few violent seconds, Hari could halt the rapid, efficient progress by blowing everything up himself. But disaster engineers combing through the wreckage afterward would figure out what he did, and it would smear his name. Already the name was tenuous, because of the successful enemy strike on the Demolio facility, a defensive failure that had been his personal responsibility.

One of his three hands rested on the detonation trigger. It wouldn't take much, just a moment of courage. At least that would slow reconstruction of the immoral facility.

Just beyond a grassy rise, the debris of the former manufacturing site still remained, exactly as it had been left a few weeks ago, with destroyed torpedoes inside and the bodies of four hundred Mutatis who died in the sneak attack. Hari could have died with them. Earlier that day he had been inspecting the facility, and had left Dij by shuttle only moments before the unexpected offensive.

To a large extent the Mutatis had assumed that the previous facility would be protected by secrecy and its remote location—and they were still investigating how the young Human commandos got through. The episode had caused the Mutatis to close down their "fly trap" system of capturing and imprisoning small numbers of Humans, in order to get intelligence information out of them. Now an entire division of Mutati soldiers guarded the new Demolio manufacturing and training facility, armed with the latest detection technology. This facility could not be destroyed by outside attack again, not even if the enemy sent a huge force against it.

Following the surprise attack, his father had proclaimed the site sacred ground, and decreed that it was not to be disturbed. Just beyond the ruins of the largest building, facing the holy direction of sunrise, a monument had been erected to honor the fallen workers, brave martyrs who died in that brief but effective attack.

"Our enemy is without honor," the Zultan had announced at the dedication ceremony the week before. "They will regret this dirty business."

A crowd of well-dressed Mutatis, all in their natural flesh-fat forms, had cheered and called for the blood of every Human in the galaxy, annihilating them to the last man, woman, and child. Sitting on the stage as his father spoke, Hari'Adab had been deeply troubled by the aggressive statements, but had tried to conceal his feelings. Certainly all human beings could not possibly be evil. He'd heard of their magnificent historical religious leaders, such as Jesus, Muhammad, Buddha, Mohandas Gandhi, and Mother Theresa, any one of whom matched the stature of the greatest Mutati prophets.

And by all accounts, one of the most altruistic of modern Humans was Noah Watanabe. Not openly religious, he nonetheless professed a deep reverence for the sacred, interconnected nature of planets, and for the need to restore them after the damage caused by industrial operations. Such Humans did not deserve to die. The galaxy would not be a better place without them, or without future leaders like that.

Hari'Adab could not condone genocide.

Sadly, his own father and other Mutati leaders were so filled with blind hatred toward their enemies that they had lost touch with decency, with altruism. Instead, they continually looked for passages from *The Holy Writ* to support their positions, citing scripture that called for the complete destruction of all enemies of the Mutati people. But *The Holy Writ* had plenty of other passages that called for compassion and justice as well, and for reasoned diplomacy instead of warfare. The Mutati leadership, however, was only citing passages to support their militaristic positions, while ignoring other, even more significant scriptures.

In their fanatic zeal, they had become tunnel minded.

The Mutati Kingdom's Demolio program was the exact antithesis of everything that Noah Watanabe stood for. If Watanabe learned about this deadly technology, the whole idea of cracking planets open would chill him to his soul, and Hari felt the same way. Such a program had no basis in morality. And yet, Hari found himself managing the industrial facility that built the torpedoes, and the training program for Mutati outriders.

As the Zultan's eldest son, the Emir would assume the throne from his father someday, but that would be too late. Already, psychotic Mutati military commanders had destroyed three enemy planets, and many more were planned. It was terrible, just terrible. He didn't care if the technology could be the turning point in the centuries-long war, swinging the tide decisively in favor of his people.

Winning that way was not victory.

One of the Emir's closest friends had even suggested that they arrange to have the Zultan killed, for the sake of the Mutati Kingdom, and to prevent continued bloodshed. No one could even remember why Mutatis and Humans were mortal enemies. A regime change seemed like the only way to break the continuing cycles of retribution and violence.

At first Hari had refused to consider patricide, one of the very worst sins that a Mutati could commit. In a huff, he had sent his friend away, and had not spoken to him since.

But maybe the idea had merit. It might just might end this folly once and for all. What if he brought the Zultan up here, along with some of the top generals, and blew them up with the Demolio facility? Hari would need to set up a political coup team to take over during the power vacuum, since he would not be around to run the government himself.

He'd always disliked his father anyway, couldn't ever recall feeling close to him. The explosion would solve a lot of problems at once.

Hari loathed the Demolio program his father was sponsoring, could not comprehend the suffering and death one of the planet-buster torpedoes inflicted on human beings when it hit a planet. That was a fate he wouldn't wish on even his most-despised enemies. He hadn't even been aware of the diabolical extent of the program when his father commanded him to supervise it. The Zultan had only told him that it was an important military operation, and a secret that he didn't want to entrust to anyone but his own son and heir apparent. The trust had been surprising considering their lack of closeness, but somewhat flattering, of only for a short while until he discovered what horrors the Demolio program entailed.

Still, the Emir had accepted the wishes of his father. In Mutati society, the young—even if they held an opposing opinion—were expected to show respect for their elders. Now Hari was in too deep to slide gracefully out of this Demolio assignment. His father would brand him a coward, and a traitor to the cause. The repercussions were severe if he didn't do what he was told, if he didn't carry on the militaristic family tradition of following orders and never questioning them.

But the repercussions were even more severe if he looked away, if he didn't follow his conscience.

Thus far he had, at least, refused to wear the Adurian minigyro that his father gave to him. A proud young man, Hari did not need a mechanical device to help him make decisions. He'd never trusted the bubble-eyed aliens anyway, and certainly didn't want their technology interfering with his thought processes.

If only it was possible to reach a peace accord with the Humans. The fighting didn't make sense to Hari, just killing an enemy because it had been that way for a long time. There had to be a better way.

Chapter Seventy-One

> There are many ways of getting from one place to another. When it comes to space travel, however, the options are strictly limited to podships—if you want to get there efficiently, not wasting time or money.
>
> —From a merchant prince transportation analysis

Despite the tragic loss of his foot, Noah insisted on leaving the grid-plane. He had just shaved and cleaned up. "It's cramped in here," he said, hobbling around with a pair of crutches that Subi made by fusing together pieces of scrap alloy. "I need fresh air."

"There's something I'd like to discuss with you," Tesh said, looking at him earnestly. "It's very important."

Noah nodded, though something about her still bothered him. For an unknown reason, he wasn't sure if he could trust her. He would rather be alone to sort through his thoughts, and the shocking medical procedure that had been performed on him. But he had trouble saying no to her. Even trying to look past her beauty, he found her an intriguing, persuasive woman.

Leaning on the crutches, Noah led the way into the cargo hold of the former podship, then hobbled through an airlock to one of the sealed walkways of the pod station, where the air was breathable.

For several moments, he paused to stare through a filmy window at the podship in its berth, trying to comprehend some of the mysteries of the sentient creatures.

Intruding on his thoughts, Tesh said, "Your bunker on Plevin Four was actually a podship that crashed centuries ago, and then was modified. After the podship regenerated and shifted its skin back into position, the window walls fell away, and so did interior rooms that your Guardians added. The vessel now has a typical passenger compartment and a cargo hold, containing your grid-plane."

"This podship lay dormant for centuries?"

"Yes."

"And how do you know that?" Noah looked intensely at her, deep into her emerald green eyes.

Without answering, she began to walk beside the podship.

Keeping up with her, Noah almost fell, and she reached out to help him. Pushing her hand away, he supported himself on his own. The stump of his lower leg throbbed with pain.

"You said you were in a navigation chamber," Tesh said, as they made their way along the walkway, past empty berths in the docking bay. "What did you mean by that?"

"Are you in the habit of responding to a question with a question?"

"I need you to bear with me, Noah. I know it's difficult, but please trust me."

"I trust you."

"I don't think you do, not entirely."

He hesitated, then said, "The navigation chamber may have only been in my dream, but it seemed fantastically real. I felt as if I was at the controls of the podship, speeding through deep space. Without touching anything, I was using my brain signals to direct the vessel. It responded for awhile, then wouldn't anymore. It was like. . . ."

"Like what?"

The two of them were standing outside the waiting room of the pod station. Noah considered how to answer her, but his thoughts drifted away, like balloons floating up on a sudden breeze, just beyond a child's grasp. He stared at the wall next to them, then looked along the walkway.

Like podships themselves, pod stations were mottled gray and black, with not-quite-clear, filmy sections for windows. He'd heard that pod stations were also living creatures, just as the podships were, but they didn't travel the podways of deep space like the ships. That left open the question as to how the pod stations—which were much larger than the sentient spacecraft—ever got sprinkled around the galaxy in the first place.

Perhaps the stations had once been spacefaring vessels themselves, and went into retirement. Or maybe they were amalgams of retired podships, having fused themselves together into different shapes. In any event, all of the ships and stations had an obvious symbiotic relationship, like different parts of one immense galactic organism. Noah had more questions than answers.

With a start, he realized that Tesh had been saying something to him.

"I'm sorry," he said. "Guess I'm not totally out of my coma. As I said, when I was asleep all that time, I had strange, vivid dreams."

"You thought you were in some kind of a navigation chamber?"

"That's right."

"You said the podship responded for awhile, and then wouldn't do so any longer. You were about to say something more."

"Well, it seemed like someone else was in the chamber too, fighting me for control of the vessel."

"You *did* have a strange dream," Tesh said.

"Now tell me how that thing changed from a bunker to a podship," Noah said, nodding his head toward the vessel.

"Perhaps that's best answered inside," she said, leading the way back to the ship.

Intrigued, Noah hobbled along beside her, thumping the crutches on the walkway.

Just as they stepped from the airlock into the cargo hold, Anton greeted them. He looked nervous and upset.

"We need to talk," the young man said to Tesh.

"This is a not a good time," she said. "Maybe later?" Tesh looked at him inquisitively, as if concerned about his welfare. This was one of the things that Noah thought he liked about her, the way she seemed so caring, so nurturing. Assuming it was not all an act. He didn't think it was, but couldn't quite overcome his feelings of doubt.

"We used to be close," Anton said, trying to move in front of her. "What went wrong?"

"I'll talk to you later," she promised. "I told you, this isn't a good time."

As she attempted to walk on, Anton grabbed her arm. She shook him loose, raised her voice. "Well, what is it?" she demanded. "What's so important?"

"It's about us, about our relationship."

"And you've chosen to interrupt me when I'm busy? Why is it so urgent?"

"It's urgent to *me,*" he said, "but I can see it isn't to you."

"That's not true at all!"

"Then why are you and my uncle acting so cozy?"

"The green of jealousy is not a good color on you, Anton. . . ."

Noah leaned against a bulkhead of the cargo hold. With

his arm he felt the leathery flesh of the podship, and he pressed his face against the creature. In the background of his consciousness, the voices of Tesh and Anton continued, but faded and blurred. They were occupied with their mounting argument, and weren't looking at the man with the cane.

They did not notice that Noah's eyes were closed, and that his eyelids were fluttering, as if in a REM dream state. But he was not sleeping. Far from it. . . .

Chapter Seventy-Two

It is said that success in life is about focus, and lacking that, nothing meaningful can be accomplished. But is that old adage really true? Can't the wandering heart, the questing soul, achieve even more? Aren't the highest achievements in God's universe the simplest, the most pure?

—*The Holy Writ* of the Mutatis

From the open hatch of the grid-plane, Eshaz had been watching Tesh and Anton as they engaged in an animated conversation, and saw Noah Watanabe with them. Despite his injury, Noah was showing grit and tenacity, a desire to continue his life and not complain about his personal misfortune. He had lost his foot, but thanks to the healing nutrients of the timehole, he was out of his coma.

The man had come back from the dead.

If the Council of Elders ever discovered what Eshaz had done, he would be in a lot of trouble. His mission was to repair timeholes and no more, using proven methods of patching up damage to the sacred web, anywhere in the galaxy. He was not authorized to go beyond that, not sanctioned to use any ancillary skills he had developed over the nine hundred and eighty thousand years of his lifetime. The reason was clear, and he understood it well. Primarily, it was all about concentration, about adhering to priorities. If he did other things, by definition that meant he was neglecting his essential Timeweb maintenance duties.

But Eshaz was, among other things, a timeseer, one of the few Tulyans with the ability to see—though imperfectly—into the future, and into the past. If ordered to do so by the high council, he used that skill for the benefit of the Tulyan race and Timeweb. On occasion, he even did it for other galactic races, for the sometimes-arcane political purposes of the Tulyan Elders. One thing in exchange for another.

Eshaz also knew how to draw beneficial nutrients from a rip in the web, as he had done for Noah's sake, but this was one of the greatest infractions a Tulyan could commit. Only the most ancient of the ancients were authorized to do that, Tulyan sorcerers who were much older than he was, and who knew much more. He had learned the skill from one of them, with all of the dire warnings that went along with it. A mistake, holding the web open improperly, could result in a huge cataclysm, the collapse of an entire galactic sector.

Thankfully, that calamity had not occurred in this case, and he had repaired the web defect after the healing procedure, along with others he found in the vicinity of the planetary explosion. Still, he could not conceal his transgression from the Elders. The next time he visited the Tulyan Starcloud, he would have to tell his superiors what he had done, and face the consequences.

After healing Noah with the Timeweb connection, Eshaz had noticed a change in his own body, as the aches and pains in his muscles and joints diminished. Physically, he began to feel more like his old self again.

Following the radical procedure, Eshaz had tried to take control of the podship himself, by gaining entrance to the sectoid chamber and merging into the flesh of the creature in the way of his people, but he was prevented from doing so. A Parvii already had it. . . .

Now, as he stood watching the argument between Tesh and Anton, he noticed that Noah was leaning against a bulkhead, and not looking at all well. His eyes were closed, and he seemed about to fall over.

Eshaz ran to help his friend.

Chapter Seventy-Three

> By deeds does a man measure his own personality, and his own worth.
>
> —Anton Glavine, *Reflections*

Following the harrowing escape of the treasure crew from the Adurian planet, Acey and Dux gambled their remaining bonus money, and lost all of it to their more experienced mates. Even so, the young men didn't feel they had lost anything at all. They had begun the space adventure with no assets, only their lives and the clothes on their backs, and now they were distinctly ahead of that. They possessed a newfound wealth of experience, something that could not be purchased at any price or found in any treasure chest.

On the bridge of the *Avelo*, the crew huddled around Captain Yuell as he examined one of many parchments in his possession. In his early years the gray-bearded old man had been the heir to a great merchant prince fortune, and had used much of his money to purchase old documents, especially galactic treasure maps. Eventually, his family had fallen into political disfavor and had lost their property and fortune. So, in his middle years, he had run off to space, taking his precious charts with him. He had spent the decades afterward exploring the galaxy, following the documents and discovering that most of them were either erroneous or fraudulent.

But a few were accurate. He had already proven that at Wuxx Reef, and at other spots around the galaxy, according to stories the teenagers had heard about him.

"There," the old adventurer said, pointing out a star system at the top right corner of the parchment. "We go there!"

On the way, a two day journey to a region where podships supposedly did not venture, Captain Yuell regaled the crew with tales from his own treasure trove of lore. He told of the most unusual aliens in the "wide, wide galaxy," of Wolfen midgets and lighter-than-air creatures, of humanoids five meters tall, and of the renowned mind-readers of Eleo.

Then, just as the battered but venerable *Avelo* entered a small solar system whose red dwarf sun glistened off the hull of the craft, the captain said, "But none are more unusual than the Gamboliers of Ovinegg. That's their primary planet," he said, pointing to a world that glistened a dreary shade of brown in the diminished light. Moment by moment, the oval shape of Ovinegg drew closer.

An air of anticipation filled the passenger cabin of the ship. Thus far, however, as the world loomed larger and larger, Dux was less than impressed. Through the hazy atmosphere he didn't see any bodies of water down there at all, and wondered if they were brown and polluted, like the seemingly treeless landscape. From the edge of the atmospheric envelope, he didn't see mountains or any other topographical features, either.

"It looks like a misshapen rubber ball," Dux said.

"Is that why the people are called Gamboliers?" one of the men asked, "Because they bounce and jump around on the surface?"

"Nice guess," Captain Yuell said, "but that's not even close. The Treasure of Ovinegg awaits us, lads, but the question is, which of you are brave enough to go get it?"

"I am, sir!" Acey said. "And so's my cousin Dux." The two of them stepped forward, but Dux did not feel as enthusiastic as his cousin. He hoped Acey's bravado didn't get them into trouble.

"I'm ready too, sir," the Hibbil Mac Golden said, pushing the youngest crewmen aside. "Just tell us where to find the goods, and we'll bring 'em back."

"Well," the captain responded with a broad smile, "the goods are just lying down there for the picking. Piles of priceless gems, and they don't even need to be mined."

"If it's that easy," one of the crewmen said, "why haven't we heard of this place before?"

"Because you're stupid," one of the men shouted.

Laughter ensued. But all around, Dux heard his mates talking about how none of them had heard of the Treasure of Ovinegg, or the Gamboliers, or this solar system.

"Here's how it works," Captain Yuell said. "The Gamboliers don't allow foreign spacecraft to land on their homeworld. All visitors must leap from a shuttle no closer than two thousand meters above the planet."

He paused, and looked from face to face. "Without parachutes," he added.

"We just jump like rocks?" Mac Golden asked in his squeaky voice. Nervously, he adjusted his eye patch, and inched a couple of steps back.

"They're supposed to catch you. The Gamboliers are quite expert at catching people as they fly out of the sky, with fire rescue nets and other techniques. After you land, they bestow great wealth on you for your bravery."

"Why don't we just sneak down there and gather treasure?" Acey asked.

"Because they'll catch us and kill us. They promise a

horrendous death for anyone who doesn't follow the rules. Oh, one more thing. I didn't mention it before, but I never got any money from being in a wealthy merchant prince family. I made my whole life story up. Actually, I got my money here on Ovinegg when I was a young man, not much older than you two. I earned it and spent it, and now I need to replenish my stockpile."

"And the rules are still the same down there?" one of the crewmen asked.

"Those rules have been around for millennia, and when I was there I saw no sign of anything changing. That was forty-four years ago, not long to a civilization like theirs."

A palpable, worried silence filled the cabin.

"I'd like to see us all go home rich," Captain Yuell said, "but if I'm the only one going, that's fine, too. In case something goes wrong, you'll find my will on the ship's computer, with my virtual signature. I leave the *Avelo* to all of you equally."

Again, he looked from face to face. "Are any of you still with me?"

At first, no one answered.

Then Acey said, "I'm with you, Captain. And so is my cousin Dux." He looked at Dux, and smiled. "Right, buddy?"

Reluctantly, Dux nodded.

There were no other volunteers.

At Captain Yuell's command, the pilot steered the vessel into position, cutting down into the atmosphere, a couple of thousand meters above the surface. Then Yuell and his two young devotees jumped into the hazy sky and plunged downward.

Chapter Seventy-Four

No matter the excellence of your skills, no matter how superior you think you are, there is always someone who surpasses you, and there is always someone to outdo him as well. It is this way across the entire galaxy, and throughout every eon of time. Most of us think there is only one zenith of attainment, in God Almighty. But is he the supreme being of only one galaxy? Or are there other galaxies, and superior gods?

—*Scienscroll* Apocrypha

Probing with his mind, Noah determined that someone had sealed the entrance to the navigation chamber, undoubtedly the mysterious, barely discernible adversary who had taken control of the podship away from him. He remembered being inside the core room, and now his memory scanned over every feature he had seen in there earlier, the glowing, pale green walls, with veins of gray and black, and a small, bright green patch high on one wall.

During the struggle for control of the vessel, his tiny opponent had moved with blurring speed, climbing a wall to the bright green section, and had done something there to take control away from him. But what had been done there?

As he continued to probe now, he could not see that section, or anything at all inside the navigation chamber. His thoughts moved around the outside of the sealed enclosure, and he noted how it was connected by a thick membrane to the rest of the sentient spaceship. Finally, he noticed that a small portion of the mottled gray exterior of the chamber was a slightly different color, a shade of bright green.

Could this be the other side of the green patch? He wasn't certain. Previously, the spot had been high on a wall, and this was lower. But could it have shifted position?

Focusing all of his energy on the bright green section, he tried to use it as an entrance to the chamber. He visualized penetrating it and going through, as if his thoughts were a laser cutting device.

Moments passed, with no apparent effect.

Then, abruptly, the thick flesh began to pulse and throb, and Noah heard a squeal, as if from a yelping animal. The flesh quivered, and parted to reveal an opening. Noah shot through, into the interior of the navigation chamber.

I'm in! he thought.

But looking back at the patch, which was also bright green on this side, Noah saw to his dismay that he had injured the creature. The flesh was torn and oozed clear liquid, giving the surface a sickly sheen. Cautiously, Noah's shadowy, remote-controlled form floated back to the spot and placed a hand over the wound. He felt moisture, a bit of warmth, and the agitation of the podship.

I'm sorry, Noah thought.

The creature shuddered. Then, as if able to read the intruder's thoughts, the podship grew calmer. In a few seconds, the wound began to heal, and the injured tissue faded, closing the opening.

Cautiously, Noah withdrew his ghostlike touch, and drifted back to the center of the chamber. There could be no more exotic control center in the entire galaxy than the one he occupied now. All his life he had wondered how these sentient space vessels operated, and now he felt the mystery revealing itself to him, opening up like the petals of a magnificent flower.

Physically, he knew he wasn't really inside the navigation chamber at all, and that he still stood beside Anton and Tesh in the cargo hold of the podship. He had extended himself to the chamber by what he could only call mental projection, an expansion of his mind that permitted him to travel telepathically, just as he had previously journeyed across vast stretches of the galaxy. All of it had all been very real, not a dream at all.

The days when Noah had performed ecological recovery operations with his Guardians seemed like long ago to him, but they weren't, really. Only a matter of weeks, or perhaps months. He had lost track of time, at least the way he had measured it previously. It all seemed like a prior incarnation to him, operating under different, less meaningful, parameters.

He sensed something around him now, the powerful psychic presence of very alien creatures who had been inside this chamber before him . . . commanding the mysterious podship, piloting it across the galaxy. Then a powerful thought projected itself into his awareness, overwhelming all others.

I am the first of my race to accomplish this.

He found the realization exhilarating, and something else even more so. He didn't understand how he knew it, but he had an eerie, undeniable sensation that his power to command podships was greater than that of any other pilot in history. For awhile—as he developed his extrasensory ability—an unknown adversary had been able to keep him at bay and maintain control of the vessel. But that time was gone. No one could ever do it to him again.

The sensation gave him pause. He needed to use his new power well, and carefully.

His vision clouded over, then cleared. In his mind he held the image of the podship's interior, from bow to stern, as if he could see through the creature's tough skin. He felt his power and dominance permeating the entire vessel, entering every cell of the sentient creature.

He saw Tesh running across the cargo hold, then into a passageway.

What is she doing? he wondered.

Abruptly, she seemed to disappear.

Refocusing, he saw her in a much smaller form, climbing walls like an insect, frantically looking for something she could no longer find. The entrance to the navigation chamber. Now he knew the identity of his adversary.

And he smiled to himself. . . .

Noah's mind controlled his body.

In itself, this was not a revolutionary concept, since the minds of all creatures controlled their bodily movements. But in Noah's case, his cognitive center could roam great distances beyond his corporal form, and still move the body by remote control. After Tesh ran off, he sent a telepathic command, causing his physical self to walk calmly to the grid-plane and climb the short staircase into the craft. It was a peculiar sensation, like a puppet master operating strings.

Then, filling the navigation chamber with his mental energy, he set the podship into motion. Following his thought commands, the vessel hyper-accelerated onto the podways.

Another extraordinary event was about to occur.

Thinking back on it afterward, Noah would not recall

being aware of the crisis beforehand. Perhaps the temporary fusion of his mind with the consciousness of the podship had caused a state of hyper awareness, an ability to see something far away and react to it in a fraction of a second. Maybe time stood still and permitted it all to happen, something to do with the vast galactic web and the space-time continuum. In his mind, the possibilities were as limitless as the stars in the sky.

Anyone looking at a chart of the galaxy would see that the remote region where Tesh had taken the podship was a long way from the scene of the crisis. But podships could cross great distances in little more than the blink of an eye, so the customary ways of thinking were not always useful. Alternate thought processes were required, different ways of looking at things.

Certainly, all was not as it appeared to be, and Noah was not the only one to notice it, and wonder at the possibilities.

According to Eshaz, Noah Watanabe was the most remarkable human being ever born, and his life had been well worth the risk the web caretaker had taken in saving it. Only a short time after receiving the mysterious healing treatment administered by the Tulyan, Noah had been able to take a fantastic mental journey across the galaxy . . . and perhaps that continuing ability, combined with his innate sense of goodness, led to the remarkable events that took place in the hazy atmosphere over a remote planet. . . .

Ovinegg.

A world where the inhabitants used to wait for treasure hunters to fall out of the sky and save them with nets, had become a ghost planet, its population devastated by plagues. But many of those facts would not surface until later. Still, on some level of consciousness Noah, and perhaps the podship to which he was linked, might have had this information, at some plane of awareness.

Or, in a universe of chance, that's exactly what it was. Mere happenstance.

But no matter the reasons, which were always debatable, the reality could not be denied. Only seconds after three people tumbled out of a spacefaring vessel that had entered the lower atmosphere of Ovinegg, a flash of green split the sky beneath them, and the daredevils never reached the ground.

The podship absorbed them into its skin and dropped them gently into its passenger compartment. Then it continued on its way, leaping back onto the podways and accelerating.

Noah could not explain what had happened, but in the moments after the rescue he felt that he again had control of the vessel. With uncertainties and questions swimming through his mind, he directed the podship across space to the pod station orbiting Canopa—a cross-galactic journey of only a few more minutes.

Inside the grid-plane, Noah sat in one of the passenger seats, with his eyes closed. He felt an odd sensation as his thoughts occupied two places at once, and he sensed that even more was possible. The idea amazed and frightened him. In the passenger compartment of the podship, he saw two young men leaning over a gray-bearded man who lay on the deck, tending to him. Something seemed to be wrong. The image faded.

Opening his eyes, Noah saw Tesh seated beside him. She was speaking to him but he only saw her lips moving, and didn't hear her voice. She seemed upset. Something clicked in his ears, like a pressure change, and he heard her.

"Why aren't you answering me?" she demanded.

"What?"

"What do you know about this?"

"About the trip to Canopa, you mean?"

"That's where we are?"

"We'll discuss it later," he said. Then, looking at Dr. Bichette, he said, "Go to the passenger compartment of the podship and see what you can do. A man needs your attention."

Bichette frowned. "But all of us are aboard this grid-plane, in the cargo hold."

"It's someone else. Go! Now!"

Looking perplexed, the doctor hurried away.

Turning to his rotund adjutant, Noah said, "When Bichette returns, Subi, I want you to off-load this grid-plane from the podship."

"Are we going down to Canopa, sir?" The big man slipped into the command chair, began checking the controls.

"That is my intent," Noah said.

"But it's too dangerous down there," Tesh sputtered.

"I need to check on the Guardians," Noah said. "They're at risk because of me, and I need to go to them. The Doge and my sister have captured some, and others have taken refuge in the forests near our compound."

"How do you know all that?"

Without answering her, not telling her what he had overheard Francella and the Doge say during Noah's own fantastic mental journey through the galaxy, he said instead, "Maybe I can find enough of our people to organize a resistance movement. This may be too dangerous for the rest of you, so you can leave anytime you wish."

Noah's companions fell silent, as his comments sank in.

Presently, Noah took Tesh and Anton aside, and said to them, "Remember, you told me the Diggers made a tunnel system that honeycombed much of my compound? Could you draw me a map, using the ship's computer system?"

"Maybe," Anton said. "We've been in those tunnels chasing the Diggers and shutting them down, but they just burrow in all directions, without any organized plan."

"If you could recall the main passageways, including any beneath my old administration buildings, that would be a big help." It occurred to Noah that he might journey there mentally, but he did not feel entirely comfortable—or safe—in that realm yet. The rapid growth of his paranormal powers opened up an exciting new realm to him, but it was also terrifying, like walking a tightrope between extreme mental clarity and complete lunacy. For now, he preferred to obtain the information this way.

"I think we might do that," Tesh said. "Between the two of us."

"All right," Noah said. "Get to work on it."

Presently, Dr. Bichette returned to the grid-plane, accompanied by two teenage boys. "We've got a dead man in the passenger compartment," the doctor said. "These young people were with him, and are telling a fantastic story, that they were plucked out of thin air and taken aboard. It sounds like a lot of gibberish to me, but I want you to hear it for yourself."

Gazing beyond the doctor, Noah met the gazes of the two youths he had previously remote-viewed in the passenger compartment. They appeared to be confused, and were obviously quite upset at the death of their companion. They exchanged introductions with Noah and the others, then repeated their story for Noah, adding details.

After listening intently, Noah had little to say in response. He decided privately that the matter would require more thought and analysis, in a manner that he could best do on his own.

"You're free to go," Noah said to the boys, "or we can take you into our organization." He identified himself and provided them with basic information about the Guardians and their ecological mission, but didn't mention what he had in mind yet, an attempt to reestablish his operations on Canopa.

Acey Zelk described again how he and his cousin had jumped out of the treasure ship with the captain, and asked what had happened to them, how they had been pulled out of the air.

"I'm not sure," Noah said, and this was mostly true. He saw no benefit in speculation, or in saying anything more about the matter.

"We're treasure hunters," Dux Hannah said, "but I'd say we're out of a job now. Speaking for Acey here—and he's gotten me into trouble by speaking for me—I'd say you have two new recruits, Mr. Watanabe."

"First I need to tell you more about what you're getting into," Noah said. "I'm heading into real danger, going after the people who stole my property and killed the Guardians who worked for me. Our enemies are powerful, the Doge Lorenzo himself, and my own turncoat sister."

Acey whistled. "Sounds worse than jumping out of a ship with no parachute."

"Could be," Noah said. He looked around the compartment, at the others. "I think I know what Subi's answer is, but I'm giving all of you, including him, the opportunity to leave right now. If necessary, I'll proceed without any of you. I can fly this grid-plane myself, maybe not as well as Subi, but I can get it down to the surface, and the on-board scanning system should enable me to elude the Doge's surveillance grid. The risk is obvious, but it's critical for me to get down there and rally the Guardians against the schemes of Lorenzo and my sister."

"I'm with you, Master Noah," Subi said, without any hesitation.

"So am I," Anton said, from a chair at the computer terminal.

"We are, too," Dux said. Beside him, Acey nodded.

Looking at Eshaz and seeing him nod his large, scaly head, Noah didn't need to hear him speak to know he would risk his own life with theirs. The two of them had an affinity that transcended galactic races and star systems, and even time itself. Noah felt like they had been friends forever, though he knew that could not possibly be the case. The Guardian leader sensed extreme dangers ahead of him—it could be a suicide mission—but he had to face these particular enemies himself and not flee or send in surrogates to do his bidding.

"I'm not getting off this ride yet," Tesh said. She made an adjustment to the tunnel map that Anton was drawing on the computer.

Staring at Dr. Bichette, whose silence had been palpable, Noah said, "We have no real need for your services any more, so I wish I could allow you to return to your home on Canopa. Unfortunately, I can't do that, though, because you're a security risk. Even if you tried to keep your mouth shut, the Doge would take you in for questioning in his notorious Gaol of Brimrock."

The doctor shot a lingering look at his old girlfriend, then scowled and asked, "How old are you, anyway? You've never told me."

"And I never will," she answered, with a sly smile.

Noah thought about her broken relationships with Dr. Hurk Bichette and the shaky subsequent relationship with Anton Glavine. He didn't want to be the next victim on her trail of broken hearts, but couldn't help the feelings of attraction that he felt for her.

Standing in front of Noah with her hands on her hips, Tesh said, "The only reason I'm sticking around is because you have some explaining to do."

"I see it the other way around," he snapped.

She bit her lip and muttered to herself. A mixture of emotions played across her face: shock, anger, and confusion.

As Noah saw the situation, the two of them were growing farther and farther apart. In one respect, he thought this was a shame, since he was attracted to her, though he would never admit his feelings to anyone, or act on them. Honoring Anton's obvious love for her, Noah wanted to keep his distance from any entanglement. In the past she had been flirtatious toward him, but he couldn't imagine having any relationship with her.

"So, you're with me, Tesh?" Noah asked.

"I just said I was." Angrily, she looked away.

With an exasperated sigh, Noah gave instructions for Anton and the boys to bring the dead captain on board the grid-plane, so that they could make proper arrangements for his body.

Half an hour later, Subi guided the grid-plane out of the cargo hold and into a docking berth of the pod station, where they connected and awaited their turn to depart. There were other grid-planes in the berths of this busy facility, and bigger merchant vessels. Four large podships loomed in the central docking bay, including their own craft.

"Uh oh," Subi said. He pointed through the front window, and Noah saw around a dozen Red Beret officers on a nearby platform, looking at Noah's grid-plane and talking among themselves.

"Our ship is still painted Guardian colors," Anton said.

The Red Beret commander did not take long to make his decision. He and his men hurried to board their own ship, several berths away.

Subi activated his weapons system, causing panels to slide open on the side of the grid-plane, revealing high caliber puissant guns. The barrels glowed blue. At a nod from Noah, Subi backed out into the airless vacuum of the docking bay. Just as the Red Beret vessel attempted to do the same, Subi opened fire on it, riddling the hull with holes.

A weapons panel opened on the Red Beret craft, but too late. Subi's shots struck their mark, and the vessel exploded in a ball of blue and orange. Debris and the bodies of the Doge's soldiers floated in the docking bay.

One of the nearby merchant vessels was hit by the explosion, and within seconds small robots scurried onto the hull, making repairs. The damage appeared to be superficial, and not near the engines. Then an odd assortment of sentient machines streamed out of that craft and others moored by it, scurrying through airlocks onto the walkway. The machines were dented, scuffed, and dull. They looked like refugees from a scrap pile, but were moving efficiently, and took positions on the walkway.

Just then, more Red Beret soldiers appeared on the walkway, running toward empty airlocks, including the one where Noah's grid-plane had been berthed. The men wore breather shields over their faces, which would permit them to open the airlocks and fire through them.

But the sentient machines lifted their robotic arms in synchronization, and their hands became an assortment of glistening weapons: guns, mini-crossbows, and dart shooters. They opened fire on the Red-Berets, cutting them down on the walkway and in the airlocks.

"We have unexpected allies," Noah said. He and Subi scanned the ships and walkways, looking for more opponents. None appeared. The machines mopped up the rest of the soldiers, killing them to the last, while only losing a couple from their own ranks.

"Who are those guys?" Anton said.

"I don't know," Noah responded. The engines of several machine vessels were firing, glowing orange in their exhaust tubes.

Then he recalled the fantastic mental excursion he had taken, when he saw podships crossing the galaxy, and one of them was filled with robot ships journeying from the Inn of the White Sun to Canopa. These must be the same sentient machines, a small army of them. And they had come to his aid. But he kept the information to himself for the moment.

Now most of the armed robots reboarded their ships, but some stayed on the body-strewn walkway. One of the machines became apparent now, the flat-bodied robot that Noah remembered seeing in his earlier vision. The others gathered around him and waved their mechanical hands—no longer showing weapons—in the direction of Noah's grid-plane.

"Pull back into the dock," Noah ordered. "Let's see why they helped us."

Chapter Seventy-Five

> One of the great delights of life is the discovery of new friends.
>
> —Noah Watanabe

The leader of the robot force was one of the most peculiar sentient machines that Noah had ever encountered. His flat-bodied appearance was somewhat seedy—dull gray with a small dent on the front of his face plate, and numerous scuff marks. Most robots that looked that bad were no longer operating. His companions didn't look any better.

The robot featured a hinge arrangement at the center of its body, by which Noah had earlier seen him fold open and closed. "I am called Thinker," this one announced. "We saw you blow up the Red Beret vessel, and noticed the green-and-brown colors of your grid-plane. Obviously, you are Guardians."

Noah did not reply, nor did those who stood with him, his companions on the trip here.

"And you are Master Noah Watanabe," Thinker said.

Stepping up beside Noah, Subi feigned a laugh and said, "He just resembles Watanabe."

"We might point you in the right direction, though," Noah added, "but first tell us why you want to see him."

"I must contemplate this," the leader of the robots said. Abruptly, he folded shut again, tucking himself away like a metal version of a turtle.

Scowling, Subi rested his hand on a holstered pistol that

he had put on, just before going to talk with the machines.

Moving close, Tesh walked around the flat-bodied machine, which was now motionless. The other machines stood nearby rigidly, but in non-threatening postures. "What's he doing?" she asked.

They didn't answer.

Moments later, the machine leader folded open. His metal-lidded eyes blinked yellow and then green. He faced Noah, and said, "I have considered the facts, and I was not mistaken. You are Noah Watanabe."

Noah did not respond, nor did his companions.

"Your identity is obvious to me," the machine said. "Even without the vast amount of data available to me, you are a well-known fugitive."

"Why did you help us?" Noah asked, ignoring the assertion.

"Consider it our employment application," Thinker said. "We wish to join the Guardians, and thought this battle would look good on our résumés."

"We want to be Guardians!" the machines shouted in unison.

A chill of delight ran down Noah's spine, but still he hesitated. Calmly, he walked from machine to machine, examining them closely, looking into their metal eyes and checking their blinking, multicolored sensors. Halting at one of the heavily armored sentient machines, he did a double take.

"This is not a machine," he announced. Through the visor of the face plate, he saw the unmistakable glint of Human eyes, and the skin of a Caucasian.

Moving to Noah's side, Thinker said, "Quite right, my new friend. This is the brother of your famous inventor Jacopo Nehr."

"Giovanni Nehr?" Noah said. Surprised, he looked more closely.

The armored man nodded.

While Noah had never met the younger Nehr, he had seen him in public, and knew his reputation as a proud man who never got along well with his famous brother. Because of the strained relationship Noah had with his own father, a renowned man like Jacopo Nehr, he thought he might have something in common with this strange soldier.

Suddenly the armored man appeared to get very nervous, and looked in the direction of Acey and Dux, who were whispering between themselves and pointing angrily at Nehr.

Then, before anyone could stop them, the boys rushed at Nehr. They knocked him down and began pummeling him through openings in his armor. Robots pulled them apart.

"It seems that we have a minor problem," Thinker said.

Giovanni Nehr, despite his superior size and armor, appeared terrified of the boys. Blood trickled from his nose.

"What's the problem here?" Noah asked. He glared at the teenagers.

"Nothing we can't work out ourselves," Acey said.

Dux didn't add anything to that.

"What do you have to say?" Noah said, looking at the man. All three of the combatants had been released by the robots now, and looked very angry.

"Same," Nehr said. "Just a little misunderstanding, that's all. We'll work it out. I promise you, sir, this won't happen again."

"They don't seem to like you," Noah said. "I want to know why."

"Uh," Nehr said, "we were in an airvator together, escaping from a Mutati prison moon, and the guards shot us up pretty good. I was just trying to keep my balance and almost pushed Dux out through a hole, entirely by accident. I didn't mean to stumble against him. Fortunately he held on, but he was understandably angry."

Dux muttered something.

Turning to Dux, Noah asked, "Could you have been mistaken? Is he telling the truth?"

"Sir," the young man said, "speaking for myself, I'm prepared to let the matter drop. I promise you that. Whatever I thought about him before is nowhere near as important as the mission you want us to accomplish. We'll set our differences aside."

"Right," Acey said, nodding. But his expression, and Dux's, looked less than convincing.

"One of the disadvantages of your race," Thinker said, stepping closer to Noah. "Personalities inevitably get in the way." The lights on his face plate glowed a cheery orange. "Now my machines, on the other hand, have no such problems. I tell them what to do, and they do it."

"Your point is well taken," Noah said.

"We have come all the way from the Inn of the White Sun to join your force of environmental activists," Thinker said. "We even have our own flying ships," he boasted, "faster than your grid-plane." He pointed at the battered vessels berthed in the docking bay. "We have many ships at this pod station, filled with more than thirty-five hundred fighting machines. The Red Berets only discovered us today, and began asking questions. We cannot remain here now."

Noah could not believe his own ears. Pensively, he rubbed his chin. "So you think I'm Noah Watanabe, eh?" he said, resting a hand on Thinker's shoulder.

"I know you are . . . sir. In my data banks, I have images of you, and voice prints, to mention only a couple of the identity markers."

"Welcome to the Guardians," Noah said, with a broad smile. He clasped the metal hand of the robot and shook it briskly. "I hereby formally commission all of you."

"And we formally accept." The machine leader raised both hands over his head, and the pod station filled with the roar of thousands of machines.

"Well, here's something that's not in your data banks," Noah said, with an intense stare. He took Thinker aside, and told him where he would like to land on Canopa, and that he needed to scout the area first by making a low fly-over with the grid-plane, while the other ships waited a safe distance away.

"We're going around to the dark side of the planet," Noah said. "We'll be looking through infrared, with the ship blacked out and our scanning system activated. Do you have those capabilities?"

"Are you kidding? We've got the latest gadgets, and even the latest gadgets for our gadgets. Well, maybe I shouldn't boast too much. Everything's a few years old, but we do have night vision capability and the ability to evade surveillance grids. When you activate your systems, we'll do the same."

"Good." Noah provided coordinates to the leader of the sentient robots, and the two of them agreed upon arrangements for the scouting and subsequent reconnoitering.

Moments later, the motley-looking force of spaceships taxied toward the exit tunnels.

Chapter Seventy-Six

> Noah Watanabe is unable to conceal the locations of many of his ecological recovery projects and other enterprises. We found documents and computer files concerning his galactic operations, and employees who responded to our questions, though only under torture. Still, we suspect there are more Guardian facilities, as yet unrevealed. He's out there somewhere, with the ragtag remnants of his company, but we don't know where. He's like a ghost in the galaxy.
>
> —File NW27, Report to the Doge Lorenzo del Velli

Noah's grid-plane led a procession of ships down toward the surface of Canopa. Seated by a porthole in the passenger compartment, he was struck by the raw natural beauty of his homeworld as he entered the atmosphere, with its deep green forests, pale blue seas, and snow-capped mountains. To the west, the late afternoon sky glowed a soft golden hue, rimmed by an orange line along the horizon. Such a glorious view. He was glad to be back.

He was just thinking that the planet must be putting on a show for his benefit, in honor of his return, when he looked to the north. In that direction the weather was quite different, with roiling clouds and jagged flashes of lightning. At the controls of the small ship, Subi reported that the storm was heading toward them. It was an unusually deep disturbance, he said, with powerful winds in the upper and lower atmospheres.

"Can we outrun it?" Noah asked.

"I don't know if we want to. This weather could actually be a blessing in disguise, covering our approach."

Noah glanced at the navigation desk, on one end of the instrument console. Anton and Tesh sat at the nav-computer, putting finishing touches on the tunnel map that Noah had ordered. A half hour ago, they had shown him an earlier version on the screen. Based upon that, Noah had decided to scout the southwest corner of his former ecological demonstration compound, looking for a possible landing site there. With luck, he would be able to enter the tunnels and set up a base there for his resistance operation, in a place where the Red Beret and CorpOne forces would never to think to look.

"We can fly through this storm, then?" Noah rose and went over behind Subi, where he held onto the chair-back and looked over the adjutant's shoulder at the instrument console, with its dials, meters, and gauges.

"We can, but I don't know about those space jalopies behind us."

"I suspect the machines may be tougher than they look," Eshaz said, clumping heavily across the deck and standing by Noah. "And their vessels, too."

"We're about to find out," Subi said. "Take your seats, and get into your safety harnesses."

As Noah got into his own harness, he saw the big Tulyan showing Acey and Dux how to engage theirs. He had developed a liking for the boys, had told Noah privately that they were brave young adventurers, and he thought they were fine additions to the Guardians.

Eshaz barely had time to put on his own large harness when the grid-plane rattled as it entered the storm and bumped through the air currents.

It grew darker outside Noah's window. He squinted as a flash of lightning lit up the sky, like a high-powered ethereal spotlight.

When the flash dissipated, he could see a portion of Canopa clearly, but the view was framed by dark, rain-saturated clouds.

My beautiful Canopa, he thought.

Of all the worlds he had known in his travels around the galaxy, this one was by far the most pleasing to the eye. Even more important than that, it held a special place in his heart.

Without a moment's hesitation, Subi plunged the grid-plane through the slot in the clouds. Looking out the wide aft porthole, Noah saw the machine ships following. He counted them, and none were missing.

He had never expected to find so many recruits awaiting him upon his arrival at the pod station, and now he took a few seconds to consider his good fortune. Thinker, while unusual in his appearance and mannerisms, just might prove to be exactly what Noah needed, perhaps breaking the string of bad luck he'd been going through.

Inside the aerial tunnel, lightning flashed on all sides, brilliant orange zigzags in the clouds. Behind him, he heard Dr. Bichette cry out in surprise and fear.

Noah thought back to the images of Mutatis in merchant schooners that he saw in the cosmic web. They had been floating in space near pod stations in Mutati territory, and he had not been able to determine why. It had seemed like an odd dream, but one that overlapped into reality.

What did I see, and why was it accessible to me?

Aside from his desire to rescue any Guardians who had been captured or who had fled into the countryside, Noah had another reason for returning to Canopa. He felt mentally and physically stronger on his homeworld, as if invigorated by the living energy of the planet. Even before landing (and despite the bumpiness of the ride), he felt more animated, more able to carry on his important work. He knew the large planet well, and looking down saw the rugged canyons where he often went on retreat in earlier years. One day he would like to take new Guardian recruits there to teach them about ecology, the interdependence of life forms in harsh environments. He had made detailed notes on how such classes might be conducted, but had not yet put them into effect.

The grid-plane leveled out and headed toward the night side of the planet, crossing over a remote, unpopulated region that was only intermittently visible through turbulent, swirling clouds.

On the way, Noah noted how Subi was able to adjust the guidance and power to make the ride more smooth, like a person in a groundcar avoiding ruts and potholes. Noah also knew that the smoothness was not entirely dependent on the pilot's skill. Some of it was attributable to a computer program that reacted to the gusts of wind with equal and opposite forces. Elementary physics. But there were always surprises, both in intensity and direction, and some time ago Subi had explained to him that Humans were frequently better at reacting to unexpected situations than machines were.

In less than an hour, they began to pass into darkness.

"Switching to night vision," Subi finally said. Thirty seconds later, the passenger cabin changed to an eerie infrared darkness, including all computer screens. Looking through the aft porthole, Noah confirmed that Thinker and his robot force had done the same. The ships were shadows against the starlit night sky.

Down on the surface of the planet, Noah made out only

occasional lights, marking widely spaced Human settlements.

"The descendants of ancient Canopans live in wild, hostile regions down there," Noah said. In the darkness of the cabin, he saw his companions as ghostlike shapes, from the infrared mechanism that provided interior and exterior visibility for the pilot and passengers. "With our scanner on, it probably wouldn't matter if we switched on our lights," Noah said, "but I don't want to take any chances."

Presently, Subi reported that they were approaching the plateau where the robot ships were to wait, by prearrangement. He circled the area, then looped upward and sped off. Thinker's ships went into holding patterns.

Noah went to the nav-computer and studied the tunnel map. A small screen on one side showed the terrain of this region of Canopa, with them flying toward the Ecological Demonstration Project compound. Subi, ever conscious of security, had fitted this grid-plane with its long-range scanning system, one that could not only detect hostile forces at a great distance, but would also neutralize the surveillance features of the planet's electronic grid system.

"All clear in the southwest corner of the compound," Subi reported. "I'm picking up activity over at the main administration building in the center of the compound, but that's what we expected."

Noah's ecology complex was immense, covering many hectares of land. As the grid-plane swooped over one corner of the facility, he saw the maintenance building that Diggers had damaged, and gaping holes from the activity of the rampant machines and the counter operations of his own commandos.

From those missions and the new computer map that he now had, Noah knew that there were hundreds of deep tunnels beneath his compound and the adjacent land, and that all Diggers down there had either been destroyed or disabled. Anton and Tesh, commandos themselves, had shown him how to gain access to a network of burrows in the remote hills east of the maintenance building, far enough away that they might go undetected. With that as his base of operations, Noah intended to organize a resistance force, hoping to eventually regain control of his land and space station.

"Let's go get our new army," Noah said.

Subi nodded, and accelerated out toward the plateau where the machine ships were waiting. As Noah's aircraft rose up to the top of the plateau and burst into the sky, he was pleased to see the twelve machine ships still in a holding pattern. They blinked their infrared lights, and followed Subi's lead.

Undetected by Canopa's electronic grid system, Noah's force skimmed the ground and reached the eastern hills. After landing, they tucked their wings and hover-floated into the largest burrow, which led to an immense cavern. The burned-out hulks of three Digger machines were near the entrance.

As Noah stepped from the grid-plane to the floor of the cavern, he saw Thinker and summoned him. The scholarly robot clanked over, and bowed slightly. "Sir?" he said.

"Send robots back to seal the entrance behind us," Noah commanded. Looking back at Tesh and Anton, he ordered them to go with the robots, and to help Thinker supervise the operation.

The three of them marched off, and at a signal from Thinker they were joined by many sentient machines. While the physical camouflage work was being accomplished, Subi set up a multi-function scrambling device to prevent scanner detection from above. He was quick to say as he activated the system, however, that it still needed to be calibrated to the surrounding terrain and tunnel system, which could take several days.

Studying the scrambler machinery, Thinker said, "Perhaps I can speed up the calibration, and even improve the system. I will work on it."

"All right," Noah said.

Thinker and Noah accompanied Subi as the beefy adjutant made final settings to the scrambler system, which was supposed to erase heat and sound signatures, making them undetectable to their enemies aboveground and in adjacent tunnels. Finally the robot folded his body flat, saying he wanted to contemplate how to improve the system.

"What do you say we call this place Diggerville?" Subi asked, looking at Noah. "Our new headquarters . . . or should I say, our new digs?" He looked tired, and seemed a little giddy.

"Fine, fine." Noah smiled stiffly.

Leaving Thinker where he was, Noah and the crew of his grid-plane settled in for their first night underground, sleeping in the cabin of the aircraft while the machines stood guard.

Just before Noah drifted off to sleep he thought of Tesh, who slept not far from him on the carpeted deck. He heard the regular breathing and snoring of his companions, but in the shadows could only identify the intermittent, deep snorts of Eshaz, and saw his hulking form profiled against the low light of the instrument panel.

At the first opportunity, he wanted to have a conversation with Tesh. The two of them needed to clear the air.

Chapter Seventy-Seven

> All living forms are dying. Life is a vast and glorious empyrean curve, gaining strength and vitality, reaching a zenith, and then fading.
>
> —Noah Watanabe

In the darkness of the grid-plane cabin, Noah cried out in his sleep, but no one seemed to hear him. He sat up, or thought he did, and wondered why he could no longer hear the snoring of his companions, and why he could no longer see the slumbering form of Eshaz profiled against the light of the instrument panel.

He barely made out a flickering light that seemed to be way off in the distance. Presently it came into focus, a tiny pinpoint of illumination. Then another appeared beside it, and another, and another. With a start, he realized that they were stars, and that he was gazing into deep space. He felt the intense cold of the void, but could endure it nonetheless.

His mind told him that he was underground in a Digger burrow, and that this should not be happening, but he recalled his previous experience in which he cartwheeled across the galaxy on a fantastic cosmic journey. At the time, he had wondered if it had really occurred, or if it had only been a vivid dream. Subsequently, however, he'd had another paranormal experience, in which he took control of the podship and flew it to Canopa.

Now, he realized that he only had his left eye open.

Lifting the other eyelid, his body shuddered at what he

saw, a strange split vision in which the tableau of space and the interior of the grid-plane cabin were superimposed over one another, as in old-time double photographic images. He heard rumbling breathing, and saw the broken image of Eshaz in the shadows, and this time he saw Tesh as well, and Anton. All were asleep, breathing and snoring regularly.

Noah closed the eye with which he had been peering into space, and abruptly the cosmic panorama disappeared, leaving only the interior of the cabin, with its warmth and Human noises. He felt queasy, then uncertain and fearful. A shuddering shock shook his body, and it took him several moments to stop shaking.

Testing, he looked through one eye or the other, and sometimes both, to confirm the bizarre reality that had overtaken him. Why this was happening he could not determine, but through each eye he beheld a different reality—confusing double images. Each eye saw something entirely different, along with alternate sounds, smells, and other senses. All of his senses were now oddly linked to his vision.

First I journeyed across the cosmos in my mind, he thought, *and then I did it physically when I piloted the podship.*

So odd, two realities—one ethereal and the other physical—overlapping at times and separate at times. His brain had capabilities that he had never imagined possible, and now each eye seemed to be linked to different aspects of that brain. He felt freakish, as if he was splitting into parts, with no control over the changes.

Opening only one eye at a time, he found that he could completely change his reality. With his left eye he saw—and telepathically *entered*—the cold cosmic-web realm, while with his right eye he saw the low light of the grid-plane cabin, and felt the warmth and nearness of his friends. This at least was an aspect of control, albeit minimal, as he could open and shut the two realities. But he couldn't make his brain and eyes stop generating the peculiar, disturbing phenomenon.

Abruptly, he felt something odd where his left foot used to be, a tingling sensation where nothing remained any longer. Noah had heard of that happening to injury victims, in which they seemed to feel missing limbs and appendages. Looking down along his body, he saw a faint illumination around the bottom of his left leg, where he knew the stump was.

He moved his left leg, and to his amazement saw what looked like his missing foot in the soft ambient glow.

Not possible. I'm only imagining this.

The illumination faded, and with it his foot seemed to disappear, and he felt nothing there at all. Darkness enveloped him and he saw nothing, heard nothing and felt nothing, not even the warmth of the cabin or the hard carpet under him. He found himself unable to reach out and check, or move his body at all. With one exception.

His eyes.

Trying to sort it all out, he closed both eyes and sat in the silence of his thoughts. But something interfered, refusing to leave him in serenity. He felt drawn outward, as if by a magnet. Cautiously, he opened his left eye just a little, and peered through the slit between his eyelids.

Noah could not resist the temptation to see more of the bizarre cosmic domain, to *experience* more of it. Once again, his thoughts surged out into the mysterious void of space, along a mystical cosmic webway. Every element of the web surrounded him, enfolded him, welcomed and embraced him. He was part of it, and looking back found that he could observe himself. There was no ground beneath him and no sky overhead, only the gossamer strands connecting him with every other point in the galaxy.

He was a Human inside a navigation chamber; he was a podship itself; he was every member of every galactic race.

By following the curving web, spinning through it, Noah found that he could reach virtually any point in the imagination of the Supreme Being who had created this wondrous kingdom of stars—and that he could move from point to point almost instantaneously. Everything floated around him, as if he was underwater. He did not seem to breathe or to have a heartbeat.

As before, he became aware of other cosmic voyagers spinning along the web—people, podships, and passengers going this way and that, passing over, under and through him, just as he did with them, in a realm that seemed to be non-physical. Who were these web travelers? Were they like him?

During his first paranormal voyage like this, he had wondered if he was dead or dying, and if the others out there were as well. He had been deathly ill then, in a comatose state. His health was much improved now. Or was it? In his sleep, had he again slipped into a coma?

And out in the cosmos, in the non-physical realm, he felt his missing foot again, and knew his body had grown a new one. In an epiphany, he realized that his corporal form had undergone a remarkable transformation. He was not dying at all. It was exactly the opposite. His injury had been healed by the web when Eshaz connected him to it. More than healed. His genetic structure had been altered in the procedure, with the gene that activated the aging process switched off.

I am immortal.

But how could that have happened? The answer did not come to him, but another did. In its original form it was a wordless answer, but the Human portion of his mind translated it for him, so that he could begin to understand.

The magical realm that saved him was an eternal continuum in which vast distances were covered in infinitesimal fragments of time. Time began billions of years ago, but the complete life of the galaxy might encompass only a few moments. Before him, the webbing expanded, folded, compressed, and took shapes he could barely imagine—while unimagined secrets remained concealed from him.

From somewhere far away Noah heard voices, and almost recognized them. They were calling for him by name, asking if he was all right. He struggled and opened both eyes, lifting the lids with great difficulty as if they were very heavy.

The split images returned, one tableau superimposed over another.

He heard himself cry out again, and saw Dr. Bichette and the robot leader Thinker standing over him, engaged in a worried conversation about his welfare. They seemed to be floating out in space, no longer on the deck of the grid-plane. Like a Human-sized god or an angel, the doctor hovered over Noah, and began checking his vital signs.

As moments passed, the split images ceased, and with both eyes he saw that the doctor and Thinker were standing in the grid-plane cabin again, this time with Tesh, Anton, and Subi.

"Are you all right?" Tesh asked. Noah felt the warmth of her hand in his, and knew he had returned to the living. He was lying on the deck, with his legs under a blanket.

Slowly, deliberately, he moved the blanket and looked at his own left leg, where there had been a stump.

The foot was there, and when he saw the expressions of horrified fascination on the faces of the others, he knew it was no apparition. Even Eshaz, who rarely showed any emotion at all, looked utterly astounded.

Chapter Seventy-Eight

Life is a sea of darkness, scattered with islands of light.
—From a Sirikan folk tale

The following day, Noah experienced no recurrence of the split visions, the odd straddling of two dimensions, the one physical and the other ethereal. It had all been like a dream, but a tangible souvenir of it remained.

His regrown foot.

He felt emotionally lifted, and excited. Something truly remarkable had happened to him. He knew this for certain when he confirmed over and over that the body part had in fact regenerated, like the appendage of a reptile. Squeezing the flesh of the new foot and toes with his fingers, he felt the remarkable bone and tissue growth beneath his left ankle. It was almost as if the doctor had never amputated, but the new growth was tender, and he limped when he tried to walk on it. He still had to use the crutches that Subi had improvised for him.

Noah wondered if this miracle was an aspect of his immortality.

Encountering him in the cavern outside the grid-plane, a bewildered Dr. Bichette said, "I want to bring a bone specialist in to look at you." Eshaz, Tesh, Anton, and Subi were with him. Earlier, he had examined the foot.

"And what would he tell us?" Noah asked, waving one of his alloy crutches around. "That it's impossible, that it couldn't have happened? I'd be put under a microscope, asked to go on a medical sideshow tour as a freak."

Bichette stared at the regenerated foot, which Noah had covered with a sock and a shoe.

"I don't have time for all that nonsense," Noah said. "I have more important things to do now; I need to maintain security and lead the resistance movement." He looked from face to face, and settled on the scaly bronze countenance of Eshaz, whom he had always considered as much a friend as an employee. "You know what happened to me, don't you?"

"Some will say I should not have done what I did," Eshaz said, "that it was too dangerous."

"And what did you do to Noah, exactly?" Tesh asked.

The big Tulyan hung his head. "I've said all I can say here. I must report to the Council of Elders, and accept their punishment. You will probably never see me again afterward."

"Whatever Eshaz did to me," Noah said to the others, "I'm grateful to him. But I don't want the rest of you to discuss my medical condition with anyone, not even the robots. Is that understood?"

He waited until he got a nod from each of them, but didn't notice when Subi shook his head afterward.

"Tell everyone I have a prosthetic foot now," Noah said. He walked away stiffly, but was beginning to feel a little better with each step.

After the group separated, Tesh switched off her personal magnification system and in her tiny form began to spy on Noah in the cavern and connecting tunnels, scrambling around behind him unseen.

Rounding a corner, she came face to face with a roachrat. The creature, around her height, stared at her with dark, beady eyes. Its antennae twitched, and it bared its sharp teeth. A moment later, the animal squealed and ran away.

Noah slipped into a small side cavern. Then, looking around to make certain no one was watching, he drew a knife from its sheath and slashed his own left wrist. Pointing the wrist away from his clothes, he watched in fascination as the blood flow stopped and the wound healed itself, in a matter of minutes. No sign of the injury remained. He even felt his internal chemistry converting reserves and restoring the lost blood.

Taking a deep breath to summon his courage, Noah then attempted something even more drastic.

Holding the handle of the knife with both hands, he plunged it into his own heart, feeling it crack through bone and cartilage and pierce the organ. He gasped and cried out, then toppled over onto the ground, with gouts of blood spurting from his chest. All bodily functions ceased.

Seconds passed.

Then, like Lazarus, he rose from the dead and stood in his own blood, as his cells regenerated themselves.

In horror and fascination, Tesh watched Noah's drastic self-experimentation and a walking frenzy he went into, hurrying this way and that around the cavern. She saw him throw the crutches away and actually begin to run around the cavern, slowly at first and then faster. Noah looked elated, and this frightened her.

What sort of creature is this? she wondered. *What has Eshaz done to him?*

Unexpected thoughts assailed her. Tesh began to consider ways to destroy Noah, incinerating his body in such a conflagration that he could not possibly regenerate himself. In her lifetime, and from what she had been told by Woldn, there were no immortal creatures in the entire universe. Even those that seemed to be were not. They all had an Achilles heel.

Somehow, Noah had embarked on a dangerous, intrusive course of evolution, a fantastic mutation of the genetic process. If his dangerous bloodline was permitted to continue, there could be others like him, a race of powerful Humans who could commit terrible acts, including taking podships away from the Parviis who had held dominion over them for hundreds of thousands of years. Just as Tesh's Parviis had once replaced the Tulyans, so too could another race prove itself superior and gain dominion. Woldn, the Eye of the Swarm, had long warned of this. It was the subject of legends.

She just hoped it was not too late to stop the mutant. . . .

Later that day, she crept away from the tunnel compound, a minuscule form that none of them noticed leaving. Like an insect, Tesh emitted a faint, wingless buzzing noise and flew all the way to the orbital pod station. (In swarms Parviis could fly much farther, even across the galaxy, but not by themselves). The tiny airborne humanoid reached the podship, but found herself unable to gain entrance to the sectoid chamber, unable to make the vessel move at all. The stubborn vessel proved unresponsive to her commands.

In the ancient podship's passenger compartment and on the walkway of the pod station outside, she scuttled about like a bug, eavesdropping on Red Beret officers, scientists, and others who wondered why the sentient vessel did not depart like a normal podship and resume its route around the galaxy. The investigators were poring over it, trying to discover its secrets. So far they had not found the hidden passageways or the sectoid chamber, and Tesh didn't think that they could.

But she'd never thought that a full-sized Human could have piloted the spacecraft, either. The Parviis had long known that there was more than one way to control podships. Long ago, Tulyans had their method, and Parviis had their own. Now the likelihood of yet another terrified her.

She envisioned a universe of untapped secrets.

Thinker thought the four Humans and the Tulyan were behaving strangely. That evening he watched as they slipped into a shadowy side tunnel. Moments later he heard them arguing, their voices escaping from the darkness into the dimly lit main cavern. Listening, he picked out their voices—Tesh, Subi, Anton, Dr. Bichette, and Eshaz.

Abruptly, a rotund man emerged from the tunnel and hurried across the cavern with surprising speed, heading for the main entrance. Moving as quietly as he could while maintaining his distance, Thinker followed.

He watched as Subi Danvar used his own code to bypass the security system, then slipped around large rocks and shrubs that the robots had placed over the entrance, and disappeared into the night.

Chapter Seventy-Nine

> All of us see life through the lens of personal experience, and how limited those experiences are! The sum total of all Human knowledge is but a pinprick in the universe. So it is with each star system as well, in relation to all other star systems. A universe of pinpricks.
>
> —Master Noah Watanabe

As required under the most ancient procedures of his people, Eshaz prepared to send a message to the Council of Elders, informing them of his unforgivable transgressions, violating the most consecrated of rules. In the transmittal, to be sent by touching the web and sending a telepathic transmission through it, he would not attempt to mitigate what he had done, because that would only make matters worse. It was hard to imagine how he could be in more trouble, considering the risks he had taken to save just one life, and that of a mere Human. The web was the most sacred object in the entire galaxy, and tampering with it was a most grievous offense. Since time immemorial there had been carefully prescribed regulations for its use and maintenance, and he had always followed them.

Until the episode with Noah.

Just before one of the prescribed times for telepathic transmissions, Eshaz prepared to place a scaly bronze finger against a strand of web. He was about to reach out of the commonly perceived physical dimension and touch another that was on a higher, more ethereal level.

Timeweb.

His fingers moved close, but he did not yet make contact.

Subi Danvar knew the back ways well, for he had walked and driven them for years as one of Noah Watanabe's faithful Guardians. But this evening was like none other. He was alone out here, in a moonlit wilderness of unknown perils, running along a paved road, breathing hard, pushing his physical limits.

Reaching the shuttle landing field at the perimeter of the compound, he saw half a dozen stock groundjets parked behind a storage building, and no visible security. With one of those vehicles he could reach Rainbow City, and obtain a good doctor for Noah. Ever conscious of safety measures, Subi thought it would have been too risky to take Noah's grid-plane or one of the robot ships on this mission. They were better left where they were, since he had just received an intelligence report that Doge Lorenzo was making improvements to the planet's surveillance grid system, and he wanted to find out what had been done before going airborne again.

He ran for one of the groundjets, staying low, hugging the shadows.

For moments, Eshaz had been reconsidering, forming all sorts of rationalizations in his mind for delaying his transmission or not making it all, defenses he might use if ever summoned before the Council of Elders on this matter. Of utmost importance, he wanted to protect Noah Watanabe, the remarkable Human who had shown more concern for the interrelationships between planets and star systems than anyone in the history of his people. As only three races knew—the Tulyans, the Parviis, and the Aopoddae—the entire galaxy was connected by a gossamer but strong and essential web that spanned time and space. This made Noah's own concept of galactic ecology all the more remarkable, though he could not possibly know how right he was. Eshaz wasn't sure how to tell him, either; Humans were not one of the privy races, so Noah was not supposed to be informed about such secrets.

Still, Eshaz felt Noah had already expanded the knowledge of his race with what he had done, and that he had the potential to do much more. In Eshaz's mind, this was linked directly to his own primary assignment from the Council of Elders, which was to protect and maintain the web. He felt he had done exactly that by saving Noah's life, but his bold (the council might say brash) decision would still require considerable explanation on his part.

The prescribed time arrived, and Eshaz placed a quivering fingertip against a slender strand of web, touching it ever so gently. He did not transmit, but felt the coursing energy of the web, the distant podships traveling on their various routes, along with the mental communications of Tulyans who reported to the Elders and received orders from them. He also heard the subtle but disturbing noises of breakage in the web, the disintegration that was continuing, no matter the efforts of the Tulyans to prevent it.

At the very last possible second, a message arrived from the Council of Elders, sent to him personally like a whisper across the cosmos: *Return to the Starcloud immediately.*

His heart sank. They must know, or suspect what he had done, and intended to interrogate him.

In fear, Eshaz removed his finger from the web and hunched over, his entire body trembling. The next transmission time would not take place for seven galactic days, and the Elders wanted him to report sooner than that. He could reach the Tulyan Starcloud today if he made the next podship, and tomorrow at the latest. The pod station here at Canopa was one of the busiest in the galaxy, with ships arriving and departing regularly, connecting the world with all points of the astronomical compass.

Now he would have to confess under less-than-ideal circumstances, enduring the suspicious glares of his superiors. It would have been better if he had volunteered the information.

Eshaz expected the worst, although they probably didn't have the evidence against him that they needed yet. If they'd had it, they might have dispatched someone to execute him on the spot—a punishment that had been used in the past, on rare occasions. If they did have the proof already, the Elders might still want to conduct a public tribunal and use him as an example, to keep anyone else from tapping into the web improperly. He felt certain that he would be declared one of the worst criminals in the history of his people, and that his name would go down in infamy.

At his trial, he could at least explain why he drained critical nutrients from the web without first asking for permission from the Council, and how he'd needed to move quickly to save Noah Watanabe's life, since the Human's vital signs had declined rapidly and he was on the verge of death. Eshaz doubted if it would do any good to present a defense, but if given the opportunity he would lay it all out, including the full and remarkable story of Noah Watanabe . . . a man whose life mattered much more than his own.

Schemes flowed through Giovanni Nehr's mind like the currents of an ocean, deep beneath the surface.

The day before, he had overheard Acey Zelk and Dux Hannah telling Noah how they hid inside the storage compartment of a food delivery robot to escape from a slave crew in the Doge's Palazzo Magnifico. The story had given Gio an idea.

During the time that he had worked with Thinker's army of robots, Gio had learned a great deal about machines and their internal operating systems. Moving quickly, under the guise of fine-tuning two large robots, he had programmed changes into them. These were unmarked mechanical units, of a type that the Guardians planned to send into nearby towns on reconnaissance missions, in conjunction with Human operatives.

Then, in the shadows of a tunnel, Gio had knocked the teenagers out with drugdarts, using one of the weapons that Thinker had given to him. He then stuffed Acey into a large compartment inside one of the robots, and Dux inside the other robot.

Giovanni Nehr did not dislike the boys, and did not wish them any real harm. But he needed to deal with them for his own survival and advancement, which were his highest priorities. Other stories that he'd heard the boys telling the Guardians would provide him with an excellent cover, in particular their boastful tales of stowing away on ships and vagabonding around the galaxy. People would think they ran off for more adventures.

Gio didn't have the stomach to kill the teenagers, and hoped they didn't die because of his actions. But he knew he was putting them in danger, casting them into the perilous ocean of space. Now he watched on a remote camera screen as the robots did their work, and projected images back to him. . . .

The sentient machines, carrying their unusual cargoes,

entered the nearest shuttleport, and studied the electronic labels on space-cargo boxes in a storage yard, showing that they were being shipped to a variety of star systems and planets. As programmed, the robots selected the farthest, most remote destination.

When no one was looking, the sentient machines loaded the motionless bodies into a cargo container filled with crates of computer parts, after removing some of the contents and then making sure there were air holes in the box.

Observing it all on the small screen, Gio thought, *If they're meant to live, they'll live. If they're meant to die, they'll die.* He had done everything necessary to keep his own conscience clear, taking steps to save their lives by assuring them of air.

As programmed, the robots waited in shadows while a mechanized crew loaded the containers on board a shuttle. Satisfied, Gio watched while the shuttle lifted off. Now he didn't have to sleep with one eye open. If the boys survived, they had no assets and would have a hard time finding their way back here. He didn't expect to ever see them again.

Subi slipped into the command chair of the groundjet. Taking a deep breath, he activated the controls and saw the instrument panel light up with shimmering, lambent colors. His fingers moved expertly, and he waited to hear the engines turn over.

But they didn't start, even though the hydion charges were full.

He cursed, hit the backup button. Nothing happened.

Spotlights lit up the parking area outside. Men shouted, and he heard the sounds of boots running on pavement.

Red Beret soldiers surrounded the vehicle, and took him into custody.

Chapter Eighty

Each of us must face a judgment day.
—Ancient Saying

The following afternoon. . . .

After crossing space and arriving at the pod station over the Tulyan Starcloud, Eshaz passed through an airlock. Pausing, he watched four robots loading space-cargo boxes onto a walkway. In other places around the galaxy, especially at merchant prince worlds, this would not have been extraordinary, since products were always being picked up and delivered. But in this remote star system it was highly unusual. Largely self-sufficient, Tulyans did not import very many articles.

Working hurriedly, the robots accidentally dropped one of the large boxes as they were trying to hoist it on top of the others, and it split open. To Eshaz's shock, two Human bodies tumbled out, along with crates of computer parts, which spilled their contents all over the walkway.

Eshaz saw one of the bodies move, and then the other. He recognized Acey Zelk and Dux Hannah. As they struggled to their feet, the teenagers looked dazed and confused, and had bumps and cuts on their faces.

The robots chattered among themselves, and sent beeping electronic signals back and forth. Then, leaving the mess behind them, they hurried back through the airlock and reboarded the podship. Moments later, the vessel departed.

"You boys all right?" Eshaz asked.

"I think so," Dux said, as he looked at his shorter cousin, who was testing a bruise on his forehead.

"I have a terrible headache," Acey said.

"Me too," Dux said. "I think we were drugged."

"I don't know about that," Eshaz said, narrowing his already slitted eyes, "but there may have been low oxygen in the cargo hold of the podship. Whatever the cause, this should make you feel better." Bringing a small bag out of a body pouch in his side, he opened it and scattered green dust on the boys. Within moments their injuries healed, and the teenagers said their headaches were gone, too.

"How did we get in that cargo box?" Dux asked, as he and Acey accompanied the Tulyan along the walkway.

"You didn't crawl in yourselves?"

"No disrespect intended," Dux said, "but I wouldn't have asked the question if we had."

"Maybe someone doped you and put you in the box," Eshaz said. "There is a likely candidate, but you should not jump to conclusions."

"Giovanni Nehr," Acey said. "I can't wait to get my hands on him!"

Showing that he was the more introspective of the two, Dux said, "We need to cool off before we deal with him. I don't think we should go back to Canopa right now, or we might do something we'll regret."

With a nod, Eshaz said, "That would be wise. The personal feud between you and the inventor's brother could be destructive. Keep in mind, too, that Master Noah does not need that sort of conflict around him, not with all the important matters he must attend to."

Acey sulked as he walked along.

"There is no proof that Gio did it," Eshaz said, "but perhaps the truth will surface."

"Where are we?" Dux asked.

Eshaz answered the question, then offered to put the boys under his protection for a while. "I feel responsible for you now," he said, "and I won't hear of letting you go off on your own."

"So we have no choice in the matter?" Acey said.

"Sure you do." Eshaz stopped on the walkway, and briefly touched the faces of Acey and Dux, one after the other. In this manner, he read their thoughts, and confirmed the story they had told him, that they had not run away from the Guardians. It was one of the abilities that Tulyans had in interacting openly with their own kind, and secretly with other galactic races.

As Eshaz removed his hand from Dux, he noted intelligence and sincerity in the boy's dark brown eyes.

"I'm going to catch a shuttle now," Eshaz said, "and you can either go with me or wait for the next podship ride. But you'll be missing out on a great place if you go. I think I can get you into a fantastic facility that's usually reserved for visiting dignitaries. At no charge, of course."

"We qualify as dignitaries," Dux said with a broad grin.

"I think we should hit the podways," Acey said.

"Aw, come on," Dux said, nudging his cousin in the side. "If we don't like it around here, we'll go somewhere else."

Hesitation. Then, "All right."

"I'll send a message to Noah," Eshaz said, "and let him know you're both safe."

"It might be better not to," Dux said. "We don't want the perpetrator to find out where we are. But if it is Gio, do you think he's a threat to Noah? Or do we just have a problem with the guy?"

"I will need to give that some thought," Eshaz said.

★ ★ ★ ★ ★

Eshaz was not allowed to bring visitors to any of the worlds in the Tulyan Starcloud, so he left the teenagers at the orbital Visitor's Center, floating in space over the mist-enshrouded starcloud below. The guests were each given an opulent suite, the kind usually reserved for ambassadors and other high government officials. The Tulyan desk clerk and a security officer appeared to be surprised upon seeing the young Humans, but acceded to Eshaz's wishes, in deference to his position. Eshaz told them he was personally responsible for the boys' safety, after having rescued them, and that they worked for Noah Watanabe, as he did himself. Then he hurried away by himself, to meet with the Council of Elders.

The Visitor's Center was globular, like a pod station and around the same size, but the resemblance stopped there. This was a glittering spacetel, not a mottled, gray-and-black docking station. As they followed the bellhop into a room, he explained that the rooms were interconnected in what he called suites; the boys had never heard of anything like this.

The bellhop, a tall Churian with thick, white eyebrows and a guttural voice, said, "This is Mr. Zelk's suite. Yours is next door, Mr. Hannah."

The boys exchanged surprised, pleased glances.

The Churian showed them through room after room, in just the first suite. Impressively, each room had a view of the misty Tulyan Starcloud below, which the bellhop explained was a trick of electronics. Dux scratched his head. It looked incredibly realistic, and he couldn't see how it worked. Soft music played in the background, blending into different tunes in each room.

"This place is bigger than the entire crew quarters on our ship," Acey said. Leaning over, he touched the plush black carpet in the sitting area, then laid on it and said it was softer than any bed on which he'd ever slept. "I'll just sleep on the floor tonight. I don't want to get too comfortable, or I might not be able to go back to my real life."

Dux laughed, but the Churian, a very proper alien, frowned intensely, causing his bushy eyebrows to cover his eyes. To Dux, this looked very comical, but he tried not to smile, or laugh anymore. It looked like the fellow had hairy eyes. For several moments, the bellhop paced around without crashing into anything, so he must have had some way of seeing where he was going, or perhaps a backup sonrad system.

A lone reptilian figure stood before a bench with twenty robed judges seated at it, gazing down at him sternly. Eshaz had a solid floor beneath him, but could not see it under his feet; he seemed to float on air, with the curvature of the inverted dome visible far below him, and the stars of space twinkling through the ethereal mists beyond.

He knew that the Visitor's Center staff had probably reported him, so he expected the aged leaders to ask him about the boys. Eshaz had an explanation ready—that he couldn't just cast them adrift after their narrow escape from death—but he hoped he didn't have to defend himself on that issue. He was already in enough trouble.

Nervously, the web caretaker gazed from face to face, searching for something in their expressions to tell him what to do. He wanted to spill all of the information he knew but resisted the urge, and instead awaited the comments and commands of his superiors. The council members looked hostile, with downturned mouths and glaring expressions.

"Reports have reached us that give us grave concern

about the condition of the web," First Elder Kre'n said, rubbing her scaly chin. One of the oldest Tulyans, she was reputed to have been the first of her race ever to pilot a podship across the vast reaches of space.

Eshaz steeled himself, waiting for the hammer of authority to smash down on him.

"Truly, this is a dire crisis," she said. Then she paused and conferred in whispers with the Elders on either side of her.

Eshaz's mind raced with visions of horrible fates, as he imagined the worst things that could happen to him.

"For hundreds of thousands of years, you have been one of our Web Technicians, responsible for the care of the connective strands, and we can ill afford to lose your services when they are needed so much now."

She's regretting what they're about to do to me, Eshaz thought. He wished he could be anywhere but here. Even dead.

Kre'n nodded to a towering Tulyan on her left, whom Eshaz recognized as Dabiggio, one of the more severe Elders who had been responsible for strict sentences in the past. Eshaz steeled himself, then jerked in surprise when the robed dignitary said, "You will remain at the Starcloud until further notice."

Scrunching up his face in confusion, Eshaz said, "But there is no punishment facility here. It's on Colony L."

"Who said you were going to a punishment facility?" Dabiggio asked.

"I thought you were going to pronounce sentence on me for something I did wrong. I, uh. . . ."

"Personally, I do not approve of your behavior," Dabiggio said. "As a web caretaker, you took a risky, unprecedented action with respect to Noah Watanabe, but you have your supporters on this council."

"You know what I did, then?"

"I have my sources," the imposing Elder said.

"But now is not the time for punishment," Kre'n interjected. She locked gazes with Dabiggio, and Eshaz detected some disagreement between them.

"I was about to transmit my confession to you," Eshaz said, "when your orders arrived for me to report to the Starcloud. I am prepared to tell all now." Convinced of the correctness of his actions, Eshaz lifted his chin confidently. "I offer no excuses, only an explanation."

At a nod from Kre'n, Eshaz went on to describe Noah on the verge of death, and the crisis Eshaz faced, with only one way to save a remarkable man who had come up with his own theory of the interconnectedness of the galaxy. Then he said, "To me, Noah Watanabe has always seemed more Tulyan than Human, he might be the one spoken of in our legends, the . . ." He paused, afraid to utter the word.

"A *Human* Savior?" Dabiggio exclaimed. "How utterly revolting and preposterous!"

"With respect sir, our legends say the Savior will appear from an unexpected source. Given the selfish and destructive record of humanity, could there be a more unexpected source?" Eshaz noticed several other Elders, including Kre'n, nodding their heads, just a little. At least they seemed open to the possibility.

"We have already decided to defer the matter of your punishment," Kre'n announced, with a thin smile. "Your long and illustrious record has not gone unnoticed by this council, and we are willing to reserve judgment during this time of crisis."

"I appreciate that very much," Eshaz said, dipping his head in a slight bow. "One thing more. As you know, I used a web defect to heal Watanabe—an early stage timehole in the vicinity of the destroyed planet. I also found other defects around the site of the explosion, and repaired them."

"We are aware of that," Kre'n said. "Your peers found similar web damage around the Earth and Mars debris fields, and they, too, implemented repairs. The question is, did web defects cause the planets to blow up, or was it the reverse?"

"The chicken or the egg," one of the Elders said.

"And why are merchant prince planets the ones affected?" another asked.

"These are disturbing questions," Kre'n said, staring at Eshaz. "But now we have another important assignment for you, as a timeseer."

Eshaz lifted his eyebrows. The last time he had been asked to timesee, he had been blocked—either by chaos in the universe or by his own failing. It disturbed him to look into the future, because he didn't know what he would see there. Especially now, with the rapid decline of the web, which portended ultimate, if not imminent, disaster on an immense scale.

He heard a drone, and looking toward a side door saw what appeared to be insects flying into the large chamber, a swarm of them in various shades of color. As they drew closer he identified them as Parviis, each dressed in an ornate outfit. They looked like tiny flying dolls, and set down on top of the judicial bench. The buzzing sound in his ears was not from wings, because Parviis had none, but from their hyper-accelerated metabolisms, which enabled them to fly in some mysterious fashion.

"I'd hoped I wouldn't have to do this again," Eshaz protested.

"Then you should not have demonstrated your talents so

well," one of the Parviis said in a tiny, high-pitched voice.

Eshaz recognized him as Woldn, their leader. He wore a carmine red suit, with billowing sleeves and trousers. The Tulyan felt anger welling up inside, but knew better than to say anything more. This was a political matter, perhaps involving an exchange of his services for Tulyan captives taken by the Parviis in their constant raids around the galaxy. He hated providing such a valuable service to the enemies of his people, but had to do as he was told. The last time he had demonstrated his limited prescience for the Parviis, they had treated it like a carnival side show act, an amusing diversion.

"You will accompany the delegation to an antechamber," Kre'n said. "And there you will tell them what you see."

While wishing another Tulyan timeseer had been summoned in his place, Eshaz nonetheless said nothing. Deep in thought, he traipsed toward one of the many smaller chambers ringing the central council room, enclosures that had clear walls, floors, and ceilings, and were only discernible by faint construction outlines around the edges. As before, everything he said would be recorded, so that the Elders would have the information, too. Theoretically, Eshaz's timeseeing report would not benefit either side. In many ways, however, this seemed worse to him than the most serious punishments he had imagined for his Timeweb infraction. It seemed like treason, even though technically it wasn't, since he was being ordered by the Elders to do it.

Still, a citizen could disobey an order if he found it unconscionable.

Chapter Eighty-One

> Sentience [one of 56 definitions]: A thinking creature with the ability to deceive another of its kind.
>
> —Thinker, Reserve Data Bank

As days passed and Subi failed to return, Noah asked constant questions, so many that the others could not maintain the lie. "We were concerned about you and sent him for a bone specialist," Tesh finally admitted.

The two of them sat in a small lunchroom that the robots had built in the main cavern, using scrap parts from the damaged hulks of Digger machines. Adjacent to that structure, the robots had also constructed sleeping quarters for the Humans and for Eshaz, who still had not returned from his visit to the Tulyan Starcloud.

"Another doctor?" Noah exclaimed. "I ordered you to keep my condition a secret!"

"You've been behaving so strangely," Tesh said. "We're worried about you."

"And where is Subi now?" Noah demanded.

"We don't know," Tesh said. She stirred a bowl of soup with her spoon, didn't taste it.

"And those young men—Dux and Acey—any sign of them yet?"

She shook her head. "People think they ran off to space again. They probably stowed away on a ship, looking for a new adventure."

"Maybe not. I wonder if they're with Subi instead,

wherever he is," Noah said.

"Doubtful."

"I wish you'd gone instead of Subi," Noah said. He glared at her. "I hold you personally responsible for anything that happens to him."

"You've never liked me, have you?"

Noah continued glaring, didn't respond. Then he lunged to his feet and stomped away.

Weeks passed, and still there was no sign of Subi Danvar.

During that period, several of Thinker's robots were able to blend in with other sentient machines in the cities, and used their new contacts to obtain food, construction materials, and various supplies needed by the Guardians. The robots paid for the articles with earnings from the lucrative Inn of the White Sun, and from the popular computer chips that Thinker manufactured for resale. The robots also obtained intelligence reports on the movement of Red Beret and CorpOne troops.

While Noah felt deep sadness at the loss of his loyal adjutant, he was heartened when Human Guardians in dirty, ragged uniforms began to filter back into his ranks. Some had escaped from the space station, while others had been in hiding in the woods and hills surrounding his commandeered ecology compound.

He sent out Human agents in plain clothes, along with robots, to look for Subi, but nothing turned up. Not a clue or any sign of him. Noah tried to hold onto slender strands of hope, but felt his grip slipping. There was no sign of the missing teenagers, either, and no word on their whereabouts. Maybe they ran away to space, as people were suggesting. Worrying that the location of his underground headquarters might be compromised because of the missing Guardians, Noah ordered the implementation of even more security measures, developed by Thinker. Primarily this involved additional covert patrols and hardening of the entrances to the tunnels and chambers. He also reviewed a report that Subi had given him before leaving, concerning unknown improvements that the Doge was making to the planet's surveillance grid system, and how this made air travel riskier than normal for Noah's and his forces.

Each day Noah went for walks around the perimeter of the cavern, past piles of scrap metal that the robots had scavenged and organized. He was walking normally or running now, without any pain. The regeneration of his foot was a minor miracle, and so was his recovery from the self-inflicted knife wound to the heart. He had even given himself a poisonous bioshot, and had survived. He had confirmed his own immortality.

Despite his astounding new physical powers, Noah found the expansion of his mental resources even more remarkable. At will, he could go in and out of the alternate, extrasensory realm and journey across the galaxy in his mind—without having to undergo the oddly disconcerting double visions he'd experienced earlier, which seemed to have only been a transitional phase. Now he just had to close his eyes and focus, and his thoughts vaulted into the cosmos . . . a dimension and reality that allowed him to see his own physical form as a tiny mote in a vast galactic sea.

The physical is part of the ethereal, he thought in an epiphany. *My body is an aspect of something far greater.*

All sorts of possibilities occurred to him. While he could journey in his mind, the excursions didn't always provide him with answers, at least not those that were of huge importance to him, and which should matter to all sentient creatures. He felt like a tourist in the galaxy, seeing and experiencing things on a limited basis, while not learning much about what lay deeper. There were gaps in his abilities: places he could not go and places he could not see.

So many twists and turns, he thought, *trying to unravel the mysteries of existence, the meaning of life.*

Abruptly, he reeled his far-reaching thoughts back, like a fisherman about to head home for the day. "The meaning of life." Such a cliché, but that did not make it an insignificant line of inquiry.

In the caverns, the Master of the Guardians stood watching robots construct more of their kind from scrap parts. On one side, Thinker was in his folded-shut mode, as if he, too, had been contemplating matters of great import.

Noah was making no further attempts to pilot the podship that had become so familiar to him. For the moment, Canopa was where he wanted to be physically, and he came to the realization that he had been holding something back in his cosmic journeys. He feared getting lost out there and finding himself unable to return to consciousness, to his familiar corporal form and all of its traditional links.

As just one example, he could have made attempts to commandeer podships as he saw them flying by on the web, but had not, and had no intention of doing so. He did not want to interfere or inflict himself on anything, did not want to cause harm to the galactic environment.

Even so, this did not prevent Noah Watanabe's mind from taking fantastic, dreamlike journeys each night as he slept.

Upon awaking one morning and looking out into the cavern, Noah saw the robots moving around, as they did constantly to complete their myriad tasks. For several minutes, he stood at the window of the improvised structure, watching them. He wore shorts and a tee-shirt.

To his amazement, he suddenly saw Subi Danvar limp into the cavern, carrying a large black bag. Thinker and another robot hurried to the man's assistance, while Noah ran out of the small sleeping structure, still dressed in his night clothes.

"Subi!" he shouted. "I thought I'd never see you again!"

The adjutant hung his head. "Look," he said, "I'm sorry, but I tried to get medical help for you." His right leg was bandaged, with the trousers cut away. He had shadows under his eyes, matted hair, and a stubble of beard.

"I already know about that, and I appreciate it."

"Your loving sister and the Doge have turned the top level of our administration building into a prison and torture chamber," Subi said. "They put me in there, but I escaped. No one knew who I was; they thought I was just another Guardian."

Noah nodded, knowing that Subi had always maintained a low profile, so that the background information on him was limited. "I assume you checked for tracking devices before coming back here?"

In a perturbed tone Subi said, "You don't even need to ask."

"Don't take offense, old friend."

"All right. Guess I'm just tired and irritable."

"So the rumors are true about our old headquarters." Noah shook his head sadly. "Did they torture you?"

"I decided to cancel the appointment they had scheduled for me." Subi grinned. "This leg is nothing, just a minor injury I got when they captured me. It took six of them to take me down."

"You've lost a little weight," Noah observed.

"Yeah. I didn't like the chef." The big man scowled. "Some of our guys are still in there."

"Are those teenage boys there, Dux and Acey?"

"No. They're not here?"

"They disappeared shortly after you left."

"I hope they're OK," Subi said.

"We'll get even for this," Noah vowed. "Already we've found thousands of our Guardians who were living off the land, and we have Thinker's loyal robots. I promise you, my friend, we'll get justice."

"Maybe this will help," Subi said. He zipped open the large bag and brought out a black-and-tan machine that was perhaps a meter and a half tall, which he placed on the dirt floor of the cavern. "This makes my whole trip worthwhile. I borrowed it from our friend the Doge."

Crouching, Noah looked the machine over. It had what looked like a hopper on top, and a chute on one side that could be pulled out to make it longer. On the side opposite the chute were control toggles, buttons, and what looked like a voice-activation speaker.

Tesh and Anton joined them, and greeted their comrade. "What have you got there?" she asked.

"It's a hibbamatic," Subi said, "a popular diversion in royal courts around the MPA, this one can create any number of small devices. Larger models are also available."

Nearby, Thinker made a hissing sound. He stared with the metal-lidded eyes on his face plate.

Retrieving several small pieces of metal and plax from a nearby pile, Subi stuffed them in the hopper, then made settings and spoke into the voice-activator. "Salducian dagger," he said.

The machine whirred on, and the raw materials were sucked noisily down into the hopper. Moments later, an object clanked through the chute and landed in Subi's waiting hand, a dagger in a red plax sheath. He slid the shiny silver weapon out and showed it off. The handle was made of the same material as the sheath.

Subi continued to demonstrate his new treasure, making progressively more complex objects: a pair of night-vision goggles, a projectile gun, and a heat-and-motion sensor that he said could fly around, watching for intruders.

"Most impressive," Noah said.

"I beg to differ," Thinker interjected. "It is just a novelty item." The hissing noise increased, and he spoke over it. "Hibbil products have become increasingly inferior. Their new robots are always breaking down, whereas old models like myself—with minor tune-ups, of course—are much more reliable."

"Very well," Noah said. "As commander of my machines, you are in charge of this one, too."

"Is that wise?" Subi asked. "We could get a lot of use out of this thing."

"The hibbamatic is not even sentient," Thinker scoffed. The hiss stopped, and he added, "All right, I will agree that it is an interesting product, and of potential use. But the units require constant maintenance by Hibbil technicians. This one appears to be out of adjustment."

Thinker retrieved the dagger from the ground where Subi had left it, and smacked the blade against a piece of scrap metal. "Look at that," the intelligent robot said, holding the blade up afterward. "It chipped."

"Can you get the machine working properly?" Subi asked.

"Perhaps, but we might not be able to manufacture more of them. Hibbamatics contain materials that are not easily obtainable, especially the rare Ilkian fiber optics in their scan-eyes." Orange lights around his face plate glowed. "Of course, the hibbamatics can't make anything that we can't make ourselves, assuming we can locate the necessary raw materials."

Noah watched as Subi nodded reluctantly. Obviously, he had gone to a lot of trouble to obtain this device, adding to the peril of his escape.

Emitting a little click, Thinker sent an electronic signal to a robot that stood nearby, and the subordinate took the hibbamatic away.

In ensuing weeks, Subi and Thinker supervised the training of the Human and robot Guardians, turning them into a cohesive fighting force. On one training exercise, they located two non-functioning Digger machines inside a deep tunnel, units that had gotten into trouble on their own or been decommissioned by Noah's commandos.

Hearing of this, Noah went to investigate. The silvery machines appeared to be intact, although some of the drill bits studding their hulking bodies were broken or chipped.

"I think we should reactivate them," Thinker suggested, standing at Noah's side. "They could be programmed to do beneficial work."

"What about their tendency to go off on rampages of destruction?" Noah asked.

Abruptly, Thinker closed in a clatter of metal so that he could consider the matter in absolute darkness and silence. In less than a minute he opened back up and announced, confidently, "It's nothing a good programmer can't straighten out."

"Do it, then," Noah ordered.

"Very well. Oops." Thinker's internal programming whirred and made a little popping sound. On the robot's chest, a screen flashed on with an image of Noah and the tunnel surroundings. Their entire conversation was played back, sounding somewhat tinny. At the end, as before, the recorded Noah said, "Do it, then."

"You've been recording all of my words?" Noah asked.

"Not just yours. I absorb data from all directions. That's why I'm so smart. I used to travel around the galaxy collecting data and storing it away. Now I'm too busy for that."

Opening a panel below the screen, the robot tinkered with the controls, then slammed the cover shut and said, "Sorry about the little glitch. If you ever want me to play anything back, just let me know."

"I don't know how I feel about being recorded," Noah said, scratching his freckled forehead.

"Would you like me to disconnect it whenever you and I talk?" Thinker inquired.

"No. I hereby designate you our official historian, along with your other duties."

Soon the restored Diggers began to excavate large underground living chambers out of rocky areas, upgrading the previous barrack arrangements. They also made improvements to the labyrinthine tunnel system beneath the woods and hills outside his former compound, and even explored existing tunnels that were directly under the old administration buildings. At Thinker's command, Giovanni Nehr supervised much of the work, improving upon the original subterranean map that Anton and Tesh drew up.

Noah came to rely on the new armored Guardian, although Gio seemed somewhat vain and self absorbed, constantly admiring his shiny armor in any mirror he passed. But little did Noah know that Gio was also a shameless opportunist, intent on watching for the perfect time to take advantage of his surroundings . . . like waiting for fruit to ripen on someone else's tree.

It must be noted however, that Giovanni Nehr's feelings were not simplistic by any means. While he looked out for his own interests above all others, he was still a long-time admirer of Noah Watanabe. The discontented son of an industrialist, Noah had tweaked the noses of the merchant princes on more than one occasion—including Gio's own famous, insufferable brother Jacopo. So, Gio was loyal to the man the Guardians called "Master," but only as much as an egocentric person like him could be. . . .

Noah had a mission in mind, and not necessarily the obvious one of retaking control of his Ecological Demonstration Project and orbital EcoStation, at least not right away. First he intended to lead his Guardians in guerrilla raids against industrial polluters, with the hope of making Francella, Doge Lorenzo, and their allies suffer.

Chapter Eighty-Two

> Even after seeing all of the evidence, it remains difficult for me to believe, and brings tears to my eyes. But the truth is that my brother attacked CorpOne headquarters and mortally wounded our father. One of the great merchant princes and industrial geniuses, Saito Watanabe, is gone forever because of Noah's treachery. I promise you this: his crime will not go unpunished.
>
> —Francella Watanabe, speech to CorpOne employees

Despite his paranormal abilities, Noah Watanabe still had significant blind spots.

One morning he explored the subterranean tunnels and caverns, probing ahead with a flashbeam visor, and did not notice Tesh—tiny and silent—following him everywhere, watching everything he did, listening to everything he said. Noah had dual realities, an ability to venture into two dimensions, realms that at times overlapped and folded over one another in ways that he had not yet fully sorted out. He was in the physical reality now, running at a good clip over dirt and rock, rebuilding his strength.

Earlier, after taking control of the podship away from Tesh, he had secretly watched her in her tiny form as she tried to regain control of the vessel, but found herself unable to reenter the navigation chamber that he had sealed. Now, though he remained alert and looked around, he did not see her at all. She wasn't invisible, but she could move so quickly that she approached invisibility in this dimension.

Deep underground, Noah slowed and walked through one of the older burrows that the rampant Diggers had excavated. He was taking the time to wander, but not aimlessly; he had a purpose in mind. Through an internal survival mechanism that had surfaced recently, he found that he could not get lost, at least not physically. No matter how far off the subterranean map he ventured, he always seemed able to find his way back to the main cavern and his companions.

This gave him increasing comfort, and he was thinking about reentering a podship and taking control of it to surge out into the vast reaches of the galaxy, where the power of his mind controlled his reality. In that mystical realm, he could stretch into the cosmos mentally, or he could take his body along, and not just as an afterthought. There actually was a physical aspect where podships traveled and carried their passengers to fantastic places.

But the domain of podships, while astounding and intriguing, gave him considerable pause. It was so infinitely beautiful out there, so alluring and yet so dangerous.

As he wandered the tunnels now, he recognized that the scene before him was not entirely corporeal. He only saw it, felt it, smelled it, and heard it because his mind permitted him to do so . . . and his mind could change focus. He wondered how many other realities remained unexplored. The possibilities enticed him.

Previously when he piloted a podship, he had done so by extrasensory means, while inside the cargo hold. From there, he had mentally projected himself into the navigation chamber and caused the vessel to lurch into motion, taking him physically and cerebrally across space.

Now it was different. He was not inside any portion of

the podship, but he wondered if he could still reach out with his thoughts, if he could still seep like a mist into the operational core of the spacecraft and take control of it, if he could still guide it across space.

But even if he could do that, Noah remained cautious. If he piloted a podship again, and tried to get lost, would his internal compass continue to function, always permitting him to return?

Moments passed, as temptation and curiosity buffeted him. He could not avoid thoughts that drifted in and out of his conscious mind. Now that he'd had the paranormal experiences, he needed to experience them again.

Summoning his courage, he dipped into the ethereal web, and on the internal screen of his mind he saw the faint green cosmic filigree stretching into infinity, wavering ever so slightly, as if from a gentle breeze. Focusing closer, he again saw flickering images of the podship he had left at the Canopa pod station, with Red Beret officers and scientists continuing to crawl over it, still not finding the secret passageways or the navigation chamber.

But as Noah seeped into the podship now, the interior was a little out of focus. Like a phantom, he floated silently through a wide corridor, then darted into a narrow one that the Red Berets had not been able to enter, or even see. Just ahead, Noah made out the entrance to the navigation chamber that he had previously sealed, to keep Tesh and any other intruders out.

Mentally, he gave the instruction to unseal it, so that he could pass through the flesh of the podship, into its most sacred and sheltered chamber, the heart and mind of the creature. Cautiously, Noah's ghost-self moved forward, and pressed itself against the entryway.

He entered the navigation chamber.

But something was happening back in the tunnel, where his physical form remained. . . .

Shifting his focus, Noah felt something cold and hard against his jugular.

"I should cut your throat," a woman's voice whispered. "But would you die?"

With a quick movement, Noah grabbed the knife by its razor-sharp blade, cutting deeply into his hand. Despite the blood and pain, he tried to pull the weapon from her grip, but could not. She was extremely strong. Blood spurted from the hand as he pulled it away, but within seconds it coagulated. In the low light, he watched with her as the skin healed. The searing pain stopped.

She withdrew the knife from his neck. "Talk," Tesh demanded, glaring at him.

"I am indestructible. You cannot kill me. I cannot even commit suicide. I've been doing little tests lately, self-inflicted stab wounds, even injected poison into my arm. I always heal perfectly. Do you know why this is happening to me?"

"I don't know *what* you are," she responded.

I don't know what you are, either, Noah thought, as he remembered seeing Tesh in her tiny, secret form, trying to gain entrance to the navigation chamber. "Let's go for a walk," he said. "We need to talk."

She sheathed the knife at her waist, and followed his lead.

The two of them trekked upward along a circuitous route of tunnels to the main cavern, crossed it and went out through the camouflaged main entrance, after using Noah's security alarm code. It was much warmer outside, with the foliage and ground baked by a late afternoon sun. They climbed to a knoll and sat on it, gazing out across the countryside toward the southern edge of his former ecological demonstration compound.

From this vantage, Noah could not see any of the buildings, only the familiar sloping hills and dark green trees of his beloved land. He longed to have it back, to free himself from the yoke of the misfortunes that had befallen him. If only he and his father had not become estranged, perhaps this whole unfortunate chain of events never would have occurred.

"I have something to tell you," Tesh said. Sunlight sparkled on her long black hair, and her emerald eyes were filled with concern.

"And I have a lot of questions," he said.

They talked well past sunset, when a cool night breeze began to pick up, rustling the nearby shrubs and canopa trees. Noah offered her his coat, and then he sat there shivering without it, while trying to keep his mind on other things. High overhead, the moon peeked around from behind a cloud, casting low illumination on the landscape, creating strange shadows around them.

She revealed to him that she was a Parvii, a major—but clandestine—galactic race that had held dominion over another race, the Aopoddae, since ancient times. Tesh spoke of her magnification system, and demonstrated it as they spoke, but Noah did not admit having previously seen her in her natural state.

"We Parviis do not confide in other races," she said as she switched the magnification system back on. "But in view of my unparalleled experiences with you, and the unfortunate condition of the galaxy . . . I must trust you. Please understand, it is not easy for me."

Pausing, Tesh looked at him. He saw her eyes glint in the low light. The wind blew her hair forward, and with one hand she brushed it out of her eyes, and continued.

"In part from time dilation during space travel, my people live for centuries. Before dying, our oldest person attained the age of three thousand and eighty-eight standard years, while I am more than seven hundred myself. Even so, we can still die of diseases and injuries."

"My story is not so clear," he said. "You and I seem to have shared a paranormal experience in which we fought for control of a podship. I suspect that each of us has information . . . and abilities . . . that the other does not."

"I agree," she said. "It's all part of a vast galactic puzzle, and we must solve it together." She paused. Then: "You are . . . or *were* . . . a primitive Human on the evolutionary scale, but Eshaz altered that with one brash act."

Even when he'd seen Tesh in her tiny size, she'd looked Human to Noah. Was that the future of humanity—to get smaller and live longer?

"Eshaz should never have granted you access to Timeweb," she said, "which he did when he healed you. He committed a terrible, dangerous act, and will surely pay the price for it. His action is unprecedented, and so, to my knowledge, are you. I do not believe that you are immortal, however. Our leader, Woldn, has always told us that there are no deathless creatures in the universe. Some are just harder to kill than others, that's all."

Noah actually did feel immortal, but said only, "Well, I'm definitely hard to kill. Anyway, I didn't try to do anything wrong, so don't be angry with me. I still don't understand what happened to me, or . . . you called it Timeweb?"

She nodded. "It's a vast web that holds the entire cosmos together, but it's extremely fragile. Think of an immense ecosystem, with planetary and other organisms intricately woven together and utterly dependent upon each other . . . a large-scale version of what it is like on each world. Your concept of galactic ecology is very close to the truth."

He struggled to comprehend. "But it sounds more complicated than anything I imagined."

"The old ways of the galaxy are in chaos, and this may have permitted you to gain unprecedented access to the web. I cannot say, but I do know this. You and I must journey into Timeweb in a podship . . . together."

"With you?" He wasn't sure how he felt about that idea.

"I sense great danger, and we must move quickly. Do you know that our podship has been sitting at the pod station, exactly where we . . . where you . . . left it?"

He nodded. "I, too, sense peril, but have not known how to deal with it, or if I am the right one to deal with it."

"We might be able figure it out as a team. Something is afoot in the galaxy, and we must discover what it is."

Noah considered her proposal, wondering if it might be a trick, so that she could take control of the sentient spacecraft away from him. In the moonlight, he stared at the knife that she had sheathed.

As if to answer his unspoken concerns, she smiled gently and said, "You are, as we have learned from our podship experience, stronger than I am in Timeweb."

"But you know your way around better than I do."

"Perhaps I only know different aspects of it than you do."

He told her about the fantastic vision in which he journeyed in his mind across space, and saw Francella and the Doge Lorenzo del Velli in a podship, and overheard her saying she wanted Noah killed. Noah also told of seeing Thinker and his small army of robots in another podship, and of seeing Mutatis at the controls of ten schooners that were painted with merchant prince colors, all with unidentifiable tube mechanisms built into their hulls.

"The Mutatis were in orbit over their own planets," Noah said. "Some sort of defensive operation, I guess, maybe listening posts. But why are they using merchant ships?"

"They probably stole them," Tesh suggested. "But with that devious race, nothing is as it seems. Woldn has long warned of Mutati treachery, saying they are a danger to the entire galaxy, and not just to Humans."

"Sometimes I wonder if the galaxy would be better off without Mutatis or Humans," Noah said.

"Don't say that. You know the goodness of humankind."

"And the evils."

"We'd better get out there and see what the Mutatis are up to," she said, pressing.

He didn't respond, and didn't tell her he had been conducting a remote experiment when she interrupted him, to see if he could get into the core while not physically on board the podship. He'd proven to himself that he could, and had no doubt that he could also pilot the ship remotely. But the less she knew about his powers the better—this Parvii female probably had more tricks than he could imagine.

"Will you go with me to the podship?" she asked.

"You could shrink yourself and sneak past the guards at the ship," he said.

"That wouldn't do me any good. You sealed the navigation chamber, and I can't get in without you."

"So it seems." Looking into her seductive, moonlit eyes, Noah wondered if he could ever trust her. "I need time to process all of this," he said.

"When will you have an answer?" Her voice sounded anxious.

"I'll let you know. You can't get into the navigation chamber without my help."

"So it seems." She touched his hand. He felt warmth from her, which was remarkable considering her magnification system.

Gently, Noah pushed her hand away. He gazed into the night sky, scanning the twinkling, distant stars. Doubts about her assailed him. She was using her physical beauty and charm to get what she wanted, obviously a method she was accustomed to using.

She pulled his face to hers, and their lips met—or seemed to—but for only a fraction of a second. Quickly, Noah pulled away. The more attraction he felt for her, the more it worried him.

Tesh tried again, and this time Noah was more forceful in response. "I will make my decision logically," he snapped, "not emotionally."

And he stalked off.

Alone in the darkness of his room, Noah probed the vast cosmic domain, his thoughts skipping along the faint green filigree of Timeweb. He needed to conduct an experiment to discover if he really could pilot a podship by remote control, but he decided it would be best to try other sentient vessels, not the one at the Canopa pod station. He didn't want to disturb that one now, not until he determined how best to put it to use. Aside from his concern about keeping information from Tesh, he was afraid that something might go wrong in a remote takeover attempt, preventing him from ever controlling that ship.

At random, he selected a podship speeding along the web, and zeroed in on it. His mind seeped inside, first into the passenger compartment and cargo hold, and then into the green, glowing navigation chamber at the core of the vessel. He saw a Parvii clinging to a wall there, guiding the ship along one galactic strand and another.

Focusing all of his mental energy, Noah tried to commandeer the ship, and for a moment he felt a mental linkage with the mysterious creature, though not as strong as he had experienced previously, with the other vessel. This time he caused the podship to slow, just a little. Then he felt increasing resistance, and noticed that the tiny humanoid had moved to another section of wall, a bright green patch.

The podship followed the Parvii's commands now and disregarded Noah's, no matter how much he tried. Finally giving up the effort to overcome the other pilot, Noah wondered how much his difficulty had to do with the remote connection, and if he had more power when he was actually on board a craft before attempting to pilot it.

Moments later, the podship pulled into a pod station and docked.

While passengers and small vessels unloaded from the ship, Noah again touched the core with his probing thoughts, and once more he experienced a mental linkage with the sentient creature. The Parvii resisted him as expected, but only briefly this time, before losing the battle.

I did it! Noah thought.

He waited for the unloading to finish, but before any passengers or cargo could be loaded, he ordered the podship to close the entrance hatches and leave the dock. To his elation, these commands were followed. He then took the vessel out on the podways and guided it along one strand and another, as he pleased.

Eventually he let the connection go, and allowed the disturbed Parvii pilot to resume control.

During the next hour, Noah conducted additional experiments on other podships around the galaxy. In each case he found that he could not maintain control of a pod that was already in motion, but he could if the vessel was docked when he made the attempt.

Noah was gaining skills in Timeweb, like a child learning how to walk.

Chapter Eighty-Three

There are countless ways to destroy a foe . . . and to destroy yourself. You must take care that one does not lead to the other.

—Mutati Wisdom

Two Mutatis stood high inside one of the spires of the Citadel of Paradij, gazing out on the jeweled buildings of the capital city, the glittering colors in afternoon sunlight. One of the shapeshifters—the Zultan Abal Meshdi—was the more massive, though his son could not be considered petite.

In the time that had passed since the enemy attack on his Demolio manufacturing facility, the Zultan had restored the program. Now there were hundreds of doomsday machines, and they had been dispatched to strategic locations in the Mutati Kingdom and in other star systems, where their outriders had been told to await further instructions.

Those final commands would be sent via his new instantaneous cross-space communication system. Pursuant to the information received from the turncoat Giovanni Nehr, the Mutatis had established deep-shaft emerald mines on a number of planets, and had been harvesting the piezoelectric gems that were required for nehrcom transceivers.

The new communication program was ancillary to the overall doomsday plan, and would facilitate the obliteration of merchant prince planets. Meshdi could have distributed the deadly torpedoes without the instantaneous communication system, by sending outriders with predetermined attack schedules (as he had done in the past), but he had been waiting for instructions from God-on-High.

Finally, while inside his gyrodome the day before, the Zultan had been told what to do. The blessed Creator of the Galaxy had appeared to him, as if from a cosmic mist, and had commanded him to make Humans suffer by destroying them progressively—rather than all at once. But unknown to Meshdi, it had not really been a divine directive at all. Rather, it had been the result of psychic influences exerted by the Adurian gyrodome and minigyros—mechanisms that swayed his decisionmaking processes and caused him to preserve the most valuable merchant prince worlds, which the clandestine HibAdu Coalition wanted as prizes of war.

Abal Meshdi had been feeling disappointment all day, and had summoned his eldest son Hari'Adab to this private meeting, to discuss what to do next. Now the Zultan snapped his fingers, causing a clearplax door in front of them to slide open. He led the way out onto a balcony, and felt the floor flex under their combined weight.

"I wish you hadn't asked for my advice this time," the younger Mutati said. He placed three hands on the balcony railing, and gazed blankly out on the city. "You know how I feel about your Demolio program."

"As my heir apparent, you must accept it anyway, just as I must accept the will of God-on-High. Each of us has our superior, you see, and we cannot alter what is meant to be, the natural order of affairs. If I had my way it would all be over quickly. I would attack every enemy world simultaneously, blasting them all to oblivion." He paused. "Beyond oblivion, I hate Humans so much."

Hari'Adab did not respond.

"We will annihilate them," the Zultan said. He tasted the destructive word and smiled to himself, forming a tiny curvature of the mouth atop his impressive mountain of fat. Such a delicious, salivating sound to it.

"We will *annihilate* them!" he repeated.

"If I had my way, Father, I would negotiate with the merchant princes and form a lasting peace. Our militarism only generates more of the same by our opponents. I say this to you with all respect, My Zultan, for the ultimate decision is yours and I would not think to question it. I only offer my humble opinion."

"I've heard this all before from you, Hari, and you would be wise not to press me further on that issue, considering how far you have to fall if I decide to tip you over the railing." He grinned at his son, and caught an angry glance in return. Then Hari'Adab looked away and stared into the distance, as if wishing he could be anywhere else.

Shifting on his feet and feeling the balcony floor move again, Meshdi said, "Maybe I shouldn't be so disappointed at the order from God-on-High. Perhaps it is for the best, after all. By inflicting anguish on our enemy in stages, we will strike more terror into their black little hearts. Think of it, Hari! They will know the end is coming without being able to stop it!"

Almost imperceptibly—but not quite—the young Emir shook his undersized head, but said nothing, obviously trying to show the proper respect for his elder, as required in Mutati society. Hari had, however, refused to wear the Adurian gyro that his father shipped to him. A proud young terramutati, he'd said that he did not need a mechanical device to help him make decisions. It had been another disappointment for Abal Meshdi, and he had been struggling to overcome it.

But at the thought of making his enemies suffer, the Zultan cheered up and trembled with excitement. “Let them scramble like ants from a fire, trying to save themselves,” he said. “It will do them no good.”

Chapter Eighty-Four

The symbiosis of man and machine. That may be the best way to describe my relationship with the robot leader.

—Noah Watanabe

In the weeks they had known one another, Noah and Thinker were developing a surprisingly close friendship, something neither of them had anticipated, since they seemed so different. This is not to say that they failed to notice one another's faults. Early one morning as they ventured outside the tunnel complex, the robot commented that Noah had a tendency to be overly trustful of people he met, always trying to see the good in them, even if he had to struggle to do so.

"Perhaps you're right," Noah admitted, feeling the comfortable warmth of the sun on his face. "Essentially I'm an optimist, I suppose, looking for light instead of darkness."

They walked a path that led into the canopa woods. The deciduous trees were in full leaf, deep green from the seasonal rains. As the forest embraced them, Noah felt secure, sheltered by its living force.

"Maybe that's how you got your environmental recovery company going," Thinker said as he clanked along. "Pessimists aren't usually successful."

"I'm not much of a success any more," Noah replied. "Hopefully some of my company is still operational, but I'm sure Francella and Lorenzo are scouring the galaxy, searching for anything associated with me."

"But you have new friends," Thinker said.

They paused at a clearing where gray-and-brown mushrooms grew, and Noah made his own observation in return. "I appreciate your loyalty, but I must say, you're overly boastful and egotistical at times."

"I don't boast and I have no ego whatsoever," Thinker said, "for those are Human frailties, and have nothing to do with machines."

"We could argue that point for a long time, because I have seen signs of emotions in machines. Call them internal operating programs or whatever you want, but the result is the same."

"It is possible to refute everything you say," Thinker said.

"I'm sure you're right."

"As for your accusation about an ego, I simply tell the truth, and here is an example: I am the smartest sentient machine in the entire galaxy, with a virtually unlimited capacity for data absorption."

"Speaking of that, do you recall our discussion a few days ago, when I found out that you were recording everything we said, and that you could play the data back?"

"Of course. I never forget anything."

They scaled a steep, wooded hillside together. Noah knew the area well, and kept off the main trail to avoid detection. For a long while, he said nothing as they tramped along, and Thinker did not press him. The Guardian leader thought of Tesh's proposal that they explore Timeweb together, and of the possibilities—and perils—this presented. Preliminary evidence suggested to Noah that he had become immortal, but as he considered this at length he had reservations. His own tests had been limited, and perhaps there was a way to kill him after all.

He cared little for his own personal safety, but his legacy was a different matter altogether. It had importance beyond the breaths he took and the beating of his heart. It meant something to the entire galaxy.

He smiled bitterly to himself as they approached the crest of the hill, where the trees thinned out and it was brighter. A short while ago, Noah had accused Thinker of being egotistical, but he had that fault himself. In a sense, though, and Noah hoped he had the right edge on it himself, an ego could be a good thing, for without it his word would mean a lot less to his followers and his message might not always be respected.

"Hold it," Noah said, raising a hand.

Thinker went motionless beside him.

"Wait here," Noah said. Keeping low, he crept ahead as silently as possible, avoiding sticks, making the minimum amount of noise possible. At the edge of the trees he peered beyond, toward a grassy expanse dotted with low trees and the doberock remains of a long-dead settlement. For several minutes he stood silently, scanning in all directions, listening intently to the calls of the birds and the sounds of the wind, until satisfied that it was safe to proceed. He wondered if weapons fire would erupt anyway, and if he could still heal himself, no matter the severity of the wounds.

Safety was only a matter of degree, he realized. Nothing was completely secure. If his entire cellular structure was destroyed, he might be rendered incapable of regenerating himself, thus leaving no mechanism for him to come back.

That is, if the renewal process actually worked that way, if it was a physical, cellular phenomenon. Or was it a form of miraculous recovery, a resurrection? He shivered at the thought. In any event, he could not conceal himself forever in the tunnels of Canopa, or here at the edge of the trees. He had to take risks.

That's what life is all about, he thought.

With a wave of his hand, Noah strode boldly out of the trees, onto the sunlit grass, which sloped gently upward. Thinker followed.

At the rock pile of a fallen-down building, Noah said, "This is an ancient archaeological site, where the original inhabitants of Canopa once lived. It's very spiritual here, a place where I like to think about important matters."

"I simply fold into myself whenever I want to do that," Thinker said. "Much more efficient."

"Perhaps," Noah agreed, "but efficiency is not always the best thing."

"I must contemplate that," the robot said. With a small clatter of metal he closed himself, folding neatly into a box. He did not move.

While waiting for him to return, Noah sat on an adjacent rock and recalled coming to this site not so long ago in terms of time, only a few months. So much had occurred since then that it seemed like much longer. The people he used to know were like specters from the past, like the phantoms of this long-dormant settlement.

Presently, Thinker folded open and said, "Efficiency is always best. You have made an inaccurate statement."

"We'll debate it another time, my friend. First, I want to ask you something about your data collection and playback system."

"Do you want to see and hear something you said to me, perhaps information you are having trouble remembering?" Thinker asked. "I can put you on the screen right away."

"No, it's not that. Well, it is, but in a larger sense." He hesitated. Then: "Can you dig into my memories, sort of like an archaeologist, and resurrect all of the events I've experienced? Things that occurred before I met you, and which you could not have recorded?"

"You have already made me the official historian of the Guardians. Now you wish me to be your own personal archivist as well?"

"Can you do it?"

"Possibly. I've been working on a method of interfacing with Humans, similar to the way I do it with my own kind, to download data. When Giovanni Nehr joined my army, it occurred to me that I had no way of analyzing the thoughts in his brain. Since then, I have come up with a method, and I even constructed the biotechnology to accomplish data transfer."

He hesitated. "But I have encountered certain . . . internal programming obstacles. You might refer to them as moral issues. As a robot, I find that I do not feel comfortable forcing the probe on a human being, not even one who is ostensibly under my command. Humans created robots in the first place, before Hibbils ever got involved, and we honor that fact."

"That's a nice sentiment," Noah said.

As if ashamed, the robot looked down with his metal-lidded eyes and added, "I fear that my researches have gone too far."

"Could you transfer my thoughts without harming me?" Noah asked.

"Of course. All of my internal operating tests confirm this."

"Then, what if I give you permission to download my memories?"

"You would permit yourself to be a guinea pig? Don't you consider that dangerous?"

"Not at all," Noah said. "I have supreme confidence in your abilities. And in your friendship."

A tentacle snaked out of Thinker's alloy head and hovered over Noah. "This is an organic interface," the robot explained. "Are you sure you want to go through with this?"

Noah took a step back, and said, "I've been wondering if a mental replica of me could be made. As Guardian leader, I've been thinking about my own mortality, and I want to make sure my philosophy is imparted clearly to my followers, in case something happens to me. I have written a number of handbooks, but it would be nice to leave something more personal behind."

"But you are still comparatively young, with much of your life to live."

"I am a hunted, wanted man. And even if I weren't, I've been doing dangerous things, guiding podships across the galaxy and the like."

"Even so, I see great strength in you, an ability to survive and overcome great obstacles. You are no ordinary man, Noah Watanabe."

"Perhaps not." He looked up at the organic interface, with its array of needles, and shuddered. But he stepped forward, so that he was again directly beneath the tentacle head. "I'm ready," he said. And he closed his eyes.

A moment later, Noah felt the tentacle connect to the top of his head, and needles of pain all over his skull. In a surge of panic, he wanted to pull away, but could not move. The sharp points of pain reminded him of stars in distant space, and how his own mind could expand into the cosmos and take incredible journeys. . . .

Thinker sent the probes deeper into Noah's brain, and data began to flow into the machine's data banks, downloading every bit of information comprising Noah's life, including not only his memories but the chemical makeup of his body. After several moments the robot withdrew, and Noah's excruciating pain ceased.

"Now I know what you had for breakfast on your fifth birthday," Thinker said.

Noah opened his eyes, squinted in the sunlight. "And that was?"

"A poached trubik egg. You only ate half of it, and said you were full. Then you sneaked into another room and gorged yourself on a stash of candy."

"I'd almost forgotten all that," Noah said.

"What would you like me to do with the information? I can erase it, analyze it, or store it."

"Store it," Noah ordered. "I want you to keep a backup copy of me, and update it regularly."

In his Canopa office, Pimyt considered the coded nehrcom message he had received within the hour, on a sheet of folded parchment. Enraged at the terrible news, he had been stomping around the room, muttering and cursing to himself.

On every merchant prince planet, the influential Hibbil had sent fake communiqués, ostensibly from the Doge. They had been passed through Jacopo Nehr and resulted in the dismantling of many Human military forces, and the positioning of others in out-of-the way locations without adequate armaments, thus rendering them useless. In addition, Hibbil officers were in key positions throughout the armed forces of the Merchant Prince Alliance, ready to take the necessary actions when ordered to do so.

My part of the plan is in perfect order, he thought.

Disgusted, the covert agent kicked the parchment under his desk, trying to get it out of his sight. The problem had to do with the Adurian side of the conspiracy, the control they were supposed to be exerting over the Zultan Abal Meshdi and all military operations of the Mutati Kingdom.

Despite being under the influence of Adurian gyros, the Zultan had still dispatched an outrider to attack and destroy Timian One, the wealthiest of all merchant prince worlds. This was a big potential setback for the HibAdu Coalition, a planet-busting torpedo that could not be called back. Meshdi was supposed to send it against another fringe planet, not the MPA capital world!

Across much of the Mutati Kingdom, the Adurians had used gyro-manipulation to twist the thoughts of the Zultan and his minions, causing them to overlook certain military anomalies, such as the preponderance of Adurian officers in leadership positions. Gyro-manipulation had also been used to establish and carry out the essentially futile Demolio torpedo program, which had diverted Mutati military assets into dead ends and permitted the shapeshifters to destroy three Human fringe worlds that were of little value—Earth, Mars, and Plevin Four.

Now came this unexpected problem involving Timian One, which should never have happened, since the HibAdu Coalition wanted to preserve that valuable planet and others for their own uses after their great victory. Many of those worlds had important assets that the wealthy merchant princes had set up, and some had untapped natural resources, minerals that were only valuable to the Hibbils and the Adurians. They were supposed to be spoils of war.

To prevent further undesirable losses, the Adurians were making emergency adjustments to the signals being transmitted to Mutatis who used gyrodomes and portable gyros for decision-making. Pimyt hoped it worked.

Upon returning to the underground encampment, Noah

found Tesh waiting for him, just inside the entrance. She rose from a rock where she had been sitting and said to him, "Well? Do you have an answer for me yet?"

"As a matter of fact I do," Noah replied. "My friend and I had some business to take care of first."

"I'm not asking where you were," she said in an impertinent tone.

He looked at her calmly, while Thinker stood beside him.

"Your answer is no, isn't it?" Tesh said.

"My answer may not be what you expect." Noah smiled stiffly, then brushed by her and went toward the cafeteria.

"That's all you have to say?" she yelled after him.

"Be ready to leave first thing in the morning," Noah shouted.

"Did he say what I think he said?" Tesh asked, looking wide-eyed at Thinker.

"He answered yes," the robot said. "I see no other alternative, even though I do not know the question. Perhaps you asked him to marry you, which is something Humans are known to do."

"We're not quite ready for that," Tesh said.

Chapter Eighty-Five

The future is a tapestry woven with disappearing threads. Sometimes it seems to come into view, but only ephemerally, providing titillating but confusing glimpses of what is to come.

—From a Parvii Legend

Disguised as ordinary travelers, Tesh and Noah took a crowded city shuttle up to the orbital pod station, ostensibly to await the next podship from deep space.

In reality, they were looking for the one that still sat in its docking berth, where they had left it. Uniformed Red Berets and technicians were poring over the craft, searching for answers. Never before had a sentient spacecraft remained in place for so long.

As they approached the vessel, Tesh reduced her pace and touched Noah's arm, causing him to slow as well. The two of them were dressed in black robes, like the garb of a religious sect.

"What is it?" he asked in a low tone.

"Nothing, nothing," she said, lying. They proceeded together, more slowly. The walkway was crowded with passengers and Red Beret soldiers.

She couldn't tell him what she was feeling. Despite the fact that she had invited Noah to accompany her into space, it troubled her that this sacred spacefaring vessel was being violated by so many nosy, meddling Humans. She hoped they had not been able to gain access to the innermost secrets of the creature, its sectoid chamber and other workings that she knew so well as a Parvii.

In the past, whenever podships were abused by Humans, Vandurians, and certain other races, the sentient vessels reacted, sealing themselves up and closing off all sections to intruders, suffocating anyone aboard and then speeding off into space. Now, however, this creature was behaving differently, and Tesh didn't know why.

Throughout history there had been examples of Parvii pilots taking heroic actions to save their vessels. In his younger years the Eye of the Swarm, Woldn, had done so himself, saving an entire herd of rampaging, panicked podships.

Tesh wondered if the battle she and Noah had fought for control of this vessel had confused or traumatized it. Perhaps it would take the two of them to restore balance to the creature, or the harm might be irreversible. She hoped not, prayed that it was not too late.

Unknown to either her or Noah, Anton Glavine had followed them in a separate shuttle, and now he was mingling into the crowd at the pod station. Attired in a dark blue cape and liripipe hat, the typical garb of a nobleman, Anton watched with considerable interest as Noah and Tesh found a place off to one side of the walkway and conversed in low tones.

The young man was no longer jealous, and had all but given up any hope of having a close relationship with Tesh again. But he was seriously concerned about her, and wanted to make absolutely certain she was safe. It was more than just concern, he admitted to himself now. He loved her. And he only wanted the best for her, even if that meant giving her up entirely.

* * * * *

Perhaps twenty meters from the podship, Tesh and Noah were keeping an eye on activity around the vessel, watching for the first opportunity to slip on board.

Tesh had her own complex feelings, but they were for the man beside her. She cared deeply for Noah with an unrequited passion, but he was an interloper in Timeweb and had control of a podship that should be hers. It made for an internal tug of war between her personal and professional needs.

The two of them had not spoken much that morning, with tension still lingering in the air. Now they exchanged only terse comments about the movements of the investigators and soldiers who were going in and out of the passenger compartment and cargo hold of the podship.

They fell silent for several long moments. Then she said, "We Parviis express ourselves differently than our larger Human cousins, a race we call 'humanus ordinaire.' When we find a person we like, we are quite aggressive. If I have offended you I am sorry, but that is our way."

He glared down at her with hardness in his hazel eyes.

Seemingly unperturbed, she explained with surprising frankness how Parviis and Humans—she kept calling them "humanus ordinaire"—could have sex together, and that it was potentially quite pleasurable. They could not, however, conceive children . . . even though the Human race was a genetic Mutation of the Parviis, a split that occurred millions of years ago. Now they were two of the major galactic races, none of which could interbreed.

"I'm trying to figure out where a galactic playgirl fits into all of this," he said, "scattering hearts across the cosmos."

"That might have been a fair comment about me once,"

she admitted, "but not anymore. Not since I met you."

He looked at her skeptically.

As she continued to speak to him, he said little in response. In his sparse words and demeanor he appeared to be trying to maintain his emotional distance from her, but in his eyes she detected his difficulty doing that. Periodically, he locked gazes with her, and seemed to soften. Then he would stiffen and pull away.

From a personal standpoint, these were good signs to her. It was only a matter of time.

When the technicians and soldiers wrapped up their work for the day, two black-robed figures took advantage of a lapse in security. Slipping through the airlock, they sneaked aboard the disabled podship. In a shadowy corner of the passenger compartment, Noah pressed a hand against the interior wall, touching the rough, leathery skin of the sentient spacecraft. It felt unusually cool, but he sensed life.

The faint pulse quickened, and he withdrew his hand. But as he did so, he still felt the pulse.

"Follow me to the navigation chamber," he said. But he did not move physically.

Closing his eyes, Noah watched while Tesh became small and ran behind his own ghostlike form as it entered a passageway that led to the core of the podship. He was making her think he had to be in physical contact with the ship before being able to get into the navigation chamber, still not revealing his earlier remote entry.

At the end of the passage, he hesitated, then seeped through the wall of the central chamber, leaving her behind. Seconds passed, and he sensed her impatience growing.

Then he released the seal on the entrance and let her in. . . .

* * * * *

Outside, Anton Glavine approached the podship, but was noticed by a Red Beret guard who had just gone on duty. "Stay back," the soldier commanded tersely. "This vessel is out of service."

Obediently, Anton backed up. "Sorry," he said. "I thought this was my ship."

"Read the destination boards and pay attention to berth numbers, you idiot."

"Yes sir." Anton blended back into the walking, milling traffic.

In the soft green glow of the navigation chamber, at the nerve center of the podship, Noah concentrated the power of his mind, and felt the ship pulse into motion.

Just inside the enclosure, Tesh stood motionless, not challenging him.

Under Noah's direction, the vessel proceeded slowly through the docking bay. From the walkway, Red Beret soldiers fired puissant rifles at the craft, but to no effect. Some of the uniformed men scrambled into a pursuit ship and fired up the engine, making a flash of orange in the exhaust tubes.

But the podship surged away from the orbital station and leapt onto the podways with surprising vigor, then accelerated out into the frigid void, leaving the Red Berets far behind.

From the passenger compartment, Noah shared the joy of the creature.

And he felt the podship still under his control, turning this way and that along the cosmic filigree. Presently, he brought the vessel to a complete halt in outer space, and as he did so he sensed the creature come to a new awareness, watching warily with its visual sensors, looking for the approach of other podships.

Noah commanded the sentient vessel to disengage, and it floated free of the cosmic web, into the vacuum of space. He felt the creature grow calmer.

Keeping his eyes closed, Noah gazed telepathically into the boundless galaxy. He was startled to behold a sea of shimmering suns in much better focus than before.

"It's so clear this time. I can't believe it."

His mind soared, and he began to see other podships speeding along the pale green webbing. As before, he could only probe one of the sentient vessels at a time, so he telescoped in on several in succession. Again he saw their passengers and heard them speaking, but in much sharper visual and auditory clarity than previously. Now he could hold the links more strongly, as if his mind had suddenly grown talons and he was digging them in deeply. But the conversations were innocuous, and of no interest to him.

Instead, he let the podship connections go, and zoomed in on one of the red-and-gold merchant schooners he had seen earlier, the one that had gone into geostationary orbit over the Mutati world of Ilbao. Inside the vessel, he again saw the Mutati pilot, and once more Noah scanned the interior of the hull, where the peculiar array of gleaming alloy tubes remained.

This time, the tubes looked far more sinister. Able to probe deeper into the tubes themselves, he saw even more cylinders inside. These were smaller, filled with dry chemical powders that were interspersed with unknown, solid elements and liquid-filled capsules, all connected to multiple warheads and trigger devices.

The schooners were not listening posts at all. They were warships, mobile bombs.

Agitated, Noah stretched his mental power and searched the other Mutati worlds where he had seen the strange vessels. Previously, there had been ten. Now he saw hundreds of them around the Mutati Kingdom, each orbiting a different planet. Expanding his search radius, he found more of the schooners in other star systems. In all cases, the vessels were near pod stations.

Another even more disturbing pattern became apparent to him: Mutati warships were surrounding the Merchant Prince Alliance.

In a frenzy, Noah zoomed one by one to the Earth, Mars, and Plevin Four debris fields, where worlds had exploded under mysterious circumstances. It was all becoming clear to him. The Mutatis intended to stage a huge attack against every Human-ruled planet, striking from all directions!

A woman's voice came to him from afar. Tesh. "Terrible weapons!" she exclaimed.

"You can see this?" Noah asked.

"I've been with you all the way, by touching the nerve center of the podship."

With his voice drifting across the cosmos, Noah told her how he had seen only a few of the schooners earlier, and how there were many more now. "They're getting ready to do something big," he said. "Each ship seems to have enough explosive power to destroy a planet, taking everything in the vicinity with it . . . podships and pod stations have been wiped out, too."

"That's why you examined the three debris fields," she said.

"Exactly. Those planets may have been destroyed in a weapons testing program. But why are you seeing this with me? Previously, I was able to take a mental journey through the galaxy on my own. And why is my vision so much clearer now?"

"I'm not sure, but maybe I'm boosting your power. During my career piloting podships, I have occasionally had paranormal experiences caused by my mental linkages to the creatures. From what we call sectoid chambers—and which you have been referring to as navigation chambers—we Parvii pilots gaze out at the galaxy through the eyes of the creatures. Usually, we see visions of deep space, the galactic webbing on which we travel and the like. But occasionally the podships seem to peer into alternate dimensions for brief moments, and we are taken along with them."

"What do they see?"

"Woldn teaches it could be the future, the present, or even the past, since Timeweb is linked to time and space." She paused. "Eons ago, Tulyans such as Eshaz held dominion over podships, before we took control of the sentient vessels away from them. Some Tulyans of today are known to have timeseeing abilities, but not all of them, only a few. Woldn theorizes that this power is linked to the abilities of the podships themselves, and that the capacity of the Tulyans to peer into time is weakening . . . from the lack of connection to their ancient allies."

"Regarding the Mutati war schooners, are we seeing them in the future or in the present?" Noah asked. "I assume it's not the past."

"They are in the present," she said flatly.

"How do you know that?"

"I am trained to know," she said. "There are certain indicators, which I am not at liberty to discuss with you."

"I'm supposed to trust you, but you keep secrets from me?"

"If I could reveal them, I would."

"They are Parvii secrets, then, not personal ones?"

"That is correct. But I do not have all the answers, not even close. It is most unusual—unheard of—how we are sharing the Timeweb experience. Perhaps it is because we are working together now, while previously we were at cross-purposes. Perhaps I am boosting your power, and you are doing the same for me. We are in turn mutually enhanced by our connection to the podship itself, since we are looking through the eyes of the spacefaring creature."

She went on to explain that the multiple eyes of the big, whale-like creatures were concealed in its mottled exterior skin, and didn't look like eyes. But they were, nonetheless.

The two of them fell silent for awhile. As Noah and Tesh focused, the faintly green strands of the web appeared to them, only slightly visible and dancing ever so faintly in cosmic winds.

"We are seeing what is not visible to the naked eye," Tesh said. "An alternate dimension. Legend holds that it is one of many layers of Timeweb, that it goes deeper and deeper, beyond anything a Parvii has ever seen or experienced."

"Legends," Noah said. At his impetus, the image shifted, and he gazed at a miniature Tesh where she still stood inside what she called the sectoid chamber. He zoomed in on her tiny features, saw the classic loveliness of her face, the seductive green eyes.

"There are many ancient legends," she said. "Perhaps one of them involves what is happening to the galaxy now. If we survive this, I will ask Woldn. He knows all of the old stories."

"We must return to Canopa and tell the Doge what we have seen," Noah said. "Sadly, there are bigger enemies than

Lorenzo or my sister. I fear a plot against all of humanity."

The eyes of the miniature woman widened. "Are you crazy? Lorenzo will kill us."

"I intend to go alone. Remember, I am somewhat difficult to kill."

"Alone? You'd leave me in control of this podship?"

"Yes. Contemplating the worst, I've also left Subi Danvar in charge of the Guardians . . . he understands the possibility that I might never return."

"Don't say that!"

"At a time like this, I need to be realistic. My Guardians are important, even critical, but I must give the Mutati threat an even higher priority." He paused, and added, "You may take the helm now. Just drop me off at the pod station."

"I hope you know what you're doing," she said.

Without responding, Noah relinquished his mental hold on the craft. He watched Tesh move into position in the sectoid chamber, and heard her utter the ancient *benedictios* of her people, like magic words.

The sentient spacecraft lifted onto the webbing, then came around like a galactic sailboat and pointed back the way they had come, toward Canopa.

With his mind separated from Tesh, Noah wondered if she had penetrated his thoughts moments ago, the inner workings of his mind, especially his intentions. He had been unable to read her thoughts at all, even though they had shared images of the cosmic web, and information from it. He hoped she could not read his mind, because if she could, she would not be pleased with what he intended to do. Noah had omitted certain key details from the plan he had related to her.

Since the Merchant Prince Alliance was surrounded by

Mutati warships, Noah's ability to remote control podships was not enough. He could only pilot one of the sentient vessels at a time in that manner, while the shapeshifters were poised to load their superweapons into different podships and strike from many directions at once. To counter that, Noah had to take drastic action.

His podship sped toward Canopa. He just watched, anticipating that he could take control of the vessel away from the Parvii woman again if necessary, even if he was not physically on board it. But it occurred to him now, as it had before, that she might have new ways to block him, more than she had shown him before.

Noah had never felt entirely comfortable with Tesh, and didn't think he ever would. She and her people harbored secrets that went far beyond the brief time that he had been formulating his own.

Chapter Eighty-Six

Our universe is in chaos.
—From Eshaz's timeseer report to the Parviis

To avoid attention, Tesh brought the podship into one of the secondary docking bays of the Canopa pod station, where fewer vessels went and the walkways were not so crowded. As they connected to a berth, Noah saw no sign of the Doge's Red Berets.

Wearing a khaki tunic and dark, billowing trousers, Noah disembarked and passed through an airlock to the sealed walkway. He waited for Tesh to leave, then strolled to the other side of the pod station, making no attempt to conceal himself. Instead, he marched right up to one of the red-uniformed officers, identified himself, and demanded to see the Doge.

Within seconds, Noah was surrounded by uniformed men. They searched him for weapons and bound his wrists behind his body with electronic cuffs.

As they completed the arrest, Noah was startled to see the Doge Lorenzo del Velli emerge from an unmarked grid-copter just down the platform, leading an entourage that included the blonde Princess Meghina and a Hibbil attaché.

Just then, Francella Watanabe stepped onto the walkway from another vessel, and walked briskly to join the royal entourage. Suddenly she saw her twin brother, and stopped dead in her tracks.

No one noticed the young man in the dark blue cape

who stood off to one side, gazing about furtively.

Anton Glavine had a lot on his mind, much more than the personal safety of Tesh Kori. Over the years he had seen Lorenzo del Velli at public appearances, without knowing that this powerful man was his own father. Anton had seen holo-images of his mother as well, Francella Watanabe, and had also been completely unaware of his own connection with her. At the moment, he stood only a few meters away from both of them.

His heart pounded as he watched his parents approach the prisoner. . . .

"I am going to say something that sounds unbelievable," Noah said, "but I ask you to hear me out." He looked at the Doge as he spoke, then at his scowling sister.

"He's a madman, sir," one of the soldiers said, keeping hold of Noah by the arm. "A raving maniac. Shall I take him away?"

Lorenzo the Magnificent held up a hand. "Just a moment." And to Noah, he said, "You have two minutes."

"I can see far into the galaxy," Noah said, "into the very heart of the cosmos. Danger lurks out there . . . Mutatis lying in wait, piloting vessels that look like merchant prince schooners, planning some kind of an attack. They have terrible planet-buster weapons. That's how they destroyed Earth, Mars, and Plevin Four."

"Your words fall short of proof," Lorenzo said. The muscles on his face tightened, smoothing over some of the wrinkles.

"The entire galaxy is interconnected," Noah said, "in ways I never imagined. Somehow it allows me to travel mentally through deep space." Leaning close to the Doge, he exclaimed, "I can pilot podships!"

The soldier jerked Noah back and slapped him hard across the face. "See what I mean, Sire? A complete lunatic."

Flashing his gaze at Francella, Noah said, "Do you think I'm a madman, too, dear sister?"

As if thinking he had a weapon concealed somewhere and that he could still get to it, she slipped behind one of the Red Berets, and peered around the man at her handcuffed brother.

"I have bad news for you, Francella," Noah said. "I was near death and received a special healing treatment that changed me . . . it made me immortal."

With that, the Doge and Francella laughed, as did the uniformed men with them.

"I think he's rather cute," Princess Meghina said, stepping forward and passing a hand through Noah's curly, reddish hair. "I'll bet I could kill him with love."

Narrowing his eyes, Noah smiled and said, "I'd have to be crazy to take you up on that offer, Princess. I hear your husband is quite a jealous man."

"Sometimes he is, and sometimes he isn't." She tossed her long blonde hair over one shoulder, and shot a bittersweet smile at the Doge.

Noah knew something about the dynamics here. Meghina and Francella despised one another, and were in competition for the affections of Lorenzo. The Princess was legally married to him and had born his daughters, but she was a famous courtesan, the lover of many noblemen. He had only married her for political reasons, to join the assets of two great houses. Reportedly his true affections were for Francella, but Noah couldn't understand how anyone could love *her*. Even Lorenzo deserved better.

"How about a little lie detector test?" Francella asked. With a sudden movement, she grabbed a puissant handgun from the holster of an officer and pointed it at her brother. The bright yellow energy chamber on top of the barrel glowed as she activated it, showing it was ready to fire.

"Go ahead and shoot," Noah said.

A soldier ripped open Noah's tunic, revealing that he wore no body armor.

"Mother, don't!" someone shouted. All eyes turned toward the young man in the blue cape and liripipe hat, who had gone unnoticed until now. He raised his hands in a halting gesture.

Two soldiers tackled him, knocking him to the deck.

Francella hesitated, and looked closely at Anton.

Noah could only imagine what his loathsome sister was thinking. She had never gazed upon her son before, not even when he was a newborn. But she might be noticing something familiar in him now, wondering if he could be the one she had left with foster parents. For a fleeting moment, Noah thought he detected a mother's love on Francella's face. Then she turned to stone, and ordered the soldiers to place Anton under arrest.

Coolly, Francella looked back at Noah.

"I don't think you should shoot him," Princess Meghina said, stepping between the brother and sister. "After all, he is a nobleman's son, and deserves a fair trial."

Francella's eyes turned feral. She shoved Meghina aside and fired a bright yellow charge at Noah's chest, ripping through flesh and searing a ragged, bloody hole. He fell back on the walkway, shuddered, and stopped moving. The electronic handcuffs sparked, and lifeless hands flopped loose.

Meghina and Anton cried out, as did several travelers who had gathered to see what was going on. One of them quipped facetiously, "You don't want *her* mad at you."

Francella glared in that direction, then looked down at her brother, with fascination burning in her brown eyes. An officer knelt to check the victim's carotid artery, and announced, "He's dead. Shot straight through the heart."

Slipping the gun back into the officer's holster, Francella said, "Just tidying up a little family business."

Doge Lorenzo grunted in amusement, then pointed down and exclaimed, "Look! He moved!"

On the walkway, Noah felt his own body regenerating, and the intense, burning pain of the chest wound fading. His cellular structure repaired itself more quickly than before, fusing bones and organs together and sealing the injury with new skin, while leaving blood on his clothing. In less than a minute, he rose to his feet and smiled stiffly at his sister. He still had nasty, bright red scars on his chest, but they were changing with each passing moment.

With a squeal, Francella stumbled backward, as if she had just seen the devil incarnate.

"I guess he passed his lie detector test," Princess Meghina said. "Bravo!"

"For your own good, you'd better listen to me," Noah said, stepping toward the Doge. "We need to set our differences aside and work together on this." The pain of the wound was already gone, lingering only as an unpleasant memory.

Reluctant to touch Noah, the soldiers did not attempt to intervene. Everyone stared in disbelief as the scars on his bare chest continued to smooth over and fade.

In his bloody, ragged tunic, Noah stood face to face with Lorenzo, and said to him, "I want you to send nehrcom messages to every planet in the Alliance. Tell them to fit all pod stations with customized sensors to detect arriving podships, and guns to blow them out of space the instant they appear. This needs to be done fast!"

Noah glanced over at the Doge's Hibbil attaché, who had been attempting to conceal himself in a forest of much larger onlookers. "I understand there are Hibbil machines called hibbamatics," Noah said, "used for entertainment in every royal court. Can those machines be set to manufacture what we need, in a hurry?"

The Royal Attaché shot an uneasy glance at Lorenzo, but received no response from him.

"I think he can arrange it," Noah said to the Doge. "Have the sensors set to blast every podship to oblivion. Don't let anyone disembark, and don't let them off-load any ships—especially not any merchant schooners. The Mutatis have planet-busting bombs aboard them."

"This is preposterous!" Lorenzo said. "I will do no such thing. The Merchant Prince Alliance needs the podships; we can't destroy them. If the Mutatis have a scheme, we must deal with it in a different manner."

"There is no other way!" Noah shouted.

"The podships are living creatures," Lorenzo said. "If we start killing them, they will signal their brethren, and they will no longer serve our transportation needs." He stared with wild fascination as Noah's body continued to heal itself, eliminating the scars.

"Podships have already died," Noah said, "one in each planetary explosion."

"Then we should capture the disguised merchant ships," Lorenzo said. "The moment each podship docks at a pod station, we move in and . . ."

"We don't know how much time elapses between the arrival of a podship and the destruction of a planet," Noah said. "Maybe the Mutatis don't wait for each podship to dock."

Without warning, Noah felt a change of air pressure, and heard a firm click. A podship floated into one of the docking bays and connected to a berth.

Hanging over the walkway, a glyphreader panel flashed, calling for all Timian One passengers to board.

"Your ship, Sire," one of the officers said.

Lorenzo did not move.

Noah was agitated at the podship's arrival, and hoped that he had not given his warning too late. Were there any Mutatis aboard?

The passengers began to offload through an airlock, while vessels in the cargo hold slipped into the docking bay. There were no schooners, and no signs of Mutatis. But the shapeshifters were tricky, and might have disguised the vessels he had seen earlier.

Just then, a Red Beret lieutenant ran from the Doge's grid-copter, which had remained in a protective position, with its weapons activated. Reaching the Doge, the officer said, breathlessly, "Timian One has been destroyed, Sire! No one knows how." He held a mobile transceiver in one hand. "The planet and its pod station have been wiped out, leaving only space debris. We have eyewitness reports of people who barely escaped with their lives. The crew of a conventional spacecraft saw a huge explosion from outside the star system, then went to our nearest base to make a report."

"Sire, issue your commands to all planets!" Noah said. "Set up defensive equipment at the pod stations! *Now!*"

Reluctantly, the Doge nodded. "Fire off a nehrcom message to General Poitier," he said to his Royal Attaché. "Tell him I need sensor-gun specifications, exactly as Mr. Watanabe described."

The dispatch was sent, and a short while later the reply

came, with the needed information.

Suddenly animated, Doge Lorenzo barked orders to the Red Berets. All over the pod station, uniformed soldiers jumped into action. Urgent messages were relayed to the Canopa nehrcom station and dispatched all over the Merchant Prince Alliance. The podship floated out on its regular schedule, and Noah watched it disappear in a glimmer of green, into another dimension of Timeweb. Without the Doge or his entourage.

Noah hardly noticed his sister slinking away.

A short while later, the Doge's troop transports arrived, eerily silent in the vacuum of space. Hundreds of soldiers disembarked.

Soon the Royal Attaché was operating a hibbamatic to create the necessary sensor-guns, and furry little Hibbil technicians hurried to install them around the perimeter of the pod station, set to pick off any podships automatically as they came in. Merchant prince warships moved into positions in orbital space, near the station.

Noah felt a terrible emptiness in the pit of his stomach. Timian One! Billions of people had been killed.

Only moments after the defensive mechanisms were set up, a podship emerged from deep space in a burst of green light. The guns opened fire and the sentient spacecraft broke apart, scattering thick pieces of the fleshy hull in orbit, along with passengers and fragments from on-board vessels.

From the pod station, Noah gazed out on scattered particles and broken bodies floating in the airless vacuum of space. A vessel that looked like a merchant prince schooner floated by, with its hull split open to reveal gleaming alloy tubes and a dead Mutati pilot. Soon, two more podships appeared, and were blasted away. Then they stopped coming.

Almost oblivious to Red Beret guards beside him, Noah felt immense pain and sadness for the loss of life, but knew he could not have taken any other course of action. As a galactic ecologist, he hated having to interfere with the podships in this way, but he was convinced that the measures he recommended would save more of the beautiful creatures than they would harm. The same held true with respect to the members of other races who had to be sacrificed. Many more of them would die if he did nothing.

Noah's future was as uncertain as that of the rest of the galaxy. He expected to be taken into custody and blamed for the huge economic fallout that would result from the cessation of podship travel. Through their political wiles, Doge Lorenzo and Francella would undoubtedly spin the facts to make it look as if the entire crisis was Noah's fault. They would fabricate a web of deceit.

But deep in his psyche, a part of Noah no longer concerned itself with such details, for he was evolving into something unique in the annals of history, changing moment by moment.

About the Author

BRIAN HERBERT, the son of Frank Herbert, is the author of multiple *New York Times* bestsellers. He is the winner of several literary honors, and has been nominated for the highest awards in science fiction. In 2003, he published *Dreamer of Dune*, the Hugo Award–nominated biography of his father. His earlier acclaimed novels include *Sidney's Comet*; *Sudanna Sudanna*; *The Race for God*; and *Man of Two Worlds* (written with Frank Herbert). Since 1999, he has written six Dune series novels with Kevin J. Anderson, all of which have been major international bestsellers. In 2004, Brian published *The Forgotten Heroes*, a powerful tribute to the U.S. Merchant Marine. He has been interviewed by radio and television stations all over the United States and Canada, and has made many public appearances. *Timeweb* is the first novel in his fantastic new science-fiction series.